## THE LONE WOLF

"A million dollars' worth of heroin," Delgado said to the silent men. "Let's call it what it is, gentlemen ... the most addictive and dangerous of all the hallucinatives used by humanity, a drug whose mere private possession in your country is a crime with severe penalties... and you have hijacked a plane in flight, imprisoned the crew, imprisoned a man named Wulff who was in original possession of these materials, and then have brought all of this within our borders. And what are we supposed to do, gentlemen?" He kicked the desk drawer closed. "What are we supposed to do?"

"This man left fifty people dead in Las Vegas."

"Which man?"

"Wulff. The one we brought here."

They had brought Wulff to Cuba. That was their first mistake.

"Hang on for a wild ride through the dangerous darkness of America in the Seventies!"—George Kelley

# THE LONE WOLF #5:
# HAVANA HIT

# THE LONE WOLF #6:
# CHICAGO SLAUGHTER

## by Barry N. Malzberg

STARK
HOUSE

**Stark House Press • Eureka California**

HAVANA HIT / CHICAGO SLAUGHTER

Published by Stark House Press
1315 H Street
Eureka, CA 95501, USA
griffinskye3@sbcglobal.net
www.starkhousepress.com

ISBN-13: 978-1-951473-93-8

Text design by Mark Shepard, shepgraphics.com
Cover design by Jeff Vorzimmer, ¡caliente!design, Austin, Texas

First Stark House Press Edition: July 2022

# 7

Some Notes on the Lone Wolf
By Barry N. Malzberg

# 11

The Lone Wolf #5: Havana Hit
By Barry N. Malzberg

# 117

The Lone Wolf #6: Chicago Slaughter
By Barry N. Malzberg

# 225

*Afterword:*
The Truths of the Matter
By Barry N. Malzberg

# 223

Barry N. Malzberg
Bibliography

# Some Notes on the Lone Wolf

By Barry N. Malzberg

Don Pendleton's Executioner series started as a one-shot idea at Pinnacle Books in 1969. By 1972 George Ernsberger, my editor at Berkley, called it "the phenomenon of the age." Eventually Pendleton wrote 70 of the books himself and the series continues today ghosted by other writers. Mack Bolan's continuing *War Against the Mafia* (the working title of that first book) had sold wildly from the outset and less than three years later, when Pendleton and Scott Meredith had threatened to take the series from a grim and obdurate Pinnacle, New American Library had offered $250,000 for the next four books in the series. Pendleton stayed at Pinnacle—the publisher faced a lawsuit for misappropriated royalties and essentially had to match the NAL offer to hold on—but the level established by the properties could not fail to have inflamed every mass market paperback publisher in New York.

A few imitative series had been launched by Pinnacle itself—most notably The Butcher whose premise and protagonist were a close if even more sadomasochistic version of Pendleton's Mack Bolan. It was Bolan who had gone out alone to avenge his family incinerated in a Mafia war while Bolan was fighting Commies in Southeast Asia. Dell Books launched The Inquisitor, a series of books on the redemptive odyssey of Simon Quinn (by a then-unknown William Martin Smith, who under a somewhat different name was to become famous in the next decade), Pocket Books and Avon began series the provenance of which is at the moment unrecollected and Ernsberger at Berkley, under some pressure from his publisher, Stephen Conlan, was ready to start his own series.

What he needed in January 1973 was someone who could produce 10 books within less than a year and although my credentials as a Pendleton-imitator were certainly questionable (they were in fact nonexistent), there was no question but that Ernsberger had found one of the few writers close at hand who clearly could produce at that frenetic level. In 1972 I had written nine novels, in 1971 a dozen, in 1970 fourteen; ten books that quickly were not an overwhelming assignment. What he wanted was a series about a law enforcement guy, say maybe an ex-New York City cop, thrown off the force for one or another perceived disgrace, who would declare war upon the drug trade. The cop could be a military veteran with (like Bolan) a good command of ordnance; it wouldn't hurt if he had a black sidekick either still on or just off the force so that they could get some *Defiant Ones* byplay going in those pre-Eddie Murphy days, and the violence was to be hyped up to Executioner level as the protagonist, after an initial festive in New York, took his mission throughout the States and maybe overseas. Ten novels, $27,500 total advance with (it is this which caught my total attention) 25% of it payable upon signature of the contract. Only a brief outline would be necessary and the tenth book was due to be delivered on or before 10/1/73.

I had never read a Pendleton novel in my life.

Hey, no problem; $6750 for a five-page outline at a time when I perceived my nascent career to be in a recession-induced collapse cleaved away scruple and, for that matter, terror. I read Executioner #7, which struck me as pretty bad, mechanical, and lifeless (like most debased category fiction it depended upon the automatic responses upon the reader, did not create characters and an ambiance of its own), wrote the usual promise-them-a-partridge-in-a-pear-tree outline, signed the contracts and began the series on 1/16/73. The third of the novels was delivered on 2/14/73.

Incontestably I could have delivered the entire series by May (the early plan was for Berkley to bring out the first three novels at once, then publish one a month thereafter) but George Ernsberger asked me to stop after *Boston Avenger* and wait for further word. There was a problem, it seemed. In the first place, I had given my protagonist, Wulff Conlan, a name uncomfortably close to that of the publisher whose name at the time I had not even known, and in the second place Conlan's victims, unlike Mack Bolan's, were real people with real viewpoints who seemed to undergo real pain when they were killed which was quite frequently. Would this kind of stuff—real pain as opposed to cartoon death that is to say—go in the mass market? Berkley dithered about this while I sulked, wrote a novelization (never published) of Lindsay Anderson's *O Lucky Man!* for Warner Books, and waited around to accept an award for a science fiction novel, which award caused me much difficulty, you bet, in the years to come. (See the letter column of the 2/74 *Analog* for any further information you want on this.)

Eventually, Ernsberger called—during dinnertime, in fact, on 3/16/73—to say that I could go ahead with the series and would I please change the name of the protagonist? Grumbling, fearing that I might never get back to the center of those novels, I started again and in fact did deliver the tenth book on 10/1/73 after all. (The first three were published in that month.) As is so often the case with imitative series, sales steadily declined from volume #1 which did get close to 70,000) but held above unprofitability through all of those ten, and I was allowed two sequels in 1974 and then two more in conclusion (at a cut advance). I insisted upon killing off Wulff in #14 against the argument of Ernsberger's assistant, Dale Copps, who reminded me of Professor Moriarty.

I signed off on #14: *Philadelphia Blowup* in 1/75. That means that I am now at a greater distance from these novels than many readers of this anthology are from their birthdates ... and for that reason my opinion of the series is not necessarily any more valid than would be the opinion of Erika Cornell on her essays in ballet class in the mid-seventies.

The purpose and development of these novels would, in any case, be clear to anyone, even the author. It is evident to me now as it was then that Mack Bolan was insane and Pendleton's novels were a rationalization of vigilantism; it was my intent, then, to show what the real (as opposed to the mass market) enactment of madness and vigilantism might be if death were perceived as something beyond catharsis or an escape route for the bad guys. As the series went on and on and as I became more secure with the voicing and with my apparent ability to circumvent surface and not get fired, Wulff became crazier and crazier. By #13 he was driving crosscountry and killing anyone on suspicion of drug dealing; by #14: *Philadelphia Blowup*, he was staggering from bar to bar in the City of Brotherly Love and killing everyone because they obviously had to be drug dealers. Finally gunned down for the public safety by his one-time black sidekick, Wulff died far less bloodily than many of his victims while managing a bequest of about $50,000 to his overweight creator. The novels sold overseas intermittently—Denmark stayed around through all 14; the other Scandinavian countries bailed out earlier; the gentle Germans found it all too bloody and sadistic and after editing down the first 10 novels quit on an open-ended contract, paid off and shut it down. I haven't seen anything financially from these since 1979 but entries in various mystery reference sources and the invitation to discuss the series in this anthology suggest that it might have found a particle of an audience. (My real pride in this series, beyond its ambition and sheer, perverse looniness is that I was able to run it through the entirety of its original contract and manage four sequels as well; no Executioner imitator other than those published by Pinnacle went past four or five volumes.) The

vicious Rockefeller drug laws ("drug dealers get life imprisonment")
were being debated and eventually rammed through the New York
State legislature at the time I was writing through the midpoint of the
series. It was a propinquity of event which led to some of the more
profoundly angry passages in these novels and imputed a certain
timelessness as well. (The laws were horseshit and we are still living
with their existence and terrible consequence.) Calling a crazy a crazy,
no matter how anguished may have been the aspect of the series which
was the most admired but for me the work lives in the pure rage of some
of the epigraphic statements, notably Kenyatta's. Writing these brought
me close to some apprehension of how Malcolm, how H. Rap Brown, how
the Soledad Brothers might have felt and how right they were: The Lone
Wolf was my own raised fist to a purity and a past already obliterated
as they were written, rolled over by the tanks and battery of Bolan's
ordnance. (Operating under Bolan's pseudonym: "U.S. Government.")
Bolan killed to kill: I think Wulff killed to be free. It all works out the
same, of course.

# THE LONE WOLF #5: HAVANA HIT

## by Barry N. Malzberg

Writing as Mike Barry

Going through those back streets then, seeing all of the aspects of the night, watching the forms heaving their way through those streets or standing, doomed, broken against the stones, their faces the geography of damnation, the insight came to me clearer and clearer yet: the country had been under bombardment for a long time and now it was a free-fire zone. Now the enemy was coming in freely. Now the territory had collapsed to its perimeters. It was a war and America was occupied ... and America had lost.
—Paul Von Partin, *Ascension*

They've delivered death by the inch through the veins of this country. It's time to turn the needle around. Kill the brutes. Kill all of them.
—Martin Wulff

# PROLOGUE

TO THE COMMISSIONER: Supplement to our earlier report and containing a further description of the subject's activities since that time. Your request for "further information," however, puzzles me because I thought that background on the subject in that earlier report was fairly complete ... and was based upon the same access to confidential PD files which is held by your office. Are those files now unavailable?

Incorporating, then, information embodied in the earlier statement and carrying it forward: the subject, Martin Wulff, thirty-two years old, was until August 1974 a ten-year veteran of the NYCPD. (Two years spent in US Army, most of them in Vietnam combat, were credited as per procedure to working time for the purposes of pension rights, seniority, etc.) Wulff served as patrolman, TPF member and in various other areas and upon his return to active PD duty in 1967 was assigned to the Narcotics Division where he remained for several years until, in August of 1974, for reasons which are still being investigated, lower echelons abruptly removed him from Narcotics Division and transferred him to local patrol car duty pending further hearings.

On the night of 8/15/74, files indicate that Wulff was ordered by radio unit to report to an upper floor of a single room occupancy dwelling on West 93rd Street where a girl, subsequently identified as one Marie Calvante, was found dead of apparent heroin overdose. Source of the call was anonymous and has never been identified. Wulff's partner on patrol car duty that night was David Williams (see file) a rookie patrolmen who was the driver and who reported that immediately upon parking in front of the dwelling, Wulff left the car rapidly and in a state of high agitation. When he did not return to the car for several minutes Williams followed him upstairs to find him kneeling by the corpse. It was at this point that Wulff, announcing his intention to quit the PD, left the apartment, giving Williams no word of his plans or destination. Later that day Wulff telephoned in his resignation. Proper forms were never filed, procedures were not followed and subject was not located at listed address.

*It is indicated that Marie Calvante was affianced to Wulff and that her* death—the circumstances of which remain mysterious, be it suicide or murder—was somehow connected with Wulff's duties in the Narcotics Division. No further information can be developed on this. Certain crucial files which would be expected to contain information on Wulff's difficulties with narcotics division are unavailable and may be presumed to be missing or stolen.

From this point on, only hearsay information may be developed, some of this information obtained from a mixture of informants who range in degree of reliability. It appears that Wulff—whose background in PD and combat gave him an excellent working knowledge of ordnance and guerilla techniques—embarked almost without pause upon a campaign to "destroy the international drug trade," which he saw as directly responsible for the death of his fiancée and against which he felt his efforts in the ND to be completely ineffective. Beginning in New York, traveling then to San Francisco, back across the country to Boston and back yet again to Las Vegas—all within a period of less than four weeks—Wulff appears to have been solely responsible for the deaths of several hundred operatives involved at all levels of the national and international drug trade. At least three of them, Albert Marasco of NYC, Louis Cicchini of Revere Beach and a man identifiable only as "Lazzara" who was murdered in Las Vegas, appear to be at the highest perceptible levels of the network. In San Francisco, fire aboard and subsequent sinkage of a large freighter seems to be Wulff's work. So does the destruction of a townhouse in NYC, a series of residences in Boston and the gutting of the Paradise Hotel, a major resort and gambling center of Las Vegas. And, one of our informants has indicated, Wulff may have appropriated a major shipment of heroin that arrived on the San Francisco-bound freighter. Even more significantly (but here the informant is particularly unreliable and the level of inference is quite great), something over a million dollars of hard drugs taken, as you know, from the evidence room of the NYC criminal division, may have been traced to Las Vegas by Wulff in the wake of the mysterious disappearance of Lieutenant Bill Stone who might have been tied in with those thefts. These drugs *may* be in Wulff's possession.

It cannot be sufficiently emphasized, however, that all information on Wulff's activities past his resignation from the PD are contrived wholly from hearsay information and any of the specific details listed above may be erroneous.

What is clear—and memos intercepted by our informants do make this beyond dispute—is that Wulff's "war" against the drug trade has had or is having significant results, that he has already severely damaged the network of supply and distribution in this country, and that the many murders have demoralized suppliers and distributors at key points. *Nevertheless there is no truth to the allegation that Wulff may have the sympathy and covert assistance of law-enforcement personnel.* Certainly the man is a felon, engaged in criminal conduct, and no efforts will be spared by reputable officers and departments nationwide to arrest him.

He is, in the bargain, apparently marked for execution at all levels of the network and despite the apparent success of his initial shock tactics, cannot go on much longer. It is sincerely hoped that legitimate law-enforcement personnel will apprehend him before employees of the network, since only in that way are we liable to interview him to obtain specific details.

On the other hand, the subject is extremely sophisticated in all phases of weaponry and is not only extremely dangerous but probably would not permit himself to be taken alive.

A fuller report is being prepared and will be on your desk within the next day or two but in line with your request to deliver an "informational noting the highlights," the above is submitted.

We remain in the closest contact with usual informants, of course, and will pass on further information when and as it develops.


# I


Crazy. The detector at the passenger gate was supposed to find weapons in hand-luggage, but Wulff doubted that probability very much; these things were full of shit anyway and there was no such thing as a dependable detector at this early stage of technology. But whether or not they could find weapons they were certainly not attuned for drugs; a million dollars or close to it of pure heroin had passed through the detector without a blink, and now the valise was up front, on the rack behind the first class section and he was sitting at the end of coach, airborne, drinking, safe.

Well, it had been risky of course; putting a million dollars of pure shit through the X-rays had been nervous-making for Wulff but then again what else could he do? He had to get out of Vegas fast and he had to have the shit with him. Between those two poles of the equation there was only the understanding that he had left a blasted hotel behind him, six men dead in the desert, half a hundred more perhaps dead in the vicinity of that hotel. But this most lethal of all the death-injections he had given the enemy could only be a temporary fix itself. They would be coming after him now no longer in squads but in battalions. He had maybe an hour of time or a little more before the fresh troops rolled in from west and east and the great wars would begin. They were beginning anyway. They would show him less mercy than he had them and that was little enough. He had killed maybe three hundred since his Odyssey had begun and only with the feeling, all the time, that he was just clearing the way for the great confrontations, the more serious business of his war.

But for the moment it was not necessary to think of this. He was airborne; they would be in New York in five hours or a little less and he would take the valise with him off the plane and disappear, for a little while anyway, into the ragged periphery of New York, deciding what he would do next. He guessed that he would take the valise to Williams, though. Yes, he would like to do that. He would like to take this valise into pure, comfortable, secluded little St. Albans in Queens where Williams was. Willaims, the black man who was all for the system because the system was holding them off him. Wulff would open it and shove it into his face. *There's your system*, Wulff would say, *there's your fucking system*. It makes death and it shares death and it pumps death all through the country but you want it to go on just this way so that you can pay your fucking mortgage. Well what next, Williams? When your shitstorm comes and half of your people are walking around with the death inside them—where are you going to be?

Enough of this. He settled back and into a thick sleep, heavy waves of recollection coming through him: dead faces staring up at him from a field like flowers, pulped bodies turning inside out in the opening bursts of fire, the look of the town house on Eighty-Third street as it had gone down, the look of the casino as it had gone up, buildings impacting and fragmenting like grenades and memory became apprehension, the waves turned thick and moist, shaking him inside out on the seat, the voices of the dead overtaking him and he opened his eyes then, strangling from the dream, to find that it was not a dream at all and that he was confronting an open, spreading artery of terror. The plane was shaking in the air, shaking and shattering like a child's rattle and moving up and down the aisles of the coach section was a man holding a revolver, flicking it over the faces of the passengers. The passengers, what few of them there were—this was off-hours and a thinly-populated flight—were in the usual postures of air-travel, some looking out the windows, others looking through newspapers, only a very few risking short, sidelong glances at the man who more than anything else seemed bored, not really in possession of the cabin so much as merely considering it.

Wulff felt his muscles tense against the hard, slick edge of the seat. His first impulse was to spring at the man but that was inconceivable; the man had him in full range and was looking directly at him now with an expression which seemed to take in not only the moment but that series of actions which might come from it. He had ditched his revolver on the way to the airport, of course, presuming that New York would yield him a better one. No point in taking chances. He was, Wulff realized, almost entirely helpless.

The passengers were beginning to realize their own helplessness. Wulff had no idea how long all of this had been going on; not too long at all, obviously, because the passengers were just focussing, one by one, into a kind of attention goaded by the pacing of the man and the shaking of the plane which started again now even more ominously; the plane coming up, the plane going down, moving like a roller coaster on the first series of dips, and now, for the first time, a young girl across the aisle, a couple of rows ahead began to scream. She screamed delicately, mouth behind hand and this seemed to kindle the others. Instantly the coach section was in chaos, passengers putting aside newspapers to grip the seat backs ahead of them, the sounds of retching coming through. The stewardesses, huddled up in the galley were holding on tightly; a sound of clattering coming from there as things shifted, then the plane took another nauseating roll, dipping forty-five degrees wing to wing, banked deeply, shuddered and came out of it.

Only the man in the aisle seemed untouched. Through the trembling he had kept his balance, spreading his legs slightly, balancing on heels, holding the gun before him with that curious, absent grace which Wulff had noticed already, his eyes very keen, poised, sweeping through the cabin, the gun hand steady. Everything was focussed on that gun. Wulff could see from long instinct that the man was a professional. You might kill him but you would not otherwise stop that steady hand on the trigger from driving death home. *All right*, he conceded to himself at some level where he could think almost without words, *we're in for it now. Nothing to be done.* There was nothing to be done. He wedged himself back in the seat as the plane steadied, as the girl's screams arced to whimpers and then went away, and he made no move.

"Ladies and gentlemen," a flat voice said through the amplification system, the gunman's head swinging toward the public address system but that hand, steady, continuing its sweep, "we've encountered a few difficulties as you should surely know by now. We've had to rapidly adjust our altitude and flight plan. There seem to be a couple of people aboard who don't want to go to New York and until we can work things out with them we'll be heading in a different direction." The speakers whined, there was the sound of someone yammering in the background, the captain—Wulff guessed it must be the captain—cleared his throat and said, "I can only advise you to relax as much as possible; we'll try to keep it steady up here now and get you down as quickly as possible."

The gunman smiled at this. Something in the announcement seemed to have granted him an obscure relief; if the passengers were not relaxing the gunman was, visibly, and with the steadying of the plane he began a measured, even pace up and down the corridor, his pace as detached and exact as if he were a prison guard casually working out the moments of his duty. Wulff, battling impulse, forced himself back into his seat yet again, drawing deep even breaths, willing himself to control while around him he could see the scattered passengers responding in their own way. The girl who had screamed now curled in upon herself in her seat; a businessman across the aisle lit a cigarette with a hand that fluttered, the rest of him very composed, almost rigid in place but the hand telling all; the stewardesses, still huddled in the galley now consulted one another. The plane flew on with slow grace. Wulff lifted his head and caught the gunman's eye.

The man came over slowly, shorter than a hijacker ought to be, perhaps in his early twenties although the long sideburns, the thin mustache were deceptive; he might have been older than that or then again only struggling for maturity. Below the level of the eyes the face was very peaceful now, even detached. Probably on uppers, Wulff thought, uppers or downers it did not matter but something was cooking through the man giving him this calm. "Take me up front," Wulff said carefully.

"You stay in your seat, mister," the gunman said in a quiet, flat voice, "and don't get taken anywhere."

"You don't understand," Wulff said, "don't be a fool. I want to go up front. How many of you are there? I want to talk to the others."

"You know what a bullet can do in a pressurized cabin?" the gunman asked. "It can blow the plane up. Take a tip from me, just sit back in that seat of yours and shut the fuck up. When you're ready to be told something you will hear it."

"Leave him alone," the businessman said to Wulff, leaning across the empty chair on his side. "Don't you understand what we're in? For God's sake—"

"We're in a hijacking," Wulff said. "I know all about it," and as he spoke he stood, bracing himself by the calves against the seat rear, rising to an uneasy posture. The gunman's eyes blanked. He backed off a pace or two in the aisle and levelled the gun.

"Now *you* don't be a damned fool," Wulff said quietly while the passengers turned and looked at him with the expressions of people who were now seeing either the beginning or the end, "you don't want to shoot any more than I want to get shot and you don't have any instructions. You're not going to put a bullet in this cabin until you feel that I'm attacking you and I'm not doing that." He began to move slowly, balancing himself in the aisle, the trip rockier than he had thought, the plane adding a slight side-to-side motion against the persistent rocking, the uneven pounding of the jets as it sought more altitude. "I just want to talk," he said, "I want to see what the hell is going on."

The gunman settled in behind him. Wulff felt the prod of the gun deep in his pelvis, but that was all right, then, the gesture was its own completion. He was not going to be shot. If the man was going to shoot him it would have been done already, when he had been in the posture of rising, the bullet thudding into him from that angle, destroying his organs and lodging harmlessly on exit into the seat. He walked, holding on for support, the stewardesses, bland faces now riven by uncertainty watched him go, past the luggage section where his own valise sat, that valise untouched which was either significant or not ... but meant, probably, only that they had not had a chance to ransack the luggage yet but would. In first class there were only three passengers, a fat man with a briefcase on his lap, his eyes glittering wildly as he rubbed his hands over them and he was saying over and again, "I wouldn't have believed it, who would have believed it, this can't be happening," but indeed it was, Wulff could have pointed out to him; and a young couple, newlyweds perhaps although not to sentimentalize they might only be a whore and her pimp bound out of Vegas with the proceeds, sitting, holding hands, their faces against one another. And he walked, the gunman behind him, into the cabin where the captain, copilot and flight navigator, all of them looking strangely young were being watched by a heavy, disheveled man who was holding a rifle on them, sweeping the confined spaces of the cabin with the same gesture as had the one with the pistol. *They must have a school for hijackers*, Wulff thought foolishly, *teaching them the motions; I wonder if it's a correspondence course*, and the heavy man looked up at him, raised the rifle; in that instance Wulff thought his head itself might be coming off but, no, the man lowered the rifle, his motions suddenly ponderous and he looked toward the gunman behind with a quizzical expression.

"He wanted to come up front," the gunman said, "I took him up front."

"Listen," the pilot said, his voice not the flat, controlled tenor heard through the loudspeaker but rather a high, almost wispy sound in the cabin, "I've got to concentrate on flying this plane. I can't—"

"Shut the fuck up," the heavy man said almost casually and the pilot turned back toward the console. Neither the co-pilot nor the navigator looked up. "What do you want?" he said to Wulff.

"That's not the question. What do *you* want?"

The gunman said, "Let me take him out of here." It must have occurred to him that there was no control back in the cabin section. There were only the two of them, then. That was something on his side,

Wulff thought, although not very much. Not too damned much. They had the guns, he had none, they were in control of the plane and any attempt to shift the balance was not worth the risk. A lot of people could get killed, the plane itself could be lost. As if in confirmation of this, the cabin shook again hitting a stream of turbulence, dived convulsively like a beast caught in a trap and then came out of it reluctantly, the pilot struggling with the controls, bright little droplets of sweat coming off the co-pilot.

The pilot looked up and said almost desperately, "Could you let me fly the goddamned plane? Could you just leave the cabin, all of you, and let me concentrate on this? I can't take much more."

The gunman who had escorted Wulff in, exchanged a look with the heavy man, muttered something which Wulff could not hear and then left the cabin. The heavy man turned toward him holding the rifle loosely, easily, his free hand dangling at his side. He had the kind of fingers that looked as if they had strangled men.

"Who are you?" he said.

"You know who I am," Wulff said, watching the other man carefully. "You tell me."

Wulff looked at the cabin, the three men jammed up against the controls trying to move a plane against panic, looked behind him to catch a glimpse of the stewardesses, like birds, fluttering down in the galley. He made a rapid set of calculations, so quick as to be subconscious, and at the end of them he knew that the decision had been made for him. There was just no other situation possible.

"I'm Martin Wulff," he said.

The heavy man sighed with pleasure, showed his teeth, held the gun on him. "I thought you were," he said. "It's a pleasure."

"What do you want?"

"What do we want, Wulff?" He tapped the rifle with his free hand almost meditatively and then pointed it again. "What do you think we want?"

"All right," Wulff said, "you can have it."

"We intend to take it."

"Let these people off. Let the plane go down and discharge the passengers. I'll go with you and the valise will go with you wherever you want."

"You sound very sacrificing, Wulff," the man said. He belched, covered his mouth with a hand and then clung to a bulkhead as the plane, hit by another wave of turbulence, began to skitter mindlessly, side to side this time, swaying like a hammock. For just one instant the man's control dropped; his implacable stare was replaced by terror and the gun slipped. But Wulff could not take advantage of the moment, he was holding onto steel himself and he hardly could see the benefit of trying to get control if the tube carrying them all would fragment under the struggle. After a minute the plane began to fly straight again at a lower level and the pilot looked up, his face almost transparent with shock and said, "You'd better let me radio in again. We've lost a lot of altitude and if they lose me on a radar track we're really in trouble."

"Where are we?" Wulff said.

"As far as I can tell we're somewhere over the Great Salt Lake. There's too much cloud cover though."

"If you don't let him fly this fucking plane," the navigator said, looking up for the first time, a much older man than the other two, (were navigators failed or washed-up pilots? Wulff found himself thinking irrelevantly) "we're going to be *in* the Great Salt Lake."

"All right," Wulff said, "let's get out of the cabin."

"Are you crazy?" the man said. "Who do you think you are? What do you think you're doing anyway?"

"I've got what you want," Wulff said. "I'm the man you want. We can do business together. But there's no reason to hold the plane hostage. I'll cooperate."

"That suits me," the pilot said. His shoulders heaved. "That suits me; you talk sense to him. But do it out of my cabin."

"Land the plane," Wulff said again, "land the plane and let these passengers off. Get a fresh pilot to volunteer and I'll go anywhere you want ... with the valise. But this can be between us."

For the first time the heavy man seemed to open a trifle, his eyes becoming luminous. "It would be easier," he said, "it would be nice and simple if we could do it that way."

"Let's do it that way," Wulff said. "Be reasonable. Do it easy." He understood the gunman now. He understood both of them. He thought that he could see their position and a dangerous and tricky one it was. They were after the valise, that was their job and about the only way they could get it, they figured, was with a hijacking but they didn't want any part of it. They were professionals, probably more so than any he had been dealing with so far and the theory among professionals was to accomplish the most with the least possible effort; if you could negotiate your way out of something you did it with a mouth not a gun and if you could get hold of a valise the easy way you didn't have to hijack a plane to do it because hijacking was a Federal rap and quite serious now.

"You'll cooperate?" the heavy man said. "You'll go with us all the way?"

"I have no choice," Wulff said, "I don't want to get people killed. I'm not in this to kill people; I'm trying to save them."

That at least was the truth. If nothing else he had not lied there; his quest was not worth the lives of the innocent. He could litter the continent with the bodies of vermin but he would not, if he could help it, make victims of those who were not culpable because if he did he was playing the vermin's game.

"All right," the heavy man said, "all right, I think we might be able to do business that way." He seemed to think, pointing the edge of the gun at his nose and for a surreal moment Wulff wondered if the equation was going to be solved by the man killing himself, then he dropped the gun to waist-level and said, "I heard that you were a pretty professional guy: I guess that's the truth."

"Let's let them get that plane down," Wulff said, "and we can find out who's professional."

"That suits me," the heavy man said. He made a gesture with the gun. "Go on," he said, "you get out, go back to the coach section and shut up. I'll stay in the cabin and help this man fly her in." There was no irony in this.

"That makes sense," Wulff said. "I think that that makes a lot of sense."

"What do you think?" the heavy man said. He shrugged; in that shrug was a great deal of understanding, more comprehension than Wulff would have wanted the man to have. "You think I'm some kind of goddamned fool?"

"No," Wulff said, "I don't. It's just business."

"That's right. Business."

On the way back to his seat then, Wulff passed the other gunman. The other gunman was in the galley, his gun held loosely on the stewardesses, his features quite lively. *Fuck* he was mumbling and the stewardesses were looking at him impassively. *Fuck* indeed. In a few moments, the man would reach below his belt, start to grapple with himself.

Well, Wulff thought, trying to smile reassuringly at the passengers, most of them already looking as if they had suspended hope, it took all kinds, even cruising at thirty-eight thousand feet. It was as much the world up here as down there and you might as well take your pleasure where you could.

## II

Delgado sat in the small room, feet on the floor and waited for the two men to come in. He tried to keep his mind empty, thinking nothing at all. Thinking only meant anticipation and rage and he could afford neither. Handle things as they came. Delgado breathed deeply, evenly, trying to suspend himself against the killing rage. It was true. He could kill them.

A security guard brought the two men inside. They contradicted what Delgado had conceived them to be. He had supposed that they would have a lurking stupidity, the clumsiness and indelicacy which he had always associated with the type of people who worked at low organization levels up north, but no they looked reasonably competent, even comfortable, particularly the taller, heavier man who seemed to have decided that he would do all of the speaking. The other one held himself against a corner under the gaze of the guard. "Listen," the heavier one said, "I'm glad that we finally got a chance to get in here. We've been waiting—"

"Shut up," Delgado said.

"I'll shut up when I'm ready to. Now you people listen to me, you just can't—"

"I said," Delgado said, "that I wanted you to shut up." He made a gesture toward the guard. The guard shrugged, came toward the desk, stood behind the heavy man and very carefully lifted his pistol.

Almost delicately he hit the man behind the ear. It was contrived to be a grazing blow, successful that way, and only a thin smear of blood came from the scalp lining behind the ear. The heavy man did not even fall. He stood there in confusion as if someone had whipped out a handkerchief and thrust it upon him and then, almost casually he moaned, staggered backward, landed against the wall.

The other man reached forward in a gesture of appeal. "Look," he said, "I don't know—"

"You keep quiet too," Delgado said. He found that his hands were curling convulsively in rage. No good. It could not be this way. If anything was to come of this he would have to remain in control. "All right," he said to the guard, "get out. Stand outside the door. I don't think that we'll have any problem here but if you hear any noises—"

The guard nodded. His English was only fair but he gave the impression of complete comprehension which was enough. He walked to the door, opened it gently and went outside.

Delgado leaned back in his chair and looked at the two men. The one that was supposed to be the spokesman was running his hands through his scalp, feeling the seam of the cut, a strange, blank expression in his eyes which was worse than fear because he had not yet judged what was happening to him. The other man stood quietly, holding his hands together, looking past Delgado out the window where he could see the mountains. They were not thoughts of escape that were overtaking him but merely a wistful desire for an openness he would never see again. Delgado knew the feeling well. He had been there.

"You gentlemen have put us—all of us," he said, "in an impossible situation. Now I am going to do the talking and you are going to do nothing but quietly listen. I do not think that you truly understand what you have done and I have been appointed to tell you."

The heavy man said desperately, "Listen, damn it, we had instructions—" and then at a look from Delgado seemed to become aware of the fact that he was speaking. He put a hand to his mouth like a child. A thread of blood came down over his eyebrow giving him a clown's aspect.

"Your instructions have nothing to do with our situation," Delgado said, "nothing to do with our situation at all. You have hijacked a major airliner with very controversial contents, have set it down in this country, have drawn international attention at a time when we want a minimum of attention, and have put my government in an impossible position. Certain agreements which were being worked out through the most intense and delicate of negotiations may have been utterly destroyed by this adventure. You have drawn maximum attention to a very dangerous situation at precisely the point where for the first time that situation seemed to be ending. And furthermore—" the heavy man seemed about to say something and Delgado raised a hand which quieted him, the man burbled to silence, the other one was looking at Delgado with an expression of absolute terror—"our government has very strong feelings about being involved in what is known by the uninformed as the international drug trade. My country has had very serious problems with this in the past and it is only through the most dedicated cleansing of the government at all levels, from bottom to top, that in the last several years we have come to assume some control over the situation. And now you have brought here and placed in our custody perhaps the largest single amount of drugs which has ever existed in a single shipment and you have also placed in our custody an extremely dangerous man who has drawn more attention. Do you begin to see now what you have done? Is there any awareness?"

Delgado sighed, leaned back from the desk and fumbled in the drawer for a cigarette, not looking at the two men now, letting them consider what he had said, trying again to reach that blankness of mind and aspect which he had had before they entered the room. It was not so much a mask now, not as much of a mask as it might have been if he had not been on the other side of this kind of desk many times in his life, knew what they were going through, knew exactly how the situation was opening up underneath them. They had a feeling of peril, of falling. It was always that way when you carried through something difficult and dangerous only to find that all along the signals had been wrong, had been issued in a different language.

"A million dollars' worth of heroin," he said to the silent men. "Let's call it what it is, gentlemen, let's not use any of your American terms like shit, smack, horse, H. It's heroin, the most addictive and dangerous of all the hallucinatives used by humanity over a period of fifteen hundred years, a drug whose mere private possession in your country is a crime with severe penalties ... and you have hijacked a plane in flight, imprisoned the crew, imprisoned a man named Wulff who was in original possession of these materials, have discharged your passengers at an earlier point and then have brought all of this within our borders. And what are *we* supposed to do, gentlemen?" He kicked the desk drawer closed with a force he had not expected; his rage was showing again. "What are we supposed to do?"

He looked at the spokesman intensely and finally, the man saw that he was supposed to speak this time and that an answer was being awaited. "Our instructions were clear," he said. "We were, if possible, to take the plane in here. We were told that all arrangements had been made at this end and that—"

"No arrangements had been made," Delgado said quietly. "There is no level of dialogue whatsoever between those people who are your superiors and my government. There has not been any for many years. You have been lied to, gentlemen, you have been misdirected all of the way. We do not want your plane in our country, we do not want your drugs and we have no arrangements whatsoever for disposition. Cuba is a free country now; it is not a backyard and a playpen for your interests."

"Look," the heavy man said, "I'm sorry; we were only told—"

"I don't care what you were told," Delgado said and came over to the man. He raised his hand and struck him in the place where the wound was, once, hard, the man groaned and spat a trickle of blood and then fell to his knees, Delgado hovering over him. Delgado kicked the man in the stomach until he arced over and then coughed, spat blood on the floor. Instantly, the rage discharged, he was calm again. He walked back to the desk. The man against the wall was looking at him in a pleading way. Delgado let the one on the floor continue to choke and spoke to this one.

"You see," he said gently, "I am here to tell you that your position is untenable. As untenable as you have made ours. We do not want anything to do with your traffic, we do not want any of your internal problems. The internal problems and politics of our country itself have changed a great deal over the past decade and some of your people have, perhaps, not caught up to this yet. You have given us an almost insuperable difficulty. The premier himself is very embarrassed. What are we supposed to do with you?" Delgado concluded quietly, his tone almost reasonable, they could have been working out the final details of some arrangement here.

The other man shrugged and looked away. With the spokesman incapacitated, however, he seemed to feel that some kind of statement was expected from him and after a moment of silence his eyes swung back, away from the mountains, toward Delgado. "I'm sorry," he said. "We had very specific instructions and no reason to feel that we would find difficulties here. This man left fifty people dead in Las Vegas."

"Which man?"

"Wulff. The one we brought here."

"Fifty people dead?" Delgado said. "I'm afraid that fifty of your people— they were your people were they not?—dead means far less to us than the fact that there were another fifty aboard that airliner and but for the grace of God *they* might have been dead and we would have had to bear the responsibility. You see, whoever is giving you your orders is a fool."

The man on the floor coughed again, spewed blood across the carpet. Delgado looked at it with distaste. It was uncosmetic, that was all. You could not have a nice, clean interrogation anymore. In the old days people understood and cooperated but then again, Delgado reminded himself and this had to be taken into account, in the old days the people who understood and cooperated were on *his* side. The enemy had never been so reasonable. "Things have changed," he said again. "Only the premier and the highest levels of the government know how much they have but this is still no excuse for you. You took orders from a fool, you have given us a most serious difficulty here and you may have set back certain facets of our international relations by several years. We will have to take the most extreme measures."

He opened the desk drawer again, this time very casually and took out a pistol. Feeling it slide into his hand, leaping into his palm almost as might a woman's breast, Delgado had a flash of recollection: this was not 1974 but instead 1957 or so and it was not he who was standing behind the desk but another man, someone in the uniform of Battista's secret police ... and this person was levelling the gun at a form which only could have been Delgado's. *Please don't do this to me; I am a loyalist,* this recollected Delgado was pleading, *don't kill me, don't kill me.* The weakness of this remembered voice poured out, gasping through every syllable and Delgado had a sudden flash of revulsion, all the more difficult because it was unexpected. The same, he thought, it is always the same, the actors and the masks and the words change but when you come to the end nothing has changed whatsoever; we have merely turned the tables. I am no different from any of the others, Delgado is like everyone else. And he reacted against this. *No!* he screamed in memory and then realized that it was not memory at all but reality which had overtaken him and facing this quivering man it was the Delgado of the present who was screaming *no!* the cry driving slivers of pain all the way from hand and elbow and then he was firing the gun into the man in front of him, firing convulsively: head, throat, shoulders, heart, spleen and the man was changing before him; he was no longer a man but a bag filled with blood, the blood spurting and leaping like fire through all the little discovered openings of his body ... and then the form was falling, burbling.

"God!" Delgado found himself shouting as the man lay before him, "This cannot be," and then his interrogator's calm returned to him as it always would (because the masks would never change and now he was the Official, the Interrogator) and he found himself looking at the corpse now, the exploding form on the floor with something that was not revulsion at all but came closer to a sense of command. "You cannot do this to us," he said in a calm, flat tone, "you simply cannot do this kind of thing to us anymore," and did not know if he was talking about the hijacking and the drugs or whether it was an entirely different matter but then his attention flicked to the man lying on the floor, the man he had beaten. Death in the room had revived this man, unconsciousness had fallen from him and he was sitting in a cramped position on the floor, arms wrapped around his knees, looking up at Delgado with the expression of a child. Yes, he had made children of both of them: that was the essence of power, to strip personality and control from people and turn them into the helpless creatures they had once been.

"No," this man said. "No, please," but although his mouth moved his eyes did not. They were curiously cold and resigned; they seemed to be saying that they were not responsible for the motions or the words of the mouth which was, after all, only performing a series of necessary gestures. You're going to do it, the eyes were saying, so do it quickly and at least allow dignity and to this Delgado could respond. He levelled the

Beretta.

"I'm sorry," he said, "I'm sorry," and he almost was because he knew what he was killing now, it was not so much these men in the room as some earlier version of himself that he had had to repudiate for survival. But every death was a recoil, every murder a lashing back, wasn't it? Wasn't it? Of course it was, that was the key to the delivery of death; you could only do it well if you knew what you were killing and then very quickly and precisely. Delgado knocked three shots off the trigger, driving them into the man's skull, deep into the brain pan. The expression of the face did not change, the eyes did not change at all but only held that curious, cold glimmer of knowledge and then the man sprawled out below him on the floor, sinking away, the mass of his blood pooling with the other's on the floor. And in that posture, dead, he was no longer Delgado but merely an anonymous man who had been killed.

Delgado put the pistol away in his drawer, closed it, and then went to the door. He opened it. The guard looked at him, caught in a posture of listening, his face looking very wet and strained. "Is it all right?" he said.

"It's all right."

"I would have done that," the guard said. "There was no need. I would have—"

"It's perfectly all right," Delgado said. "It wasn't necessary. I had to do it."

"All right," the guard said. "Should I—"

"Of course you should," Delgado said. Tension broke his voice and then he was screaming. "Clean them up!" he said, "get them out of here! Do you think I want corpses in my office? Do you think that I want blood overtaking everything? Get them out of here!"

He pushed past the guard, shaking and walked down the hall, toward the administration offices. He would tell them what he had done. He would tell them that he had followed orders. Now the problem was theirs and he hoped, hoped very strongly, that he was out of it. But there was just no way of knowing. There was no way of being sure.

As the revolution had evolved, there was no way of being sure of anything.

**III**

All prisons were the same. He had seen their interior a hundred times in New York, conveyed prisoners in and out of the Tombs, even once as a participant in a project had spent a night in the Tombs and another on Riker's Island so that police personnel could see exactly where the people they apprehended could go. He had never forgotten that. And he had spent a night in a jail in Saigon back in the sixties for reasons which were still obscure to him and once, long ago, he had spent a few hours in one of the well-known Mexican jails because, as an eighteen-year-old below the border on his own, he had not been able to immediately establish his identity. So he knew a little about jails, not much but far more than most people would ever care to understand and when you came right down to it, Havana was the same as New York City or Tia Juana. A jail was a place where people were held in close confinement in undesirable conditions where, if you got lucky, the only killer was boredom, but the boredom could destroy you. For many it extended through years and years, decades mounting toward a life sentence, for others it might only go six months or a year and they could pace out the time a little better, but life-imprisonment or overnight, it was a place in which you simply could not get out of yourself, where you were hurled back on yourself constantly, the real prison then being the cell of self.... And now, after two hours in this basement, nothing more, Wulff felt himself closer to an edge of panic than anything he had ever glimpsed since his war had begun. He was alone in a room with a barred gate, at the end of a hallway and he could not even hear voices. Now and then, far down, a door would slam and he would hear footsteps and curses. For the rest he sat in the cell, an uneaten meal in front of him and calculated the dimensions of what had happened. It did not look pleasant. Now, he was deep in.

At least he had been able to talk the passengers off the plane, get the stewardesses out, get in a fresh crew who had had experience with something of this sort and had the training to do their jobs. It could have been a major disaster; at least he had saved them that although there was no saying what was minor or major, not in a situation like this, not ever. The flight to Havana had been sullen, the last hour on the edge of an explosion of some sort because the two gunmen, initially confident, had seemed to lose assurance progressively as the plane came toward Havana. Maybe it was only the first awareness of what they had done sinking through; maybe it was the suspicion that they had not had prepared for them at Havana the most riotous of welcomes but there had been a point, almost when they were about to land, when the gunmen had seriously discussed turning the plane around and being taken anywhere else, perhaps Canada. They had been so agitated that their voices had risen and they had made no effort to conceal from Wulff what they were worried about. They were worried that there was going to be no protection from the authorities at landing and that the people, whoever they were, who had sent them out on this were in no position to make guarantees. "We're being played for fools; I tell you they just want that shit and that son of a bitch out of the country!" one of them had said and the situation had become even uglier because they had discussed then the possibility of killing Wulff, getting the plane turned around and escaping with the valise themselves, possibly to Canada. Sitting alone in the passenger cabin, gripping the seat Wulff had found himself judging the chances he would have in taking them on right then and only by a small margin had he decided that he could not, there was too much risk, they were armed and even in their panic could probably overwhelm him. As long as there was the slightest possibility that he could get out of this whole he could not attempt suicide. But the realization that the gunmen were beyond their depth, that they were functioning on orders which were confused and probably issued from a level which could become treacherous had been very much with him in those last moments and although there were good things about it— because he could at least hope now that the landing in Havana might not be a death sentence for him—there was the matter of surviving through this.

But they had decided at last to go in, decided that Cuba looked safer for them at least than an unknown destination and he had been able to relax, at least until the plane had taxied in front of a dismal administration building somewhere at the far corner of the airport and they had been instantly surrounded by police in full riot gear. Well, that would have to be expected, notification to the authorities; the gunmen had until that last moment of fear, been convinced that they were heading toward a haven and there had been no attempt to block the crew from explaining who they were carrying and where they were landing. But when the police had charged aboard the craft, moving past Wulff in fact to seize the gunmen first, clap them into handcuffs and take them roughly off the plane before they came at Wulff in a more restrained manner ... when all of this happened Wulff allowed himself to see that not only the gunmen but he had misread this situation. Nor was there any reason for this: he should have anticipated as should the others that the public landing of a million dollars' worth of shit in Havana was not something with which the authorities could cooperate.

They had taken him off the plane then, less roughly than the hijackers but firmly enough and sped him through the bleak back streets of Havana, toward confinement of some sort he had supposed. But for a moment, sitting in the back of the official car, his limbs cramped, his stomach convulsed from the profound tension of the last day, he had allowed himself to think that it would not be jail at all, had entertained the fantasy that they would turn him loose somewhere in the vicinity

of the capitol buildings for apologies and congratulations of some sort
after which he would be put on a private plane for return to the states
and a destination of his choice .... Yes, it had been something worth
thinking of anyway, even though he knew at the more rational levels
of consciousness that nothing like this could happen. They were no fools
here. It was possible that the gunmen would not get the warmest of
greetings, that was quite likely in fact—there had just been too much
pressure on this government recently—but that hardly meant that
things would be going his way. They owed him no favors, none of them,
he was the one who had, from their point of view anyway, been
responsible for the hijacking simply by presenting the gunmen with an
irresistible opportunity ... and things would be getting a lot rougher
before they became easier. If they ever did. Wulff had eased back in the
car, closed his eyes, tried to resign himself but resignation was difficult;
resignation was the most difficult thing of all to cultivate when you were
in a situation which was literally out of control and in which you were
controlled by others. That was something which had not so far happened
in his war; he guessed that he would have to learn. There were many
things which he would have to learn indeed, no one ever reached a point
of utter knowledge, but then again he would have been crazy if he
thought that this was going to be easy. Remember, he had counselled
himself, remember that you're a dead man; they killed you on the fifth
floor of a rooming house and you'll never be alive again but he was not
even sure that this could be taken as a truth. What was death? what
was killing? who was he to deny that he could be reached by pain when
there was pain all around? Well, no point to any of this. As best as he
could, he reconciled himself.

They took him into a large, grey building near what seemed to be the
center of town and he was escorted by three solemn guards into this cell
and there he had been left. The guards were dishevelled, sweating
heavily from what appeared to be more a personality defect than any
tension: Havana had deteriorated through these days. Wulff, who had
never been here, supposed that in the Battista days it had been a resort
center; a place whose gaiety might have been shallow but which had,
however manufactured, been the pose which the city had adopted, the
gaiety oozing out even into the slum sections which ringed the city and
in the slums, which were part of every city he had ever seen (except Las
Vegas which had no neighborhoods but was merely a condition, laid in
brights against the desert) they had probably accepted that condition
as well so that from stem to stern the town had danced, danced in mud,
danced under the armaments of the dictator's police, but however
wavering, the dance had gone on until the Revolution had come. And

now the revolution had clamped, in this decade, a lead cover over those waters and the city had been baked dry. Empty rubble, ruined buildings, staggering forms passed by Wulff as they drove through the back parts of the city. It looked like New York now or like any large population center in the western world, like an occupied zone. Nevertheless it was still here; it was working after a fashion.

Now he sat in a cell in the jail, looking through the bars and thinking of the price he had paid, the risks he had taken, the men he had killed to get this far. It did not seem worth it. Looked at in perspective nothing was worth it; you wound up in a cell or in the grave but somewhere you had to try, if you cared, to make a contribution and he wanted to believe very badly that he had made a difference. Still, if they simply left him here forever, would anyone notice? After a long time David Williams in the PD might remember that Wulff hadn't checked in and use informants to start a thin network of inquiry. But what would it matter months from now, long after they had had their chance at him? He shook his head, bit his lips, looked at the walls and then away. He would not even consider this. You lived, rather, moment to moment like the drug freaks themselves, trapped within the cycle ... and hoped, somehow, that there would be a reckoning.

The guard was a fat man somewhere in his upper sixties. He carried weight as clumsily as age, his flesh weaving on him like a barrel, his ruined head and appendages protruding from the mass. He came down the hall, jingling like a music box, and poised in front of the cell. He put his hands on the bars, clamped them like an animal: an ape peering through these bars, pleading for attention as if he were the prisoner and Wulff the guard, and said, "You come with me now."

"Must I?"

"Of course you must," the guard said almost peevishly. "That is regulation."

"Do you live by regulations?"

"We live by anything we can get."

The guard's English was unaccented; despite his ragged speech pattern the words did not sound malformed. Everybody here seemed to speak an unaccented English. If Havana were truly to be cleansed of *Yanqui* it would be more than a ten-to-fifteen year haul. At the heart all of them were Americans; that, Wulff thought, was why the government here was a battering ram, their back streets gutted as they led into the heart of the cities. For two decades everything had been America; face up to it.

"Let's go," the guard said.

"I don't think I have any choice," Wulff said. The gate was opened.

"Should I resist apprehension?" The irony was lost on the guard. Everything was lost on them; they would take anything without expression. The basic humorlessness of all authorities was worldwide; then again, Wulff thought, there was very little for them to be whimsical about. Was he? The stakes were too high. The guard probably thought that he could be killed at any instant.

They walked through the narrow halls of the prison. Apparently Wulff was in a special section; either that or Havana had become law-abiding under the new regime. The cells were empty. Row after row of empty cages confronted him; he kept on walking, three paces ahead of the guard, knowing that the man had his gun out, was following him one hand on the trigger. Even so, he could take him. The guard had fallen into lockstep; if Wulff stopped suddenly and hurled himself backward the man would be caught completely unaware. The gun would be jammed back against his body; before he could get off a shot, Wulff could roll over him on the floor and take the gun away. Easy. Nothing to it. Still, he thought, why bother? Wherever the guard was taking him would be more interesting than this alley. It would be difficult to break out of a prison; they could seal him in here. Go to high ground. Try to make escape from there. Who knows? he thought, there may be no need for escape whatsoever. They might want to deal with him. Their position was not too happy a one; there had been too many hijackings and he suspected that the gunmen had hardly been greeted with a procession.

"Up the stairs," the guard said unnecessarily and Wulff climbed a long winding flight leading to a shallow landing, paused there, climbed another row of stairs and yet another, ascending toward the high ground exactly as he had hoped, seeing windows now, jutting spokes of light. At yet another landing he paused, waiting for the guard to catch up with him. The guard was gasping; turning pale with the shock of effort; a little more effort like this and he would collapse and die, probably of arterial blockage. They had some security here. Regimes might change but the basic incompetence of these people would go on. Incompetence would go on anywhere; that was the only thing you could count on ... that the organization itself, the enemy, mostly did not know what the hell they were doing. Groaning, the guard gestured Wulff toward a door off the landing which led down a long hall ringed by officers. At the end of the hall was a small room, an open door. He slowed to allow the guard to catch up to him; then went the rest of the way almost side by side. A man was waiting for him at the doorway, a man in military uniform whose face looked closed in and purposeful. He motioned toward Wulff and Wulff went past him, into the bare room with the one window looking out on mountains. Behind him he heard the small man dismiss the guard. Wulff sighed and fell into the chair behind the desk. The man closed the door behind him, came briskly around the desk and sat. He opened a drawer, withdrew a pistol and held it lightly, like a professional, the point turned from Wulff toward the wall but obviously poised.

"That isn't necessary," Wulff said. "I'm not going to do anything."

"I wouldn't think so, Mr. Wulff. I'm sure you wouldn't."

"Still, you've got to make the display."

"Perhaps. If you call it that." The man laid the pistol neatly in his lap, looked briefly out the window and then turned back toward Wulff. "My name is Delgado," he said, "and you have given us a very difficult problem, Mr. Wulff."

"Not me. Not me at all. The people who brought me here have given you a problem. I wouldn't be here on my own, you know."

Delgado seemed to smile, a man sparing of his gestures but probably deep inside, Wulff thought, all heart. That twisted little smile would become an ebullient chuckle as he kicked someone to death. "That is questionable," he said.

"Don't question it. I was going back to New York."

"You were on a New York bound flight. Whether you intended to go there we simply do not know."

"Don't you?"

"For all we know you might have been in collaboration with the hijackers. It might have been prearranged for you to land this shipment of yours in Havana. It certainly is nothing you would have wanted to take into New York."

"Don't bet on it," Wulff said. He stretched his legs in front of him, tried to settle back in the chair but it was one of those constructions, made for interrogation no doubt, where it was impossible to sit with dignity. "What do you want?" he said.

"You should be asking *us* that, Mr. Wulff? The question is what do *you* want?"

"That's simple. I want my valise back and I want to get out of this country."

"Ah," Delgado said. He cupped his hands, leaned forward. "An international crime has been committed," he said. "Hijacking is an offense punishable by the death penalty both in your country and mine. Are we expected to ignore it?"

"I'm quite sure you advised the others of that," Wulff said, "so you can spare me. This is not your problem. It has nothing to do with you; it's an internal, private situation and I'd like my property back."

"You are aware of what your property is?"

"I am perfectly aware of what it is," Wulff said.

"Ah," said Delgado again. He leaned back in his chair, still commanding the situation. His chair was quite a different piece of furniture. "You have really given us an insuperable problem, Mr. Wulff."

"Not me. I've had nothing to do with this."

"What are you doing transporting uncut heroin? A man of your credentials and background could hardly be in the supply business. Or are you?"

"You've done some research," Wulff said, "so you know who I am."

"A little," Delgado said, "just a little. Actually I know nothing of you except that you are a very dangerous man and that there are a number of people, I would estimate them to be at least a thousand, who would like to see you dead and are prepared to kill you on sight."

"They're not very desirable people."

"But neither are you, Mr. Wulff," Delgado said carefully and then leaned forward again, gestured with a finger and began to talk very precisely. "You see, the difficulties here are enormous. If we release you and your shipment we are, by proxy, in the supply business ourselves. You don't think that your government is unaware of what has happened by now, do you? This is major news."

"I'm sure that you've hardly broadcast my presence on board the plane."

"We did not," Delgado said, "you are a clever man. We certainly made all efforts to conceal the apparent motive for the hijacking or your presence on that plane, let alone the shipment. Still, people even in your government, to say nothing of millions who read newspapers, can put two and two together as you say, no? We have been trying very desperately in the last several years to obtain real credibility in international relations for the sins of our lamentable and disreputable past and now we are put in a position, so to speak, of reliving a nightmare."

"You have nothing to do with this," Wulff said quietly. "Neither you nor your government. Give me the valise and get me out of the country." The thing to do in dealing with the Delgados, he knew, was to say one thing at a time, to say it patiently, repeat it over and again, and finally convince them of your single-mindedness. The bureaucrats could only consider one thought at a time, one line of discussion in a conference; there was no way in which they could see complexities. As bureaucrats go, Delgado was probably of a higher order—for one thing your average bureaucrat did not carry on interviews holding a gun with the option of killing his interviewees—but the principal held. It always would. It was not a man that he was dealing with here but a system. Wulff thought of the cell from which he had come and made a decision right then in that room; he would not go back. He was not going back there under any circumstances because this time they might just leave him there and forget about him. Better to leap on Delgado; take the one chance in ten that he could overpower the man and bull his way out of here ... but he was not going to be incarcerated. He was already in the cell of his mind; two levels of imprisonment would kill him. "Get me passage out of the country," he said again.

Delgado looked at him implacably. "With your valise?" he asked.

"Do you want it?"

"Do you?"

"Your whole point was that you didn't want that shit in your country," Wulff said, "so I'll take it with me."

"I didn't quite want to give that impression," Delgado said. "Of course we don't want it in our country. Why should we? We are a government of revolutionaries; our drug is change itself, we would have no need for anything of this nature in our society. But can we condone delivering it back to your country?"

"It will never be used."

"Won't it?" Delgado said. The smile was back. "Perhaps our sources misread you Mr. Wulff. You may be no so-called activist against the international drug trade. That may be a clever story. Actually you might be a purveyor."

Wulff came half out of the chair, unthinkingly slapped Delgado across the face. The little man was surprisingly resilient; the blow streaked his skin, made his eyes whiten but he did not move. He sat still poised in the chair, then held the gun, levelled it, looked at it carefully. Wulff stood there motionless. There was too much distance toward the gun; if he went for it Delgado would blow his hand off. He held his position, looked at the man. The streaks on Delgado's cheek began to puff.

After a very long time or what seemed to be a very long time, Delgado lowered the gun. His respiration was uneven, the breath rattling around his rib cage. His eyes blinked. "That was unwise," he said. He tried to keep his voice flat and calm but the effort showed. Wulff slowly sat in the chair, palms extended. Give then no additional provocation. He showed lack of provocation in every gesture. "Very unwise, Mr. Wulff," Delgado said and in that tone Wulff could hear the outcome. Delgado was not going to kill him. If he was going to he would have done it already.

"No one calls me a drug purveyor."

"It was just a suggestion."

"Do you know what I am?" Wulff said. "Do you know what I've done? There are two hundred bodies behind me; there are a lot of broken buildings. No purveyor got that suitcase out of Las Vegas."

"He might have."

"If you call me a peddler or organization man I'll have to try to kill you," Wulff said calmly, "I mean that. I won't hear anyone say that to me, not after what has happened. Do you understand that?"

Delgado looked at him bleakly, then nodded. "All right," he said. "I understand that."

"I want passage out of your country, I want the valise. The rest is up to you."

"You apparently think this is your interview, Mr. Wulff," Delgado said. His confidence was returning slowly, little pieces of it jutting together to form again the puzzle of self. "But it isn't."

"There's nothing more to discuss. We understand one another now, I trust. I want transportation out of this country and I want the valise back."

"And if we do not take these terms, Mr. Wulff?"

"Then we'll deal with the problem as we face it."

Delgado put a hand to his cheek, rubbed it absently, already far removed from the pain. "You are a decisive man," he said. "You really believe yourself to be in control of situations, don't you?"

"Some of them."

"You have put us in a very difficult situation. At the moment I have been instructed to work out the easiest way of solving this for all of us." Delgado looked at the pistol again. "Certainly one of the easiest measures would be simply to kill you. That would eliminate our problems right there."

"You're not going to kill me," Wulff said flatly, "because if you were going to do that you would have done it already. Certainly when I struck you. You are under orders *not* to kill me."

Delgado shook his head and looked downward. "All right," he said, "you are a perceptive man. You are a very difficult man as well which you probably have been told."

Very carefully, showing Delgado every motion before he made it, Wulff stood. He laid his calves against the chair and gently pushed it away from him. "I think that this interview is finished," he said. "There's really nothing more to say, is there? Get me out of the country, Delgado, and give me my valise."

"And where do you propose that we drop you? At the border? Or would you like direct conveyance to New York?"

"I think that the border would be a very reasonable proposition. You wouldn't want to go into any major urban center, now would you?"

Delgado sighed, slammed a palm on the desk and stood. "No," he said, "we would not want to do that." Something in his cheek stabbed him and he raised his hand there again, rubbed the area, his eyes darkening. "I have been instructed as you probably know," he said, "to do just that. To get you and your valise out of this country as quickly as possible. Those were my orders before this interview even began."

"I thought as much."

"But you have made things very difficult, Mr. Wulff. You had no business striking me."

"You had no business—"

"You'll get out of the country," Delgado said, his eyes glowing, "about that we can be fairly sure. Instructions, after all, must be respected; we are now living in an incorruptible regime. But there will be a reckoning."

"I'm not interested in reckoning."

"Ah," Delgado said, "but I am. I am very much, Mr. Wulff. You are a violent, irresponsible, reckless man. The fact is that most of the people with whom you deal deserve that treatment but you have not learned to discriminate."

He came away from the desk, stood over Wulff then, a tall man as well, not as tall as Wulff, perhaps—make him six feet one or so—exceptionally tall for a Cuban and through some intricacy of balance maneuvering himself so that he was able to look down upon Wulff. "I am very serious," he said, "this is a personal, not an administrative manner. We will deal again."

"I am sure of that."

"You should be sure of that," Delgado said. He walked toward the door, opened it and found the guard sitting in a cramped position against the opposite wall. "Take Mr. Wulff away," he said.

The guard looked up questioningly and Delgado said something in Spanish, the short, intense syllables somehow ferocious. Wulff could pick up a little of it; wandering through Manhattan you learned a little pidgin Spanish anyway but not enough to disclose much information. Delgado was saying something about a helicopter, that much was clear.

The guard motioned; Wulff went toward him. Delgado moved from the doorway as Wulff passed him, looking impassive. Wulff ignored him. Already his mind was on other issues. The guard made a gesture with his rifle, Wulff fell into place in front of him and they walked down the corridor that way, the feeling of Delgado's gaze burning into the back of his neck, an unpleasant heat which Wulff felt sustaining him all the way as they went outside, into another corridor, out the corridor, to a different level and there poised on a roof was a helicopter, body shaking, blades chattering, a small ramp laid out below it like a carpet.

Wulff walked right in, found a man sitting in the cramped passenger compartment a rifle draped across his knees. Wulff nodded to the man, sat across from him, folded his hands and waited. Through an aperture he could see the back of the pilot's head, the head nodding as he acknowledged instructions of some sort. Then the sound of the engines shifted from a groan to a whimper, a series of whimpers, a series of knives cutting across his consciousness and slowly, gracelessly, the thing lifted into the air; looking out through the window he could see the ruined city of Havana suddenly opening underneath him and then they were heading north, riding in the air as if it were fire.

# IV

The voice on the other end of the line said, "But how can we be sure? How can we—"

"You'll have to trust me," Delgado said. He felt the earpiece sliding against his temple, slick with moisture. He was sweating. Delgado never sweated but now he was. He took a handkerchief out of his pocket, cleansed his face, looked through the window at the mountains. Haze was settling. It would bring visibility down to only a few miles shortly. Good that was good.

"It's not a matter of trust," the voice said, "it's—" and then it faded out again. The international hookup was impossible nowadays; new regime or not the wiring had been rotted almost clear through and the maintenance and repair could just not keep ahead of the deterioration. "Worried," the voice said fading in again.

"I'm worried too," Delgado said, rubbing the place where the man had hit him. "Everybody's worried. Nevertheless, the situation is under complete control. The man is in our custody and will be disposed of shortly."

"He'd better be."

"Don't give me orders," Delgado said quietly, "you're in no position to give me orders. You're two thousand miles out of here and all of this is your own fault. All of it and now we have to muck up your messes."

"All right. All right," the voice said after a pause. Delgado wiped his face again and waited. "What are you going to do with the shit?"

"I don't like that term. I told that to your friend. It is a term out of my vocabulary."

"Goddamn it," the voice said and then it faded out again. Delgado waited patiently, working on the creases around his temple, holding the phone lightly against his ear. A long rest. He would have to take a long rest; he was pushing himself very close to his limits. Even he could see that. But there just seemed no way out. "—disposition?" the voice said, apparently ending a sentence.

"In due time," Delgado said. "The ultimate disposition is the disposition of Wulff himself and that is being handled right now."

"We want them back."

"And maybe you don't."

"You have no need to keep them."

"We do not condone the dissemination of drugs. The regime, the premier believe very strongly in the rational sectors of the human being, our ability to come to terms with reality; the necessity to accept the world as it has been given us. Drugs are a symptom of decadence and this is not a decadent regime. It is—"

"No political philosophy," the voice said quietly. "We assume that you're making disposition and we'll wait to hear from you on the other matter."

"Yes," Delgado said quickly, "yes you will wait to hear from us," but the other side had already hung up. He took the phone away from his ear, stared at it for a moment and then smashed it viciously into the receiver, toppling the stem, shattering the plastic into splinters and driving a wedge through his finger. Blood came instantly.

Cursing, Delgado put the handkerchief against the cut, pressing it in, looking for a fast clot. The blood, sopping rapidly into the handkerchief was a spreading, open stain, a web of darkness and implication springing from his flesh, he shoved the hand in his pocket, putting the stain away from him and for a while simply leaned back in the chair, eyes closed, thinking of Wulff, the son of a bitch who had hit him. Orders were orders. The man would be disposed of in the helicopter.

But it was a shame; in a way it was really a shame because Delgado wanted to do it himself. He wanted to confront the man, show him death in his hand and then destroy him. *You can't do this to Delgado*, he would say and understanding would at last break over that face and Wulff would fall before him. *Cannot do it, cannot do it*, the blood went into the webbing of the handkerchief; he was shaking, his eyes seemed to be filled with some peculiar moisture.

Face it: it had been ten years since anyone had done this to him. More than ten. They must have been in the mountains the last time he was struck like this.

Delgado realized he was crying.

**V**

Wulff knew that something was wrong almost as soon as the helicopter had gained altitude. You had a feeling for things like this; it came with the training. The helicopter was not heading smoothly north or in any particular direction but was merely hanging there, stationary in the air, the man across from him staring impassively, now twirling a gun in his fingers, the aperture to the pilot's nook closed by canvas. Something was going to happen and Wulff guessed he knew exactly what it was. The man across from him—a short type wearing the uniform of the police—was impassive. He seemed to be chewing gum. Now and then, he checked his watch almost secretively, his gaze never really flicking away from Wulff.

Wulff was pressed back in the cabin. He held his buttocks tight against the walls feeling the protuberances; his shoulder blades likewise were pressed against something that felt like wiring. If you had any experience with helicopters (and Wulff had been in his share in Vietnam) you knew that every motion within them had to be cautious and calculated beforehand. You just did not move suddenly; if you did you might overbalance and even more dangerously the overbalancing might affect the copter itself so that the machine could swing in the air. In the hands of an inept pilot it could even fall out of control. But if he knew this instinctively by now, the man sitting across from him did not. His face, as a matter of fact, was riven in terror. Only his hand on the gun was steady; the rest of him was trembling. Now and then he cast glances toward the canvas but the pilot was not coming out. Early up, as soon as they had achieved altitude, he had dropped the canvas and now the gunman was on his own.

Wulff held himself in place there. He felt utterly calm as he had not with Delgado. The calmness came from the sure knowledge that they were supposed to kill him. The interview with Delgado had been filled with doubt; doubt of the context, doubt of exactly what the interrogator wanted from him and it had been this more than anger which had caused him to strike the man, the lack of sureness, feeling that the situation was shifting beyond him. Now, though, all questions had been resolved. It was a double-cross, had been so from the start. The only reason that he had been in Delgado's office was to be pumped for information; Delgado thought that he knew Wulff's situation but wanted to make sure. Perhaps Wulff was not who he seemed to be but an operative for the organization itself. You could not be sure. From

Delgado's point of view the whole thing might have been a test of his own loyalty. How trustworthy was he? How dependable? Delgado was a smooth and professional operator; he would want to check things out to his satisfaction. Now he had.

He had sent Wulff into this copter and the copter had taken him into the air to die.

All right. He had been up against death many times; the odds were certainly better here than he had confronted before. In Delgado's office he had had, strictly speaking, no chance at all, not against a professional with a gun. Earlier, in the hijacked plane there had been nothing to do but negotiate out the passengers and see what could be managed from there. Any chance would have been no chance at all; he might have been able to take control of that airliner but there had been forty passengers on the flight. Maybe forty-five.

But these odds, Wulff thought grimly, were just a little better. The pilot with the canvas had sealed himself off; the man before him was obviously terrified of flight. Obviously they were waiting for some prearranged point in the journey to be reached before disposing of him, maybe a signal through the radio, otherwise they would have done it already, would do it while the thing was hovering in the air. Maybe Delgado was making one last series of checks before he sent through the killing message. That was most likely. Regardless, the two men were locked into position now. They had no freedom of action; they could not move until given the signal, whereas Wulff had options.

That was very bad procedure. Wulff could have told Delgado that himself if only the man had asked. You never sent out an assassination crew without the full freedom to execute as they saw fit. Any two-bit runner up north could have told him that. No hit man worth a dime on the dollar would take an assignment where he could not make the conditions of the hit, run it out at his own pace, make the necessary decisions.

Things had not really changed that much here after all. The players were different; the ideology had a different label but it was the same thing. If the brutality persisted so did the stupidity.

Wulff measured himself and leapt at the man across him.

He came at him flat and low, compensating for the sway of the copter by carrying himself straight forward and dove into the man's stomach. The man screamed, his gun hand flailing and he tried to bring the gun down on Wulff's neck but the surprise had been total and he was terrified of flight anyway. Even the hand that struck him harmlessly on the back trembled like a violinist's, darted away and the man whimpered with a dog's wail. Wulff came up then, still carrying himself low, using his head like a bull's to straighten the man up and fling him against the wall. Something projecting from a bulkhead caught the man in the armpit and he shrieked again, a sound of utter desperation and loss and at this instant Wulff grasped the man's arm in a lover's grip, brought his palm down and wrested the gun away. It came into his hand so easily that it might have been a baby playfully handing over a rattle. Wulff felt the gun in his hand curling authoritatively deep into the palm, he stepped away and let the man simply fall.

The man fell straight away from the wall, whining, hitting the deck unevenly, the copter shuddering momentarily. His face was overtaken by pain: somehow he had hurt himself against the bulkhead. Wulff looked at him lying on the floor: a short, anonymous man in a police uniform glazed by his own sweat, the eyes too filled with pain even to plead; Wulff balanced off his decision within a second or less; it was not pleasant but it was necessary. There were only a certain number of unknown factors he could handle at a given time. Granted them not being airborne, granted there not being the presence of the pilot ... he might have let the man live or settled only for a shot that would injure. But he could not do it now. Add another body to the list, add another heap to the slag pile of humanity he had left behind him ....

He shot the man behind the ear, levelling the pistol close in there so that the bullet would not emerge but go deep into the skull, tear the tissue of the cerebrum, penetrate down past the cerebellum to the throat, carry beyond that all the way into the internal organs, finally lodging somewhere in the hip. Make the man a receptacle. The bullet must under no circumstances emerge from the body because he could not be sure of the stability of the copter if anything was hit.

The shot went in cleanly, inaudible under the shrieking of the propeller, the screaming sound of the copter looking for altitude, and the man died quite silently on Wulff's shoes, only a small, bright coil of blood to show the violation of the body. His face, terrified under the first impact, smoothed and became a child's. His uniform looked like a costume.

Wulff cocked the pistol and stepped back, swaying, jammed himself against a bulkhead for stability. The copter was indeed working a swift ascent now, struggling for height, everything not tied down in the cabin swaying and clattering around him, little pieces of metal, burlap, wire stumbling through the cabin. The pilot, aware of what had happened, was trying some desperate maneuver of his own now; he was undoubtedly trying to freeze Wulff with panic but if there was any panic in this copter now it surely was that of the pilot himself for they were beating at the air now like an insect, weaving uncontrollably in a series of motions which betrayed more a loss of control in the cockpit than a reasoning effort to unsettle him. Kicking the corpse aside, Wulff dived through the burlap, looked for the first time at the pilot.

The man was bent over the controls, working desperately lever by lever, playing the copter like an organ, trying to assert some control and Wulff understood in that instant before he charged forward that the pilot had had no plans to panic him at all, that the motions of the copter were purely those induced by his terror. Hearing the shot, knowing no doubt what it meant, the pilot had succumbed to nothing more complicated than the fear of his own death and it was this fear which was looping the plane through. He was a small man, even by the standards of the revolution he would have had to be considered underweight, no more than five feet one, hunched over the controls, flinging switches as if they were darts. His mouth was open and over the noise of the craft Wulff became aware that the man was screaming. The copter twisted sideways in the air like a stricken, wounded bird, then began a long, graceless plunge and the pilot, battering at the switches in the midst of his screams seemed almost unable to control it. Wulff closed in on him, showed him the pistol. The air clamored. Above the sounds he shouted. "Level it off!" he said. "Level the damned thing off!"

The pilot said nothing. Frozen at the controls he was dead weight, baggage; quickly seeing this Wulff pushed the man to the side. He fell like a sack to the floor, his hands curling. Wulff looked over the controls quickly, equated them in memory with what he had dealt with in Vietnam, and reaching for what he hoped was the proper lever, shoved it all the way back. The craft hung in the air—its descent braked as if by a giant palm upraised and then backed off—then started to gasp for height. He took the seat behind the controls, ignoring the pilot, ignoring for the moment even his own pistol which he placed beside him, using both hands now to work the switches and, hovering somewhere between recollection and instinct, he balanced off the craft in the air, hung it into a stationary position, the propellers beating over him now like a wing, feeling as if he were suspended by some awkward bird throbbing above and then set all of the switches on stationary, the craft balancing off finally to hang in stasis.

Below him he could see the city shrouded by the same plumes of fog and mist which all of the great cities of America were swaddled in. Further out he could see the backyards, the plains, the dry, empty farmlands and these were, he noticed, nearer now. They had gone from Havana to the outskirts in this wild ride, moving no more than four or five thousand feet in the air; now, suspended, the copter seemed to be both part of the city and removed from it. He reached for his pistol again and then looked toward the pilot. The man was crouched on the floor, hands above his head, features absolutely immobile.

"Don't shoot me," he said in unaccented English. "Just don't kill me."

"Why not?" Wulff said. "Why shouldn't I kill you?" Strangely, he felt no pressure now. He would have exactly as much time as he needed; no more but no less. Everything waited for him on the ground but there was no hurry. He could come into it at will.

"I have nothing to do with this," the pilot said. He held his crouch, showed his palms. "They just asked me to fly the copter. I'm not even Cuban."

"I didn't think you were," Wulff said.

"I'm just a hired hand," the pilot said. "My name is Bill Stevens and I'm from Detroit. Sometimes I fly helicopters and sometimes I work on heavy equipment. You could say that I'm kind of a mercenary if you want." He tried a smile but it was ghastly underneath the tension of his cheeks; the cordiality at which he was aiming looked as if it could be shattered by one movement—say, the raise of the pistol. "I have nothing to do with this at all," the pilot said again weakly.

Wulff looked at the pistol in his hand and then past the pilot to the corpse lying in the cabin. It was bleeding richly now, the blood mingling with burlap, the stink of it beginning to fill his nasal passages above the smoke and decayed-wood scent of the plane in flight. The man would have to be pitched overboard in self-defense if they were to be airborne much longer. "Where's my valise?" Wulff said to the pilot.

"Valise? What valise?"

"They told me a valise was being taken aboard."

"I don't know anything about that," Bill Stevens said. He put his palms flat on his head protectively, as if expecting a bullet. "I just take orders and do my work. But I guess that I won't be doing any more work for these people now, will I?"

"Will you?" Wulff said, "I don't know if you will. You can tell me where my valise is."

"I don't know anything about your fucking valise," Stevens said. The copter lurched in a wind current, his face paled. "You better let me off the floor if you want to keep flying in this thing," he said.

Wulff raised the pistol by the point and hit the man over the shoulder with the barrel. He did it almost gracefully, just pulling the impact at the last moment sufficiently to bring pain but no incapacity. Stevens whimpered, a high, desperate sound in the compartment and then fell full-length, rising to his knees only after he had struck himself on the point of the chin. His head weaved; he seemed about to faint. "That wasn't necessary," he said, "you shouldn't—"

Wulff worked on the controls, levelled off the craft again. They were hitting turbulence; with old instinct he could sense that at some intricate level the very metal of the craft was parting under the strain. They had been sent up in half a copter for half a kill these men; they had no luck, that was all. But Wulff was not going to have any luck either unless he came to terms with the situation. "I'm going to put this thing down," he said to Stevens, "then we'll talk."

"You'd better let me put it down if you want a soft landing."

"Can you fly?"

"I can fly dead," Stevens said. He came into a crouch, then used his hands to come into a standing position. "That's about the only fucking thing I can do. I sure as hell can't do anything else." He rubbed his jaw. "Teach me not to take a job like this again."

"Will it?"

"Maybe I'll learn something someday. Most likely I won't." He gestured toward Wulff. "You want to get away from the controls so I can drive this thing? You can stand over me; you can watch closely, but believe me, I'm not going to try anything. It's my ass in this thing too, remember that."

Wulff moved away. It was a calculated gamble, everything in or out of this world was but he trusted Stevens. The man visibly had nothing more to lose nor did he have anything to gain by setting the machine anywhere but straight down. A box on a plank above the controls beeped and began to make sounds, very casually Stevens extended a palm and knocked the box to the floor. It smashed.

"Sons of bitches are trying to get through," he said, "this is a hell of a time."

"They're in radio communication?"

"Of course they are," Stevens said. "I suppose they're giving final orders or something like that." He hit a lever; the copter began to move down vertically as if it were descending an elevator shaft. "I don't give a shit."

"You just work for them."

"I'm a so-called mercenary," Stevens said. "I go where they pay me but I drew a real piece of shit this time around, didn't I? That'll teach me."

Wulff looked out toward the floor of the cabin. Everything was as he had left it except that the corpse was visibly exploding with blood; the blood released in death had coated the body and was pluming toward the sides in little rivulets. He had seen death in many ways before but never, in one body, so much of it. Some died quietly and some like this one disgustingly. You just never could tell.... In that sense death was like sex; you could not tell from appearances how the person would take to it. "What I'd like to know," Stevens said, working the helicopter in its delicate descent, "is exactly what your plans are from here on in."

"That's no concern of yours," Wulff said.

"I didn't say it was ... I didn't say it was, friend. I just wonder if you plan to kill me when we get down."

"I honestly don't know," Wulff said, "I hadn't thought of it."

"Because if you're going to, I'd appreciate if you'd make it quick and clean. I can't stand suffering. I have a horror of physical pain as a matter of fact—which really makes me a bitch of a mercenary, doesn't it?"

"Fear has nothing at all to do with it. The more scared some men are, the better."

"Yes," Stevens said nodding, "that's surely true but I don't know if it applies in my case. Well, that's hardly the point, is it?" They were about five hundred feet in the air and settling toward a clearing now in what appeared to be a light forest of some sort. Neatly, Stevens headed the copter toward a part in the trees, his hand now working over the controls with assurance and accuracy. He was good, Wulff thought, no question about that. Good enough to do his job without even thinking about it which was the mark of the professional in any line. "I'm sorry about your valise," Stevens said, "I didn't know anything about it."

"I didn't think you would."

"That's the key, isn't it? The valise."

"Don't ask questions. Don't think."

"I'm not thinking," Stevens said, "I'm just making conversation, just idle, casual conversation." He peered out the window, located some point which apparently satisfied him, nodded once and then dropped the copter into a shallow, straight drive: one moment they were looking down upon trees, the next they were amidst them and then they hit ground with a rolling bump, dodged through the clearing still rolling and came to a stop in what appeared to be a shallow, abandoned strip of farmland just outside the wooded area. Stevens shook his head and cut off the engine, closing switches one by one. "Closer than you think," he said.

"You did well."

"Mostly I just try to get through," Stevens said. With the machine now out of gear he seemed to have lost intensity or even a sense of purpose. He slumped over the controls, propping his chin on an elbow. "Now what?" he said.

"We'll see," Wulff said. "Sit tight."

"You going to kill me, too?"

"Not unless it's strictly necessary."

"You know," Stevens said, almost offhandedly. "It's interesting, the things that you learn about yourself when you go under the gun. Two hours ago I would have told anyone who listened that I didn't give a shit about dying; I didn't care what happened to me; that I was already a dead man and it couldn't happen twice."

"Yes," Wulff said, "I know what you mean."

"But you want to know something?" Stevens said inquiringly, looking at him, his features open, neither defiance nor irony in the small eyes. "That's all a lot of bullshit. It's crap. I'm as afraid of dying as anyone; the idea of death terrifies me. I can't stand even thinking of it and I'm terrified that you're going to kill me like you killed that cop out there. Now isn't that interesting?"

"It's interesting," Wulff said, "everything is interesting. Where's my valise?"

"What valise? What's that?"

"Delgado said that we were going to go airborne with the valise."

"I don't know anything about that," Stevens said, "All I do is take orders and carry them out. They didn't tell me anything about a valise and there's certainly none aboard this copter."

"Then that explains everything," Wulff said and indeed it did, it made everything come clear, not that there was any satisfaction in this or that knowing what Delgado had been tracking from the first made the situation here any less difficult. But he knew now what the man had been trying to do; saw the outlines of the plan. The only question—and Wulff supposed that it did not matter particularly—was whether Delgado was freelancing this one out or whether he was acting as a government agent. Did the regime itself want the valise? This was doubtful; Delgado's remarks about the new puritanism, the self-righteousness of the regime were probably well-taken. At the highest levels they would not want to deal in drugs; would probably not even want knowledge of them. That brought it right down to Delgado, then, who was walking a very tight line indeed; on the one hand he had to carry out his official capacity, on the other there were a million illegal dollars to be made. Wulff could feel a certain sympathy for the man; he was in a difficult spot and needed all of his courage and diplomatic abilities to get through. On the other hand, this sympathy was not going to make it easier for Delgado if they ever met again. Which he suspected they would. Which he was going to make happen.

Wulff said, "Stay here," to Stevens and walked through the canvas into the passenger compartment. The man in the uniform was still in the process of dying but dying had already shifted toward decomposition; the bleeding had at last slowed and his face had tensed into the first signs of rigor mortis. He looked somewhat like a dog taking a scent, the staring eyes considering the ceiling, the mouth pursed, the long nose pointed straight upwards. Wulff had seen and touched many a dead man in his time but this one gave him a stab of revulsion; he had never seen a corpse that so *actively* bore the signs of death. Be that as it may, be everything as it may, the first thing to do was to dispose of the body.

He went over to the hatchway and kicked it open. The metal fell away; smells of woods and fields drifted into the cabin, overtaking the deeper, richer odor of the corpse; they mingled with the smell of flesh and rotting blood and the end compound of odors was almost of a kind of gaiety; all they needed, Wulff thought, were a few grazing animals, perhaps a shepherd or two and there would be a delightful pastoral scene. Of course there would be. He looked out over the terrain, then cautiously stepped from the copter, prodding at the grass and feeling its resiliency, under that first springing response corruption and ooze, of course, that was Cuba for you, that was the whole damned world but what were you going to do? In the world or out of it everything was corrupt but maybe things had come a little further since the regime because in the good old days Delgado would have shot him right in the office and had the guards carry him out but now Delgado had gone to the trouble of getting a copter to take him out of there ... which was the best indication, after all, that the man was freelancing. It was not really government policy to mingle in the drug trade; in the old Battista days everybody was into it just about the way that they were into torture but things had changed a little. They had moved along.

Well, that was progress for you; no reason not to be optimistic. Now they did it under the table, the officials worked their operations on the side and bowed to policy in the capital. Not only did it show that government was turning around, it also gave an enterprising man like Delgado the opportunity to make a few dollars on the side and that was important. Why not? all of the tourist trade was out of the island, the great casinos were closed, the tree drug lines had been cut off and the least that a man could hope for was a little private enterprise. That left him squarely up against it then. It was just him and Delgado *mano a mano*; he would not have to take on an entire government, lines of militia, the premier himself to recover his valise. Just a nice, tight simple operation: probably fifty hired hands and an arsenal. Well, that was better than the entire Cuban army. Maybe not though. Maybe not. You could never be sure.

Wulff walked back to the copter, peered in the hatchway and took the corpse firmly by the ankles. He pulled and the body came loose, sliding on blood and then jammed, stalled in the doorway. "Come on," he said, "help me get this guy out of here."

Stevens looked out from the compartment. "I'm squeamish," he said.

"I'm not only afraid of death, I can't bear to look at it. I—"

"You're going to help me," Wulff said. "You're living from moment to moment right now, friend. You understand that? You're living on my indulgence."

Stevens shrugged wryly, a man, it seemed who had come to grip with vast weaknesses in the last hour and having known them, found he could never be touched by anything again. "All right," he said. He came out cautiously, stood behind the policeman and got a grip on the shoulders, then hoisted him, gasping. Wulff backed down the ramp, the body swinging in their clutch like a tent, ballooning slightly, streaming blood again, and they staggered downrange a hundred feet or so to a small raised hill, little strips of tar clinging to it. "Dump it," Wulff said. Stevens dropped the body convulsively, the full weight of it rearing into Wulff momentarily and he lost his balance—the dead feet prodding deep into his chest—and he fell heavily in the ooze, still embracing the policeman. Stevens stood with his hands on his hips, looking at this expressionlessly. Wulff got to his feet, little strips of mud and tar clinging to him and said, "He'll keep for a while. How far are we out of the capital?"

"About ninety miles."

"Where are we?"

"It's hard to judge. We'd need a map."

"You used to flying blind, Stevens?"

"I follow instructions," Stevens said expressionlessly. "I do what I'm told to do and don't think much about it and at the end of the day or week I get some money. I was told to fly south until ordered otherwise. I assume that I would have heard from our friend down here but he had an accident before he could have a chance to talk to me."

"You're serious," Wulff said, "aren't you Stevens? You're really serious about this. You don't think, you just follow orders. Something must have happened to you a long time ago."

"Nothing *happened* to me," Stevens said, "I'm not getting into personal details at all. I'm not serious. You're the one who's serious, Wulff. You're the one who goes around killing people. Me? I just work here."

He turned toward Wulff then, a precise, neat man dressed in slightly stained flight clothes, only the curl of his lips showing fear and that in such a well-controlled way that Wulff could only admire him. The man was doing well. He was doing far better than almost any of them he had faced with death so far. "Well?" he said, "are you going to kill me?"

"I don't know," Wulff said honestly. "I haven't decided yet."

"You seem to kill everyone sooner or later. You're reputation gets around. Even a guy like me hears about you sooner or later."

"I can't decide," Wulff said, "I have to get back to the capital, you see, the fastest and easiest way and I really don't know how to fly one of these things. I can fake it but it's not my area."

"Let me fly it then."

"I'm thinking of that," Wulff said, "but I don't know whether or not I can trust you."

"You can trust me," Stevens said. "I just work here. I go for bids. I don't have anything against you at all; in fact I rather admire what I think you're trying to do."

"Sure you work for bids," Wulff said. "The question is what you think they're bidding now."

Stevens motioned toward the corpse. "That's what they're bidding," he said. "I think I get the message. I live in a hotel room and I drink a lot. This year I'm in Havana but next year I'll be somewhere else. The way I figure, there's always corruption and troubles and room for a man with certain biddable skills. It has nothing to do with ideology."

"Where does Delgado live?" Wulff said.

"I don't know where he lives. You saw where he works. Somewhere in Havana I suppose. Maybe he lives in his offices. How the hell do I know? You want to find out where he lives I'll put you there in a three-point landing. I don't give a shit, Wulff. You'll reach that point sooner or later but you don't really believe that now."

Wulff looked at his pistol and then at Stevens. Easy. It would be so easy. The thing about the power to bring death is that after a while it can get to you, almost demand application. It starts small and then it grows; it begins in an alley somewhere or in some secret room and then it spreads out, moves to larger and larger stages and eventually you can end up being a Louis Cicchini. A Marasaco. Or a Delgado. He could see that in himself now: a vivid picture of what he could do to Stevens. It would take so little out of him; it would be virtually effortless. The gun raised, the shaking terror of the man, the slow desertion of life then as the realization hit him, that realization which always took them, even those killed in surprise, then the explosion, the powder, the impact, the small, neat hole or the ragged one, blood pumping through, kicking limbs, a flurry of collapse ... and Stevens would be lying next to the policeman on the grass and tar, his body stained by blood and earth, transported from the life that until thirty seconds ago had been as much his as Wulff's. The mystery of this deliverance; death as something co-existent with life, so near that it could be brought about casually. And yet men would reinforce that separation forever, do everything they could to deny the reality of death, build and destroy people or cities merely to prove that death could not overtake them.

He could not kill the man. Not deliberately, not up against him like this. All of those others he had killed had been for a reason, there had been no choice at all, ultimately, but this would be face-to-face considered murder ... and he was not a murderer. Slowly, almost reluctantly, Wulff lowered the gun. He had found and measured a weakness in himself; it was that simple. He hoped that he would not have to pay for it later. It was the same weakness that had driven him into Tamara's body in San Francisco, rutting and screaming in copulation when he had thought all desire had died with the girl in the hotel room. It was a weakness which he could not account for but would nevertheless have to live with and work around. He did not enjoy killing. He could do it if the circumstances necessitated, he could do it if the price were right, and, as on that freighter explosion in San Francisco, he could certainly do it easily enough if the victims were generalized and invisible. But face to face, unless it meant his life or vengeance, he did not like the kill.

Slowly, then, he put the pistol away inside his coat. He knew that Stevens represented no threat. If Stevens had seen a weakness in him, then Wulff had long since seen the weakness in Stevens; he was a man, simply enough, who went for bidders and he did so because he held onto life so desperately that he wanted the path of least resistance, of service rather than decision. This was true of all the mercenaries; they laughed at death, gave the illusion of great courage. But there was no courage whatsoever, merely the desire for survival, to go on and on, not to die but merely to live, confront nothing, seek nothing, merely to stagger on from moment to moment because that great Prince, Death was always there—

Wulff felt sick. He walked past Stevens, for the moment only dimly conscious of the man, and toward the copter, his feet sinking in the ooze, feeling the weight of the corpse he had carried still pressing against his wrists and shoulder blades. Nausea overtook him; if it had not been too much trouble he might have stopped there and retched.

It was just too much. It was all too much. You did the best you could and he would go on, but it was a hard thing to realize that only the enemy could enjoy his work. He had thought in New York, at the beginning, that he could turn the tables on the enemy by killing in his own joy—and the first kills had been that way—but now every death, like a fingerprint, was a stain on himself ....

He went inside and sat there quietly waiting for Stevens to return. Of course the man would return. He had nowhere else to go ... and he worked for the highest bidder.

Wulff was the highest bidder.

# VI

Williams was working interrogation in the basement of the station house when the phone call came in. It was a simple, routine kick-the-shit-out-of-the-guy type of interrogation; the subject an eighteen-year-old junkie moving now deep into the withdrawal stages and panic. The collar had been made while the kid was in the act of ripping a handbag off a fat woman in daylight at Broadway and 107th Street in front of the patrol car, an act so stupid that the kid obviously had been far gone to even consider it. Soon enough they would book him in on something or other and throw him into the Tombs where like it or not he would go into his private withdrawal program, but there was a chance before they gave up and took him upstairs that they might get the kid, in his panic, to blurt out some information they could use: something about sources of supply, connections, quality of drugs and so on. You could never tell with these things; you worked every angle you could. Nothing would happen or the junkies would be stupid and then, suddenly, you could fall into a great deal of information, enough to break open a pending case. What the hell: you tried. Williams didn't mind this kind of work; it got closer to reality then most aspects of PD and because he was a black man he might be able to work on the kid's confidence a little more than the white ones could, not that black or white made much difference in the present structure of the street or the PD. That kind of shit had gone out five or six years ago.

Still, you gave it a whirl. You gave anything a whirl; nothing ventured, nothing gained and like that, and even though procedures had tightened quite a bit in recent years you could still put the screws in at least a little. It was mostly the *threat* of the screws which got the job done anyway. Williams hit the kid backhanded, pulling his punch carefully while the other cop sitting in the corner on a stool watched absently, chewing gum, letting this one be Williams's party. Even in the basement, the black man got to do all the work. The kid screamed and backed further away, kicking the chair against the wall. "I don't know shit," he said, "I don't know nothing about anything. I been off that stuff for months; I'm clean. I kicked all that shit; I'm just trying to stay alive now." His voice cracked. "Please leave me alone," he said, "you can't fucking *do* this to me; I got my rights."

"You ain't got no fucking rights," Williams said, falling into the kid's slang. Fordham Law School rhetoric wouldn't take you far in a basement. "Your fucking rights are the rights I decide you got, and right now you ain't got none." He closed in on the kid, a nineteen-year-old, address 411 West 111th Street, furnished room, no friends or relatives. Bullshit about going to 411 to find anything out. Better to pound them face to face. "Who's supplying you?" he said.

"No one," the kid said. His eyes rolled; his cheekbones almost transparent. At his best he weighed a hundred twenty on a six foot frame; a year ago he might have been almost double that. You could tell, you could see a big weight drop; the kid moved like a heavy man. "I told you I'm clean."

"You ain't shit," Williams said and hit the kid backhanded again. The kid screamed, a high wail; the cop on the stool looked at Williams in an inquisitive way. *Go easy*, the look was saying, *but then again go hard; it's not my problem is it?* What it came down to was just two niggers in a basement working each other over, am I right? Williams shook his head and plowed down on the kid, feeling a sudden explosion of self-loathing. What was he doing here after all? Wasn't he merely another black man tearing at a brother while the white man watched? Was it true what some of the militants said, that at the root it was always a race issue? Don't think of that now, fuck it; he had a mortgage in St. Albans and a pregnant wife. The system gave him shelter. Choking on his rage he hit the kid once more, a little bit harder this time than he might have meant and the boy fell over, weeping. He squirmed on the floor like an insect. "All right!" he said, "all right! I'll tell you what I know, I don't know nothing," and weeping, head bowed he began to mumble names, addresses, quantities, whereabouts, all of the information which Williams had worked out so patiently ... and he couldn't hear a word. It was frustrating, that was all. He nodded to the cop on the stool who came off quickly, moved over to the boy and bent an inquisitorial ear, the kid scrambling around on the floor while the cop tried a juxtaposition of heads, trying to get close enough to make sense of the babbling. And Williams withdrew. He simply could not bear to get close to them. Hitting out at them was not a closeness but merely an expression of revulsion; diving into them though meant that he was coming into a closeness that he had dedicated his life avoiding. That was the whole principle, to build distance. That was what the system was giving him.

The cop groaned, shrugged, nodded as the kid whispered to him. Williams found himself losing interest, walking toward the door, feeling a detachment surging through him that was the next thing to disgust. Face it: if there were any satisfactions in this at all they came in breaking them down, ramming through to the corrupt, empty hearts of them, establishing control. But what came about as a result of this meant absolutely nothing to him. The interrogations were interesting but the interesting parts had nothing at all to do with the information disclosed. Let me face it, Williams thought suddenly, looking at the kid who was now embracing the other cop, rising to his knees, his head extended as he whispered horrid confidences, I am a monster. In certain ways no different from theirs, I am absolutely monstrous. Police work could do this to you, it could do it to anyone. Still, you could go back to the mortgaged home in St. Albans and act as if this were not so ....

An elderly woman clerk looked in through the door, jabbing Williams in the back with the knob; he jumped away. Clerks would come in anywhere; the interrogation rooms meant nothing to them. That was civil service for you: there was nothing that could be done to interfere with the career-&-salary plan. "David Williams?" she said.

"I'm David Williams."

"You're David Williams?"

"I'm David Williams," he said, again. "Don't I look like David Williams? Don't I feel like David Williams? That's who I am."

The kid broke off from his whispering into the white patrolman's ear. "Get me out of here," he said to the clerk, "they're torturing me."

"That's a police matter. There's a telephone call for David Williams upstairs."

"All right," Williams said, "I'll take it."

"They really can't do this to me," the kid said. "There are constitutional things, aren't there? They're not allowed to torture you for testimony."

"Shut up," the patrolman said.

"I don't know anything about the Constitution," the clerk said, "that's not my concern," and walked out of there. The kid slumped on the floor shaking his head as she went away.

"I'll be back," Williams said.

"I don't like it," said the patrolman. His name was Thomas and he had been on duty with Williams for a fortnight and he didn't like anything. Then again, Williams conceded, there was no particular reason why he should. "I don't want to be alone with him."

"Be a man," Williams said. "Consider the stakes; we're going to break up the international drug market on the strength of what information is divulged here tonight." Thomas did not know quite how to take this. His face suffused with confusion. "I'll be back," Williams said. "It's probably my wife; she's five months in, you know; this kind of thing can happen anytime." This seemed to mollify Thomas; even the kid looked impressed. Williams went up the stairs directly behind the room two at a time, not bothering to close the door. Once he was out of there, he knew, Thomas was going to back away from the suspect with an embarrassed expression, pull out cigarettes, even offer the kid one maybe, trying to take the pressure off. Odd but all the sympathy for the kid would come from that quarter; Williams was the one who had put the knife-edge in the scene. He went through the reception room and into a back area, opened a door and went into a small, bleak office where there was nothing but a phone on the desk and a huge picture of a naked girl on the wall. The picture, in black and white showed the girl fingering herself; over this, on the wall itself, someone had neatly printed the caption ON THE TAKE. It had been hanging there for almost a week which was a record for this precinct house; probably it would hang on for another few days after which a lieutenant would come in and demand that it be taken down. Either that or the lieutenant would add his own caption which would render it instantly unacceptable to everyone else and it would be taken down. Williams turned his back on this—of course the girl was white but ten years ago she would have been black; such was the progress of interracial understanding in the department—he picked up the phone which if the clerk had been efficient had already been set into the line for his personal call. "Hello," he said unhappily.

"This is Wulff," a voice said. "You've taken long enough, Williams; where the fuck have you been?"

"I've been breaking the international drug trade," Williams said. He held the phone tightly against his ear, trying not to show surprise. "Where the fuck have you been, man?" he said. "Where are you calling from?"

"Where do you think?"

"I have lost track of you," Williams said. "I have lost track of you since you climbed on a certain flight outward bound from Las Vegas and got yourself taken to Cuba. But up until then I kept pretty good tabs on you, man. I guess everybody in the country knows who you are by now. You've made a pretty good name for yourself. You are no longer obscure."

"The hijacking got around."

"Everything got around," Williams said. He propped the telephone under his ear, looked for a cigarette, realized that he had left them in the interrogation room and cursed.

"What's that?"

"Nothing," Williams said. "Where are you?"

"Well," Wulff said and paused, "I seem to be in Cuba."

"Still. Still in Cuba, eh? Well that's fine," Williams said. The need for a cigarette was overwhelming him but he would come to grips with it somehow. Discipline. "When are you going to come out?"

"That all depends," Wulff said. "I'm still looking for a certain valise."

"You got the valise, then," Williams said. "You found it in Vegas."

"I found a lot of things in Vegas, Williams. I found about fifty corpses."

"And the valise. And you got on the plane with the valise and that was the reason for the hijack."

"Something like that," Wulff said thinly. "You ought to go into police work, Williams. You've got a lot of talent for picking up clues and following a trail. Have you ever thought of getting into the police racket?"

"How are you going to get out of Cuba?"

"I don't know," Wulff said. "I don't even know yet how I came in so it's hard to figure the getting out. By plane, probably. But I've got some unfinished business here yet."

"What's that?"

"I've got to pick up the valise. Somewhere along the line I seem to have misplaced a valise but I'm going to get it."

"Why tell this to me?" Williams said, looking at the nude picture. These things were posed by professional models, all of them, but this girl looked as if she genuinely liked her job. Funny that he had never noticed the tilt of the mouth before. The fact that he was desiring a white woman sent guilt to mesh with lust somewhere in his head; it drew a coil, his fast erection faded. "Is there any way I can help you?"

"You helped me into Vegas," Wulff said. "You helped me into fifty murders, you helped me into a hijack, you helped me into a helicopter with a man who expected to kill me. Any more of your help, Williams, and they'd carry me out of here for a state funeral."

"This is your war," Williams said, "Not mine. I don't want any responsibility for it. You were the one who started this. You asked me for help—"

"And you gave it, Williams," Wulff said. "Oh boy did you give it. Do you help everyone this way? It's a lucky thing I caught you at the precinct, you know. Your wife really wasn't sure where the hell you were. But I had a feeling, Williams. Old cop instinct, you know? I figured that you were downstairs in the stationhouse, probably beating the shit out of some suspect. Upholding the system, of course."

"I got no time for this," Williams said, "I'm on duty now. I don't know what you want but there's nothing—"

"I'm calling international wire," Wulff said, "and it's taken me about fifteen minutes to get this one through so don't think that I'm going to keep you. I'm not going to keep you at all. I got a big problem down here. I just wanted to tell you one thing, though."

"What's that?"

"Are you sure you want to know?"

Williams took the mouthpiece slightly away from his lips and said, "I have no time for shit, man. I don't know what position you're putting me in, what you're trying to make me but you've got this wrong—"

"I don't have anything wrong. I have most things right, Williams. Do you know what I'm going to do? I'm going to get out of Cuba with that valise. Nobody thinks I'm going to make it now but I'm going to do it."

"I hope so. I really hope so, man."

"And you know what then? I'm going to take that valise straight up north to your pretty little living room in St. Albans, Williams, and I'm going to dump it at your feet and open the clips one by one and show you a million dollars of shit, most of it stolen from the property clerk's office in the good old municipal court. Have you ever seen a million dollars' worth of shit?"

"No I have not."

"Well neither had I, Williams," Wulff said almost gaily. "So don't take it personally. There are very few people walking around, even top-type organization people who have even seen a quarter of that. A tenth of it is pretty big stuff nowadays. And you know what I'm going to do after I've got the clips open on the valise and you're staring down at all that stuff? You know what the next move is?"

"I couldn't imagine. I simply couldn't imagine, Wulff, so you tell me what the next move is."

"I will. I'm going to ask *you* what to do with it, Williams. I'm going to let it be your fucking decision because I've had enough decisions for the time being. I'm going to rest on this one. You're the one who sent me out for the shit; *you* can make a decision on what to do with it next. You always knew all the moves, Williams: you got the mortgage and the pregnant wife; you're the one who loves the system so you make a decision *for* the system. What is best in terms of your fucking system, Williams?"

"Enough," Williams said and withdrew the phone from his ear.

"Think about it over the next few days," Wulff said thinly, "because I'm getting off now but I guarantee you, I absolutely guarantee that I am going to come out of here alive and I'm going to have that stuff with me. What is it going to do if it gets into New York? Can you throw it into the sea and say it doesn't exist? Can you toss it into the market and watch what it does to prices? Do you want to take it back to the property office and say that, here, they can cover their tracks; we've pulled them out of an embarrassing situation? Do we go with the system or against it? And if we go with it do we know what's right? It's time you did some thinking, that you came up against it. I have in the last couple of days, Williams. I've learned a good deal about myself. Now it's time you did the same thing."

"All right," Williams said.

"All right yourself," Wulff said, "all right yourself, you middle-class son of a bitch," and cut the connection. Williams stood, holding the phone at arm's length, looking at it with astonishment and then, with a total abandonment to fury, he lifted the thing over his head, heaved it up several feet in the air and with all his force smashed it down on the receiver, brought it down so hard that the plastic split, the desk shook, the picture on the wall shook. Two deskmen came sprinting into the room to see exactly what the hell was wrong but one look at Williams' stricken face convinced them. They turned and got the hell out of there.

So did Williams. So did he. He went back to the basement and finished up the interrogation; the kid completely broken babbling out names and addresses now as if he were giving a list of people invited to his funeral. Small potatoes, but all of it would entail careful checking. It would keep a few men busy for a few days; give the narcotics division something else to be hopeful about.

Things, in short would proceed, just as if Wulff were not coming back with his valise.

But Williams knew he would.

# VII

The call had been out of a hotel room in the back streets of the shabbiest, dirtiest slum Wulff had ever seen. Backyard Havana. How Stevens had managed to sneak them back into the city without detection, avoiding what must have been heavy surveillance was beyond him but Stevens had done it. He had not been kidding when he said he was the best damned pilot in the history of aeronautics or at least of the helicopter. The return from the countryside had been done at high cruising range, far above the maximum operating efficiency for altitude and the copter had groaned and bucked all the way in, Wulff clinging to sides of the cabin, trying to hold his balance and not become sick, as Stevens did what he had to do. The man was remarkably gifted; Wulff had to admit that. His skills were beyond almost any other copter pilot's and he had flown with a few in his time. Part of it had to do, he supposed, with Stevens' admitted cowardice. The man wanted desperately to live; it was survival technique which he had been applying to the controls and as jolting as the ride had been, it had all along been controlled by the bottom line of necessity.

What Stevens wanted to do, he had explained, was to get them back to some kind of safety; they had to get out of the countryside because at this moment, no doubt, there would be a massive sweep and the place of safety, oddly enough, would be the central city itself, in fact in the dismal hotel in which Stevens had been living for some weeks. "They'll never think of looking for us there," Stevens said, "they're just not very organized, there's no organization anywhere along here, they don't know what the hell they're doing." And that at least Wulff had been willing to agree with. The likelihood was that if he could get under cover, Stevens said, get the helicopter out of sight they might decide that the helicopter had ditched somewhere and all of them would be written off for dead ... which would, from the viewpoint of anyone, be a convenience.

It was a question, though, Stevens pointed out, of how much official support Delgado was getting for this adventure or whether he was freelancing it out strictly. Stevens simply did not know that much about the operation; he contended that he was a mercenary working on a strictly job-to-job basis and knew about as little on the internal workings of things as Wulff did himself. Wulff did not know whether or not to believe him, whether to believe any of this but past the initial decision to trust Stevens, at least for the moment, there was nothing to do but ride along with it. The man, at the very least, could fly a helicopter, he could get them out of the countryside which was a very dangerous place to be, and he could provide a few leads on Delgado. Not many but better than none. It was obvious that Wulff could hardly walk into the administration building and take on Delgado face-to-face; no amount of courage or anger could make anything like this possible. He would have to find the man's home and would have to come in behind the lines, so to speak; even then it was probable that Delgado had a great deal of security and that in light of the situation he was not going to be easy to get now. Nevertheless, Wulff was going to try. He wanted Delgado dead. That was personal, that was one killing which he would enjoy, but on an impersonal basis, he had to have him dead because he wanted the shipment back ... and knew that he was going to have to kill Delgado to get it.

According to Stevens—who kept the helicopter at high altitude, bouncing and jouncing through the air but for all of that showing complete control over the machine—a strictly telephone contact basis was absolutely essential. He would stay in his hotel room drinking and thinking; now and then a phone call would come in with instructions for a job and he would go out and perform it. That was all. All equipment was provided; Stevens had to bring nothing but himself. Stevens refused to say exactly what the jobs had entailed or how many men he had seen murdered. For that matter, he would not even say exactly how long he had been in Cuba except that it was more than a year but less than a couple, and that he was in some kind of trouble with the American government which had made this kind of exile necessary, but the trouble was not his fault, and had to do with false charges. Wulff decided that he would settle for this. For the moment he was willing to settle for anything which Stevens wanted to tell him. He had much more serious problems on his mind.

Stevens knew exactly where to go. He came in, under the cover of night, into a dense, damp plain on the outskirts of the city, landing without lights, peering through the screens to negotiate a hand-landing and in the last thirty seconds he went for a straight descent, cutting the engines for quiet, the copter dropping down straight and plunging into mud with such force that it was half-taken into the slime by the impact and rolled there, held only by the ledge of mud created. Insects twittered and smashed themselves against the sides of the steaming copter. Wulff shook his head, raised it for the first time since the steep descent had begun—flight training or not what the descent had generated was simple nausea—and unfastening the safety gear, followed Stevens out the hatch, leaping into the mud, feeling himself settle into it quickly and it was a struggle to pull himself against the grip of the mud to slightly higher ground, the earth gripping at him like small hands. "Where are we?" he said at last when they got to a clearing and Stevens pointed in front of them. "We're in the big backyard," he said, "the big backyard of a ruined city. We can go to my hotel."

"Can we?" Wulff said. He looked back toward the copter. Even here, just a hundred yards away or less, the machine was barely visible, a dark animal against a darker background. It was possible that by morning it would have collapsed all the way into the mud.

"It will," Stevens said, following his gaze. "It will sink. It should be up to the prop soon. Besides, no one comes here but derelicts and the gangs that kill them. They'll never look for it and if they did they sure as hell wouldn't go around reporting it. It's about a mile to the hotel," Stevens said. "I live in one of the most distinguished sections of town. Let's hike it."

"Why?" Wulff said. "Why should I trust you?"

"We've gotten this far, haven't we?"

"You had to get onto the ground too. You say you work for the highest bidder, Stevens. Then why should you work with me? I'm offering you nothing."

"I don't feel like getting into philosophical discussions," Stevens said. "We've had a very rough ride and I'm ass deep in mud. Let's go back."

"You piloted a plane that was supposed to take me on a death flight.

So why should you turn around?"

"Because *you* don't understand," Stevens said. "You're the one who says that people don't dig, don't follow your deep message, Wulff, but you're the one who's missing now." He turned toward him, even in the darkness, his eyes were luminous. "You've got to trust me," he said.

"Why?"

"Because I got you this far, that's why."

"I had a gun on you."

"That didn't matter," Stevens said.

"Sure it does. You were the one who said it mattered. You're the one who's afraid of dying."

"Listen," Stevens said, "are we going to have to stand here in this goddamn mud and discuss attitudes or can we get the hell back? This can't go on, you know. It just can't go on at all."

"I don't understand anything about you, Stevens," Wulff said but this was not true, not exactly because he thought that he understood Stevens very well. Stevens reminded him very much of David Williams. The two of them were playing the same game, it would seem, and almost for the same reasons except that Williams was working inside the system, Stevens on the edge. But they were high-bidder men. They were for sale. It all came down to a question of self-protection.

"All right," Stevens said. A curl of wind took him and he shuddered standing, a light opened up in the distance, sending little splinters of flame through the clearing and Wulff instinctively ducked, looking back toward the copter. Stevens was right. The machine was already shrouded; by morning it would be up to prop level. "I believe in you. Okay? That's all." His voice had dropped perceptibly, become hoarse. "Do you think I'm a fool?" he said, "I'm a lot of things but not that. I know who you are. I know what brought you here and why Delgado sent you out. I know what you represent and what you've been going through. Don't you think that everyone here knows?"

"I don't know."

"You're right," Stevens said, his voice still in that peculiar monotone. "You're hitting them at their own level with their own weapons. You're not going to put up with the shit anymore; you're going to get right at them where they live. I can admire that. I'd do the same thing myself if I had the guts."

"I'm touched," Wulff said, "I'm really touched." Stevens was right. There was no question about it; this was no place to stand and hold a discussion. The light was beaming in again, the splinters shaking. A probe, no doubt. Soon enough, if they stayed here, the beam would pick them up.

"You want me to say more?" Stevens said. "You want me to get a violin accompaniment? Well fuck that anyway; you'd just think that I was begging for my life. I'm not begging for my life, Wulff, I just want to get out of here. You want to kill me, I'm as prepared for it now as I'll ever be; just draw your gun and get it over with. Get it done now; I won't crack but five minutes from now I might. Otherwise let's get the fuck out of here. These people are no idiots. They're going to get us on a tracer, damn it."

"All right," Wulff said. "All right, enough of it, let's get the hell to ground," and Stevens, wanting to hear no more turned and began to trudge from the clearing. Wulff followed him, head down, hands in pockets, stumbling after him in the ooze, smelling the night and the insects swarming around them, wondering exactly how crazy this could get. How far out of control it would slip. Did he really think, following Stevens to a hotel room, that he was going to get anywhere? Did he really think, following this mercenary blindly, that he was in any position to deal with Delgado? Fuck that: screw it, Cuba was death country, Havana oblivion city. They had sucked him in here and beaten him as bad as anyone since they had almost gotten him at the tollgate heading into Boston. Boston had been a sucker play but at least he had been working his own territory there: what the hell did he know about Cuba? Cuba had been a foreign country for fifteen years now, a country controlled by the enemy, and now he was so deeply in trouble that he did not even know where his adversary *was*, he was dependent upon a desperate mercenary who had been piloting a death-plane, he had absolutely nowhere to turn ... and in the bargain, Wulff thought wryly, he was absolutely at the end of his physical rope. Even he had to rest, the tensions and pressures had been so great that he felt that he was caving inward, slowly.

But he trudged behind Stevens. There was nothing else to do and he had a kind of wistful, crazy faith in the man now, the same faith that Stevens for all he knew might feel for *him*. They went into the back section of Havana, a slum so crude, ragged, disjointed and mean in all of its aspects that Wulff decided it had to be, there was just no alternative, the worst he had ever seen short of Saigon which was of course in a different category altogether. The people staggering around these streets seemed to be suspended at the last edges of humanity; street scenes in Harlem were bad enough but at least the junkies there had drugs to hold them up for a while. Here, Wulff suspected, there was not even that. Drugs along with hope had dried up with the coming of the revolution; these people had nothing to buffer them from the stones except the conviction that as bad as today was, tomorrow would certainly be worse and next week inconceivable. They reached out hands toward them as they went through, these people did: some of them Wulff supposed were old and others were not so old but they all looked the same age, a ruined, beaten point of chronology where all of the organs, one by one, were ceasing to function. Not only did they look the same age, these people all appeared to be of the same sex, neither male nor female but something in between, something horridly complex which drove them past biology and made them part of the landscape and it was the landscape itself which persisted in Wulff's mind, which he knew would last far longer than anything else he would take out of Cuba, even the valise if he got it because the landscape proved beyond a doubt that revolutions did not work. They simply made no difference. Movements, people, regimes came and went but the landscape was eternal; it was the only politics that any of them would know, here in the backyard of Havana, and Wulff felt himself retreating into a tunnel of revulsion as he and Stevens, step by step, trudged through those streets.

No one assaulted them. No one seemed very interested in them at all; the reaching of the hands was more a reflex action than anything else. Tropism they called it, at least the botanists did, the vegetative turning of flora to and away from light, depending upon the season, and these people, he thought, had no more minds than plants had. Still, they were terribly important; in their name murders had been committed, vast shifting flux, the rising of castles, all of this had come in the name of the people even though these people, in no true sense, could be said to exist.

Enough. He had a job to do; he was not a social revolutionary. Even if he had been, where would you begin? Where would you try to make these people right? Even if you could cleanse all drugs out of the vein of the United States, New York City would still look like an occupied zone toward the end of wartime. It would take fifty years to make any changes even if the root causes themselves were instantly removed; most of these people would have to die off before anything could be done. The sickness bit too deep. Everything did after a while; the answer was not politics.

They went into Stevens's hotel. It was a hotel only by Havana standards Wulff supposed; it was a crumbling, rotting three-story hulk on a street even more depressed and rancid than those through which they had walked. There was no clerk sitting on the bottom level, only a lobby in which in various attitudes of despair or catatonia a scattering of men sat, staring at the walls, a few of them singing to themselves in aimless little voices. "It's not much," Stevens whispered, "but it's home," and they went up a winding flight of stairs, beating at insects for purchase on the landings, up one more flight and down the hall into a small, dirty room in which there was a bed, a chair, a bulb dangling from ceiling wire and an old-fashioned telephone propped next to the bed which Stevens pointed to with a flourish. "All of the conveniences," he said, "the phone is particularly important; that's how I get my assignments." He locked the door on an unsafe, insecure bolt, kicked it and walked back toward the windowsill where the bottles stood like little dishevelled troops, removed a gin bottle. "You want a drink?" he said.

"I don't think so," said Wulff.

"I do."

"You go right ahead."

"If any man ever was, I'm entitled to a drink. I never thought I'd see this place again." Stevens uncapped the bottle and drank from it straight, groaning as the gin hit his stomach, then doubling over, half-retching. "Never thought I'd see it again," he said and collapsed on the bed holding the bottle, falling straight back, clutching it as his head hit the blanket. He put the bottle in his mouth and drank again. Wulff could see that as far as Stevens was concerned the night was over; he would use the gin to drink himself into stupor and then that would be the end of all things.

"What are we supposed to do?" he said.

"I don't know," Stevens said, "that's kind of your problem, isn't it? I told you that I'd give you a place to hole up, a place to get underground while you decided what to do next, and that's exactly what I've done. It's your move, isn't it? I don't see how I can help you."

"I've got to find Delgado."

"I know you've got to find Delgado and don't you worry about it," Stevens said, shaking his head, giggling, taking another swallow from the bottle. "You are in the right place to find him because don't you think he'll be calling in here sooner or later? He's going to want to know where the fuck I am; that phone is going to ring."

"I thought that you said he'd take us all for having been killed someplace."

"He will," Stevens said, "he definitely will, that's exactly the way he thinks you see but he's a man who covers all his possibilities first. He'll call, check in just to make sure that I'm not here by any chance. That's routine surveillance procedure, isn't it? I mean, it makes sense that he'd check to see if by any chance I've returned."

"So you'll set up a meeting with him."

"If you want," Stevens said, "you see, I don't give a shit about this anymore. If you want to use me as a setup you can go right ahead and do that because I'm finished. Do you mind if I pass out, Wulff? If it's all the same to you I think I'm at the end of the line. You can use all the conveniences here. You can even go out in the streets and go looking for Delgado if you want. Help yourself. There are a couple of pistols on the bottom panel in that bureau in a dead compartment but I don't know if they work or not. I've never touched them; I just carry them around for show. Actually I'm afraid to even handle a gun," Stevens said and this seemed to bring forth his giggling all over again, the giggling became a wild, uncontrollable fit which clawed and heaved at him; he rolled on the bed groaning with the convulsions. "I wanted a quiet life," he said, "a quiet life, a simple existence, no pressures, no politics. Look at me. Look at it now. I had it all figured out, Wulff. I'd freelance or soldier of fortune myself into a permanent crippling injury by the time I was forty and then I'd find myself a nice foundation to take care of me for the rest of my life. The whole thing was to get an injury or illness which wasn't too painful but had a good foundation back of it so that you could get free room and board and plenty of sympathy. Muscular dystrophy? Retardation? Polio? But they wiped out polio years ago and anyway I'm really afraid of physical pain. In fact I'm afraid of almost everything," Stevens said and quite neatly passed out on the bed, the gin bottle plopping to one side, his empty hand to the other, his mouth open, fishlike he groaned in air through his mouth, looking at the ceiling with fixed eyes and then his eyes closed. He slept.

Wulff looked at him. He had really bought it this time he decided. But bought or not it seemed that he had a companion. Stevens was right, for all of his posturing the practicality of the man was awesome. There was nowhere else to go now. He was safer in the hotel room than he would be elsewhere. And Delgado would be checking in.

He went to the bureau and just as Stevens had said, in a compartment slatted in above the bottom drawer was a small, rather seedy array of pistols, four of them in various stages of age and finish, looking up at him. He checked them out one by one and they seemed to be operative. A full clip was in each; the clips themselves were in the drawer. Probably the pistols would work if they didn't blow his hand off first. He was not going to pump a few shots into the walls or ceiling to find out, that was for sure.

Wulff put the stuff in his pockets, secreting armaments like jewels in various crevices of his body. Then he looked at the sleeping Stevens and at the floor. The floor looked more inviting; he could probably get a few hours rest here.

Then his attention was caught by the phone. It was there; it leered at him temptingly, surely in a place like this no one could possibly perform a tap. Technology, even with the new regime, had to be at least forty years behind the United States here. They had not yet had the advantage of defoliants, phone tracers, organized systematic distribution of drugs ... Oh, they had a lot to look forward to if only the regime could keep on going and bring them to the point where America stood. Probably they could make it. If nothing else, in a few years one of the corporations or a mass of them would simply buy up Cuba wholesale. For a tax write off.

He picked up the phone.

That was when he called Williams.

## VIII

Delgado was trying to stay calm. Stay calm, he was telling himself, do not panic, but it was difficult to contrive this mood, more difficult than it had been in a long time and he knew that he was showing the visible signs of a man disintegrating. Only the fact that he was in his office, that the door was locked, that there were definite orders that he should not be disturbed for any reason were preventing everyone from seeing his deterioration. His hands were shaking, sweat was pouring from his cheeks. He was not acting like an old revolutionary but like some nineteen-year-old peasant, trapped in the hills by the militia, pouring out his heart and guts to them for fear of being castrated by their knives. He could not go on this way. He had to get hold of himself.

The copter was missing; the men had not returned. Their whereabouts were unknown. Obviously something had botched the job; they had not killed the American. It had been a simple flight, a simple assignment: two men should have been able to handle it easily. What was there to do? The American was unarmed, helpless, he had been sent up with a skilled gunman and an equally skilled pilot. Two against one in the air and the American weaponless. Nevertheless the assignment had not been carried out. Somehow the American had overcome the situation, probably killed both pilot and gunman and had gotten the copter down and away.

Where had it gone wrong? Had he gone wrong? Should he have sent out more men? But that was the problem; he was playing this situation as close as possible: the more men he sent out the higher were the chances that he, Delgado, would be found out. Still, two men had obviously not been enough. He should have taken the risk. He could have found another and another, two more reliable men. One risk outbalanced the other. His mistake. He had underestimated the

American. And he knew who the man was. What he had done! How could he have been so stupid? A streak of self-loathing went through Delgado like an electric bolt, so jolting that it was almost purifying, it cleansed him in a way. It was his own fault. There was no one else to blame. He stood alone; he took the blame, he would now have to save the situation himself.

Somehow the American had escaped and doubtless was bearing down upon Delgado. He would be looking for vengeance. This man was a killer. It was not enough for him to merely escape; this man killed because his purposes as he saw it was to abolish evil and Delgado would seem evil, at least from his point of view. The American would not leave Havana let alone the country until he confronted Delgado and although that was bad because Delgado did not want to face a man who would kill him it was also good because it provided a certain sense of security. There would be no loose ends. He would not have to think of the American somewhere in his own country, outside of the borders of Cuba, planning for revenge—waiting months and years for *that* hammer to strike. No. It would not be that way. The American would not leave until he had performed his mission and that meant that the situation would be settled quickly and between the two of them. All right. All right, he could deal with that.

The drugs were in his possession. He knew exactly where they were and he could get his hands on them instantly. The temptation would be strong, Delgado thought, to take that valise and make his own run for freedom. A less judicious man than he would have done it. He would already have arranged his flight, plotted out the means of disposition. This less cautious version of himself would be in the United States by now, frantically seeking connections through which he could unload close to a million dollars' worth of heroin. This less cautious version of himself would have been killed, too. The American was no fool. The arrangements which Delgado would have been trying to make would have drawn attention like carrion drawing the restless animals of the desert. The American would have picked up the rotten scent and closed in. No, there was nothing to do but wait. Take care of that business first. First things first as the Americans put it. Until Wulff was out of the way he would sit tight, make no moves, attempt no disposition. It should not take long. Then, Delgado thought, then he would be home free.

He would have the drugs then and no one who knew their possessor, no one trying to take them away. His title would be clear. It would be absolute; the interests in the United States, if nothing else, respected property rights and the fair interest of the holder and they would be doing business with him, not threatening attack. They respected property these people. Once the American was out of the way: clear sailing. And how could he lose? He had the full and righteous force of the government behind him. The American was a felon, in two countries now. He had no rights, no means, no defense. The full force of both governments were mobilized to find and kill him and Delgado not only had the valise, he had government sanction to use all forces to kill him. How could he lose?

He couldn't lose. All that he had to do was to keep the search parties going, cover every alley in Havana, which he could do with a telephone and meanwhile stay under the perfect security which was afforded him by his office and his rights as a public official. He represented the government of the country; in his defense all force could be exerted and against that what could the American do? He had no troops, armaments, possessions, plan. All that he had was an imperfect knowledge of the situation, so could it be more than a matter of time until Delgado closed in on him? No. It could not. It could not be, the situation was totally in control, he had everything in hand and why then, Delgado thought, having reached this completely optimistic and absolutely true assessment of the situation ... why was he shaking like this? Why am I so frightened? he asked himself.

Because—the perfectly reasonable interior voice of the old revolutionary he had carried around inside himself like a jack-in-the-box for fifteen years said—because, the old revolutionary told him, the American is of a type with whom you have never dealt before.

That's ridiculous, he said. I was in the mountains.

You were in the mountains; a lot of people were with you in the mountains. You were sustained there by others. Also, you had faith which is something that you do not have now. You had a deep and persistent belief in the feeling that you were right.

That has nothing to do with it.

It has everything to *do* with it. You had an ideology then, you were fired by political idealism. What are you fired by now except greed?

Idealism has nothing to do with it either, he told the old revolutionary. Idealism is for the young or for the disenfranchised. It has no connection to those who have or are near power. Which is the situation that applies to me now.

That is why you are a fraud, Delgado. You are no longer what you were. You have been abandoned, you have completely abandoned yourself.

I have abandoned nothing.

You have abandoned everything.

I see a reasonable chance to make a new life for myself, he told the old revolutionary. The drugs can give me a way to a new life. It is not as if I am doing anything that would not be done otherwise. Americans are deeply involved in the drug culture, the people who sell it are merely answering a human need. Is it wrong if I get some of this for myself? It will change nothing. It is not as if I am taking drugs myself or I am creating a sickness that does not exist.

You are a liar, Delgado, the old revolutionary said. You are a cheat, you are a fraud and you are also very frightened. And do you know why you are frightened? Because you no longer are held up by idealism, by a series of beliefs. That is why you felt no fear in the mountains and why you are dying inside this time. Because you have become one with the Americans. It is not belief but merely the lust for money which is driving you now.

That is insane foolishness. You are talking to me like a schoolboy.

All idealists are schoolboys, Delgado. Why are you sweating? Why are you shaking so, why are you terrified of what the American, despite all the protection around you, might do to you? I will tell you. It is because in the mountains you felt no guilt, you knew that you were on the side of justice, and now you do not have that sense. You are guilty. What is holding you up now, Delgado? What do you have other than guilt?

The revolution is finished. Idealism is finished.

This revolution is finished. But the revolution as an abstract goes on forever. You have fallen away, the government has fallen away, but that does not mean that the revolution no longer exists. Just as in 1958, it is up there in the mountains. But you can no longer seek it, can you? You are crippled.

Go away, he said to the voice, I do not wish to continue this further.

Do you think that I really can go away, Delgado? I am yourself, I am as much a part of you as you are.

Nevertheless I want you to go away. I want no more part of this.

But you do, the old revolutionary said, you were the one who summoned me up, Delgado. I can do nothing unless you want me to speak.

Why won't you leave me alone?

It was your decision, Delgado. All along the choices were yours. You have no one else to blame; you cannot pass off the responsibility.

Enough! Delgado screamed. Enough: get away from me! And the old revolutionary laughed, he laughed maniacally through all the alleys of Delgado's skull and he rose from the desk to seize the old revolutionary by the throat and shake him to death and only then, only then did he realize that the revolutionary was indeed inside but the screaming had been outside and two security guards posted outside the door had come in to look at him with faces as blank as dishes, as puzzled as the animals that had scattered before them in the mountains fifteen years ago, the mountains that he could still see before him ... and would never touch again. Finally, he went to the phone.

# IX

Wulff awoke from a clotted doze on the floor to the shrieking of the telephone. Half suspended in a dream he thought for a moment that he was back in the precinct, doing desk duty, taking an emergency call. Your girl is dead, someone was saying to him, your girl is dead, and he awoke fully, bellowing, to find that he was in the room with Stevens and that it was Stevens reaching for the telephone, not he. The man's face was coarse with sleep but his eyes were alert. He looked at Wulff and made a motion indicating that Wulff should settle back and, breathing in a shallow fashion, he did. It came back to you, all of it, sooner or later. He would be living with one emergency call forever.

"Yes," Stevens was saying into the phone. "Yes, everything's all right. I was going to call you in just a few minutes. Everything worked out. No, the helicopter is ditched."

He paused, listened to something coming over the phone. It was a loose, syrupy babble with occasional peaks and Stevens withdrew the telephone from his ear, shaking his head at the sound, blinking and rubbing a hand over his free ear. "No," he said, "he's dead. I'm afraid that he was killed in an exchange of gunfire but we were able to get him anyway. They're both dead. Yes, both of them. I was able to get the copter down somehow and walk away from it. It was in the dark; I can't give you the exact location but it's somewhere pretty near here."

He paused again, looked at the wall, eyes dead. "Yes," he said, "that would be a very good idea. I'll get over there myself, don't send anyone here. It's best if you just let me get over by myself; I'll be there shortly," and then hung up the phone with a clatter, pushed it away from him and stood, backing his calves into the bed for balance. "He doesn't believe a word of it," he said to Wulff.

"That was Delgado?"

"Of course it was Delgado. He doesn't believe that you're dead; he doesn't believe that the policeman is dead. I don't even think he believes that he was talking to me. He wants me to come right over and see him."

"Well," Wulff said, "you can go over and see him."

"He's no fool. You're all wrong if you take this man for a fool. Delgado knows what the hell is likely to happen."

"Does he?" Wulff said, "then why isn't he sending someone over to escort you?"

Stevens started to say something and then hesitated. He shook his head, his eyes became abstracted. "I guess he trusts me," he said, "also he's trying to attract as little attention, make as few waves as possible. This isn't exactly a government-sanctioned project you know."

"You mean he's freelancing."

"Probably. He's probably doing that."

"If he's freelancing there's only a minimum amount of troops he can throw into this. Also, he's not likely to get much help, is he?"

"He's no fool," Stevens said again, "I'm telling you, he knows what he's doing."

"I've been dealing with people who know what they're doing. It doesn't help them."

"All right," Stevens said, "I don't know why I'm arguing with you. That's pretty stupid, isn't it? You're the one holding the gun. I don't want to fight this out. What do you want to do?"

"I think we ought to go over and see him," Wulff said.

"Just walk in there, the two of us? Do you really think that we'd get two steps into the building? They'd kill you."

"I'll take that chance."

"I don't understand you," Stevens said. "We can't walk unarmed into that building and expect to get into Delgado's office."

"I didn't suggest being unarmed," Wulff said.

Stevens's glance swung over to the drawer in which the armaments had been and then back to Wulff. "That's ridiculous," he said. "That's no real firepower."

"There may be enough. You were the one who said that he's freelancing this thing out, remember? He wants to draw as little attention as possible. Probably no one ringing that building, none of the security force knows what's going on."

"That's crazy," Stevens said, "that's absolutely crazy. You can't take this man."

"Can't I?" Wulff said. He looked at Stevens in level fashion. "Are you sure of that? I took you."

Stevens held his gaze for a moment and then, convulsively, looked away. "All right," he said. "It might work. But Delgado isn't me."

"Yes he is," Wulff said.

"I doubt it."

"Delgado works for the highest bidder too," Wulff said, "and he's freelancing. There's no one behind him. I detect if I may say so a certain absence of conviction ... he doesn't understand drugs, you see. All that he understands is money."

"What do you want?" Stevens said. "What exactly are you after?"

"I want my valise back," Wulff said. "I went to a lot of trouble to get that valise and then they hijacked it away from me. I still consider it my property. I'm getting a little tired of losing valises full of smack. The last one that was stolen from me cost about ten people their lives. You'd think that they'd learn their lesson by now, wouldn't you? But they've got to learn it over and over again. The turnover in the world is fantastic."

"All right," Stevens said, "all right then," and began to pull himself together. He went to the small closet, took out a set of clothes, began to dress. "I've got no choice, do I? I've got to come along."

"Of course you've got to come along," Wulff said. "You're the one who's going to get us into the building." He went to the small table where he had left the armaments for the night and carefully began to check them over, checking the stocks, the action of the triggers. Everything seemed to work. Stevens finished dressing and went to the door, stood there in a reluctant position, one hand on the knob.

"He wants to see me now," he said. "I guess that we should be going."

"I guess we should," Wulff said. He scooped up the pistols casually, began to fit them into various pockets. Thirty-two caliber, they hardly made a noticeable bulge anywhere yet at close range they would be as deadly and effective as machine gun fire. For the first time since he had boarded the plane in Las Vegas he was really armored again; there was a feeling of security in that. The gun, that was all they understood, there was no other argument which could draw pity or fear from them, and so if that was what it came down to, then it was that with which he would confront them. Stevens stood by the door, looking at him, his glance curiously lustreless. "I don't like this," he said.

"I don't like it either," Wulff said. "I just want my valise back."

"He's a deadly man. It's a deadly business."

"You don't want to go there?" Wulff said. He looked at Stevens directly. "Then what use are you to me?"

"When you put it that way—"

"I haven't decided what to do with you yet," Wulff said. "I can't decide if you're to be trusted or not. Probably that doubt will always exist. So if you can't be of any use to me, I can settle out the problem right now."

"I'm sick of being threatened," Stevens said, the lustrelessness passing down from eyes to voice. "I've been threatened for years, Wulff. I'm so tired of it. I can't go on living this way anymore. There's got to be some peace. I came to Havana for peace."

"All of you people are crazy," Wulff said. "Right down the line you don't want to be involved in what you're involved in but you'll do it, won't you? Of course you will. You love it; you wouldn't know what to do if you didn't have defeat, Stevens. You'd have to face up and accomplish something, admit feeling, have pain if you couldn't hang onto defeat. Come on," he said, "let's get going."

"I'm not afraid," Stevens said, not moving. "Right now, this minute, I'm not afraid. A minute from now I might be but now I'm all right. You ought to kill me, Wulff; I'll never die better."

"I wouldn't do it," Wulff said, "I just wouldn't do it," and he made a motion toward Stevens; Stevens caught it, acknowledged it and then with the aspect of a man binding himself together opened the door and preceded Wulff down the stairs. From behind he was not nearly such a large man, shrunken in fact, his shoulder blades prominent, his walk awkward, the tilt of his head that of a man many years older who had suffered an injury of some sort.

Into the jaws of the enemy, Wulff thought.

There was just no other way.

He knew that Delgado would be waiting.

## X

The capital was only a short distance from the hotel. Urban sociology, Wulff thought, was a constant: all cities in all parts of the world seemed to be fabricated in the same way. From the central city, the gleaming center of commerce with its relatively aseptic streets, the city spat back residents; the people living just outside the circle of the central city lived in the filthiest, most dangerous area of all because real-estate values back of the central city were such that housing could be accommodated only by cramming the largest number of people into the smallest possible space. That meant poverty and filth but it also meant residents, because no firm or governmental office wanted to be on the ring outside of the central city; it was either straight downtown or it was sprawled out ten miles from that ring. Havana was typical of such construction; the hotel in which Stevens lived was in that ring but as they walked through the streets the very air seemed to lighten; it came off them like a glassine sheet or cellophane, rather than like the gelatinous material which had clung to their faces further back. It even seemed to Wulff, as he stalked Stevens four or five paces to the rear, holding his hand lightly on a pistol within his pocket, that Stevens himself was gathering courage, looking better the further he moved from his dismal quarters toward the capital. The capital itself loomed up before them, a series of flat buildings which rose above the skyline of the city and approaching it from the rear this way they were able to close in utterly unobserved. From the rear the buildings looked unadorned, unpatrolled, all of the security forces so common in these countries were clustered toward the front because they could see matters only in terms of frontal protection. No wonder any group of guerillas numbering more than three with more than five dollars in backing could make a good run at the regime if they wanted. The only reason the government here had stood so long was probably that no one else would have it: it was simply too much trouble to inherit the difficulties for oneself.

They stopped by a low wall ringing the near building, Stevens halting, letting Wulff catch up to him. "This is the building," Stevens said. "He's on the third floor."

"I know that. I was here, remember?"

"I don't remember. I don't remember anything. As far as I'm concerned your entire life is a blank up to the point I met you on the plane. All right?"

"Suits me," said Wulff.

"So what do you want to do?"

"What do you think I want to do?" Wulff said, "I want to go in there and take him."

"I tell you again, you're crazy. We won't get anywhere."

"You don't understand," Wulff said, "you just don't understand what's really going on here. If we keep it low-key and matter-of-fact we have a reasonable chance."

"Don't say *we*. I'm just a hostage being brought here under duress."

"Oh," Wulff said, "in other words if this thing doesn't work you'll jump back to that side."

"I'll jump back to any side," Stevens said, "I'll be on any side which will have me. Survival is the name of the game, do you understand? I won't betray you and I'll work with you but if I can save my ass I'd like to. But I'll walk in there fronting you and try to get us in."

"You're an honest man."

"It's the only goddamned virtue I have left," Stevens said. "The rest of it went a long time ago, but yes I'm honest. I try to be according to my lights, anyway." He pushed off from the wall again and Wulff fell into position. They traversed the wall of the building and came out then on a sudden, glowing street, sun bouncing off the hard cement, an explosion of traffic and uniforms. It was stunning, as if the street had been scooped up and hurled in their faces and for just a moment Wulff found himself taken by it, from the rear the building was death stretching into the backyard and rubble but from the front—ah! from the front it was the gleaming center of a thriving, industrious government. Washington, D.C. was the same way, crawling in from the drug-smeared ghetto to the abrupt sweep of Pennsylvania Avenue and the White House and these people had certainly taken their lessons from American administration, either that or both of them had learned from some common source .... Well, it was very complex and interesting, but having nothing to do with the primary thing, which was not to speculate on urban sociology but to get hold of Delgado and proceed from there. The uniforms ringing the steps did not even look at Stevens and Wulff as they climbed upwards; they looked straight out ahead, one of them chewing gum, a couple of others conversing, a gleaming display of governmental authority except that they did not hold themselves correctly and surely did not know what was going on. Stevens walked through a glass door, held it open for Wulff and they went into a huge lobby, stone figures ringing the walls. There at last a guard stopped them; a man whose face under the ornate cap was both young and stricken, showing a kind of personality which officials should never have.

"Yes," he said, holding his hand out, then his arm extended so that Stevens walked into it and stopped. "What can be done for you?"

"We're here to see Raoul Delgado," Stevens said.

"Have you got a pass?"

"No," Stevens said, "we have no pass at all. We do have an appointment. He asked—"

"Who is this gentleman with you?"

"I'm his assistant," Wulff said, "I assist Mr. Stevens."

The guard's eyes flickered. "I'm afraid I do not understand that," he said. "I will have to call up to Mr. Delgado to—"

"It is not necessary," Wulff said flatly. "We have an appointment."

"You may very well have an appointment but there is no verification—"

"This is our verification," Wulff said. He took out a pistol and aimed it at the guard's stomach. The man looked down at it and seemed to shrivel.

"Keep quiet," Wulff said. "Don't say a word. I don't want to draw any attention."

The guard seemed fascinated by the gun. There were two others in the lobby but they had their backs to them, seemed to be examining the walls. That was governmental efficiency for you. Still, at least they were English-speaking which was something. It made business easier to transact. Trust this government; they would, all of them, make English their second language. They knew where the money was.

"Lead us to Delgado," Wulff said. He held the gun close in against him with old practice. Anyone looking casually would not even see it. "I really would like you to lead us there," he said. "Otherwise I'm going to have to kill you and that would draw a crowd."

The guard gulped. He appeared eighteen years old now, probably exactly what he was. "You'll never manage this," he said, "it's impossible—"

"Nothing's impossible," Wulff said. "Check him out," he said to Stevens.

Stevens had been looking at this with awe. Now, impassively enough, he stepped forward, ran his hands up and down the guard's body. His eyes kindled with a little expression of pleasure and he reached into a side pants pocket, took out a small gun and drawing it against him like a professional, passed it to Wulff.

"Keep it," Wulff said. "Is it in working condition?" he asked the guard.

"I don't know," the boy said. He was gasping, his cheeks turning greenish. "I've never used it."

"Well," Stevens said, "we'll just take our chances. Probably it fires backwards."

"No doubt," said Wulff. "All right," he said to the guard, "you're going to escort us to Delgado's office now."

"I'm what?"

"You heard me. We want an escort."

"I can't do that. I'll be killed."

"That's possible," Wulff said.

"It's possible that we'll all get killed," Stevens said dryly. The activity seemed to have soldered him into courage; the man looked imperturbable now. "Life's a temporary state at best. Get moving."

"I'll get killed," the guard said again, almost wonderingly. "But I don't want to get killed. I want to live."

"Not at this rate," Wulff said and prodded him gently in the buttocks with the pistol. The guard's body yanked forward, then he moved into a slow, perilous walk. The two facing the wall did not even turn. They walked through the lobby: first the guard, then Wulff, Stevens in the rear, all toward a winding flight of stairs at the rear, then the guard stopped and turned. "You want the elevator?" he said. His eyes were shrouded as if he had just thought of something.

"Not a chance," said Wulff.

"It's two flights."

"Good. We need the exercise."

The guard sighed, turned again. As he did so he cast a longing, sidewise glance at the two by the wall; he seemed to think that they might take some notice of what was going on. A dart of sheer need flamed from him which Wulff intercepted, caught that bolt in the air and then the guard sighed, relaxed: the two were paying no attention whatsoever. Shaking his head the guard led them up the steps. Looking back, casting a quick sidelong glance at the guards as he trailed, Wulff had a sudden flare of understanding himself: it was quite likely that the guards did know what was happening, did suspect that something had gone wrong ... but it made no difference. They were not going to pay attention because they simply wanted no part of it. It was a reasonable thing; it fitted in with everything that he had already come to know of Havana. These two guards were not going to get involved; it was not worth it to them. If Wulff and Stevens were assassins, if they had compelled the guard to lead them upstairs to deal with some official of the bureaucracy .... Well, if the guards could stay out of it they might well benefit. A change of order might be a promotion. That was about the only way you could make it in this kind of regime if you were at the bottom levels; hope that it would be changed over and that you might move upward in a purge.

Reasonable: it was all reasonable. They climbed one flight, then two, the guard offering no further resistance of any sort, only clambering upward numbly as if he were an actor following the rather obscure instructions of a director who he did not understand, but who made no difference to him anyway. At the second landing the guard stopped, his chest moving unevenly under his jacket, his young face beaten and now streaming sweat. He lifted a shaking finger and pointed down the hall.

"No," Wulff said. "You take us in there."

The guard shook his head. Some last vestige of resistance showed in soft pastel moving across his cheeks. "No," he said. "I won't do that."

Wulff showed him the pistol again. "Then I'll have to kill you right here."

The guard looked up; the sweat had converted his face into a mirror in which Wulff thought that he might see himself. "No," he said, "you wouldn't do this."

"I wouldn't? Try me." There was no one in the corridor. The corridor was empty. The soft sounds of typing drifted down. Fluorescence winked.

"I won't," the guard said again, with less assurance. "You know which office it is," he said to Stevens.

Stevens shrugged to show that he was out of it and nodded at Wulff. "It's up to him," he said. "I have nothing to do with it."

"I don't want to—"

"I know you don't want to," Wulff said. "You don't want to lead us in there because you'll be the first through the door and you're afraid that Delgado has been alerted or is waiting anyway with a gun and as soon as someone walks in he's going to shoot. You don't want to die, do you?"

"No," the guard said weakly. "I don't want to die."

"But you're going to. One way or the other. You're going to die in this hall or in Delgado's office you see. You can have thirty seconds more of life if you listen to me. Otherwise you'll die now."

"You wouldn't kill me," the guard said. "You wouldn't be so foolish. A shot would draw attention. You don't want any attention drawn to you now." He put his hands down, backed away, slowly, down the steps. "You won't shoot," he said, "you won't do it." Confidence flooded into his face. "You won't," he said again.

Wulff lifted the pistol and shot the guard in the throat. The guard made a sound like a frog and slowly, gracelessly, arced. His feet departed from the steps. Spouting blood he flew backwards, airborne for half a flight, then his body hit the landing. He spattered and began to roll, moving with increased speed down the steps and out of sight.

Stevens looked at Wulff and said, "Did you have to do that?"

"Yes, I had to do it."

"You're going to get all of them—"

"I'm going to get no one," Wulff said. "No one at all if we won't waste time." He waved the gun at Stevens. "I don't have the time," he said. "Show me his office."

"All right," Stevens said carefully. The nervousness that Wulff had not seen since yesterday had returned. His hand shaking, Stevens took out a handkerchief and wiped his face in short, trembling strokes. Then he turned and walked down the corridor.

It was still empty. The typewriters sounded like silk in the thin space. The shot had been half-silenced by the guard's croak; the guard's croak, the kind of sound that a fat man might make clearing his throat, had not attracted any attention. Stevens led Wulff down the corridor. At the end light spilled out from a larger opening. Stevens pointed. "There," he said, "that's it."

"Good," Wulff said, the pistol held comfortably. "Lead us in."

"Lead us in?" Stevens said, "I thought—"

"You thought exactly right," Wulff said, "you're going to lead us in there. What do you think I went through all of this for? To let you go?"

"No. I didn't think so."

"Good. Get on in there."

"All right," Stevens said. He ran his hands up and down his arms in a nervous, convulsive gesture, swallowed twice, then seemed to bring the various angles of his body together. "I never expected anything different," he said, "I knew it would have to be this way."

"No philosophizing."

"I work for the highest bidder."

"That's right. Now work for the highest bidder and walk on in there."

"Right," said Stevens. "Right. Walk right in. Sit right down." He strode out, Wulff behind him two paces, turned the corner and went into the crevice.

Delgado, in a white jacket behind the desk, was holding a gun. His hand reached out as he saw Stevens. The first shot might have gone right in, but as he was still aiming, his eye caught Wulff behind and that small instant of confusion was just sufficient to jar the gun in his hand. The shot came out screaming and went into the wall above Wulff's left shoulder. Wulff fired immediately but Delgado had kicked down below the desk, scrambling, and the second shot came viciously near Wulff's left shoulder, the one that had been injured in Las Vegas. It had been in pretty good shape; he had not even been conscious of it until now but yanking his arm sent a small explosion of pain through it all over again and he spread-eagled on the floor, the gun extended before him, gasping.

Delgado got off another shot. This one was aimed for Stevens again, but Stevens had scattered, scrambling toward the wall to the side and the shot failed, spattering into the carpet. Little filaments of dust came up. Wulff aimed through the filaments and fired again.

Delgado screamed. He reared from his concealed position and there was the sound of wood shattering as he hurled himself into the desk in some complex agony. The agony had lifted him; now Wulff saw his head and shoulders convulsed across the desk. Weakly, Delgado extended the gun for another shot. Wulff put a bullet into the gun hand. The gun fell away like an overripe fruit.

Stevens lifted his own pistol and bore in for the killing shot. Delgado whimpered, shook his head, raised his hand. "No," he said.

"No," Wulff said to Stevens.

Stevens, locked into the act of slow levelling did not even appear to hear him. Wulff got to the man from behind, put an arm around his stomach and restrained him. Stevens struggled, then dropped the gun.

"Why?" he said, turning toward Wulff. "Why can't I—"

"No," Wulff said, "not now."

"I want to kill him," Stevens said. His face was red and filled with moisture. Wulff had never seen so much emotion on it. "He needs dying."

"Not now. Later."

"Please," Delgado said. He was lying on the desk, his legs dangling toward the floor. Now and then he attempted to stand, but he skittered and whined. Blood fled down the panels of his body. "Don't kill me."

Wulff hit the man across the face. The impact was satisfying; he could feel his palm drilling through toward bone. Delgado shrieked again. Wulff lifted his hand and then in a quick spasm of indifference stepped away. It *made* no difference. Once they were hurt, once you had made them vulnerable and brought them to the level of pain … once all this had happened, they were no longer the men who had brutalized you. The brutal parts of them were gone. There could never be, then, retribution, all of it was merely a turning of the wheel.

"Let me kill him," Stevens said. He was shaking. "I want to kill him."

"No point," Wulff said. He turned, walked back quickly toward the open door and then, peering out gun in hand, checked the hallway. Empty, the purring of typewriters continuing. No one had paid any attention whatsoever. A tactic of revolutionary governments, he thought, everybody attending to his and her work. He closed the door, bolted it, and walked back toward Delgado. In pain but lucid, the man had gathered up his legs underneath, now lay across the desk curled like a paper toy.

"Where's the valise?" Wulff said.

Delgado shook his head. He opened his mouth but no sound came out.

"The valise," Wulff said, "I want the valise. Tell me where it is."

Delgado tried to talk. Wulff could see the words forming in his throat, moving up then toward the mouth but they were blocked at the lips. His eyes were dark and fixed. He shook his head violently, stricken.

"This isn't getting us anywhere at all," Wulff said. "Tell me where the valise is."

"I don't—" Delgado said faintly and then choked. He hawked, gasped saliva, his body shaking. "I'm dying," he said.

"Soon enough. Where is it?"

Again, Delgado said nothing. This time though there was no effort to speak. His eyes clouded over. Apparently he was attempting silence, now.

"All right," Wulff said, turning to Stevens who had been watching this impassively from one side of the room. "You wanted to hit him, hit him. Ask him to tell us where the stuff is."

"Right," said Stevens. He seemed made cheerful by this. He walked over to the desk lightly, stood over the shrunken Delgado. Delgado flopped on the desk like a fish. "You know what I'm going to do now," Stevens said.

Delgado said nothing. He closed his eyes.

"You thought I was a hired hand," Stevens said, "a possession. You took away any pride I had."

He reached forward, dug two fingers into Delgado's throat and pushed, gently, then with increasing force. Delgado's eyes opened. They bulged.

"But I've got a little left," Stevens said. "Just a little. Tell this man where the valise is."

He removed his fingers and looked at them as if they were blood-smeared. "I could enjoy this," he said, "I can do this all up and down your body. I'm going to take you apart, Delgado."

"All right," Delgado said faintly. "I don't have it."

"Sure you have it."

"No I don't. You think that I'd have something like that in my possession?"

"Yes," Wulff said, "I do."

"Well I did. But now I don't. When I knew about the plane going down I had to get rid of it."

"You had to get rid of it," Stevens said. He hit Delgado open-handed across the mouth. "Sure you did. Who did you get rid of it to?" He hit the man again, his hand trembling. Wulff went behind Stevens and said, "Stop it now."

"Stop it?"

"You'll kill him," Wulff said, "but not now. He has to talk."

"I gave it to DiStasio," Delgado said. His eyes had become hopeful seeing Wulff. They looked trusting. Like a child fallen down a hole, he had seen his savior and Wulff was going to get him out of this.

"Who is DiStasio?" Wulff said.

"You son of a bitch," Stevens said to Delgado. "I know who DiStasio is. Why did you do it?"

"I had to do it," Delgado said. "I couldn't hold onto it any longer. I knew that this was going to happen."

"Who's DiStasio?" Wulff said. Stevens was hovering over Delgado. He poked Stevens in the ribs, hard. "I said, who is DiStasio?"

"Intelligence," Stevens said abstractly. He hit Delgado open-handed across the mouth again. He could have been a surgeon performing an operation under Wulff's supervision. "Intelligence division."

"I couldn't handle it alone anymore," Delgado said. "You see, I realized that I had been wrong about this. Nothing like this could be handled by oneself. I underestimated you Wulff," he said. "I was wrong. Help me. You've got to help me."

"Intelligence division," Stevens said again. He spat in Delgado's face. "Sons of bitches, you're all in it."

"Who is DiStasio?" Wulff said.

"DiStasio is an intelligence chief," Stevens said. "Delgado here probably got panicky and decided that he needed help right from the top. You got it, didn't you?"

Wulff thought he heard a thin scurrying in the hallway. He backed away, went to the door and was about to open it when some instinct told him to keep it closed. He tensed himself against the door listening. There were footsteps in the hall, picking up in volume and intensity. Intermixed were voices through the poor soundproofing.

"I think the party's over," he said to Stevens. "They're coming up after us."

"They found the guard."

"Of course they found the guard. What did we expect, that he'd just lie there?"

"Well," Stevens said, "you never know about those things. You know these south of the border countries." He spat in Delgado's face again. "How do you like it?" he said. "How do you like being spat on?"

Wulff took out his pistol and held himself against the door evaluating the situation. It looked fairly grim. They were going to have to shoot their way out of the building, that is if they got out at all. "Let's go," he said to Stevens. "Do you know where we can get to DiStasio?"

"I know where we can find him," Stevens said. "If he's still there. He may have already left the country. Wouldn't you with the supplies he's got now? He's come into an inheritance."

"He wouldn't," Delgado said, "he wouldn't do that. He'd—"

Wulff looked at Delgado and then toward Stevens. He could see the desire in the pilot's eyes. "All right," he said, "kill him."

"With pleasure," said Stevens. He slapped Delgado once more in the face, almost casually, and backed off from him, levelling the pistol.

"Please," Delgado said.

"Fuck you," said Stevens and pulled the trigger. The shot tore, almost absently, through Delgado's skull, taking out pieces of bone and hair. A little halo of fragmentation hung around the man's head for an instant, then disappeared in the glow of the lights. The thing that had been Delgado rolled from the desk and hit the floor with a watery sound.

Stevens levelled the pistol and put two more shots into the neck. The corpse jumped; beyond life it was apparently not beyond pain. More blood exploded, lacing little strips of red on the carpet.

"Enough," Wulff said.

"Son of a bitch," said Stevens, "son of a bitch you just don't know—"

"It's over. We've got to get out of here."

"You don't know what it means," Stevens said and fired the pistol again. Wulff aimed, shot the pistol neatly from Stevens's hand even before he had gotten off the next shot. Stevens's pistol spanged against the wall as the man clutched his wrist, turned toward Wulff with the aspect of a man who was about to be killed.

"There's no time for this shit," Wulff said, "we've got to get out of here.

We'll never find DiStasio unless we get out of here.

"I wish that the son of a bitch was alive again so that I could kill him twice."

"That's all right," Wulff said, "but one death is the most a gun can get out of a man."

Not, however, drugs, he thought. Drugs could extract an infinity of deaths.

The voices in the hall were rising.

## XI

They burst from the room together, heading toward ground as soon as they were out of the door, ducking into the low-fire position. Staying in there was no good, Wulff had decided, not two long flights up with no visible means of scaling down the wall. They could be burned or gassed out merely waiting; when in doubt, combat training had taught him, it was best to make a frontal attack. You had, at least, surprise on your side and it was possible that the enemy would fail in courage. You could intimidate them. Even forty men could be intimidated by two if you came at them in a certain way.

The hall was filled with noise and uniforms; guards had sprung from the lower levels to fire aimlessly without seeming direction and one of them, stupidly, threw a tear-gas canister, probably thinking that this was a clever idea. It was not, however, the plumes of smoke choked and blinded the guards nearest it, the fumes dispersing harmlessly by the time that they had wafted toward Wulff and Stevens and crouched on the floor they offered poor enough targets anyway; they were even poorer without visibility. Down the hall women were screaming, the typists had come from their offices to stand in the corridors, then shriek for cover and Wulff, from the low position, fired a couple of shots above their heads, just to create further confusion.

It created more than confusion; it was total panic. The guards were trying to close in on them but they had no idea where Wulff or Stevens were. Also, the women blocked their passage, taking the guards, in the clouds of gas, to be the assailants themselves and the noise volume was rising, creating further panic. Wulff, using Stevens as a screen, got off a couple of careful shots, dropped two guards quickly, then reloaded while Stevens put fire ahead of them. The screams rose and then someone threw a grenade at them. It fell on the carpet, yards in front and went up in a sheet of flame but the flame too was protective. The attackers' luck was not with them at all this morning; the flame merely walled off Stevens and Wulff from their assailants down the hall, setting up a protected area through which Wulff could pinpoint his fire and more guards dropped. He had lost count; there must have been seven bodies on the floor, half of the original force anyway. Stevens turned toward him, his face smeared with smoke residue and murmured, "I think we can get out now."

"Not through them."

"No. Don't have to." His speech was coming in short, stricken puffs. "There's a back way." Stevens motioned behind them. "Direct to the street."

"All right," Wulff said, "give ground slowly though. Maintain fire."

"Right," Stevens said and got off another shot through the flame. Someone screamed. They had opened up an area in front of them now of at least several yards; through the dying flame they could see that the guards had retreated. Fire was only sporadic now. A clot of people at the end of the hall were wedging themselves into a staircase. "Keep it up," Wulff said, "go back step by step," and back-pedalled slowly then, holding the pistol level, imagining the guards to be pins set up in a long, flat alley, and he used the bowling ball of the gun to knock and scatter those pins, sent them sprawling one by one to lie in the refuse of that long alley. Stevens was already back-pedalling down the stairs, firing himself; Wulff held in close to one of the walls to cover from that angle, and then one of the guards, perhaps the last one standing, began to fumble inside his clothing, reached in there, took out something ominously shaped and threw it. Wulff found himself reacting before he was even sure what had happened; he caught the grenade on the fly and hurled it back at the guard, then turned, leaped down the full flight of stairs, sprawled down another, the dull *whoomp!* of this second grenade heard above him and then the upper level literally shook. Scars of fragmentation burst open above him and he heard the reverberating concussion. No dud this grenade: this would kill anyone standing within six feet of it and probably had, he thought, it probably had.

But better not to think of the destruction above. That was behind him. Wulff found himself on the first level, the door adjacent to him open. He went through it and was in what appeared to be a large convoy area to the opposite side of the building; here were a number of vehicles lined up in a huge, flat yard, some of them with engines idling. There was no one here; apparently the fury on the third floor had drawn everyone up there as spectator if not participant.

"Look at that," Stevens said to him, gripping him by the arm. He had backed off ten to twelve feet from the building, was staring upward. "Son of a bitch, look at that." His features were twisted in something approaching reverence; Wulff looked up and saw what was happening on the third floor.

Jets of flame like propeller blades were shooting from the building, arcs and circles of fire. The third floor had imploded, buckled in within itself and was now open to the air in a hundred ways, holes and jagged lines of destruction opening it up and it was through these openings that the fire sped. Even as they looked, the implosion was continuing, that level carried in upon itself like a smashed bag and within the heart of this forms which looked like ants seemed to be struggling around, black, shrivelled forms trembling in the wreckage. "Those are people," Stevens said quietly. "My God, those are people."

"We've got to get out of here," Wulff said. He inhaled, the stink carrying deep within his gut. "That whole building is going to go," he said.

"They must be evacuating the other side," Stevens said, "but they'll be back here any moment."

Indeed they would. Wulff could hear the sirens dimly now. It was the international sound just as drugs was the international currency; the universal, recognizable point of connection. The sirens carried on the wind, approaching.

"All right," Stevens said. He sprinted away down the line of vehicles, lumbered into a small jeep. Wulff watched him struggle with the clutch and levers and then the vehicle was free, rolling toward him. He put a foot on the running board and then with some difficulty got all the way in, Stevens helping him.

"We'll have to make a run for it," Stevens said. "There's no other way. We're going to have to drive right through them."

"All right," Wulff said, "you know your geography."

There was a secondary series of explosions above and the roof of the building fell down. It was as simple as that. Staring up they could see the roof settle to a different level, diving five or six yards toward the earth, held up then by the beams themselves, the beams stretching upward almost like human arms for that laborious support and then, almost as if in slow-motion or freeze-frame the roof came all the way down, swooping through the building like a cookie-cutter, compressing the first floor.

Stevens was already rolling. His reflexes were still there if not his attention. He had the jeep in full flight before the swath of destruction had been cut, and bearing left, away from the building he sent them away at fifty miles an hour, the sheer discord of metal underneath them, the bolts and joints of the vehicle slamming at thighs and back with iron hands as Stevens carried them away: away from the burning capital, away from the sirens, away from the death and the terror, into the garbage-strewn back streets of Havana where the same empty faces looked at them as they whipped past ... the faces so unchanged and unchangeable that if the burning building had been dropped on them they merely would have died without attention.

Wulff's hands clenched on the bar underneath the windshield as he held on for balance. His thoughts had already turned from the destroyed capital, had restlessly probed ahead—like blood through a sick artery— to the next point of interception.

He was thinking about DiStasio.

God help DiStasio now.

## XII

When the panicked phone call from Delgado had come in DiStasio's first impulse had been to seize the man, detain him to once. Certainly he had all grounds for reasonable detention simply based upon what Delgado was babbling. But on second thought he decided not to do this; detention was not the answer because it would put the transaction into official channels and he wanted that as little as Delgado would. No, everything had to be done sub rosa, worked out on a quiet level. Delgado was insistent about that himself. DiStasio could see the point.

So he had gone into Delgado's office, verified for himself that the man was frantic but credible and had taken the valise from him. Delgado's terms were a straight fifty-fifty split after he was able to make arrangements to leave the country and arrange for distribution. DiStasio had humored him in his heavy-handed way because he had already made another and better decision. Delgado was not going to get back those drugs. He was not going to get them back in any form or condition because he did not deserve them and furthermore, the man could not function under pressure of any sort. Already, just under the flick of the botched assassination, he was starting to come apart.

"You leave it to me," he had said to Delgado. "You just let me take care of this and we'll work out the final terms later," and Delgado had nodded weakly, reluctantly: what, after all, could he do otherwise? By calling in DiStasio he had already ceded control of the situation. Delgado was no fool; he could see that. But there had been, as DiStasio left the room clutching the valise, just a hint, a brush of indecision in Delgado's eyes which confirmed DiStasio's original estimation: he would have to have the man eliminated. There was no room in this scheme for a partnership arrangement; Delgado would ruin everything.

He had taken the valise, given it to his chief clerk Alejandro Figueroa and told him to take it to his estate, turn it over to the garageman, return. Figueroa had taken the valise solemnly, without a word of comment and done exactly that. Figueroa would do anything that DiStasio asked and do it without comment; he knew that DiStasio could have him killed by whim, and that was sufficient reason and justification for a man like Figueroa. That was sufficient for all of them; DiStasio had worked himself through risk and difficulty to a position where he held that power over a number of people including all of his staff members. And, he understood, it was the only power that meant anything at all. It came down, at the end of it, to power, the ability to inflict pain and death and if that was the world in which he lived, unfortunate as it might be, it was how DiStasio would run things. There might be a different world, a little further down the line where things other than power were the ultimate authority but until he reached that point he would settle for this.

So he had the valise at his estate and a fairly good idea of how to move from there on, but there was still the problem of Delgado. Delgado would have to be eliminated. He had pondered this decision for a little while, giving it some minutes of concentrated thought, balancing off the fact of Delgado's survival against the possibility of his death, seeing all of the implications and coming to the decision with hesitance. But once he had reached it, well that was the end, the one thing which DiStasio could not stand was uncertainty past the point of decision. Delgado would have to be killed because he was no longer necessary. From the moment at which the dangerous and valuable valise had been passed on he functioned only as a hindrance. It was not only that he would have to split responsibility, risk and income with Delgado—that was bad enough.

It was that Delgado was of an older breed, a generation back which in Cuba was a lifetime; he was of the revolutionaries who had spent time in exile and the trouble with these people was that their wasted years had burned purpose out of them and substituted a habit of thinking too much about too little. For every fragment of action which these people were able to cajole out of themselves they generated whole mounds of thought, of anxiety, of guilt and self-loathing ... and these more than anything else made Delgado extremely dangerous. He was the kind of man who at one moment could turn over the valise and responsibility to DiStasio, beg him for assistance—and in the next his old revolutionary's brain was apt to send out flashes which would illuminate all the circuits of fear, and in a torment of what he would call "conscience" he would renege upon the arrangement, take the full details directly to the premier himself ... and DiStasio would then be in serious trouble. Not that the premier minded that much as long as the activities of his subordinates did not subvert the revolution, such as it was. But the premier could hardly ignore something like this, not with the amount of difficulty which Delgado was apt to cause. DiStasio would be in serious trouble. So Delgado would have to be eliminated.

He would do it as quickly as possible and third-hand. Then he would take the valise himself and arrange disposition. He might even leave the country, try a new life elsewhere. The valise would give this to him. The drugs were very pure; DiStasio had had that much experience. The drugs were of the purest variety he had ever seen, and distributed in the proper channels might be worth far more than the million dollars which Delgado had conservatively estimated. DiStasio, the head of intelligence, had been watching the regime from one vantage point or another for almost a decade now. The regime was not going to last forever; they could not change the landscape as much as they insisted that they could. Sooner or later the landscape was going to erupt on them.

At that time the regime would fall.

An intelligent man would be better off making provisions.

So DiStasio had already arranged in his own mind for Delgado's murder, had arranged it so efficiently and with so little potential difficulty that it came almost as a shock to him when the disaster of September 15th occurred. (He knew that however long he lived he would always think of it in those terms; already the broadcasts were framing it that way: *the disaster of September 15th*). Delgado was not supposed to be assassinated, the building destroyed, fifteen people killed in the explosion, another seventy-five injured, none of this was supposed to happen. Delgado had already had another kind of death prepared for him and so complete was DiStasio's conviction within himself, so deep was his faith that he found that his primary response to the events was one of absolute fury that matters had been taken out of his hand. DiStasio was the head of the intelligence division; he controlled everything in the country. Nothing which occurred could be unexpected because he set in motion almost all of the events.

Nevertheless, there was the building destroyed and Delgado murdered. And nothing to be done about it.

How could this be done to him? Yet, almost immediately after this first reaction coming on top of the conveyance of the news, then the hurried series of phone calls through which he was able to verify that all of this was true.

Almost immediately after that, DiStasio succumbed to a different and older emotion and that was one of fear. He did not need extended analysis or any amount of reports to make clear to him exactly why Delgado had been killed and all of this had happened. It tied in with the drugs. The drugs were the key and the key to *that* was the man who had brought them into the country, Martin Wulff. Wulff was responsible for this. If the fools at the upper levels could not see that immediately, then it was their problem and stupidity, but it was obvious, should be obvious to the rankest fool exactly what was going on. Now Wulff would be coming to DiStasio in search of the valise. He understood felons of this sort. He knew their thought processes as well as he knew (or thought he knew) the internal workings of his body. Somehow, before the September 15 disaster, Wulff would have tortured from Delgado information on the whereabouts of the valise and he would be coming to retrieve it from DiStasio. He could see it all clearly. He could see everything clearly. That was one of the virtues of being chief of intelligence; your mind worked in clear, preordained channels, and there was no sense of mystery. None whatsoever. Everything fell into place.

DiStasio was home when it happened. Reports came to him over the telephone of the wreckage, the fire, the deaths. He listened to all of them impassively, managing to control his hands, his voice. No one would suspect his reaction. He was entitled to be home on that day; it was his certified leave time. Everything had been cleared through the highest levels. He said that he would immediately take over the processes of investigation. The country was in a state of emergency alert, of course. That would make it easier for the intelligence arm to function without interference. DiStasio said that he would get right to it. They wanted him to come to the capital of course but he said that he did not think that this was necessary. He would be able to assume control of the situation at home and would be in tomorrow. Certainly if a state of guerilla siege was starting (this was what the premier thought; he had no idea of the true meaning of the events, of course), it would make more sense if the government was scattered; if high officials were not seen as being concentrated in a specific area where they could, one after the other, be attacked. The caller agreed with this. He praised DiStasio's judgment and said that he would be in touch.

DiStasio hung up the phone, shaking. He called in Figueroa immediately. That was Figueroa's function: to be always available. When valises were to be dropped off he did that; when DiStasio needed counsel Figueroa was obtained. Also Figueroa served as a sexual receptacle of sorts, not that DiStasio would even think of that business now. Everything in its place. Passion could not be contemplated in this moment of extreme danger. "We're going to have to prepare to leave the country," he said to Figueroa.

"Ah," the man said. "I will make the arrangements."

That was Figueroa. Unquestioned obedience. If the premier had the kind of unquestioned obedience from subordinates which Figueroa gave *him*, the government by now would have conquered all of Latin America. Then again, Figueroa was extremely stupid. This had to be taken into account. You could not sentimentalize a man who believed that his only purpose was to make himself fiercely agreeable.

"We will probably have to go to Bolivia," DiStasio said.

"Bolivia is excellent. Bolivia is an excellent country. I have always wanted to see—"

"Then again, perhaps, we should go to Buenos Aires."

"Buenos Aires is also a good possibility," Figueroa said, "I have always delighted in Buenos Aires, its fragrances, it's sophistication, its women—"

"It will be necessary to make arrangements for a pilot and plane. It is official business, of course."

"Of course," said Figueroa.

"We will have to leave immediately. By midnight in any event. We must be airborne within six hours."

"This must be a very important mission," said Figueroa.

"It is. It involves the whole security of the government."

"Does it have anything to do with today's difficulties?"

"It has everything to do with today's difficulties."

"That was a very bad business," Figueroa said. He looked at the carpet, a delicate man whose posture gave an appearance of gravity and depth. On this basis alone he suited all of his assigned functions. "A very tragic business."

"Life is tragic," DiStasio said. He stood from his desk, looked around the enormous study. "We will have to take the valise with us."

"The valise which I brought back here?"

"Exactly. The same one."

"It must be filled with important materials."

"It is filled with important materials," DiStasio said. "All of our security may depend upon our getting them safely out of the country."

"Ah," said Figueroa. His face became very serious. "I understand."

"The stakes are enormous. We cannot afford to fail."

"We will not fail," Figueroa said solemnly. "It is absolutely impossible that we will fail." He smiled but for just an instant a whiplash of confusion crossed his face as if he had heard voices from the yard outside the huge windows. "Why are we going to Bolivia?" he said.

"Important governmental business. A vital question of alliance with revolutionary elements—"

"We are going to carry the revolution to Bolivia!"

"Exactly," DiStasio said, "and that in turn will increase our influence throughout the Americas."

"Of course," Figueroa said. "Politics is very intricate. I wish that I understood more about it. You realize that it has always been my favorite science."

"Of course," DiStasio said.

"Maybe I could have been a politician, if I had had university training," Figueroa said. He paused, the look of confusion returning. "Exactly what kind of benefits can we offer the revolutionaries—"

"That is not necessary now," DiStasio said curtly. Sometimes the man, despite his abysmal loyalty, annoyed him. It was impossible to treat Figueroa as if he were a rational person. "Just make the arrangements."

The sharpness of the tone made Figueroa quail. His skin assumed the transparency of paper. "Of course," he said, "of course." He left the room quickly, moving sidewise, trying to get to the door as rapidly as possible without showing disrespect. In the hallway, then, he broke into a full run. DiStasio could hear his footsteps and then they were gone.

Less than half an hour before flight if Figueroa acted with his usual efficiency. Surely he would; at what he did, the man was the best that there was. DiStasio went to the door, secured it with a bolt and went back slowly to the cabinet half-hidden in the wall, threw back the panels and took out the valise. For the first time since Delgado had made the transfer he permitted himself to touch it, ran his hands over the leatherette tenderly, feeling an almost sensual pleasure in the pattern the texture gave back to his palms, then slowly he opened the clips the way he might unhook a woman from her clothing and lifted the top. He looked straight into the valise.

And saw it then in its purity, the little solid bricks of it planked up under the straps, pure white and glowing, the grains at the top of it glistening.

Diluted, one of these bricks might be a quarter of a million doses, sugared and watered out with a little glycerin and a few inert materials a hundred thousand human beings would be able to take this jolt into themselves and become transported. Dreams and death lay within that case, all of them impacted into that small space, one brick a quarter of a million doses, twenty bricks two and a half million ... Two and a half million voyages, and DiStasio looking at this felt transported himself, the sheer effect of this weighing upon him. His breath was shallow in his chest, pure constriction; finally he had to unleash his hands reluctantly, one by one, and stand back from the case breathing the air of the room. He felt lightheaded; almost as if he might faint and came forward then to carefully, lovingly put the lid back into place. Only when he did this did he feel the giddiness recede. He stood there, latching on the clips, looking at the case and a flicker of understanding came to DiStasio: he had been motivated thus far by greed but it was not greed alone which would send him on this voyage for he had plenty of money. He had position. It was not greed, either, which had imploded that building; no, it was something else, another kind of desire altogether and it had something to do with the power of these crystals, a silent power which overtook men and made them mad.

What was it? What was there in this valise that would drive a man like Delgado, a cynic, a beaten man, an old revolutionary, to such an excess of behavior? What, for that matter, was there about this valise which would send someone like Wulff on a journey of terror which probably involved five hundred dead men by now? DiStasio did not know, exactly. He only knew that he felt the same reaction himself, some call within him as he looked at those deadly cylinders and squares which told him that almost every sacrifice was worthwhile if, in the end, it could result in the putting of these into the supply channels. The wealth was almost identical. DiStasio did not need the money. No, it was the need ...

... it was the need to filter the drug through those quarter-of-a-million doses because—and now he thought he had it—heroin was itself the revolution. It was a revolution taking place in ten million heads every day, four hundred thousand heads an hour were being overtaken by the sensations of the revolution, and if it began there, if the revolution could be brought home into the impacted psyches of all these users, then there was no question but that it could spread out and eventually overtake the world. So, it was, ultimately, a proselytizing drug, heroin, without it the world was a less mad, more contained place but the revolution was one step further away and if men were not dedicated toward revolution, toward the change of the conditions which bound them in ... then what was their purpose after all? I must be a little mad, DiStasio thought, a little bit mad to think this way. It is only heroin, it is only money, this is a business transaction pure and simple, an investment. But the excitement would not drain from him; instead it seemed to be building, accumulating in small worn pockets of the psyche and finally to restrain himself he had to sit with an effort of will, clamp his hands into fists and try as much as possible to block all anticipation from his mind.

There was no turning back. Once he took this valise and left the country he could never return. The finality of this oozed through him, he thought of it—no more bureau, no more administration, no more channeling of secret information directly to the premier—and balanced it off in his mind: did he really want it to be this way? Would it not be better to let the valise go, let someone else take the responsibility and return to the man he had been twenty-four hours ago, before Delgado approached him?

No. He did not want to do that. DiStasio sat there and looked through the windows, waiting for Figueroa and made an admission which he would have thought to be impossible until all of this had happened ... an impossible admission for an old revolutionary like him—but then consider Delgado ... it had been the same thing.

He was tired of the revolution.

He wanted no more of the revolution.

The revolution had ransacked the country for fifteen years just as the government before it had ransacked, the only difference being that Battista had allowed others to do it for a cut of the proceeds, whereas this regime needed no intermediaries whatsoever.

They had failed—or looking at it another way they had succeeded. But in any event the country was finished.

It was best to take the valise and make for himself the best deal that he could. It was in the tradition of the government. Of all governments. The premier, granted the same circumstances DiStasio thought, would have done the same thing.

He waited for Figueroa.

## XIII

Out on the flat back road, finally clear of the burning city, Wulff said, "Now we go to DiStasio."

"He's got an estate," Stevens said, trying to hold the wheel steady on the difficult terrain. "He's going to be sealed in there with heavy security. We don't have a chance."

"We'll have to make our chances. There's no choice. We'll go in now."

Stevens raised a hand to his face, brushed away smudge, shook his head. "You don't stop, do you?" he said. "Not for a moment."

"There's no time to stop. He's probably arranging to flee the country."

"All right," Stevens said, "so he's fleeing the country. I think it would be a damned good idea if we did the same thing."

"No," Wulff said.

"You've done what you wanted to do. You've broken them wide open. You've—"

"I want the valise," Wulff said. "They took the valise from me."

"You don't understand," Stevens said, fighting with the wheel, the jeep skittering a little, hitting cobblestones, then coming back toward the center of the road with difficulty. "He's the chief of intelligence. He's *sealed* in there. We get within a mile of his estate—"

"I don't care," Wulff said. He checked the last pistol, everything in order. "We're going to go in. We'll do the best we can."

Stevens shook his head. "It's crazy," he said.

"You want out?"

Stevens bit his lip, looked straight down the road. Little puffs of dust kicked up against them. "I don't know," he said.

"You've paid your dues," Wulff said. "You were next to me when I needed it. Everything's even now. You can go if you want to."

"What's the point?" Stevens said. "What's my future in this country? How long do you think I'd last?"

"I never even considered it."

"Not very long," Stevens said, "not very long at all. I had a nice comfortable life you know. I lived in a hotel and had all the whiskey I needed and now and then I'd do a little job for them, little risk. I didn't have to think about anything and I didn't have any responsibility. Now you've fucked the whole thing up."

"Sorry," Wulff said, "I'm sorry I mucked up your life so bad."

"Oh you didn't," Stevens said. Like all good drivers he was able to focus his perception of the road down a single, long narrow tunnel, outside of that he could converse, look at Wulff, carry ninety percent of his attention outside of the act of driving. He brought the jeep out of the country road to a long, flat narrow highway which looked off across empty fields, accelerated sharply, yanking the gears so that the jeep lost road adhesion momentarily, then seemed to settle at a newer, more insistent level of speed. The speedometer went toward eighty. "I took care of fucking things up myself .... We're about five miles from there now, no more."

"Good."

"We're going to go up against that man with four pistols and a jeep, is that right?"

"It could be worse," Wulff said. "We might be unarmed altogether. He won't like it."

"I never thought this would happen to me," Stevens said. "How did I get into a fucking crusade? I've got nothing against drugs at all. As far as I'm concerned people can shoot it, suck it, drink it, eat it or blow it up their ass. What's the difference? It's just another way out of the world, that's all."

"That's your point of view."

"I messed with it a little in the Navy years ago. Pot and cocaine." Stevens's eyes narrowed, he appeared abstracted. "It didn't do a goddamned thing to me."

"We're not talking pot and cocaine," Wulff said, "we're talking about heroin."

"Heroin too," Stevens said. "What's the difference?" A dog ran across the road; he braked sharply, swerved, accelerated out of the pocket quickly. The dog was safe. "It's a matter of individual choice, isn't it?"

"Not anymore."

"Of course it is," Stevens said. "If people want to shoot a little smack they can do it as far as I'm concerned. Why put them in prison? They should have all the smack they want; they ought to have clinics, give it away free. As far as I can tell," he said, "there's no drug problem up there. It's not the drugs, it's a drug deprivation problem. Now if they only made it available—"

"No," Wulff said.

"No? Why not?"

"Because it wouldn't work," Wulff said. "You're talking to a man who was on the narcotics squad for five years and the solution isn't to hand out drugs on street corners or in drug stores. The only solution is to get rid of them."

"Seems to me it's a matter of choice."

"Drugs are death," Wulff said.

"So are a lot of other things."

"Drugs are death," he repeated. "Heroin is death and anything that leads to it is the same. All drugs are death. The people who sell them are murderers."

"Seems to me you've got a rather simplistic view of things."

"I have a goddamned simplistic view," Wulff said, lurching in the seat, holding on for purchase. "There's nothing complicated about it at all. Certain things in or out of this world are very simple. Heroin is one of them."

"All right," Stevens said, "I don't want to get into a fucking argument—"

"No one's arguing," Wulff said flatly. "There's nothing to argue about. Certain things are very simple I said. The trouble began when people were sold on the idea that they weren't. That there were two sides to every question, that every dog had its day, that you had to consider the criminal's rights along with the victim's. Fuck that. That's not truth, it's conspiracy. Drugs are death. Have you ever seen death?"

"I've seen a fair amount of it," Stevens said quietly. "I've seen so much of it in fact that I never intend to see it again if I can help it."

"Have you ever seen a seven-year-old junkie? Have you ever seen a little girl holding a doll and so strung out on junk that she didn't know her name? Did you ever see a whole city destroyed, turned into death, converted into a bombed-out zone because of drugs. Did you ever see an eighteen-year-old kid jump off a roof in front of you because he couldn't take withdrawal anymore? Have you ever seen the soft men who peddle the stuff, the soft men in their houses on the bay, far away from all of this, laughing at it, shielding themselves from what they've done, taking the money, filling the vein—"

"All right," Stevens said, "all right then, you're a fucking crusader. See where it gets you." The road arced right and there on a hill in the other direction Wulff could see the outlines of a house, the house was shielded behind fences, gates, half-concealed by the roll of terrain so it was only barely visible at points, jutting randomly through the landscape. "You're a fucking crusader and you're going to clean all the drugs out of the world everywhere and drugs are death and you're a killer, Wulff, a real killer. But *that's* your problem right now. How are we going to get in *there?*" Stevens rolled the jeep to a stop by the side of the road and looked outward, his eyes shaded and abstract. "How?" he said.

"I'll think of something."

"You'd better think of something," Stevens said, "because that place is guarded. There are at least five men on duty all the time and they're armed and expert."

"I've gotten into worse," Wulff said, thinking of Boston, then of New York, images of the freighter in San Francisco darting through for just a moment. "I've faced a lot worse and am sure I will again."

"You're too much," Stevens said.

"Well," Wulff said, vaulting from the jeep and standing by the roadway, "it beats working for the New York narcotics squad."

He looked out into the distance with Stevens, considering.

# XIV

They ditched the jeep by the side of the road, finally, sheltering it under a clump of trees, and made their entrance on foot. Stevens had been all for sinking the vehicle entirely but Wulff had said no, they might possibly have use for it later and in any event, ditching it would be more trouble than it was worth in terms of the attention they might attract. There were woods cutting off DiStasio's estate from the road and they made their way through it with difficulty, the ooze sticking to their shoes, branches jutting out, administering small, painful blows throughout the body. DiStasio had sealed himself in pretty well, no question about it. All of them had sealed themselves in well, they were experts, these people, they knew how to cut themselves off from the very consequences of the lives they were leading. No ragged pack of citizens would come through this wood to burn and sack the DiStasio estate, no counter-revolutionaries could find a position from which to bring fire. There was only the necessity to stagger through the wood, approaching the house in a concealed fashion, avoiding the cobbled roadway which certainly was patrolled and hope that there would be some position from which to fire once they got to the top of the hill. They staggered up that rise, gasping, the pistols in Wulff's clothing slamming into him at odd intervals, making him inhale in pain so that a few times he simply had to stop while Stevens, himself in bad condition, hung against a tree trunk and breathed hoarsely.

Finally he passed over two pistols to Stevens, trusting the man finally and irrevocably and after that the climb was a little easier. They came finally to a point about fifty yards downrange from the estate and Wulff looked through the clearing cautiously. From this distance there seemed to be no surveillance whatsoever, the grounds were deserted, small plumes of smoke drifting from a chimney toward the rear gave things almost a pastoral tinge, but that Wulff knew was deceptive. Surely there was a three-hundred-and-sixty-degree surveillance conducted from some point of the estate and the moment that they came into the clear they were under severe risk. There was the sound, then, of a helicopter.

It was an unmistakable sound. Wulff could identify it instantly and he was not an old hand like Stevens who involuntarily jerked to attention and looked toward the sound. As they stared a copter appeared at some point far above them, dropping in a quick, graceful descent toward a landing point which would put it on a low, flat terrain midway between their vantage point and the estate. The machine gleamed, the sun bouncing little particles off it.

"Look at that," Stevens said. "The man is good."

Professional admiration to be sure. The helicopter was coming in delicately, easily at a rate of descent that would not break eggs. The pilot controlled the sideways motion absolutely, the hand on the throttle so steady that there was no miss in the engine even as the RPM'S dropped further. "He's getting out," Wulff said.

"What?" said Stevens absorbed in the landing. "What's that? Who's getting out?"

"DiStasio. Obviously he's planning to leave the country with the valise."

"By helicopter," Stevens said. "The boy at those controls is really good, isn't he?" His eyes were glazed, he was focused to attention. Wulff was able, almost, to envy him. It would be nice to admire something that much, to be able to generate that kind of respect for a machine.

"He's not bad," Wulff said. "He would have made a good combat pilot."

"Combat?" Stevens said. "With a hand like that he could have done stunt shows."

Gently, delicately, the copter came down on the enormous lawn. It swayed carefully, left to right as the pilot checked for balance, then came down, bobbling slightly on the wheel struts as contact was made. The pilot cut the machine down to idle and the blades revolved almost noiselessly, little wisps of smoke and haze drifting out from the cockpit to blend into the air underneath him.

"He's not getting out," Wulff said after a moment. "He's waiting."

Stevens carefully restored a branch to the front of his face and said, "That would be reasonable, wouldn't it? DiStasio should be out any moment now."

"That could make it a little easier," Wulff said. "He may come out with only a bodyguard."

"Nothing is easier," Stevens said. "There's probably an armed guard in that cockpit."

"Probably," Wulff said, "it would make sense if there was. Still, let's wait for him."

"All right," Stevens said, "that suits me. I sure as hell don't want to take the house."

*Me neither*, Wulff thought and yet that was dangerous thinking. Without Stevens he might have followed his own inclination, which was to rush the house at once and take the consequences. There would have been, then, at least the element of surprise; DiStasio could not have possibly anticipated a direct attack and they might have succeeded. However, DiStasio would certainly be on the alert as he approached the copter. That would be his only point of exposure, after all, moving from the seclusion of the house to the protection of the plane; it stood to reason that he would be geared to the highest point of alertness then.

The thing about Stevens' kind of thinking, of playing matters cautiously, functioning on the path of least resistance, was that it was so seductive. It was so easy to fall into it, to hold back, to take the safe rather than the proper path. Looking sidewise at the man next to him Wulff began to see exactly how Stevens had become the kind of man he was, why at the age of thirty he was functioning, or had been functioning, as an odd-jobs man for a corrupt official in a two-bit country. He was like most of the men on the narco squad; all that he wanted to do was to survive, to cut corncrs, to get along. It could not even be called a matter of corruption. People like DiStasio were corrupt. They devoted themselves to aggrandizement and destruction with the same energy that Wulff was trying to devote to set matters right. But it was the people in the middle like Stevens who were responsible for almost all of the problems: the people who merely wanted to get along as best they could, curry no disfavor, make it from one day to the next. And they were so reasonable in their outlook, their arguments so defensible that at almost any given point it was hard to resist them. Certainly, unless you saw the end-product here in the person of Stevens, unless you could see the exact results of being accommodating, not taking chances, cutting corners, you might do it yourself. Already Stevens had corrupted *him*. Cuba had become a nightmare of missed purposes because he had slid along with it rather than rising to the circumstances. If he had gone after Delgado immediately he might have gotten to DiStasio at the same time. Now he had to do two sweaty, nasty jobs instead of one. *Son of a bitch*, Wulff thought, looking at Stevens, *son of a bitch, he is the enemy*. This did not exactly change the situation.

Stevens tensed, seeing something even before Wulff did. "All right," he said, "here he comes."

Wulff followed the man's gaze. In the distance, two men were walking from the house, one of them holding a large, bulky object against him. This must be DiStasio, then, the object the valise. The man behind him, following in close order no more than a pace separated was carrying a machine gun. Briskly they walked toward the copter.

"Son of a bitch," Wulff said, "they don't take any chances at all, do they?"

"A machine gun," Stevens said almost reverently. "How the hell are they going to get equipment like that on a light copter?"

"Oh they'll manage," Wulff said, "they'll manage." He looked at DiStasio downrange, the little man walking almost jauntily and then reached inside his coat and took out a pistol. The man might have been thirty yards from the copter now. The blades stroked lazily.

Stevens reached out and put a hand on Wulff's wrist. "Are you crazy?" he said.

"No."

"For Christ's sake!" Stevens said desperately. "You'll never get him with a light weapon at that distance and even if you do, you'll bring fire on us—"

"Shut up," Wulff said distinctly. "Shut the fuck up." And then with assurance waved the pistol backhand, hit Stevens a stunning crack on the forehead. With a little shriek the man fell heavily. Wulff felt just an instant of remorse; he had not wanted to do it, this man had fought with him in one of the worst battles of all. But it had to be done, Stevens had to be dumped, he could no longer go along with him because the man's terror was holding him back and it was contagious as well. He kicked Stevens away, making this calculation in just an instant and then aimed the pistol quickly, bore it down on the man holding the machine gun. And he fired.

That was the only hope, to get the man carrying the gun. Stevens in his panic had not seen that obviousness; that of course the bodyguard would have to be downed. That was the only way to DiStasio. The man holding the machine gun spun as the shot hit him and then in perfect, soundless slow motion lifted the weapon clumsily against his chest, pointing it in Wulff's direction. He struggled with the mechanism, at the same time as DiStasio dove toward the ground. And then he must have found the trigger because the gun began to boom. But even as the first shots sprayed out, moving well above Wulff's head, the man had collapsed, the machine gun flung from him in the death agony, the gun rolling harmlessly on the field.

He had downed him.

DiStasio lunged toward the coper, holding the valise, and then, as Wulff came from the bushes aiming, DiStasio must have seen that that wouldn't work, there was simply no way that he could get to safety before Wulff would place the killing shot. Instead he dropped the valise reached inside his clothing and in one gesture which was almost a blur got a shot off which passed above Wulff's left shoulder, just missing him. Wulff dove, unconscious of everything but the need to find cover and as he did so the pistol, in his fall was torn loose from his hand, rolled away from him. DiStasio put the second shot a foot in front of Wulff's face and then ran toward him. Wulff tried to roll toward some kind of safety but there was none. DiStasio had him levelled. But the man was not shooting; instead he closed in on Wulff and then stood above him at a distance of six feet, holding the pistol, looking at him.

The man's face was contorted with fury. Looking up at him Wulff understood why DiStasio had not put in the killing shot. He was so filled with hatred that he wanted to see Wulff's face in the knowledge of death. He wanted Wulff to know panic before death, die with his bowels open. He would not give him that. If it all ended here, then it must, but he would not give the enemy the satisfaction of breaking him. He waited.

"You son of a bitch," DiStasio said, "you dirty bastard, I want you to beg for it. Come on. Come on beg to live." He squeezed off another shot, it landed in the dirt near Wulff's wrist. "Beg for your life," he said.

Wulff said nothing. He lay there like a patient on a hospital rack and closed his eyes. It was not true that death was the common end. There were any one of a number of ways to die and each of them refracted back upon the life that man had lived. He would not buckle. He would not beg. He had done all of his dying in New York, months before.

"You crazy, lousy bastard," DiStasio said, "you've ruined everything, everything you touch turns to shit, don't you know that? But you've come to the end of it now." He let out a maniacal laugh. "Beg," he said again, "I want you to beg."

Wulff shook his head.

"All right," DiStasio said. He was a short man with transparent features; this was a man, Wulff thought staring up at him, who found it impossible to conceal his emotions to maintain any kind of dissemblance whatsoever. Everything would show on his face the instant that he felt emotion. Right now confusion was making the changes with hatred around his lips and mouth. "You killed a good man," he said. "You killed a good man. Delgado," ready to betray him.

"Delgado was such a good man that you were ready to betray him."

"Delgado was a good man, an old revolutionary, he was one of those up in the mountains," DiStasio said, not hearing what Wulff had said. "He worked hard and he deserved better than this."

"Delgado was a dealer."

"You killed my friend. You killed Raoul Delgado."

"You don't really believe that, do you?" Wulff said and he thought yes, you do believe that, you believe it completely. You have managed to convince yourself that Delgado was your friend, that you were not going to betray him and that in killing me you are merely avenging his death. Already DiStasio had his cover story straight. Even before the commission of the act he had altered reality to accommodate his interpretation of it. No wonder, Wulff thought, no wonder that this man was the head of the intelligence division. Ex-head, of course. DiStasio would have another career waiting.

"Goodbye you filthy, dirty, rotten, murdering son of a bitch," DiStasio said and aimed the gun and gritted his teeth and something came into his left ear and his head exploded.

DiStasio's skull opened up like a pulped tomato, spitting seeds of brain and blood and he put a hand to his head, touched the explosion, brought down the hand with what was still left of his intelligence must have seen it, must have seen what had happened to him. He emitted one terrible wail like a tortured infant and then fell heavily across Wulff, the body already like a corpse, covering him like a sheet. Wulff took the impact off his haunches. Stevens stood above him, holding a pistol.

"You know," he said to Wulff with the casualness of a stranger asking someone to please get off his toes in a crowded public place, "you're just goddamned lucky that you didn't hit me hard enough to really put me to sleep. Where the fuck would you have been then, I want to know?" He sounded piqued.

## XV

In the copter, Figueroa saw everything. He saw everything but he could not believe it: his boss, the best of the bodyguards, the valise that was somehow so important to this, they were all coming aboard the copter and then in the next moment the shots had begun and then the terrible, unbelievable scene which followed. He simply could not believe it, he could not believe what was going on but he knew that he should not interfere either. DiStasio after the bodyguard was killed seemed to have the situation completely in control and he would only become very angry if Figueroa interfered. Once Figueroa had interfered in something like this and DiStasio's wrath had been terrible; Figueroa had been afraid that he was going to get killed himself. DiStasio was very private about his murders. So Figueroa merely sat hunched over in the compartment, watching all of this, giving orders to the pilot with his hands that he was to keep in place, do nothing, keep the motor running. Surely DiStasio would come aboard quickly, just as soon as he had finished his business with this man lying on the ground and he would want the motor running.

Figueroa waited it out. It could not be long now although he found himself becoming a little impatient; DiStasio was his boss and a wonderful man but he wished that he would not relish killing as much as he did. Figueroa had watched DiStasio kill five or six men now and toward the end the kills had been very slow and soft because DiStasio wanted his victims to beg. He liked begging; he was making this one beg now but probably the man was holding out, that was all.

Suddenly the two forms touched and then he saw DiStasio levelling the gun. Now at last it would be over. DiStasio would kill the man and would get in the copter and Figueroa was glad, because he always felt a little bit empty when he was not near his boss where he could see and touch him. Also he had been very frightened at the strangeness and suddenness of this attack. Surely everything would be all right now, though. He saw DiStasio level the gun and then, from nowhere, a bullet struck his boss and Figueroa saw horror.

It was pure horror; he had never seen anything so terrible in his life. DiStasio's head, that handsome, passionate head was suddenly opening up like a decayed fruit and from all kinds of openings and holes

Figueroa could see the blood lurching. It was a mortal shot; Figueroa knew it instantly. DiStasio was dead even as he lifted a hand to draw it across his bloody face and then stare at it with a shudder. Figueroa could see death in the gesture; then DiStasio fell over the man that he had been about to kill. It was a death fall. From a clearing another man holding a pistol had come and now he joined them.

Figueroa screamed. It was the scream which he had been building up within himself for thirty-nine years; a scream of utter torment and loss because now his boss, his protector, his life and guardian was gone but as he screamed he was, at some cold and efficient level of himself, working and thinking. He drew his pistol. If nothing else he would kill the men who had killed his boss, wreak a terrible vengeance upon them and then he would bury his boss and kill himself because there was no point in living. But even as he aimed the pistol clumsily through an open part of the compartment his hand jiggled and he felt himself losing aim. The copter was lifting.

"Goddamn it!" Figueroa screamed, still trying to get off a shot. But the copter was coming off the ground at great speed; they were now ten to twenty feet up and soaring, soaring. "What are you doing?" he screamed to the pilot. "You had your orders—"

"Not me," the pilot said behind the bulkhead. He was one of the best in the corps of engineers, the best that Figueroa could find but he was merely a hired man without true inner loyalty and now he sounded like one. "We must save ourselves. I do not know what is going on down there but we are taking a terrible risk—"

"Put it down!" Figueroa screamed, "you can't do this! Put the plane down! We cannot leave; he may still be alive—"

"No," the pilot said. "That man is not alive, and even if he were our primary responsibility is to ourselves and to property. We cannot remain there and risk the property. My orders are very distinct. We will return to the capital and make a full report and troops will be sent—"

"You can't do this!" Figueroa screamed. "You murderer, you murderer!" And at that moment it was indeed the pilot who was the murderer, collaborating in all of this: watching it, being held responsible and now obstructing vengeance. And something cold and terrible, a snake of purpose, seized Figueroa's wrist and he turned his arm, then wrist and hand holding the gun toward the pilot, went through the bulkhead, aimed the pistol at the pilot's head. Slowly the man turned and then he saw the pistol and the same terror was in his face that was in Figueroa's.

"No," he said, "you cannot do this."

"Murderer," Figueroa said.

"You do not understand. Who will fly the copter—"

"Murderer," Figueroa said again. He shot the pilot in the neck. The pilot reached his hand toward the sudden hole as if it were an insect bite or bee-sting, his face perplexed. Then, as the helicopter swayed in the air, he dropped his hand to the controls, instinctively tried to right it. Still alive. The murderer was still alive. "Die!" Figueroa said. He put another shot into the pilot's head, this one at the medulla oblongata. A smear of blood appeared, delicate as a spider web in the first impression, then spreading. The pilot slumped over the controls.

The copter began to fall.

"Murderer!" Figueroa shrieked. "Murderer, felon! You killed my boss you bastard!" And then the tears came, the tears because DiStasio was dead, and now, looking out at the revolving landscape beyond the windows, Figueroa understood that he was dead too because the plane was falling hopelessly out of control. In that suspended instant before impact he went for the controls himself, yanked at bolts and levers futilely, desperately tried to bring some organization to the path of the plane but nothing worked, nothing worked and the plane revolved in the air, a complete turn, three hundred and sixty degrees, everything loose in the cockpit jumbling together, wedges of metal flying, the corpse of the pilot tumbling from the seat and hurling Figueroa into the wall, enveloping him with a ghastly hug. Figueroa still had his gun, he fired and fired, sending shots into the dead man but the grip would not release. And the copter, gracefully coming out of its revolution settled in a straight plunge toward the fields, light and air streaming by, a curious soft radiance in the cockpit as Figueroa tried to struggle free and then, at the last instant before impact, there was a feeling of ascension, rising, it was exactly as they had told him in church so many years ago, there *was* some kind of radiance and he tried to embrace it, tried to move into that center and beyond pain but he could not help thinking of DiStasio dead, the flight destroyed, his own life ended, as the plane arced. And at the end, as he had always known there would be (because the church always lied about everything, that was why he had left it for that better church, DiStasio), there was terrific pain, tearing him apart, gutting him like a fish on sand and then—

Mercifully enough, and as he also had long suspected, there was nothing.

# XVI

They watched the copter hit in flame midway between them and the horizon, the lances of fire diving into the earth like Jove's bolts and then Wulff's attention returned to the situation at hand, the two corpses, the pulped head of one of them lolling at his foot. He moved away from DiStasio's body slowly, feeling the disgust, hearing the secondary explosion of the destroyed copter. Everywhere he went he brought death. But then again, the dying was just.

"That was stupid," Stevens said. "Knocking me out."

"I thought I had to."

"Well you're lucky you didn't."

"All right," Wulff said, "enough of that. You saved my life. I'm grateful."

"Are you?" Stevens said, rubbing the back of his neck, looking at him strangely. "Are you really grateful?"

"I am," Wulff said, "I'm endlessly grateful. I'll write you a recommendation. I'll use my influence with the NYPD to get you a job as a custodian. What the fuck do you want, Stevens?" He walked to the valise, perched on one end, half-buried in the ooze and tugged on it. "I thought you had no heart for it and that you were holding me back. I was half-right, wasn't I?" He struggled with the valise, got it out, put it down flat. "You have no heart for it."

"No" Stevens said. "I haven't."

Wulff opened the valise. He half-expected to see it filled with bits of waste-paper—it would be the right end to his adventure with the post-revolutionary regime—but no, he did not, it was filled with the same snowy bricks that he had seen in the Las Vegas airport. Only two days ago, that. Unbelievable. He looked at those little pillars of death and then swung his head left to look at the fire tracings from the downed copter. When he turned his head back Stevens was standing to his right, looking into the valise, the pistol held loosely at his side. "Son of a bitch," Stevens said. "So this was it all the time."

"You didn't believe there was such a thing?"

"No," Stevens said. "I did not. I admit that I thought you had made the thing up. Shit, there's a million dollars in there." He extended a forefinger cautiously, rested it against a brick.

"No," Wulff said, "not the way to do it. First you lick the finger, then you put it against the brick. That's the way you test them. If you want to test them. It's real."

Stevens licked his finger rather doubtfully, rested it against a brick, then took it up and checked the grains, sniffed them delicately. "You're right," he said, "it's real."

"Don't doubt it."

"Son of a bitch, it's real," Stevens said. His facial expression had changed, become subtly fierce and ugly. He extended a foot and kicked the valise closed.

Suddenly the pistol in his hand was levelled at Wulff.

Wulff held his ground, looked at Stevens steadily. He was not surprised. Whatever else, he had been expecting this at some level. "Don't think of it," he said.

"I have to," Stevens said. "You don't believe this but I do."

"I believe anything," Wulff said.

"You don't think it's true," Stevens said. Once again he had that confused, abstracted air. Despite the danger of the situation Wulff had the sudden insane urge to clasp Stevens by the shoulder and tell him that it was perfectly all right, but he would do better by getting some control of himself. Stevens appeared badly in need of counsel of some sort. This was not his kind of thing at all. Nevertheless the pistol appeared menacing.

"I know it's true," Wulff said.

"I've got to do it," said Stevens, "I'll never get another chance, don't you see that? It's there, staring me in the face. A million dollars."

"It's not a million. By the time it works its way into supply channels it may not be half of that. Besides, the purity is still in question."

"I don't care about the purity," Stevens said. "What does purity have to do with it? I can't live on the margin all my life, can I? Sooner or later you've got to get out. I'm forty-four years old."

"All right," Wulff said, "I'm thirty-two. What does that have to do with it?"

"Thirty-two isn't forty-four," Stevens said. "It's an entirely different stage of life. You've got options ahead of you. Possibilities. I'm going to be living in hotel rooms all my life."

"Not necessarily," Wulff said. He felt the bulge of a pistol in his hip pocket. It was the one he had retained through all of this: loaded and cocked like the others. If he could get to it in time … But he discarded the notion for the instant. Stevens was alert. His conversation was only peripheral to his purposes. A move toward that pistol now would merely give Stevens his excuse to kill. Now he was on the borderline, still talking himself into position.

"I don't want to live in hotel rooms all my life," Stevens said in that cold, empty monotone. "I mean, it's not fun living that way, no matter what you've heard. I admit that I've fallen into that habit but that doesn't mean it's right. And working for bastards and pricks like Delgado just because it was too much trouble to go out and chance it on your own. Well, this has to end."

"Don't do it," Wulff said, not to dissuade but merely for rhythm's sake. Throw in a line here, a response there, keep the man talking. If Stevens's eyes ever lost that peculiar air of alertness ...

"I lost everything in Vietnam," Stevens said, "I was only thirty you know when I went over there. I was there five years and I went in believing everything. Came out as a light colonel believing nothing. That's a hard thing to do to a man." His hand clenched on the pistol. "I've got to kill you Wulff," he said. "You're not a bad man, understand that. I even sympathize with you a little bit; you've bottled up a lot of integrity in there. But consider my position."

"All right," Wulff said softly, "I'll consider your position." The fire on the hill was out now; thick, deadly puffs of smoke indicated that ignition was over and that now it was only guttering in small sparks. He revolved his attention nearer, looked at the corpse of DiStasio which through some trick of light had already begun to cyanose, the veins puckering darkly under the skin, surfacing. The bodyguard lay behind him face-down on the ground in the embryonic position. Already the area was filled with the stink and fumes of death and of the crash. They could have been at the end of the world. "You don't have to kill me, you know," he said. "You've got the gun. You can just take the valise and get out of here. What can I do?" You'll have to kill me, he thought. You'll take that valise away over my corpse and no other way and you know it.

Stevens nodded as if he was listening to Wulff's stream of consciousness. "I have to kill you," he said. "I know who you are and what you are now. You've killed a hundred men for that stuff. You wouldn't let me walk away with it and if you did you'd spend the rest of your life getting me. The only way is to kill you."

"All right," Wulff said, "kill me."

"I want to," Stevens said very softly. "I want to a lot. I've killed hundreds of men and I shouldn't really have any trouble with this at all. But it's hard, do you know? I guess I don't really want to kill you after all."

"Good," Wulff said. "If that's how it is, don't kill me."

"I've thought of that too," Stevens said, "but it doesn't work. You have your qualities though. You really do have your qualities."

His finger tightened on the trigger. Wulff looked in the man's eyes, saw them shrink toward a small point of light. He looked for it, saw that point, deduced it and the proper moment.

"I think that someone's come off that copter," he said. "Not to bother you."

Stevens whirled, dove toward the ground facing the clearing, looking for the men who might have come off the copter. There were none but the idiot trick had worked, it had worked just as Wulff had hoped it might, knifing in toward the moment of maximum tension and reluctance as well, that delicate balancing instant in which Stevens was trying to push himself past fear toward murder and now as the man, hopelessly out of position, turned on the ground, Wulff already had the gun in his hand. Yanking it out of his pocket, without thinking, he put a shot squarely into the lower spine and Stevens bucked on the ground; his body convulsed and his own gun fell from him. Then, spine broken, he flopped on the ground like an animal, scrambling desperately as if to raise himself toward his feet, squealing in horror as he realized that he could not and finally falling on the ground, stretching out full length as if it were a bed and Wulff reached over and took the pistol that Stevens had dropped, looked at the man on the ground. Stevens, convulsing again, rolled on his back, shrieked with pain as he drew his knees up involuntarily and then looked up at Wulff through clouded eyes. Wulff stood there and looked down at the man impassively. Stevens stretched his arms out full-length, fingers twitching. "Kill me," he gasped, "you've got to kill me."

"Soon," Wulff said, "but when I'm goddamned ready."

"I'm in agony, Wulff," Stevens said. His voice was thin and soft. "You broke my spine."

"I'm sorry about that."

"I lost," Stevens said. That curious transparency of cheekbones made his face seem to glow. "I tried it but I lost."

"You certainly did."

"It was nothing personal," Stevens said, "I was just tired of living on shit. There's just so much shit a man can take and then you've got to make a move."

"Sure," Wulff said.

"I couldn't take it anymore. But you're good. You're practically the best there ever was. Did anyone ever tell you that? You're just about the best in the business."

"I'm flattered."

"I mean, the way you handled this. I couldn't handle things that way." A flash of pain went through Stevens, he convulsed again. "I'm no fucking good," he said. "I never knew what I was doing."

"Neither did I," said Wulff.

"Kill me," said Stevens. "I tried and I lost and I'm in great pain now, Wulff. Don't give me fucking dialogues. Put a bullet through my head.

You'd do it the right way, wouldn't you? You wouldn't leave me a brain-damage case."

"I trusted you," Wulff said. He had a vague feeling of incompletion. Everything was happening too rapidly. Not fifteen minutes ago, it seemed, they had been stalking the clearing, looking for a shot at DiStasio. Now at least three men were dead and another lay on the ground destroyed. Events accelerate. It must be the same way, he thought, on heroin. Yes, that is exactly what a drug jag must feel like; the compression of time, the acceleration of circumstance. "You were the only one so far I've trusted."

"Well that's too bad," Stevens said. He licked his lips. "The pain isn't that bad now," he said. "It's fading away. You must have smashed the spine altogether; after the first impact you don't feel anything. I'm all gone in the arms and legs, gone below the waist." There was a dark stain on his pants which Wulff noticed; Stevens looked at it as well. "Bladder control would go," he said clinically. "You lose all control of the sphincter, too. I'm sure that my pants are full of shit."

"I did trust you," Wulff said, "that's the hell of it. I haven't trusted anyone since all of this crap began. But I *trusted* goddamn it in you. I figured that like me you had nothing left to lose."

"I didn't," Stevens said weakly. "I had nothing to lose, that's why I did it. I'm sick, I was sick of having nothing left to lose. You're the guy that's holding on. You've got something to fight for."

"Now what the fuck am I supposed to do?" Wulff said, feeling something very much like disgust, looking at the corpses and the valise, the damnable valise lying to his right. "What the hell am I supposed to do now?"

"You can kill me," Stevens said, "and then take your fucking valise and get out of here on foot. But I wouldn't advise you waiting much longer because probably a lot of people are bearing down on this place by now. That copter may have had a radio and besides DiStasio was a very important man. He was almost premier six years ago, you know. There was going to be a coup but at the last moment people backed out of it." His eyes rolled. "I know all about the fucking politics of this fucking miserable country," he said. "I know everything about everything. It's sure as hell gotten me a long way, hasn't it?"

"All right," Wulff said. He sighed thickly, the breath uneven in his chest. He pointed the gun. "All right, I'll do it. I ought to fucking leave you on the ground to die but I won't. Maybe you wouldn't die. They'd find you here and patch you up, give you a useful life in a wheelchair. A whole new second career, moving around rehabilitation corridors. You'd enjoy that, wouldn't you?"

"Don't bet on it," Stevens said. "Medical care in this fucking country is like it was in nineteen-hundred in the States. I probably wouldn't survive the exploratory." He leaned his head to the side, vomited, a thin, clear stream of bile with little flecks of blood mixed in it. "I think I'm bleeding internally, Wulff," he said. "It's going to get very bad now. You could save me a lot of trouble."

"Sure," Wulff said, "I'm saving a lot of people trouble these days. That's a career."

"Up to you," Stevens said. He inhaled, closed his eyes. "But if you're going to do it you'd better do it now because I don't think I can be courageous anymore. I've just about used up the last of my courage." Tears sprang from his eyes. "Please, Wulff," he said.

Wulff shot him.

He put the shot deep into the man's forehead, centering it between the eyes, the purest killing shot of them all and on the ground Stevens arced, he gasped, his body tensed like a bow and then it relaxed. One pearl of blood came from the wound and he emitted a final gasp, then he lay there, empty, on the earth.

Wulff smelt the sharp odor of feces.

With a sudden revulsion as profound as it was surprising he raised the pistol over his head and hurled it into the forest. It clattered off a trunk, then vanished into grass. He knelt by the corpse, closed the eyelids, shuddering for a long time in a mood that he could not understand. Then he brushed one hand down the forehead, covering the wound with hair and stood, feeling a curious lightheadedness, an inability to focus himself.

He walked away from Stevens and toward the valise. It was just like Boston. At the end there was the valise. Bodies came and went, the fires leapt, people screamed and died, everything fell away ... but there was always a valise and within the valise was the pure, white death that had inspired it all. It laughed and mocked at them. It was the only permanency. It would survive all of them.

Wulff shuddered.

He hefted the valise; curiously warm it came into his hand. As he did so—and as he knew it would be—purpose returned. The valise was central. It would always remain. He too would die, his death was inevitable ... but the pure white death would remain. That was the nature of the situation. It could never be any other way.

For men needed death.

He picked up the valise and walked slowly away from there. The road, as far as he knew, was only a mile down and he thought that he could find it through the forest. The jeep, hopefully, would be where it had been ditched. It had been a good idea to keep hold of it after all. The jeep would put him on the road toward the capital and somehow from the capital he would find a way out. The airports would be blocked but he would somehow get a private plane, put a gun to someone's head and get out of there. You could not go as far as he had without going further. Otherwise, it would make no sense at all.

For Wulff, everything made sense now.

He got through the forest and toward the jeep. It was not too difficult, at least not as hard as he had feared it would be but it certainly would have been a lot easier with Stevens. That man really knew his terrain.

## XVII

Taking the jeep down the road he found himself running up flat against a military convoy. He could see the trucks in the distance, soldiers hanging from them, handholds on the slats, looking in his direction and in that instant he knew that there was very little time in which he could judge and control the situation. Hunched over the wheel of the jeep he used his free hand to dig out a pistol, felt the cold metal leap into his hand and then, driving one-handed he made his decision which was to attack by driving on through, take the chance that the convoy had nothing to do with him and that he might be well past them before word got through that he was the man they were seeking. In any country under any circumstance you had to have a kind of blind faith in the continuing and compulsive stupidity of the military. It was a constant. If it wasn't a constant it ought to be. He kept his head down, shoulders over the wheel, looked as expressionless as possible and wheeled the jeep toward the side of the road, decelerating on the rutted shoulder then to give the convoy the widest possible gap through which to pass.

The distance narrowed, closed completely and then he was amidst Cuban military. Soldiers hung over the sides of trucks staring absently through the trees, mumbling to themselves. In the center of the trucks men with stripes on their sleeves hung on for balance with an expression no less miserable than that on any of the soldiers. Four of the trucks passed Wulff so closely that he could feel the breath steaming from the soldier's mouths.

Then he was past them and moving over a hill.

He put the clutch in, cautiously shifted up a gear and then drove for speed. The speedometer hovered to fifty but over that point the vehicle seemed to be on the verge of coming apart, bolts and joints chattering within it ominously. Stevens had had this thing at eighty without a shake. Stevens had been a hell of a driver, that was all. Anything mechanical was obviously within Stevens' strength; it was the question of dealing with people which gave him difficulty. Scratch one for Stevens. Scratch two. A few cows on the roadway far down scattered to the sound of his horn, moving with surprising speed for cows and he drove on through. Then, behind him, he heard the sound of engines.

He turned. The truck filled with soldiers was behind him no more than a hundred yards. They were leaning out, gesticulating, waving at him to stop. Wulff floored the accelerator.

Obviously they had found out who he was and at least one of them, functioning as point, was coming on back in pursuit. No rear view mirror in the jeep; he had not even thought to look behind. He had been loping along, dreaming, already calculating his method of access to the airport and all the time they had been closing in.

If Stevens had been along this would not have happened.

He would not think of Stevens. If he allowed himself to think of Stevens, it would lead to remorse or regret, or at the very least preoccupation, and he could not afford them now. Also, there was nothing to feel guilty about. If he had not killed Stevens, Stevens would have killed him. He downshifted the jeep, put it in second and floored the accelerator. The vehicle almost stalled, taking power unevenly, groaning, protesting, but then it seemed to come together in a different way and it lurched out of its bind. He was going at sixty miles an hour. Looking behind him he saw that the truck had closed no ground; in fact he might have dropped it ten yards behind him.

The first shot came. It went well over his head; he could see the projectile whisking, disappearing down the road. Then there was a whole hail of secondary shots, scattering fire on the sides and rear of the jeep, some bullets like fish moving around his head, a firmament. The accelerator could go no further to the floor. Reluctantly, however, the jeep was still accelerating. It was going at seventy-five now and there was no shudder in the metal. Keep it in low gear then; that had been the trick all along. He bent over the wheel, opening ground. Now, on a long, flat rise he was able to maintain speed where the truck could not. It fell behind him and then out of sight. The bullets ceased. Wulff held the wheel steadily.

He found himself on the outskirts of a small village of some sort. Buildings were closer together; men sat by the side of the road in chairs, smoking. Out in the fields he could see other figures. Toiling on crops no doubt. The village made him slow, he had to do it or risk seriously injuring someone. He was not yet ready to do that. Children in the street scattered before him as the jeep plowed through. The truck was still not in sight behind him. He was going to make it. He was going to get through this.

A man stood in the center of the road holding a rifle. He raised the rifle and put a long, flat shot across the hood. He was screaming something in Spanish but Wulff did not understand it and then he was atop the man so quickly that the man just barely evaded him, leaping to one side. He levelled the rifle again. Wulff saw all of this compressed into a few seconds that seemed to take place very slowly. Driving away from the man one-handed he reached into his pocket, took out a pistol, aimed and fired.

The man fell away. Then again he may simply have ducked the shot or collapsed from sight; it was impossible to tell at this rate of speed. He put the pistol away, drove two-handed again. He had either killed the man or he had not. He had either added another to the body count or then again he had added no one. Did it matter? Bodies were all over. Life and death were academic to the people with whom he was dealing now. It was just a matter of getting through.

He was going to get through. Now, seeing signs, arrows, intersection indications he knew exactly where he was. He was no more than four or five miles from the airport at which he had landed. This airport was a military installation of some sort; it was off the main channels. Good. He would not have to deal with traffic then. He picked up a sign and got onto a two-lane highway. Here, for the first time, there was a little traffic, most of it composed of ten and twelve-year-old American cars but no one took any notice of a civilian in a jeep holding a valise against him with a single elbow as he drove. Wulff wished that he had a hat with which to conceal himself but a hat hardly seemed necessary. Everyone was concentrating on his own destination. Latins drove with complete absorption. No one was interested in him here.

No sign of the truck. He guessed that he had shaken it for good. Maybe they were investigating the corpse up ahead. The sun was finally going down now—the last sun that Stevens ever saw—dropping somewhere in the mountains. The mountains that Delgado had talked about from which the revolutionaries had come. He took a bypass road and found himself almost immediately dumped onto the airstrip. Compression. Everything in Cuba was smaller: the people, the landscape, the airfields. The lives. The deaths.

A helicopter with someone in it was revving up near the roadway on a small strip of gravel. Private area no doubt; the military's playpen. Wulff rolled the jeep down a few yards from the copter, stopped it, yanked up the brake but left the motor running. As Stevens had said you never knew when you might need the thing. He took the valise out from his side, leapt down and carried it over to the copter.

A man wearing dark glasses was in the cockpit. He looked down at Wulff without expression, then shook his head and went back to the controls.

Wulff took out a pistol and aimed it at the man, then held it until the man's gaze returned and their eyes locked. The man seemed very interested in the pistol. Wulff let him think about it for a while, simply holding it in position. The man's mouth fell open. His hands fell away from the controls and very carefully he stood.

"A ramp," Wulff said.

The man nodded slowly. He understood English. Good. That was very good. He went away from the cockpit. A hatch opened and a small ramp fell down. Wulff, holding the pistol steadily, struggled with his valise up the ramp and into the helicopter.

The man waited for him inside. He was trembling. All of his limbs seemed loose, disconnected from his body. Wulff put the valise down, eased it against a bulkhead and then straightened, holding the pistol on the man. "You will do as I say."

"Yes," the man said, "I will do as you say." His voice was unaccented. Probably American. What was an American doing here? The place was crawling with his countrymen, that was all. Cuba, like Vegas, was simply a place to go when there was nowhere else.

"I want to go about ninety miles," Wulff said.

"All right. I will take you."

"I want to go ninety miles north and east and I want no difficulty at all. If you make any difficulty, I will have to kill you."

"Not necessary," the man said. "I have children—"

"I don't care about your children. I don't care about anything except this valise. If you cooperate you'll get out of this alive. If you don't I will have to kill you, and since I know how to fly one of these things myself you will not be missed."

"I'll cooperate," the man said, "believe me, I'll cooperate."

"Fine," Wulff said, "then let's get going."

The man went into the compartment and did something with the controls. Slowly the helicopter lifted. The airfield fell away and Wulff was looking then at all of Havana.

"I want no trouble," the man said, "I want no problems. I will do anything you say." And all the way up to altitude he kept on talking, talking, inexhaustibly talking but Wulff, holding the pistol easily, listened to none of it but only to the comforting, throbbing sounds of the engines, his mind only on the valise and its destination. He was damned, absolutely damned, if he was going to get into a relationship with any copter pilot again.

THE END

# THE LONE WOLF #6: CHICAGO SLAUGHTER

## by Barry N. Malzberg

Writing as Mike Barry

Fix the pusher ... by dialing the drug hotline at any time, night or day, in complete confidence, by giving any information you may have on the pusher: name, habits, whereabouts ... you can, in safety, help the government to help you. Let's fix the pusher ... let's put him in jail.

—Newspaper display ad

So some clown is going to call up the hotline, give the name of the guy who he thinks is running around with his girl or who he owes a hundred bucks to; some clown is going to call the hotline and get the feds on his neighbor because he doesn't like his looks. How long is that going to last? Either the feds are going to put everyone into jail or they're going to give up. A little bit of both, knowing their track record.

There's only one way to fix the pusher and make it stick. It's an old message and where it lands, comes out blood.

—Burt Wulff

# PROLOGUE

Methadone stinks, David Williams thought.

Methadone stinks; it was supposed to be the promised land for drug control but it's just turned out to be another kind of hustle. Methadone was supposed to block the need for heroin in the system, remove the obsessive grinding search for a fix that was the core of the addict's existence, but actually it did nothing of the sort. It did not take the user off drugs and turn him into a non-addict but only pushed him in another direction. Methadone produced a high of its own, not the free-floating condition of heroin but a lower, steadier buzz and he had heard professionals say that in its own way methadone did not have to take a back seat to the big H at all; that you could do very nicely with methadone, it would get you off in a different way for about the same period of time. And with methadone you had a license, illegality being the big H's only drawback.

You traded in one form of addiction for another; the same principles were in effect, Williams thought. Also the same people and methods. If you could peddle heroin then you could sell methadone; if you could build up a profit-and-barter system on smack than methadone which was more freely available, distributed by the government itself, was even easier to push into the flow. Who was kidding who? Methadone was getting pushed into the street just as H was; the margin wasn't as high but the work was steadier and less dangerous. And, he thought, the methadone high was nothing to look down on. It wasn't an H high but on the other hand it was considerably better than no high at all.

It was the same corruption and stupidity that had always been, Williams thought as he brought the car to a stop a block away from the methadone center in East Harlem, yanked up the emergency brake and then, leaving the doors unlocked—shit, it was New York City PD property, this unmarked 1971 Plymouth; the junkies could only do them a *favor* by taking it—got out of the car and worked his way east. Plainclothes duty; check out the traffic around the methadone center. Maybe try to locate a known dealer or two by face and bring them in. Meth, heroin, it was all the same. It was a hustle; the same actors, the same format with a new deck of cards switched in. A stacked deck, of course. Williams supposed that he didn't mind.

Hell, why should he mind? He was going to draw his fourteen grand per plus pension, plus health benefits, plus this and that for the full twenty, no matter what he did. If they wanted to send him up to

Harlem to check out methadone that was okay; if they wanted him to sit on his ass in property and shuffle papers around he would do that too. Putting in the time, making the time: he had eighteen years and two months to go and if it wasn't bad time it was good time ... the Army philosophy.

He moved quickly on 137th toward Lenox, checking without seeing, absorbing without thinking. Street technique. You picked it if nothing else up fast. Everything looked as it always had; junkies littering the stoops, a couple of kids playing hooky scooting through alleys kicking garbage cans, sanitation workers in the middle of the block holding beer cans and bitching while the truck stood idling, doors open. They were working out their twenty, too. Everybody was on the twenty.

Shit, Williams thought, it doesn't matter to me. If they want me to check out meth I'll check it out, if they want me to deal for a little smack just show me the way; I'm just working here. I didn't make this situation, I hold no responsibility for it and it's going to be the same after I leave. Except worse. Short of dealing myself or ripping off graft I'll do anything necessary to take me through the twenty. *I don't really believe that*, he thought.

Talk of hustling, he was hustling himself. It all hurt too much, that was the point; it hurt too much for an honest, feeling man to take, doubly so if he were a black man, and if you didn't build up that armor you were wiped out. It was something that either came with your first month out on the street or sent you right off the force. Williams allowed himself to look at the intersection of 137th and Lenox for just one moment with eyes that were not shrouded by attitude and the impact of the scene. The litter, the waste, the small, nervous pool of activity radiating from a filthy storefront made him sick. He had to draw down the shroud of detachment quickly, otherwise he might have stumbled on the pavement, collided with something. It was that bad. All right then, it was that bad.

You had to seal off. Unless you were Wulff. Unless you were that crazy bastard Wulff, and Williams thought abstractedly of the man for an instant—his ex-partner, ex-cop, ex-narc, ex-combat veteran, ex-career man, ex-everything in the whole godamned world who was going to clean up the international drug-trade singlehandedly because he thought they had done something nasty to him once. Wulff was crazy, he believed in this holy war shit, he really thought that you could make a difference. And Williams could have laughed, but then he thought of what Wulff had been able to accomplish in just a couple of months of single-handed action and he was not so sure. He was not so sure at all. Moving out on his own he certainly had done more damage than a hundred agencies had in twenty years. "Watch where the fuck you going man," someone said.

Williams looked up. The man in front of him was a little younger, make him in his twenties, a cigarette coming out of one corner of his mouth, down to the butt end. The man must have been in an alleyway; he certainly had not been there just a few seconds before. Williams had that much faith in his reconnaissance even though all of it was subconscious. "Who you think you are, anyway?" the man said.

Williams stopped and looked at him. If the man was setting him up for an attack of some kind he was far gone because Williams had to outweigh him by thirty pounds or so—to say nothing of the gun that he carried inconspicuously. He looked at the man's eyes which were rolling slightly, then levelled out as they stared at Williams. Probably a junkie. You couldn't be sure, though. Half of New York had that rolling, spaced out look. If you went by the stare, there would be two million people in Nelson's fancy lockup.

"Excuse me," he said and extended an arm to brush by the man. Damn NYPD procedure anyway. Men in plainclothes were required to maintain a certain standard of dress and decency at all times unless they were on an infiltration squad. He would have attracted a hell of a lot less notice if they had let him go out on the street in the clothing that the rest of them wore, but no. No, the NYPD procedures panel was having none of it. Plainclothes but he had to wear a white shirt and suit jacket. Lucky they had not thought of a tie or that would have been included, too. He reached the arm out in a blocking gesture to bring the man to his side, uncovering the pavement so he could walk through. Elementary crowd technique. But the man did not come up into his arm and instead ducked under it. Now he was to Williams' side.

"Just hold it up there, dude," he said, "I want to talk with you a bit."

Williams stopped. The situation was getting trickier. On the corner a clump of them—dealers and customers, narcs and informers, for all he knew—were looking at him fixedly. Motion itself seemed to have stopped on the street. An incident, then, anything to break the monotony. Some outsider getting himself ripped off. He was probably the only man on the street who was not immediately identifiable. Thank the NYPD for that too ... sending out an observer cold without infiltrating the neighborhood, making him dress in white shirt and jacket. Bright, that was very bright. "What the fuck you doing around here?" the man said. He reached into his pocket and took out a small knife, pointed it at Williams. "You a tourist at the freak show or a fucking narco?"

Crazy. It was getting crazy. Williams had the vague feeling of unreality of the dreamer. This could not possibly be happening to him; it was the kind of routine mugging that might occur to the outsider he was pretending to be but not to him. Not to David Williams. Particularly not to David Williams who understood the situation as no one else did and who played carefully and with the system. No one was going to take him off. Impossible. He reached inside for his gun.

"Look here," he said, "I'm an—" And would have gone on to point out that he was a New York police officer who was going to take this man in for assault, lay it out to him simple and clear, see the widening fear in the assailant's eyes as he realized who he had had the profound ill luck to take off. He had it all plotted out in mind, in fact, knew what his moves would be leading up to using the gun to get clear to a callbox and summoning a patrol car ... but the assailant short-circuited him. Williams felt something like a pinprick in the area of his ribs, a small, neat incision of pain, then the pain began to spread, opening up like a flower and he felt the petals of hurt beginning to work through him.

"Son of a bitch," the assailant said, "son of a bitch narco." So he *did* know after all but this was doing Williams no good. The man in fact had moved into fury. "You dirty bastard," he said, "doing this to your own people," and Williams was still trying to get his gun out—should be simple, one motion and out, but it had hooked inside on a coil of thread in his jacket, either that or something had happened to him to make him weak. He felt a strange disinclination to struggle further for the gun; leave it stay where it was, it was hopeless anyway. Never get it out. He felt the pain moving upward now, toward his neck. Funny: funny thing about that, water seeks its level going downward but pain moves *up*. "Son of a bitch," the man with the knife said, "dirty, fucking cocksucker," angry, he was really angry and Williams reached out a hand to tell him to cut it out, it was ridiculous, this was no way to solve the problem and in any event he was an armed police officer who in just a few seconds was going to take out his gun and kill the man. Just a few seconds. In just a few seconds he would go for the gun; now he was still meditating the best way to do it. The sidewalk hit him on the left side of the jaw and dreamily he punched back at the concrete. Unwarranted attack. Assaulted by a sidewalk. This was quite funny; he felt himself beginning to giggle. "Son of a bitch," someone said to him again as if from a far distance but he did not care this time to find out who was saying it. They were all the same, all of them far away at 137th Street and Lenox whereas he, David Williams, was comfortably settled in St. Albans, Queens, in his mortgaged house where the system was taking care of him. He had a sensation not of falling but of rising. Funny. Strange how it worked out that way. Well, maybe death was upward-mobile too.

# Chapter 1

Wulff's plan had been to show up in St. Albans with a million dollars' worth of smack in a valise, shove it at Williams's impenetrable face and say, "Here it is. Take it back to the property office and tell them to be more careful the next time." It might have well been worth it, worth everything that had happened to him in Las Vegas or Havana to see the look on the young black man's face when he did this. "The entire NYPD, the federal prosecuting staff, the godamned FBI, none of you could trace it," he wanted to say, "but *I* got it and what does that say about your system, Williams? It says that your system sucks, that's what it does." He would have thrown the valise at Williams's feet and gone the hell out of there, back to San Francisco, maybe, looking for some more distributors he could kill. Then again he might have gone back to the girl in San Francisco and taken an honorable retirement from vigilantism, having successfully made his point, which was simply that the system had broken down twelve to fifteen years ago through incompetence and infiltration, and that short of the kind of drastic action he was taking the drug problem would *never* come to hand. Hell, his life expectancy could hardly be considered high in his present line of work. By now, he knew, every clown, hit man, pusher, doper, distributor, organizer and adventurer in the country probably had a picture of him in his wallet. There were at least five thousand highly skilled people waiting to get one shot. One shot would be all that they needed.

No, he had to dump the valise and get out of this, at least take a different battle direction. The first frontal assault, sweeping him from New York to San Francisco to Boston to Vegas had had the advantage of surprise and the enemy, unused to vigilante tactics, softened by a decade and a half of making their own way by graft and infiltration had been completely unprepared. But these people were not fools, certainly not like the authorities delegated to destroy them. And they were catching on. They had almost gotten him in Vegas and they had gotten him for sure in Havana, hijacking the Vegas flight out and incarcerating him there. He had made it out of Havana only through sheer luck and because of the confusion he had created there. But the luck was being pushed too hard now.

He had made it out of Havana on a hijacked helicopter which had dumped him in Louisiana, near the border but far enough to get him well inland and all the way back out of New Orleans in a stolen car (he had worked his last rental; he had to function completely outside of society now, dared not even risk a plane flight). He had worked the situation through in mind, worked it out through a thousand miles of blank superhighway, the car momentarily suspending him above the world and it seemed clear to him that he had gone almost as far as he could this way. It was a never-ending guerrilla war, a final commitment. He understood that and he was not abandoning it. But he had to fight another day in another way. They were coming in too close to him now. Two or three hundred of their men were dead by his hand, the northeast sector shaken, the San Francisco area battered, left leaderless. They knew now how dangerous he was and they would stop at nothing to eliminate him.

He would have done the same if the positions were reversed.

So he was going to go into St. Albans. He was going to take this valise and ram it down Williams' throat and let him, the man who believed in the system and always took the odds, decide what disposition to make and Burt Wulff was going to get out. But he wasn't after all, it seemed, because system-levers got theirs too, poised on the razor-edge of the world as they were.

Williams had been knifed and beaten. He was in Metropolitan hospital in serious condition. Admitted three days ago he had passed the point of first crisis and was expected to live, to make a full recovery in fact. But the duration of his hospital stay was still unknown. He might be in for months. At full salary, of course.

Duty injury. Williams had been on plainclothes detail in East Harlem, apparently checking out methadone traffic. He had come against an assailant who had either seen through the cover or had been too spaced out to care, or both, or neither—people could get killed in New York City by other people who did not even have a reason. Williams, going for his gun too late, had been knifed and stomped half a block from the clinic. Apparently forty or fifty street people had witnessed all of this and one had even been nice enough to put in an anonymous call for the cops. Williams had been picked off the street in view of all these interested witnesses and taken to Metropolitan where an operation had saved his heart and life. The entry wound was slightly south of the heart, otherwise nothing would have worked. Why Williams did not go for his gun or go fast enough and how he walked into something like this was not quite clear. The assailant, of course, would never be found. Traffic around the methadone clinic continued brisk. Nothing much had been changed except that a twenty-four-year-old cop had gone off duty involuntarily. That was New York for you. Take it with a grain.

Wulff learned all this from Williams' wife an hour after he hit town.

He heard it all on a pay telephone in a candy store in Rego Park four blocks away from where he had ditched the car. The car, a 1971 Delta Royale 88 had been overheating badly through the last hundred miles anyway and had probably burst a seam in the radiator. Wulff never felt guilty about stealing a car anymore. The newer cars were such completely incompetent stuff that the owner was really getting a break on the theft—collecting more on book than the car was worth in transportation value and saving the trouble of breakdowns besides. The godamned things, like the narco squad, just weren't geared up to deal with the situation.

Wulff learned it all fast. Williams' wife laid it on him straightforwardly, dispassionately, quickly. She was a cop's wife. She knew Wulff. She had met him when he had been there before the Vegas jaunt and there had been a moment of sympathy, of possible connection which Wulff had neither missed nor followed up. What was there to follow up? But he had known that in a different time, in a different way, something might have happened between the two of them. Enough. Enough of that. There had been a girl called Marie Calvante and, in a different time, in a different way, something might have happened there too but it had not; instead he had found her dead of a heroin overdose. Forget it. Abstractions. You concentrated on what you could deal with.

"I'm sure he'd like to see you," she said over the phone. "He's conscious and the pain isn't too bad. Visiting hours are anytime; I'm going to go there myself in just an hour or so. You can—"

"No," Wulff said. "He wouldn't want to see me."

"Of course he would. You don't understand—"

"I understand that he's probably got two police watching that room all the time," Wulff said. "That's standard procedure and I don't think they'd change it even for a man shot in plainclothes."

"Oh," she said, "oh." She paused. "The police patrol. I forgot—"

"Forgetting isn't something a cop's wife should do," he said. He was calling from a candy store, stacks of newspapers heaped in front of the booth and now as he looked beyond them he saw a hint of activity, men moving around rapidly, someone at the center of a small group talking animatedly, digging into his pockets to pass something to a few in the circle. Numbers payoff? It couldn't be a bookie's runner, the legalized horse parlors had put those kind out of business. It didn't matter, he supposed, but living on the run made you preternaturally alert. "I was going to bring him a present," he said, "but I don't think that I had better deliver it. Do you?"

"You found the—"

"Yes," he said, cutting her off. "I did indeed. Don't ask me anymore."

"We read about Las Vegas in the newspapers," she said. "He didn't think you'd make it but I did. I thought you would all the time. He thought that you'd go through it alive but no one would ever find—"

"Please," he said, cutting her off again. "Enough. Don't mention it. What hospital is he in?"

She told him quickly, adding the room number. "It's a private," she said, "and because he's on critical they allow him visitors around the clock but he's not really critical anymore. They just do that so I can get in when I want. Do you think you'll call him?"

"I think I'll do just that," Wulff said. The valise was an unpleasant weight against his left knee, indelicately he raised it, opening up a few inches of space. It was tough to live with a valise, he decided. It was tough to live with anything that was not a piece of yourself yet had to be treated as if it were. Old lechers with showgirls would know all about that he supposed. "After all, I need further instructions."

"No you don't."

"But I do," Wulff said, "I thought we settled that weeks ago. I'm just the tool. David directs me."

"David is a sick man," his wife said sharply. "He got knifed on the street and a few inches difference, it would have gone the other way. I don't think he's going back to active duty for the rest of his life and I'm going to try and talk him off the force."

"It won't work," Wulff said, "you know that. I'm sure he'll pull through."

"Of course it won't work," she said, "but I've got to try, don't I?"

"I guess you do," Wulff said. "I guess we've all got to try." And then he said goodbye and before the conversation could start to trace into any other channels he hung up the phone emphatically. He stared through the glass of the booth looking at the activity in the candy store. The circle had broken up into little consultative clumps. Now and then someone threw a stare into the booth although that shouldn't have been; there were a whole bank of phones here and as far as he knew only one other of them was occupied when he had come in. They shouldn't be looking inside to see if he was finished. On the other hand—

On the other hand he had had enough of this candy store. He had had enough of Rego Park Queens. For that matter, with the whole fucking city of New York. It had been a mistake to come back here. Why had he come back? Why—after all it had cost him to get that valise out of Vegas and Havana—had he brought it right back to this trap, this sewer of a city?

Because he had wanted to present it to Williams and shove it right up his ass, that was why. Show him the valise.

Enough, Wulff thought, enough, and stood abruptly, his head colliding with an overhead panel. He winced, reaching for the valise, ready to quit the booth, quit Rego Park, quit New York. He could call Williams another time, he just did not like the situation here, he needed space. As he opened the door of the booth a heavy man with a gun whose mouth looked as big as a manhole put a hand on his back and held Wulff in a tight embrace, gripping at him.

"All right," he said and his voice in that confrontation was strange: soft, sweet, delicate; he could have been whispering to Wulff of the most intimate and tragic things. "That's quite enough. Come out of there slowly and leave that fucking valise in there. We'll take care of that our own way."

It was strange to hear the word *fucking* coming hard in the center of all that softness. The inconsistency that made life so appealing, Wulff thought, that made menace the more explicit. He bent over and wedged against the heavy man, came out into the circle, keeping the valise within eyeshot, however.

Godamnit, he had gotten it out of Havana. He wasn't going to lose it in Rego Park. They would have to kill him for it ... They probably would, at that.

# Chapter 2

Williams lay in bed, hands behind his neck, painfully adjusting himself to take some weight from the bad side while the two cops guarding him murmured in the hallway, smoking illegally. He thought, it's shit. The whole thing is shit. Wulff was right all the time and I was wrong. The system sucks.

The system that set me up with a mortgage and a uniform allowance and a legal gun (imagine giving an American black man a legal gun; he had thought that the humor implicit in that was worth the whole crap of the academy, just to know what they were going to hand him). It was teasing me all the time, that lousy cunt of a system was just sucking me in, moving me deeper and deeper, helping me to close my eyes as I worked my way into that cunt, and all the time you know what was waiting for me at the end of that tunnel? A shiv in the ribs, that was it. And almost an expenses-paid funeral with an honor guard. The mayor might have been there.

That was what the system had offered him.

Williams found himself thinking more and more about it these days. Lying in the bed, after the first few hours when he knew (even before the doctors) that he was surely going to live, had given him plenty of time to think. Now the system was no longer an abstraction, that neat figment he had batted around with Wulff in their sessions. No: he could see the system now and it was a cunt all right or if not that a beast, a concrete organism that sat over the swamp somewhere and set up the conditions: my swamp, my game, my rules, your ball. Your loss. He had believed in that beast, sweated and romped with it, chased it all the way into the sewer. And had come within six inches of being ripped off by it as casually as any fifteen-year-old Harlem junkie.

Except that the junkie wouldn't even know that he had been ripped off; he would think of himself as a hustler who had lost. Whereas Williams—thanks to the coaching of the system: access to its facilities, its educational institutions, its media, the piddling little toys it offered with one palm—could at least identify what had happened to him. That was all. They had elevated him to that level of insight where he knew what was happening.

Wulff's right, he thought then.

He's right, he's always been right, the son of a bitch. It doesn't work. How can you change something from inside when the whole purpose of the thing bottling you up is to *keep* you there? Like the FBI. Federal Blackmail and Intelligence division, *that* was your FBI for you, a complicated information-retrieval and extortion business whose *only purpose* was to keep itself in existence. The FBI was no aberration, no example of breakdown whatsoever. *It was the system in miniature.* All of it shit and lies and here I lay, he thought, here I lay with a hole slashed across my ribs reaching like a hand toward my heart to prove it. I thought that all the time you could play it on the rules and make it work for you and *I* was the fool. Save a place in the palace, Huey, I'm coming to lay the bombs. The pain is just beginning because who's going to lay bombs anywhere? I'm trapped, he thought. To get rid of the pain in the chest and what was coming was only to move it upwards where it could take rest, lay its confetti of anguish up to the brain. Pain in the brain, he thought, they've given me a pain in the brain and Wulff, you crazy, vigilante son of a bitch, you were right after all.

One of the cops, bored, came in from the hall and asked him how he was feeling. He knew damned well how Williams was feeling, this fat white sergeant who had been cruising in and out of the room for a week, his belly moving delicately in rhythm with his stride. This half-dead son of a bitch who was on stuff like surveillance detail and monitoring because something had happened to his own body or mind which made him incompetent for active duty, but the department was too cheap to give up and hand him full disability, take him out of his twenty-year misery. Don't be that tough on him, Williams thought, it's just another part of the system. But it was hard to look at the man let alone answer him in a civil way. "How do you think I am?" he said. "How does it look to you?"

The sergeant shrugged and said, "Just trying to make conversation, just trying to show a little interest, you don't have to take out your troubles on *me* friend, I'm pulling duty here whether you like it or not," and went back into the hall without saying anything else. So they have me labelled as a bad nigger, Williams thought. What it comes down to is that he looks and sees just another angry, hostile black lying in this bed. *Who the fuck do they think they are?* he was probably saying to his partner out there in the hall now, his partner also white and crippled up, a thinner man with the dull eyes and abstracted walk of a man probably carrying around a piece of steel in his head. *Beats me,* the steel plate would say, *all of these bastards are exactly the same, he probably thinks that we did it to him.* And on that note they would resume their sullen sodden stumbling in the hall. They had very little to do, it was just an obligatory sort of detail so that if someone came off the street to shoot him they might have a slightly more difficult time than otherwise, not that these two clowns would pose any kind of problem to a determined assassin.

But then, Williams thought, who the hell would bother to kill him? Even assuming that someone on the street had decided that he didn't like Williams' detail and wanted to make sure that Williams didn't go around checking out methadone trade again, they didn't have to kill him. He was finished. He had reached the end. His next detail if he got one would probably be to join the steel plate and the belly out in the hallways to guard another fool. And if the purpose of the assassin was to make him suffer further ...

Well who needed to shoot him for *that?* He was in hell, Williams thought. It had all blown up on him now. He understood everything, he accepted nothing; everything that he had believed had been gutted out. He would never be the same again. Wasn't that as good a definition of death as any?

He heard steps in the hallway that sounded like his wife's and lay back, closed his eyes, breathed regularly, imitated sleep. He would make her think she woke him up. Yes. He would make her think that he had been lying here resting, relaxing, all of the pain purged and that none of this was happening to him. Because he did not know, he did not know, if he started to talk to her about all of this ... if he could pull her through it. He knew that he could no longer navigate himself.

He simply did not believe a word of the shit anymore.

# Chapter 3

Wulff came out of the booth slowly, leaving the valise where it was. Had to do it, no choice. He was being held by the big man with the huge gun. Flanking him, left and right, were a couple of others, nondescript types; both of them looked at him impassively, hands in their pockets. They might have guns in there, they might not; the only way to tell was to try them and it was too soon for that. Other than that there were only four or five others in the store now, the clumps of numbers players or whatever they were having disappeared. The owner, his palms flat to the counter was looking in Wulff's direction with astonishment; the others seated at counter seats were huddling protectively, two gripping themselves. So that was good. That was good then. Coming out of the booth he had thought that he might be taking on an entire group of men, all of the numbers players turning out to be *soldati*. But it had not been that informed a setup at all. A lend-lease operation. There was only the heavy man and his two assistants handling this, and they had waited out their time until the store had emptied because they had been as afraid of the crowd as Wulff had been.

Live and learn; learn and live. This was probably another freelance operation, a group of bounty hunters who had stumbled across the information somewhere and were trying to move ahead. Marginal types. It meant that he had a shot at this, although of course not an excellent one. Still, he looked much better than he thought he would when he came out of that booth.

"Now listen here," said the owner. He was a small man, his white apron spattered with chocolate stains. "I don't know what this is but we can't have any of that here. You take it outside. You take it outside right now or I'm going to call the police. I—"

"Shut the fuck up you prick," the heavy man said in that gentle little voice of his and pivoted, aimed the gun and deposited a cartridge in the wall. The gun recoiled on him, causing his shoulders to quiver and then a few splinters sifted delicately out of the wall, dropped on the owner's scalp. He put a hand to the bald spot trembling, brought it away, inspected it. Looking for blood. Wulff knew the feeling.

"Stay out of it now," the heavy man said. To Wulff he said, "We're all going to get out of here now. We're going to take a nice, quiet amiable little walk down the line here and out the door and into my car and then we'll see what we see. Don't forget the valise," he said to the man on his left, "take it out of there nice and easy." The other man blinked, as if the idea of touching the valise had never occurred to him; he was the kind of man who worked by the numbers and this had been an outside shot. "Don't stand their thinking," the heavy man said in that soft, sweet whisper and momentarily the gun shifted, "just do it."

So he might be a bounty hunter, Wulff thought, but he was working with recruited help. That was interesting. That was very interesting, but he didn't want his attention to narrow down exclusively to the man with the gun because this would be equally dangerous. The three had to be taken on as a team but they were not the tightest and most integrated unit. He stood there quietly, making no moves. He could go for the gun in his inside coat pocket but then again he would not. That would only draw attention to the fact that he had a gun and he trusted the heavy man's reflexes. "Go on!" the man with the gun said again. "Get it!"

Delicately, the man on the left peeled off and reached into the booth. He took the valise by the handle and then with some effort tugged it out. It caught on the lip of the stand and Wulff thought for a moment that it might jam there, the same thought occurred to the man, panic flared and then he had the valise fully, held it panting, a few inches off the ground. The other man, the man on the right smiled faintly and licked his lips.

"All right," the heavy man said with a directing wave of the gun. "The two of you go ahead with that and keep a lookout; I'll take this one out myself." That was even more interesting; he was carrying on the operation now as if he had three men under cover instead of just one, a definite, hounded aspect here and in that moment Wulff saw that he could probably take him. It was not three against one after all; it was *mano a mano* with witnesses and the heavy man did not truly have the situation under control. He was working on Wulff but doing so without a clear sense of purpose and it had to be fear which was driving him as much as greed. Certainly, not frisking Wulff had been a very poor move, it was elementary procedure ... but then he did not trust the other two to carry on the frisk competently and he was afraid to get too close to Wulff himself. So the situation was manageable. It was damned close to even—perhaps even a little better than that because Wulff would know when he was going to move but the heavy man would not.

"Come on," the man with the gun said as the other two went out the door, the valise following in grip like a puppy. "Let's get going."

Slowly Wulff moved, following the arc of the gun, went down the line of stools at the counter, heading toward the wedge of light showing through the open door. The owner stood in that frozen position, hands on the counter watching him go; Wulff passed within an inch of the man and then beyond. Out of his class here. Numbers trade was one thing but assault with a deadly weapon was another. The owner probably had established his own code of values which had something to do with the fact that anything he did was legal and morally justified but anything beyond that was not. A good system. Most people worked that way. Wulff kept on moving, not even looking back. He assumed that the gun was still on him but even if it was not, if there was some lapse of attention back there, he wanted to do the owner a favor. He would not give him a murder in his candy store in Rego fucking Park. Cops, detectives, investigations, notice and picture in the *Daily News*; it would blow his sideline sky-high. Be merciful. Render unto men in equal parts what they deserve.

He was in the street now. The valise was on the ground, the two men flanking it the way they had flanked the gunman, left and right, looking past one another. They were standing in front of an old Fleetwood, rust spots on the chrome panels, damage to the rear quarter panel, probably the heavy man's car. A banged up piece of junk; elegance corroded to bargain rates. A bounty hunter's kind of vehicle. The heavy man was behind him, prodding. There were a couple of people on the street but no one seemed particularly interested in what was going on. Why should they be? This was New York and furthermore they could be filming a television segment, the valise a portable camera. No one gave a damn; if they wanted to get involved they could see it on the box in six months.

"Open the door," the heavy man said to the one who had carried the valise. He did the heavy work; the other one was backup, probably. Hierarchy in every aspect of life: everything was the army. Sergeants and corporals. Captains. The door came open reluctantly, squeaking. Wulff turned, measuring out the proper leverage and direction by the sound of the voice and chopped the heavy man in the throat.

The heavy man gagged. Blood came into his face, suffused, dripped from his mouth. As Wulff turned, measuring him, the man tried to get the gun up but the effort seemed beyond him; it seemed for a moment as if he didn't remember what the gun was or what these things were for and his body slowly caved in. "Son of a bitch," he was trying to say, Wulff could see the motions of his throat, deduce it from the movement of the lips but the blow had taken away laryngeal functioning and now paralysis was setting in; the gun fell from his hand, he collapsed to the pavement. "Son of a bitch," he said again and Wulff bent over, took the gun and in the same motion kicked the heavy man in the head. He lay there, his eyes open, searching out parts of the sky. His mouth moved again. He seemed to be looking for some kind of explanation.

The other two already had their hands in the air. They were making no movements whatsoever. Indeed, their expressions, the way they held their bodies seemed to be a kind of anti-menace; they were sending Wulff signals in every way that they wanted no part of him. Wulff looked at the valise in place on the sidewalk and then he looked at the men and the disgust was suddenly total; he spat on the sidewalk and then spat again, forcing mucus, feeling a rage within him so thickly impacted that the only way around seemed to be to *spit* it out, God help him but that would not work either. For this. For this they had brought death up against him. They did not even know what death was.

"You stupid sons of bitches," he said and now there was no one in sight at all, not even the face of the owner staring through the mist of the candy store window, he probably having gone to call the police, "you've got to be crazy." He pointed to the valise. "Do you really want this?" he said. "Is it so fucking important? You really want to take this on?"

He stared at them and the one on the right, the one who had moved the valise out, senior movement expert number one said, "You've got this all wrong."

"Have I?"

"You've got this all wrong, Wulff," he said, looking at him almost pleadingly. The heavy man stirred on the pavement, made vomiting sounds. "We weren't here to kill you."

"Oh no," he said, "you weren't here to kill me. Just for an interview."

"Put the gun away, Wulff," the man said. The fact that he could talk without being shot down seemed to have given him confidence. If anything, his voice seemed mildly authoritative. "Cooperate. Cooperate with us. I tried to tell him that you would do it anyway if it was only explained."

"What are you talking about?"

"Wulff," the other man said, "Wulff come to your senses. Cooperate with us." He reached inside his clothing and Wulff thought for an instant that it might be a gun but then he knew that no man, not even one like this, could do something so inconceivably stupid so he held his ground. The man took a flat leather case out of his pocket and opened it arm extended, held it so that Wulff could see. "Wulff," he said, "we're federal agents."

# Chapter 4

He let the one with the credentials drive, the other one in the back against him, the valise wedged in a corner. Wulff was neither shocked nor bothered after the first half-minute of surprise; it had just shifted to a different level, that was all. He had to change his modus operandi, look at things in another context. They had left the heavy man on the sidewalk, the decision being that it made no difference what he had to say when the cops came along. Which they probably would any moment. The heavy man would reach the right people and talk his way out of it, probably without reference to Wulff. Now the thing to do was to get the Fleetwood and the other two with the valise out of there. Wulff could see the good sense of that. He even let one do the driving while the other talked. He had the gun, he had essential control of the situation. Except that the situation was mad.

They were federal agents, all right. They were loosely attached to the federal narcotics bureau, not on an actual payroll but freelancers who appeared to be paid off the books by federal funds in varying amounts. The reason for this was because the president's commission or at least a part of it had declared a war on drugs three years ago; but the war on drugs, because of the nature of the enemy, had to be highly confidential and carried on by the kind of people who generally could not pass the standards of federal employment. Also the methods that these people used were unconventional. The administration had decided that the only way to carry on the campaign was with guerrilla tactics and through means that stuffy investigatorial types might find illegal. So it was basically a covert operation, carried on by disreputable types operating under loose supervision in unplanned ways toward an unpredictable end. A typical federal operation after all, Wulff thought wryly. Except, of course, that these men were dead-serious, they were the most serious types that he had met yet. Even more so than the distributors, and there was nothing funny about them at all. If their level of competence had been anywhere near their level of seriousness and degree of energy, they might have cleaned out the drug trade months before Wulff ever got into it on his own stick. As it was, however, they seemed to be losing ground.

At least they were *willing* to admit that they were losing ground. Trapped, held at bay in the car, their superior eliminated, the two that he had with him seemed almost eager to confess their incompetence and failure as if this somehow would make things go easier on them in the long run.

"Well, we knew all about you Wulff," the talkative one said. (The driver had to bring his full level of concentration to the task simply to avoid going off the road; he was one of those people who was simply ill-equipped to get along in a post-technological situation but then again he kept on trying.) "Your name and number are just known to everyone in the network and we figured that we'd take a shot at you, not because we thought you were a double-agent or anything like that, you understand, but because we had heard what kind of stuff you were able to pick out of Vegas before you were waylaid to Havana. We could take a million dollars' worth of smack out of the market, right? But we really fucked this one up, I admit it, Wulff, we didn't know what we were up against. Guess we should have taken you more seriously, eh? Guess we thought you were some kind of clown but oh boy were we wrong, Wulff. Were we *wrong!* You're just the toughest that we've ever been up against. Boy, you really know what you're doing, don't you?"

And so on and so forth. The talker would not go into any aspect of his background but to Wulff he sounded like a type who had been thrown off a local police force somewhere for drunkenness, but because of his vast law-enforcement background had been able to convince the federal authorities that he was equal to the job. At least that was the way that these things generally went. The more removed the branch of civil service was from the street level the less competent it was, and just as the NYC force was at least close or closer to the people, nothing could be further from the realities of the drug trade than the federal government. He supposed.

He had told the driver to take them on a long loop of the city, onto the Grand Central Parkway and over the Triborough into Manhattan, the East River Drive clear down to the South Street viaduct, then up the West Side Highway, to the Cross Bronx Expressway and down the East River Drive to the Triborough again. This gave him plenty of time to consider the issue while he pumped them and decided what his next move would be .... But exactly what the hell was he going to do? What was proper? He had to fill in the background but the background seemed to make absolutely no sense.

They had tracked him, these three, from shortly after the time he had hit the border clear through to Rego Park; they had picked him up in the South and in the ruined Fleetwood had pursued him, sometimes at a gap of miles, other times close in, all the way to Rego Park. They had no other assignment except to pick up Wulff and his valise which enabled them to concentrate upon the matter at hand. Wulff would have conceived of federal agents as being busy fellows: a conference here, a meeting there, an apprehension there, a bit of surveillance now. But no: he had been their sole client and they had been following him for days, following at various distances, finally closing in at Rego Park because the heavy man who had been the nominal leader of the team had made the decision that Wulff might be arranging to rid himself of the valise.

It all sounded vaguely insane to Wulff but then on the other hand it was not insane at all; he supposed that it exactly fitted the way people like this would work. Three men on one. What had they planned to do with him after they got him under wraps? Well, the speaker was not exactly sure. That was up to the leader of the team. They hadn't discussed it.

A pretty dismal life. Wulff could imagine the three of them jammed into the old car, moving silently on their sullen pursuit. Now and then they would pause for gasoline, more rarely they would pull into some bleak motel for the night, the leader making sure to get receipts at every stage of the journey so that he could put in for governmental reimbursement. They would stay at the cheapest places, of course, and watch the budget. But then again, considering the backgrounds of these men and what appeared to be their general intelligence level, it was possible that they were doing quite well. They were on a payroll, after all, and part of the federal war on drugs. Also they had credentials and were permitted to carry firearms which for people like this would be comforting.

"I know where we were supposed to go," the driver said. He had said very little during the thirty to forty minutes that the other one had been talking, filling Wulff in on all of the details, concentrating on the job of keeping the Fleetwood on the road which, as Wulff had already decided, was something that tested him up to his full energy levels and even a little beyond it.

"I mean, I don't know exactly what we were supposed to do with you, that was up to Frank and he never told us. But we were supposed to take the valise into Chicago. There's some kind of federal prosecution there, a grand-jury investigation and so on and the valise was supposed to be taken in there if we ever found it. Of course, I don't think they were too sure that we would ever score."

Wulff could imagine this too: the man Frank, the leader traveling for days with these men and holding to himself the secret of Wulff's disposition. It would seem impossible that three men, supposedly working as a team, would consist of one giving orders and two who did nothing, but that also was the way that the government managed its affairs. "A grand jury investigation in Chicago," he said, "introducing the valise as evidence."

"Something like that," the driver said. "He wasn't too clear, we didn't get too many facts. Frank said that it was for our own good; the less we knew the less we had to bother us."

He held the steering wheel with one hand, dug into his pocket and passed over to Wulff a card with the name *PATRICK WILSON* typed on it with a couple of strikeovers and a telephone number scribbled underneath. "He's a district attorney there," the driver said. "Something like that, they weren't too specific. Anyway, we were supposed to get in touch with him. We were supposed to bring the valise to him and let him handle it from then on in. Some kind of investigation," he mumbled, "a federal grand jury, that was it."

"And what about me?"

"What's that?"

"You had the disposition of the valise all plotted out," Wulff said. "Patrick Wilson and his staff. But what was supposed to happen to me?"

"Happen to you?"

"What did Frank intend to do with me?" Wulff said. It was like interrogation. You hit the point and then you hit it again; you persisted, phrasing it slightly differently each time and eventually they folded. Or they did not.

"Why I don't know," the driver said sullenly, "I don't know at all." And as if the effort of speaking, backgrounding Wulff this far, had taken the last of language out of him, he turned his full attention to the windshield, peering out at the road, muttering something to himself. Wulff let him stay in that lapsed silence, looked out the window himself.

"What are you going to do with us?" the man in the back said.

"What's that?"

"I said, what are you going to do with us?"

"Why," Wulff said, "I don't know. I have the same difficulty in making decisions that you do. What was Frank planning to do with me?"

"We told you," the man in the back said. "We just don't know. He was giving orders, we followed along. He was the senior man, we weren't even on the payroll. We're federal agents, you know and theoretically you're still in our custody." Wulff turned around and looked at him intensely, the man's eyes dropped into an almost boyish shyness. "Well it's true," he said, "you *are* in our charge. You've overpowered one of our senior men and you've kidnapped us ..."

"All right," Wulff said, "let's pull the car over."

They had just come off the Triborough again, onto the sudden four lanes of the Grand Central Parkway opening up under the railroad trestle at Jamaica, the Fleetwood in the far left lane, the driver struggling. "What's that?" he said.

"Pull the car over," Wulff said again, "we're going to get off the highway."

"This is ridiculous," the driver said, "there are thousands of cars around here, passing this point every hour, we're two blocks from a subway station; you don't think that you can—"

"Get it off the road!" Wulff said harshly and gave the wheel a yank. The driver let out a little scream as he felt the car momentarily lurch away from control, grappled with it, brought it frantically three lanes across the highway and onto the shoulder, other cars squalling as they went past. The driver pumped the brake desperately, brought the car to a rolling stop and then, finally, put his hands back on the wheel and looked at Wulff sidelong, attempting, Wulff could see, self-control. But under the surface terror burbled. "You can't get away with this," he said.

"Out of the car."

The man in the back said, "Wulff, listen, we were just doing a job. We didn't even *know* what was going on—"

"Out of the car," Wulff said again. Interrogation procedure. Hit the point and then hit it again. He showed them the gun he had taken from Frank, a large Beretta, clumsier than what he would have liked himself but probably the ideal weapon for a federal systems and investigations man.

The two clambered out of the car, driver to driver's side, the other one taking the rear door on the far side. They stood near traffic, blinking, looking at passing cars as if each contained some aspect of salvation.

"Over here," Wulff said. He gestured with the gun.

Reluctantly, shambling they came over. They could not seem to abandon the thought of rescue from the highway; they kept on casting glances over there as if any moment an unmarked limousine would pull over and from it would pour agents of every description holding firearms, perhaps the president of the United States, riding incognito, come to present them a medal for faithful and laudatory service. "It just isn't right," one of them said again. Out of their roles as driver and speaker, Wulff could not individuate any longer. They were the same. All of them were the same. Only the labels changed. "Isn't right," the man said again like a child.

Wulff looked at them. Frozen to position, shaking, they did not look like pursuers. Under the point of the gun, assailants never did. Brought to bay, the power relationship reversed, they all came down to the same thing: vulnerability, helplessness. If only you could pull a gun on the world, he thought ... but only the Cicchinis, the Marascos, the cold men who injected the poison and lived on their sheltered mountains and sea-coasts ... only they believed that it could be done. The rest of the world had to struggle along without the relief of confrontation. "You stupid sons of bitches," he said. "You don't know what the hell is going on."

That seemed to set well with them. At least they did not seem disposed to argue, standing in attitudes of contrition by the road, traffic moving by fast, the three of them standing at the bottom of the bowl of fumes which was Queens. "What the hell did you think that you were going to do?" he asked. "What the hell was your war anyway?"

They still said nothing, exchanging one blank look of consultation in which Wulff thought that he could read everything. Let him talk himself out, that look said. Yeah, let him do that. Maybe all he wants to do is talk. We'll get him another day. Maybe. Maybe. They returned their attention to him like fish fascinated at the end of a line, slowly being hauled out of the sea. "You had to be out of your minds," Wulff said.

They looked at him. Imperceptibly they nodded. Yes, the nod said, have it your way, we were out of our minds. And looking at them in that moment Wulff had a clear flare of intimation: nothing would ever be different. He could kill them but he could not change them. Right up until the end, no less than Cicchini or Marasco, they would believe that they were right. They would die holding onto their righteousness; the Cicchinis because they had mapped out the game and won it, these two because they believed in the forces that had sent them there. No way to change them. No way to get clear and to the other side, no way to bring them to awareness of the fact that they were fools and that their mission was as doomed and corrupt as that of the Cicchinis. They would not listen. No one was going to listen. As long as he went on it would always be the same; right up to this instant of confrontation when he would come up against impermeability.

He held the revolver steady. He could kill them. He could certainly kill them. In terms of the lives they led it would probably make no difference. They might not notice the difference themselves. What was the difference between life and death for a freelance federal narcotics agent? He looked into the eyes of the near one and saw furnished rooms.

"Don't do it," that man said. He must have seen the decision forming in Wulff. If nothing else, working for the federal authorities gave one a certain acuity, a heightened sense of awareness and possibilities. "You can't do it."

Wulff looked at his gun and then he looked at the men again. Traffic was pouring by on the Grand Central Parkway. No one cared. It made no difference to anyone as long as the lanes stayed open and they kept on moving along. He could kill these two men, strip them naked, probably bugger them in sight of the traffic lanes and the Triborough Bridge. As long as the traffic moved. That was the important thing.

"Fools," Wulff said again. "Fools."

He shot the near one in the forehead, high, above the ridge between the eyes. The man gasped once. It was less agony than surprise; a vaulting surprise which momentarily gave him an impression of health, vigor. Blood sprang to the wounded part and then made its passage elsewhere. The man raised a hand to his forehead, wiped at the blood as if he was wiping sweat. Then he fell straight forward like an actor practicing tumbles at a rehearsal, blocking his fall at the last moment with an extended wrist. He did not look injured at all. He croaked once and died.

"No," the other one said. He backed away from Wulff. Wulff had lost track of identities. Speaker or driver? Driver or speaker? In the car they had defined themselves very clearly but outside of that they were interchangeable. He moved toward a clump of bushes. A truck cut into the right hand lane seeking to pass, horn screaming. The driver's face was a pale vegetable behind glass, staring, screaming. Mufflers cut out, the truck went by, got ahead of the car in the middle lane with which it had been struggling and moved out of sight. "No," the man said again. "You can't do this. You're not a killer."

"Yes I am," Wulff said. "I'm a killer."

"But you only kill pushers," the man said. He had the false calmness, the control of the man who as the result of some intricate calculations had decided that he was already dead. Wulff knew that feeling; he had died himself several months ago and now everything was being played on the margin. Still, it was interesting to see in someone else. "You don't kill people who work for the law."

"You work for the law?" Wulff said. "You're the law?"

"Of course," the man said. He skittered toward a pile of stones. "I *am* the fucking law. I'm a federal agent. You shoot me and you're messing with the federal government. You're not a fool, Wulff. You can't be."

"You don't understand," Wulff said again. Tiredly, feeling the edge of hopelessness even in the act of killing. Because you could not change. You could change neither yourself nor them; the combinations and relations merely shifted. At the base was the same ignorance. "If you represent the law," Wulff said, "if you represent the government, then we're all dead. You're not the law. You're an outlaw."

"Now listen," the man said as if calling upon some reserve of authority, "if you think—" and extended a finger toward Wulff. Wulff was able to make the individuation then; this was the one who had presented him with credentials. The speaker. The voluble one.

"I think," Wulff said. "I think a great deal."

He shot the man in the head.

Unlike the other, this one seemed eager to die. The concept of death might have excited him the way that sex was supposed to excite most men. In the abstract anyway. In any event he died as if he had been practicing it in his bed alone for a long time, rehearsing all the gestures of a graceful expiration. He had worked on it. He fell straight down, kicked once and then rolled on his back to display his empty face to Wulff. "Ridiculous," he said then as if this had just occurred to him. "This is ridiculous. I can't—"

"Yes you can," Wulff said and put another bullet into his gut. This one finished off the speaker. He died without another word, his eyes not even blinking. It was as if a series of assumptions, long suspected, had been confirmed.

The two dead men lay in the mud off the Grand Central Parkway. Wulff put his gun away feeling that in a way it was almost like old times. Home. A returning. He had left his first corpses in New York, two of them on upper Madison Avenue in Harlem. Now he had come full-circle, another two on the Grand Central Parkway. Nothing changed. The blood ran, it mingled. All of the blood of the cities. Havana, San Francisco, New York, it was all the same. The same blood.

Wulff went back toward the Fleetwood. The driver, thoughtfully, had left it in idle, the motor knocking. Lifter trouble, common with Oldsmobiles and Cadillacs of the late 1950's, a clatter in the cylinders, the high, dense sound of metal working against itself without enough lubrication. They had worked out that problem, the GM engineers, by the sixties and now you didn't hear lifters. What you heard was the uniform gasping of engines struggling under emissions control. Progress. They were rapidly moving toward that point where nothing would work.

Well. Something would work. Death still worked, Wulff thought. He got behind the wheel, put the Fleetwood into gear. Traffic went by and no one cared what was going on in the little marshes by the side of the road; chalk one up for death. Death was the true urban phenomenon; its dwelling place was the cities. Here it could stalk. If it would ever be noticeable on the Grand Central, it would only be as an obstruction to traffic.

Wulff looked at the card that the speaker had given him. Patrick Wilson. Patrick Wilson of Chicago and his merry men, the federal grand jury. All right, Wulff thought, the car rolling at fifty. All right. All right.

He had the valise. Williams was in the hospital. The two men who had been appointed to take it away from him had run into a very little difficulty of their own.

So all right and all right again. Patrick Wilson was making a presentation to a federal grand jury? Patrick Wilson wanted a look at a valise?

Don't send messengers, Wulff thought.

Wilson wanted it?

All he had to have done was to ask.

Now he was going to get it. Directly.

# Chapter 5

At around eleven that evening, give or take an hour—he was drifting in and out of the drug haze, he simply did not have at that time the cop's keen chronological sense—the phone next to Williams' bed rang. Williams picked it up, not even thinking about it. Coming out of the screen of drugs he took himself to be in a station house and here was another damned squeal coming in. The phone never quit. "What is it now?" he said.

"This is Wulff," a voice said.

Wulff? Who was Wulff? Williams had to make an effort, pull memory like a sheet around him and adjust it before it finally, laboriously, began to come clear. With the clarity was pain. The drugs could not shield the pain no matter how deep they went. "Oh," he said. "I heard about you."

"Your wife told you?"

"Not much," said Williams. His head hung back, he looked at the ceiling, for a moment he found himself falling back into the tunnel of dreams. No sound from the other end of the wire. "It's hard," he said. "It's hard to talk, man."

"I know that."

"It's very hard to talk. I got myself cut. I almost got killed."

"I heard about that."

"You got Stone's valise. You got the smack taken out of the property bureau. You nearly blew up Vegas and then they hijacked you to Havana but you got out of there too. You got out of everything. You're too much, man."

"You don't know the half of it," Wulff said. His voice sounded strange, a hard edge to it as always, but underneath it an anxiety which even through the deadening phone wire Williams could catch. "You don't know the third of it."

"All right," Williams said. A flare of pain went through his ribs, reaching with fingers toward his heart. He shifted in the bed, seeking a better position. Out in the hallway, the two new ones, the four to midnight shift, were sleeping. He could hear their snores sounding through the hallway like children waving rattles. Two fresh ones would come on at midnight. Two by two by two. Six men a day, one hundred and forty-four man hours to guard David Williams. About twelve hundred dollars a day, figuring in the fringes. Eight-thousand four hundred a week, almost thirty-five thousand a month. If he was hospitalized for a year the NYPD would go over four hundred thousand dollars just for this detail. That was very moving. It was a testimony to his value. It would be nicer, of course, if they could give half the money to him and invest the rest in an alarm system, but that was not the way the PD worked. Why should they? He shifted again. "I don't want to know anything about it," he said, "I've had it."

"No you haven't. Don't cop out now, Williams. The fun is just beginning."

"For me it's ending," Williams said. "I don't think I'll ever have any fun again."

"Don't be pessimistic," Wulff said. "You'll get yourself a desk job and you'll be fine. Don't worry about the knife, it won't have any lasting effect. You'll get double disability."

"I don't need this man," Williams said softly. "I do not need to be called at eleven at night to hear *your* fucking pep talk. Any fucking moment you're going to start singing, aren't you? *Semper Fidelis.* Get off the wire."

"I got your valise," Wulff said, "I got your smack. Doesn't that make you happy? You sent me out and I got it."

"I don't give a shit."

"Don't go dead on me now, Williams," Wulff said sharply. "You were the one who set this whole thing up."

"I do not give a shit anymore," Williams said. He looked up at the ceiling light; a fly was battering itself against the smooth, dead glass surrounding the dim bulb. A fly in a hospital? Highly unsanitary. But then again flies had a way of getting in anywhere. "Just leave me alone."

"I'm going to Chicago," Wulff said. "They are starting a federal prosecution in that town. There were some people who thought that they might be an escort service but I decided to go direct. To save them the trouble. I am taking that valise to Chicago."

"You're crazy," Williams said. It was the first thing he had said with energy in weeks. "You're out of your mind. You're turning that stuff over to federal authority?"

"Why not? You're the one who was talking up the merits of the system. Here's its chance to prove itself. I'm going to give them Exhibit A. I'm going to give the system a chance to prove itself. You ought to be very happy, Williams."

"I don't believe in the system anymore," Williams said. He put a hand against his side. The fly, driven to some frenzy by the surfaces of the lamp, its heat and stolidity, gave one last lunge and then fluttered to the bed, landed on the back of that hand. Williams flipped it off against a wall; it hit with a *tic!* "Don't tell me about the system."

"I don't believe it. You are the original systems man."

"Don't get started on me," Williams said. "I'm a sick man. I got a shiv in the ribs. I almost died; I'm not out of the woods yet. Don't start on me, Wulff."

Wulff said, "I was sorry to hear that, you know. I was very sorry about that."

"Sure you were."

"It shouldn't make you give up. It shouldn't make you change your mind."

"No?"

"No," Wulff said, "it shouldn't. If you want to give up on the system you should do it because of what you understand, what you've learned. The way I've learned. But a shiv in the ribs is an accident. It could happen to anyone."

"Sure it could."

"Sure it *did*. That's just rolling the dice, friend. I learned all about odds and percentages in Vegas, friend. All right," Wulff said after a pause, "I want you to rest. I don't want to push you. I just wanted you to know that I'm taking this thing into Chicago and I'm turning it over."

"That's going to make the PD look like shit," Williams said. "They'll love it. They've been looking for something like this for years."

"I want it," Wulff said. "I want the PD to look like shit. Don't you?"

"No. Not particularly."

"Then you still believe in the system," Wulff said. "Then you're lying to me and yourself. You haven't given up on the system, just your own luck. But you still believe in the PD and that's the crucial part. Think. Think over the whole thing, Williams. I'll be in touch."

Williams heard the sound of the phone going down.

For a few moments he just lay there and worked on the pain in his ribs, trying to coax it down, move it away from his heart. He had decided a long time ago—at the worst stages, in the beginning—that if he could keep that pain cresting south, use mental will and concentration to work it toward his groin, away from the delicate and palpitating area of the heart, then he would have a chance, mind over matter, control of his destiny. But if he were to slacken his will for even an instant, lose control over his pain, it would leap like an animal straight north, set its claws into his heart and then he would be gone.

Now it seemed closer than it had been in days. Only through careful breathing, even stroking of respiration through his body was he able to bring the pain down until it nestled in his belly like a kitten, curled upon itself and then went sleepily away. He looked at the ceiling, where the

small, dark blood spots left by the tormented fly glowed against the
light. Did he believe in the system? Was Wulff right? Had what he taken
to have been his new attitude merely been a deception, an armor
against more pain and all the time he had merely walled himself off
from an excess of feeling until he was ready to deal with it again?

He did not know. It was something to think about, however. It was
something that he would have to think about, and now, with the pain
sleeping against him, he guessed that he could avoid it no longer.

One of the night patrol came in and asked him how he was doing.
Williams said all right. No nurses ever came in to ask him this. Maybe
they were intimidated by the presence of police. Or maybe they simply
felt that the PD, alert to the task as always, had the situation under
control.

He slept and dreamed of the knife—like a snake, arcing like a wish
toward his heart.

# Chapter 6

Coming out of O'Hare Airport the first thing that Wulff saw was the
famous sign: *WELCOME TO CHICAGO, RICHARD J. DALEY,
MAYOR.* That made him smile, curled against himself in the rear of the
cab, thinking of a time when the Daley welcome had been more than a
signpost. But things had changed in six years, hadn't they? Now like the
postwar Germans most of the populace was willing to approve Daley's
purposes, if not the methods by which he enacted them. Give Daley City
this much, Wulff thought; he doubted if even the most minor civil
service functionary had ever seen, let alone used drugs. It was a tightly
held, older-generation operation. When Daley went it would be a sad
thing, not that he intended, Wulff supposed, to go any too soon.

The valise was here with him in the cab; he was going right to the
federal office building. It had been easier, easier than he had thought
it would be, just a matter of checking the directory at the airport and
phoning in for confirmation. Yes, Mr. Wilson had offices in this building.
Yes, Mr. Wilson had staff in this building. Well, Mr. Wilson was going to
have himself a visitor. The federal grand jury was going to find itself
with a surprise.

Wulff had calculated all of it after he had killed the two men, after he
had talked to Williams. He had decided, finally, that it did not matter.
He was burdened with the valise, he was sick of carrying on single-
handed a war without end. He was sickened, finally, by the act of
killing; not a single murder he had committed until these two on the

parkway had bothered him in the least because all of them had been justified, none had had any alternative. But this latest killing, he was willing to admit, had been a tough one. He probably could have let the two of them go. It wouldn't have made any difference if he had, particularly since he was going to turn over the valise himself.

But the killing had come out of disgust, a disgust more than anything else with the very real stupidity with which he had been forced again and again to deal. If the circumstances had been reversed, these men would not have hesitated to have killed him, and taken honor for it. And if he was dealing with a government so murderous, so bestially ignorant that men like these could be sent out to commit murder in its name, then truly there was little to justify the continued existence of such men. Or of the agency that had sent them. It just did not matter anymore; something like this could not be sustained.

Nevertheless, he was going to turn over the valise. Williams' near-murder had sickened him too and this one far more than he had been willing to admit. Williams was Mr. System; right or wrong he thought that the thing could still work for him, that the processes of law functioned as a kind of shield, and to listen to Williams, to hear how low he had been brought, had shocked Wulff. Williams was not supposed to give up. His belief, as misguided as it had been, had sustained Wulff more than it had seemed because Williams was no fool, and his belief made the processes of law possible. It could be said, in fact, that much of what Wulff had done had been in an effort to prove to Williams that the system did not work, that only vigilantism could swing the tide. And now Williams had given up. He had no further defense to make; he was swinging over to Wulff's side.

There was nothing left to prove.

He wanted to get rid of the valise then. Dump it on the federal authorities, let them worry about it. He supposed vaguely that there would be much more to this than simple pickup and delivery, that they were going to have a lot of questions to ask and that the sudden possession of a million dollars' worth of shit would create more problems than this particular branch of the government would want to handle. Also they must know by now, as well as the organization, exactly who Wulff was and what he had done. They would want to talk to him. They might even try to frame some kind of prosecution although there was nothing that they could bring that would really stand up because who was going to testify against him? All of the witnesses were dead. Wulff left no witnesses. Still, he would deal with it.

The simple truth of the matter was that he was tired. He had had enough. You went on and on and there were always two or three men in a car somewhere, bounty hunters or employees or federal agents, who were out to get you. He could not battle them off eternally. Sooner or later they would get him and all that he had done would be wiped out. He would be dead. Certainly they would kill him. Righteously, eagerly, greedily, defensively—for any one of a multitude of reasons they would want to kill him ... and whatever the reason the outcome was the same.

He didn't want to live, not all that much. The effective parts of him had been killed when he had seen Marie Calvante dead in a furnished room on West 93rd Street. But he didn't want to die either. Not exactly. Not in their way anyway. He was entitled to pick the ways and the means of his death and he did not like their plans at all.

So Daley City. A TWA carrier out and no one had looked at him. The valise stashed in the luggage compartment and no one had looked at that either. Fuck their x-ray devices, fuck their sky-marshals, fuck their hijacking and suicide teams. Havana had been a freak; no one had expected him to get out of New York in the way he had and as quickly. The only precaution he had taken was to have ditched his guns in a locker before boarding. Small loss. He could stock up anywhere in Chicago, if he wanted. It was an open country.

Daley City. It looked pretty much as he had seen it years ago, passing through, attending a national police seminar on riot control and the techniques of infiltration. That had been during the summer of the year when everyone had seen an international Communist conspiracy to subvert the country through longhaired, bomb-building radicals who took drugs and also fornicated with one another in the basements of abandoned buildings. The seminar had focused on the best way to control this menace and a sequence of speakers and discussion leaders had agreed that killing was the answer. But unfortunately, since there were grand juries and communist attorneys who got stuffy about this, you might as well settle for the most sophisticated and forceful means of riot control. Spray guns. Mace. Infiltration at the highest level of their filthy organizations. Clubbing and preventative detention. Well, Wulff thought, that had been a difficult summer. The war had been near its height and the nadir of its public support, and presidential candidates, right and left, were falling into the practice of stepping out of cars or into kitchens and getting themselves shot or shot at. You could explain this kind of hysteria simply by saying that it was inevitable and that it would begin at the bottom levels of the populace, slowly filtering its way up until some group of clerks, somewhere, began to write memos for high-grade clerks on what had to be done. The cops were really close to the situation, closer than the clerks; they could hardly be condemned for getting edgy. Everybody was pretty edgy. Wulff had still been a narco that summer and the informants themselves had clammed up saying that the atmosphere was so mean and tight that there was no spare information lying around. They had run out of information and the free market in drugs simultaneously.

"Like it?" the driver said, pointing to the Loop skyline, then gesturing off in the direction of the lake. The driver had been delivering a nonstop soliloquy on the advantages of Chicago throughout the clogged, rush-hour drive, probably on the assumption that Wulff was a businessman on company time who would appreciate this kind of backgrounder instead of having to think about the convention upcoming. Either that or the driver was under constant threat by the city administration to plug Chicago nonstop or face expulsion. The taxi union like everything else in town was almost a branch of civil service. "It's some godamned city," the driver said. "There's never been a godamned city like this, not ever. Your first time here?"

"Not quite," Wulff said, adjusting himself on the seat. He did not want conversation but the effort of avoiding it meant other dangers. He looked out the window into the gathering traffic, the air—for all the density of the highway and the industry of the city—surprisingly clear at this time of the morning.

"Federal offices, right?"

"That's right."

"What brings you into the federal offices? Marshal or an attorney? Something like that?"

Wulff leaned forward, elbows on the seat and stared at the driver. He was a short man with enormous, ill-proportioned wrists which lay crosswise across the steering wheel, otherwise he was completely unremarkable. "What's the difference?" he said.

"Just asking."

"Don't ask."

"All right," the driver said, "I won't ask. I won't ask a godamned thing. I try to be friendly, I try to make conversation—"

"Don't be friendly. Don't make conversation." Wulff fought for control, almost saying *just drive and shut up* and held onto himself. "I've got things on my mind."

"Oh," the driver said. "I can understand that. Having things on your mind, I mean." He leaned over, tapped the valise which lay next to him on the front seat. "Important papers?" he said. "Or do you have some stash here?" Driving one-handed, he toyed with a clip. "Might as well take a look in, see what's making you so unfriendly."

"All right," Wulff said abruptly. He felt stunned. Were all the taxi-drivers this way or was this man a damned lunatic? "Get your hands off that valise. Just drive now."

"Just curious," the driver said. He handled the car skillfully, weaving through traffic one-handed, his free hand resting on the valise. "I'd like to know what you have in here that you're so distracted. Chicago's a beautiful city, you should be able to sit back and enjoy it. Without having your mind bothered with strange thoughts."

"All right," Wulff said again. "That's it. Enough. Pull the cab over."

"I don't think so," the driver said very softly. He turned still driving one-handed, the wheel neatly balanced in a pocket of that enormous wrist and showed Wulff a gun, "I don't think that I can do that you see." He turned his attention back to the road, delicately shifted the cab into the slow lane and then with no unnecessary haste or lapse of control turned back toward Wulff and showed him the gun again. "I think we'll just have to keep going," he said.

Wulff sat back in the seat, shoulders flat to the leather and confronted the gun. He found that there was no fear, only an odd detachment. This had been rigged cleverly, he had to admit that. He had to give them their due; they had set this one up very well. Coming out of the TWA exit he had gone into the nearest cab without a second thought, even tossing the valise on the front seat next to the driver before he had gone into the back, leaving the valise unattended for that perilous instant. He had been so sure of himself that it had never occurred to him until a moment ago that the level of attention concentrated upon him now was nationwide. It was no casual factor whatsoever. Did he really think that he could get in and out of the plane unobserved and over to the government offices so easily? Well yes, he had, he had indeed. That was his mistake.

"I advise you to relax," the driver said softly, back to the road again one-handed, the gun now withdrawn to a safer distance from Wulff. The man was good, no question about it; there was no way that Wulff could reach the gun before the driver had a chance to fire. And he was handling driving and gun at such a level of skill that it was obvious Wulff was dealing with a professional, one of the very few real professionals he had run into so far. "That's fine," the driver said, "you're taking this the right way. I respect you and there's no reason why you shouldn't respect me. You know that I know what I'm doing. Now, you sit back and cooperate and we'll get you where we want to go with no conflict at all, but on the other hand if you make things difficult we won't. It's up to you. It's your decision."

The driver said nothing else. He slipped the car at high speed off an exit ramp and Wulff found himself on Michigan Avenue, driving quickly along the lakefront, the tires of the cab squealing just a little as the driver whipped it in and out of lane. It occurred to him as they pulled up to a stoplight that his way out of the cab was clear; he could jump free and evade the driver. There would be no shooting. But to jump clear would mean that he would lose the valise and he suspected that they wanted the valise as much or more than they wanted him. He was a fringe benefit, extra pay for the driver if he was brought in as well.

"Son of a bitch," he said involuntarily, "son of a bitch." He was no longer a person. He was a valise. That was about the way it had been since he left Vegas. And before that, in Boston. "Son of a bitch."

"I happen to disagree with that," the driver said almost cheerfully, "but I'll fight to the absolute death for your right to say it."

They whipped along the lakefront.

# Chapter 7

Versallo felt happy. He had got up that morning with a singing feeling deep in his chest, the kind of feeling he used to get when he got a good high going, before he had made himself quit the stuff. And all day the high was building, building within him, fed this time by nothing more than coffee, cigarettes and the sure feeling that he had got him. He was going to get the son of a bitch. He could not lose.

Sometimes you just knew it; you knew when you were on a hot streak, building and building toward something really good, a breakthrough and you had that perilous feeling of taking the wave at its highest point, moving beyond collision, simply rising. Sometimes— and it was rare but when it came it was unmistakable—you knew that you were on a streak, in the groove and nothing could beat you. Horse was much better, sex a little, but luck was all right. He had lost the one, gotten slow with the other; he would take his kicks where he could find them. Luck. He had the bastard nailed.

He knew somehow that Mendoza would bring him in. He had had no contact with the man since he had dispatched him to the airport but with that peculiar extra-sensory feel which was one of the many things which made him superior to other people he could *feel* that Mendoza had him. Mendoza was his best man, his most competent and trusted assistant; he could not have put the job in better hands than his and at around three o'clock that afternoon, give or take no more than a couple of moments, he had had a sharp jab, a *flame* almost, of knowledge. He knew that Mendoza had him. He had gotten him into the disguised cab and now he was bringing him in. They were on their way. They were coming in, Mendoza and Wulff and the fucking valise with the smack. He could have started singing, he was that happy, he was that sure. But Versallo had cultivated professionalism the hard way, working at it from the bottom. He would keep that knowledge, beating like a small bird, to himself.

So he did nothing. He betrayed no emotion. He hung around the offices and went through the motions of work instead. He dispatched three trucks to Milwaukee to pick up a small meat consignment. He took a call from city hall and verified that he was good for sixteen tickets, hundred dollars a plate, to the farewell dinner for some retiring hack sewer commissioner a week from Thursday.

He met with the union shop steward who said that the complaint this week was that the washrooms on the second and third levels were filthy and almost never provided with paper towels and the men were mutinous. They were threatening a job action of some sort. The steward wanted Versallo to know that although he did not personally condone this kind of action the men were quite angry and felt that their complaint was justified. This was the kind of thing, the steward pointed out, that, just because it was so minor, should be straightened out quickly. Otherwise the smaller resentments built into larger ones and at the time of the new contract negotiations ...

It was this last which, despite the burning happiness within him almost caused Versallo to lose his good humor and temper simultaneously. If his mind had not really been on the abduction, if he had not been looking forward to two million dollars' worth of purest whitest shit he would have gotten into real trouble with this steward just as he had with the one this guy had replaced. Lost his temper with the man, thrown him out of the office, possibly beaten the shit out of him ... which was not the most progressive way, even Versallo had to admit, to handle the union problems. As it was, he was able to keep a lid on himself, although just barely.

"These meatballs are getting seven and a half fucking dollars an hour plus fringes," is what he pointed out, trying to be mild. "So what the fuck are they worried about the fucking washrooms for."

He always used *fuck* a lot when in any kind of negotiations, be they with the union, city hall, or the men down state. They would get the idea that he was a rough, tough, abusive character and would not try to get an edge on him. Little things like that really counted in this business. Versallo did not use the word *fuck* in ordinary conversation and never anywhere around women. Although he was fifty-three years old he was still more than mildly surprised every time he heard a woman say the word. *Fuck* was simply not something which women were even supposed to *know* let alone say. Yet he had grudgingly come to admit over the years, particularly since he had two daughters now in their twenties, that not every girl who used the word was necessarily a whore. Usually. Usually a whore but not necessarily.

"Get the fuck out of here with your fucking towels and fucking soap," he said to the steward.

"It's not my say-so," the steward said. He was a young man, much younger than Versallo, and trying to do the best he could within the limits of a very difficult situation but right now he looked uncertain. "I'm just conveying to you—"

"Convey yourself the fuck out of here," Versallo said, "convey yourself back to those fucking assholes and tell them that they can have their fucking soap and fucking water, all they need, when they wash their hands to get on the fucking unemployment line. You understand that?"

"I think you're taking the wrong attitude," the steward said, still acting as if he were conducting a valid grievance session. But something in Versallo's eyes or maybe it was the set of his hands as he stood from his desk, clenching and unclenching them in a gesture only partly conscious was what convinced the steward that he was working on a difficult and possibly unprofitable path of negotiation. "All right," he said, going to the door, "all right but you've got to understand the safety valve function here, I'm acting as a safety valve, letting you know what's happening here, trying to keep you informed before we get to a serious confrontation—"

"Get the fuck out of here," Versallo said again. "Get out of here before I use some fucking soap and water on your fucking mouth," and the steward went, he left Versallo standing there. For a moment he wanted to laugh with the excitement of it, the skill he had manifested, the way that he had caused the steward to crumple and had made a fool of him. But then, as was happening more and more often these days, the mood shifted and he found that he was not so pleased with himself after all. The thing was that nothing was as easy as it had been. The mood in which he had been was fine, knowing that Mendoza was coming, knowing without being told that his best man had justified all of his trust by accomplishing the mission and bringing in the two million dollars' worth of smack along with the lunatic who had been carrying it ... but how far could the mood go? How was it possible to sustain this kind of lift when, no matter what the ups or downs there was still the same shit to deal with, the constant shit: the unions, the campaign contributions, the hundred-dollar-a-plate dinners that were oh-so-voluntary, the trucks moving in and out of the country? No, he was too old for it, too old to have to put up with all of this nonsense and now like a damned kid he had allowed himself to be bucked into a mood of optimism where he thought that a million dollar valise would solve his problems. It would not. His problems in a basic sense were insoluble. They came, he thought, from being fifty-three years old.

But all right then, he was fifty-three. Past his prime, but so what? He still had a tight hand on his affairs, he knew what was going on; he knew how to handle an organization. Versallo was no fool; no fucking shop steward or idiot politician could take him lightly. And so the mood began to swing again, it arced right back toward ebullience; now with the business of the day settled and nothing to do but bide his time and wait for Mendoza to come in with the big clown, Versallo allowed himself to be happy once more.

He called in his secretary, this one a twenty-four-year-old (he was big on knowing ages) with huge boobs and demanded that she strip. She did. He locked the doors and checking his watch decided that he could give her ten minutes. Ten minutes was more than enough for what he needed; he banged the shit out of her, working her up and down, and demanded that she finish him off with her mouth. She balked, one timid peep of resistance, but he gave her the look and repeated the demand and she went at it without another word. Drained him dry. Drained him fucking dry. He came into her mouth gasping, groaning, beating on the slick surfaces of the couch like a butterfly, forgetting for the moment that he was fifty-three years old, that he was hooked up to his neck, that most of the time he had trouble coming, that he had kicked horse five years ago and there had truly never been a period of more than an hour since then when he had not been in agony, literal agony for it ... forgot all of this beating and screaming against the couch, coming into her mouth and she held it in there when he had finished, her cheeks bloated until at a look from him she swallowed all of it with a gasp. Thought that she would be able to ditch his seed in some toilet but no one was going to get away with that.

"Better," he said, "that's better," not knowing if he was talking about her swallowing it or helping him to come off in her mouth in the first place or whether he was just talking about fucking in general as opposed to doing almost anything else but whatever he was saying she agreed with, nodding her head once, stiffly, then putting on her dress in one motion and got out of the room.

That was the way he liked it. That was the way they were supposed to be. Take what you had and get it out of you and then get the fuck out of your life. If only everything could be that simple; if only he had learned that about women a long time ago ... but enough of this. He would not sacrifice his mood for anything, nothing would take the edge off. He locked the door on the cunt. He waited.

Waited, purged, he thought of nothing at all. Semen drained, anticipation levelled off, rage tempered, Versallo whirled at idle now like a car locked into neutral or park, thinking almost nothing at all. His major problem would be what to do with this Wulff when Mendoza brought him in. He knew that Mendoza would bring him in. He would have to do something with him. Killing was the answer, of course, but it could not be anything as simple as that because this Wulff had created a great deal of trouble for many people and a simple kill would not be the answer. It would have to be something more complicated than that.

Maybe, Versallo thought, fill his veins full of his own smack and watch him thrash around on the floor; move up on and out the way that his girlfriend was supposed to have done. Yes, that would be fun. He would not mind working into something like that at all. The only problem would be that as he watched this Wulff scrapple with himself on the floor, what he would feel would not be satisfaction as much as envy. Because of the horse in the veins. Don't waste it then. Not on something like this.

The intercom buzzed. His twenty-four-year-old secretary, who seven minutes before had been on her knees in front of him, sucking and milking him dry, her breasts shaking behind the erect nipples (erect with revulsion, he thought, and that was fine with him; they *should* hate it; they were born as creatures of filth and, stained by their own ugliness, could only find salvation through realizing what they were), told him in a businesslike way that two men were downstairs waiting to see him. One of them was holding a gun on the other, she said. She said this in a totally matter of fact way which Versallo did not find remarkable. The girl had been there for three and a half weeks now, maybe four (he lost track of them early on) and had seen stranger combinations than this coming into the reception area in the dispatching room a level below. If she had any thoughts on what was really going on she kept them to herself which was the proper attitude and meant that she could stay as long as she wished. Versallo said that that was good news; could he get an identification, though?

There was a pause while the girl consulted with someone in the background. Murmurs, clattering, then the girl was back on the line and said, "Only one of them will talk. The other one won't say anything. The one that will talk says his name is Mendoza, and you're waiting, to see him. He says he's from the other dispatching office, across Michigan, and that you know who he is. Is it all right?"

"I know who he is," said Versallo. He felt the giggling beating in his chest again, felt the little bird of laughter in his heart, battering against its cage. Control, control. "Yes, I know who it is. It's all right. Send them up."

"Both of them?"

"Both of them," Versallo said and hung up the phone.

He rubbed his palms together, felt the feet of a stranger clattering on the floor. He looked down. He was dancing. His heels moved in an imperious little strut up and down the polished surfaces of the floor. Like a movie he had once seen of Hitler after he'd invaded some godamn country or other. In his throat he felt a keening which might have been song. Control, he said again. Control.

It had been long. It had been difficult. There had been moments in the last five years after he had cold-turkeyed it when he wondered if he was going to live or, for that matter, if there was any point in doing so. Why live? Why go on? What man in his fifties who had been on horse off and on for twenty years could face life without it?

But he had prevailed somehow. And now he knew why.

Versallo stood by the door and waited for his justification to walk through. And to hell with the little cunt and her almost unnecessary mouth. Shit, the way he was feeling right now, he could have finished— if he had wanted—in his hand.

# Chapter 8

Wulff had decided to go along with it. That was the only way. Mendoza was no fool; he was a professional and professionals had one trait in common down the line; they were consistent. They might make mistakes but they were moment to moment, small lapses of consciousness; overall they had a fine, consistent line of purpose and you simply could not count upon those lapses extending into a chasm through which you could throw a knife of interference. No, he had to go along with Mendoza; the alternative, which was hurling himself at the man, attempting an all-out attempt for freedom would probably result— this was his best and most calculated decision—in getting both of them killed. He could probably seize the man, choke him, get the car thrown irrevocably off-course but Mendoza would be able to get off the killing shot and even if he did not, if the shot was merely a wounding one, they would both die in the ensuing wreck. It was no percentage. Mendoza knew it too; he knew that Wulff was thinking along those lines and that there was a certain element of risk for him in this too. But with the calculation of the professional he had decided that Wulff knew what he was doing too; he was just not going to attempt anything like this. So, standoff. *Pax difficle.* Balance of terror. They drove through the Loop and into the parking area of a large, dismal warehouse on the South Side.

Here was familiar territory for Wulff. Chicago had been a strangeness, the elegance of the river, the high buildings along the waterfront looking like nothing in New York, only San Francisco could compare with this. But the South Side was pure Hunts Point; it looked like the Bronx might at the end of a murky, greasy afternoon and Wulff, looking at the way that the doors of the warehouse, streaked with obscene lettering, were closed against the afternoon, felt that he was at home for the first time since he had hit this town. He understood this warehouse, and by implication he understood the man who worked in it. It was a contrived ugliness; they were here because the man who ran things wanted to be here and would have picked a place like this given any alternative. It was the proper kind of cover. And the scene, stretching away from the warehouse on all sides was pure Hunts Point too; there was a feeling here of abandonment so profound that it had moved beyond the few stumbling human forms he saw here into the landscape itself, a landscape streaked and exhausted, wrecked and ruined by assaults compounded over fifty years. Nothing could live here. Nothing could even die here. There was not even the energy to support transition from the one state to the other.

"All right," Mendoza said, pulling into a flat, open space at the back of the parking area, removed from a bank of trucks, "that's it. End of the line. Let's go." He tapped the valise and then took it by the handle, waved the gun and showed it to Wulff. "Don't give me any trouble," he said.

"I wouldn't think of it. I wouldn't think of giving you any trouble."

"Because," Mendoza said waving the gun, "we've gone this far, it would be a shame not to wrap up the job and deliver you nice and safely. Not that I'm not willing to knock you off, you understand. I've been given a lot of latitude. But I'm a man of surpassing neatness."

"Of course," Wulff said. Not looking at the man, he got laboriously out of the taxi, felt ground under his feet, stood unsteadily. His cramped position in the cab, the tension of the drive had taken more from him than he might have calculated; for an instant Wulff thought that he might pitch to the ground. Mendoza must have seen it too because he smiled distantly and said, "Nerves will get you even if fright doesn't, eh, Wulff?"

And they had exchanged another of their looks then, the third or fourth since all of this had started, a look which said that they both knew exactly what was going on and indeed were so deep into it that either could have played the other's role. But in spite of that understanding they would act as if this were exactly serious instead of repertory theatre and not make any sudden moves against the grain. Professionalism. Wulff could understand this, he could respect a man who had this competence, this control of a situation. What it came down to at the root, he supposed, was that Mendoza was quite willing to die if he had to and the communicability of this resignation made him more threatening rather than less; there was very little you could do against a man who was willing to die and understood death this well. It was this power in himself which had made Wulff so effective. They walked, Wulff a few paces ahead of Mendoza, into the bottom level of a huge warehouse, a scattering of trucks on this level, sacks, leading bins, one of the trucks muttering away at low idle, men scurrying through the open spaces.

So these people were in the dispatching business, Wulff thought, keeping a few paces ahead of Mendoza, noting that no one looked at him. Each man seemed quite absorbed in his own task which for the most part seemed to be loading the trucks, although one group of men was working frantically on the idling engine, apparently trying to repair it before the fumes blanked them out. "That's nice," Mendoza said behind him, "that's very nice, just keep on walking that way and everything will be fine. You're a cooperative gentleman, do you know that? Really quite a cooperative gentleman," and then prodded him once, guiding him right. Wulff found himself walking into an enormous service elevator, the cage open, the handle unattended. Mendoza poked and prodded him into a corner, closed the gate one-handed and then cranked on the handle, meanwhile holding the gun poised on him in that single, absent gesture. The man knew what he was doing. The man was not to be faulted; he did his job about as well as any Wulff had ever seen. The elevator went up to the second level, hovered there for a moment and then with a crack Mendoza stopped it, opened the cage. Wulff found himself looking into a long, low hallway, oddly stark and well-lighted for a building of this sort. Whoever worked on this level obviously had a good sense of his prerogatives. "Come on," Mendoza said, standing by the handle. "Start walking."

Wulff went past him. For a moment there was an opportunity; the gap between them was only a couple of feet and he might have been able to have extended an arm, closed that gap, knocked Mendoza off his feet. It was at least a possibility and for a moment Wulff indeed did consider it but then kept on walking. He did not like the odds. It was even money or a little better than that that he might have been able to overpower Mendoza, wrest the gun away, take control of the situation ... but fifty percent or a little more was not good enough. Simply stated, he was not that desperate. He had a fair chance of getting out of this alive or at least staying alive for a while, he did not have to do anything drastic. Besides, Mendoza had the valise. The valise was somewhere in the man's possession; he had left it with the men in the booth controlling access to the parking area but it wasn't going to stay with them too long at all. He was sure that Mendoza was going to get it back and transfer it up the line. Funny thing about this man; Wulff did not think of him as a messenger but as a quality in his own right.

Mendoza snorted now as if he had gauged everything in Wulff's head, had calculated it so well that he knew what Wulff was going to think before it had been thought. Of course. A professional: he had left that possibility of attack open to Wulff—not really to taunt him because he knew that Wulff was too much of a professional himself to try it. Only one professional could do it to another; it was a tribute that Mendoza had given him. A weaker, a less intelligent or experienced man might have sprung at his abductor then. Wulff shook his head with disgust and walked down the hallway.

At the end, a door opened before him as if this had been prepared, as if his coming had been observed. He walked through into an office. He saw the man who had held the door for him and then he saw Mendoza come through and close that door as the man went back to his desk, sat, sighed, put his hands behind his head and looked at Wulff with cold, measuring eyes. Then the man sighed again, the coldness in his eyes turned into a soothed pleasure and he leaned further back, put his feet up on the desk, smiled and said, "Mendoza, that was good work. It really was."

"Thank you," Mendoza said. "It was my pleasure."

"I knew you would do it all the time. I never doubted that you would bring the son of a bitch in. Someone else, yes, I wouldn't have been sure. But not with you. I've just had the feeling coming over me for hours that you had scored."

"I scored," Mendoza said. "That's for sure."

"Where's the smack?" the man said. His eyes gleamed. Wulff, looking at him, thought that he had never seen such corruption before, not of this variety, but then again there was no judging from appearances. The man in front of him, heavy, in his early fifties, dressed in a blue business suit that seemed to cover rather than to shape him looked like he had spent half his life in the process of breaking people and now, at this stage of the game, had just begun to move into the period where he could have other people do this work. Still, he thought again, if you could look at a man and fully judge him there would be no need for painstaking detective detail work, there might be no need for a police force at all.

Maybe the man in front of him was a saint who operated this warehouse to give the handicapped a station in life and was kind to animals and small children. Of course. Absolutely. The pressure is getting to me, Wulff thought, it is really getting to me and this much he knew was the truth; fatigue was one part of it and the other was that he had already spent too much time in too many rooms, confronting people like this. There were limits to what one could take and he found himself wondering almost clinically if he might have passed them. But then what?

"Where's the smack?" the man said again, more hoarsely. He brought his palms together. "Come on, Mendoza, where'd you stash it? Don't tell me that you didn't—"

"I gave it in at the gate," Mendoza said. He pointed toward Wulff. "I didn't want to carry it up here with him; I thought that I had enough to handle here."

"Well," the man said, his palms beginning to rub together in an unconscious gesture of tension, "that was good thinking. Mendoza, why don't you get out of here? I think I'd like to have a conference with this man."

"I wouldn't advise that," Mendoza said.

"Oh?"

"Let me keep him covered. It's better that way."

"What do you think?" the man at the desk said to Wulff, abruptly. "Should your friend Mendoza stay here and watch you while we talk? Or can we make this a private conference?"

"That's up to you," Wulff said. The man was baiting him. Little saucers of light inverted in his eyes, twinkles of liveliness at the corners of his mouth. He knew that if he could come close to the man he would hear a ragged intake of breath, find irregularities in respiration. It excited him. Fear, pain, hurt excited this one. Of course, he was no exception. Most of them liked to deal with people in this way, otherwise why would they do it?

"I think it would be sensible," Mendoza said. "He's a rough character."

"A rough character," the man at the desk said softly, "a rough tough character, Burt Wulff. Your reputation has preceded you, you are a famous man." He moved his hands below eye-level, there was the sound of a drawer opening, and then the man came out with a gun which he showed to Wulff with the same absent tenderness that he might if he were demonstrating it for sale in a firearms shop. "What do you think of that?" he said.

"Nothing," Wulff said, "I think nothing of the gun at all."

"Can we have a calm and reasonable discussion here?"

"I never said otherwise."

"Get out of here, Mendoza," the man said. There was a sly, cruel overlay in his voice. "We'll talk privately."

"In other words I've done my job."

"In other words you've done your job," the man agreed comfortably, "and it's time to go."

"All right," Mendoza said. He left the room abruptly. The man behind the desk made a flourishing gesture to Wulff, half-inclined in a bow and said, "Would you mind checking to see if the door is locked? I'd like this to be a private conversation." He showed the gun to Wulff again like a demonstrator.

"All right," Wulff said, "I'll do that." He walked to the door, checked the knob, walked back.

"No," the man said, "there's a bolt there too. Throw it." His face was alight. A smile almost genial came from him. "You'll do that, won't you?"

"Surely," Wulff said. He went back to the door, threw the bolt that he found there and went back to the desk. He stood there then while the man made little circles like smoke rings in the air with the point of the gun.

"Good," he said, "good. Now let's discuss things, Wulff. Tell me all about your career."

He leaned back as if to get more comfortable, the gun held lovingly in his hand. "And when you've filled me in on all the background," he said, "then we can discuss your future."

# Chapter 9

The man with federal credentials leaned over the bed and said to Williams, "You've got to cooperate. You're not helping us at all."

"I don't know a thing," Williams said. "I tell you I don't know a damned thing." He wanted to throw the covers in the man's face, get out of the bed and stalk away, but of course, he could not do that. Non-ambulatory condition. The surveillance man, standing against the wall in uniform, crossed his legs, sighed, but made no move to come over. "Listen," Williams said to the cop, "give me a break. I'm a sick man. Tell this clown to get out of here and come back and ask me questions when I'm well."

"I'm afraid that won't wash," the federal man said. He was even younger than Williams, all of twenty-two, Williams estimated, with that strange, bleak cloak over the face which all of them seemed to have, but he was sweating and not quite as impassive as the manual called for. "You've got to cooperate with us. This man has apparently murdered two of our agents."

"I'm sorry about that," Williams said. "I'm sorry that he murdered your agents. Believe me, I'm sure that he had his reasons. Wulff is a reasonable man." He turned his face toward the wall, closed his eyes. "Quite a reasonable man," he said again. "Why don't you leave me alone?"

"We know that you've had contact with him," the federal man said, "since the time that he left the New York police force. We're quite aware of that. Don't you think that it's as much in your interest as ours to try and cooperate? We simply don't know what this man might do next."

"I told you," Williams said, "I don't care. I don't care what he does next and I have no idea of his whereabouts."

"You admit that you had contact, then?"

"Not recently."

"There's been no phone conversation? He never attempted to call you?"

The cop at the door said, "They monitor phone calls coming in. If he called you, they'd probably know about it already."

Williams shook his head and faced the federal man again. "I got a shiv in the ribs," he said. "I almost died in the performance of duty. Isn't that enough for you now?"

The federal man seemed to quail slightly and for a moment the impassivity slipped away altogether and Williams found himself staring at a young, frightened contemporary, probably in over his head and not even sure how this had happened to him. "No one's out to get you," he said, "believe me, this really doesn't involve you and we're not harassing. We simply believe you had contact with Burt Wulff recently and we're looking for him. This man is a felon. He's a murderer."

"I'm sure he had his reasons," Williams said again. "If anybody got killed it was because they were trying to kill *him*."

"Well then," the agent said, as if dropping one line of discussion, opening up another, "what about the drugs?"

"I don't know anything about drugs. What are you talking about?"

"We have reason to believe that this man had in his possession at the time of the assault a considerable quantity of stolen heroin."

"Is that so?" Williams said. "That's very interesting. What would he be doing with a considerable quantity of heroin? Shooting it?"

The federal man shifted in his chair and then in an abrupt gesture, stood. "I don't think this is getting us anywhere," he said, "I had hoped that you would cooperate; this is a very serious affair—"

"I don't *know* where the fuck he is," Williams said. "I'm not saying that I've had contact with him or not but even if I had, I wouldn't know where the hell he is." He felt a pain beginning in his ribs then, moving like a growth toward his heart and lay back stiffly, *deep breaths, easy,* he told himself and after a moment it passed. "And I don't know if he's got anything in his possession."

"He did," the federal man said. "He had a considerable quantity in his possession. As a matter of fact we believe that the murders were committed when our agents attempted to relieve him—"

"You don't know anything," Williams said. He struggled for breath, gasped, grappled with the sheet at the side of the bed and managed to rear into a posture of confrontation. The surveillance man looked at him with dismay but made no move to help him. "You don't know what the hell's going on, that's your trouble; this man took to the streets because people like you didn't know what was going on. What drugs? What drugs are you talking about?" *But he got it,* he thought, *the son of a bitch did get hold of it and what does that say about the system? What does it say then, eh?*

"A large quantity of uncut heroin which was stolen from the police property room in this city," the federal man said. He was already on his way to the door. "I see that you won't cooperate, Mr. Williams," he said, "and I'm willing to accept that. It will be noted that you failed to cooperate but beyond that—"

"What the fuck are you talking about?" Williams said. "Who the fuck are you people to talk about cooperation, non-cooperation, you and your fucking damned federal war on drugs. If Wulff shot any of your men it was because they would have shot him if they had the chance; you've got a bunch of assassins on that payroll. These aren't police personnel you got there; I know what kind of men—"

"I won't discuss it anymore," the federal man said quietly. He bent over, whispered something to the cop against the wall. The cop nodded briskly, said something back. They went into a short conference and then the federal man, swinging his briefcase was through the door and into the hallway.

Williams lay there in the bed, pulsating with rage. He had only one thought at this moment, that if he ever got well, if he ever survived to get out of this bed, which was not likely if he did not get control of himself, but if he ever lived to see the end of this he was going to go down to headquarters. He was going to go to headquarters and throw their fucking credentials in their teeth because he could not take it anymore. He could not take collaborating in a world in which people like the federal man had power.

No. No way. He would not collaborate. He had reached, it would seem, the end of the line at 137th and Lenox; it was not only his body which had been knifed. They had torn open his sensibility, turned over the clean pan of his consciousness through which he saw the world whole and had shown him instead exactly where they were, where *he* had been every step of the way.

He had been their nigger. That was all. They had used him, even—and this was the cunning of it—made his feeling that he was using *them* part of their scheme.

He thought of Wulff, he thought of the two federal agents that Wulff might have killed and he thought of the valise. Mostly, he thought of the valise. If Wulff had actually dug Stoneman's stolen drugs out of Vegas then it justified everything, because it showed that Wulff could work where the federal man could not. That was something to hold on to.

Fuck them.

Go get them Wulff, he thought, get them all with their hearings and commissions and surveillance and taps and filthy thugs who work on commission and judges and representatives and businessmen and legal protectorates all of them working toward only one goal which was *to keep themselves going.* And to do that demanded that they hold on to the drugs no less desperately than the meanest junkie would crawl into a shooting gallery with a bag to unload some cheap death in his veins.

Maybe singlehandedly Wulff could clean the whole thing up. If he couldn't, Williams thought, one thing was sure: it could only be accomplished by a man who worked singlehandedly and who had nothing to gain or lose anymore.

"That guy was really pissed off," the cop confided, "you get out of this, you're going to find yourself in a boiling pot of hot water."

Williams said he hoped so.

# Chapter 10

Mendoza went away from Versallo raging. He had knocked his brains out to get the big clown in. Did Versallo think it was so easy to take on a job like this and bring it off? Then let the son of a bitch try it himself. Let *him* pick up a car disguised as an ordinary city taxicab, get hold of a uniform, time his arrival at the airport, cooperate with the paid-off dispatcher there to make sure that he made the pickup when the guy came off the plane. Let Versallo deal with the bullshit worry of whether that guy was going to walk off the plane in the first place, whether the tip they had gotten out of New York was a blind lead. Mendoza didn't need this shit. He was entitled to better.

Wasn't he? Wasn't he a better man than one who had to put up with this kind of crap? Taking this shit, wiping Versallo's ass for years and then pulling off this, maybe the biggest job of his life and being thrown out of Versallo's office like some nineteen-year-old asshole who was getting his first chance to prove himself on a major assignment! That wasn't right. Versallo had no right to treat him like that.

And taking the guy in. Bringing him into the warehouse with nothing but a gun and guts; a guy like this who had a record of maybe two hundred bodies behind him. What did Versallo think? that this was all in a day's pay. It was a miracle, that was all, a fucking miracle that he had been able to bring the thing off. Bluffing the thing through successfully every step of the way, holding this guy in check, dealing with the possibility that at any moment he would lose control of the situation and take a slug through his neck. And for what? For what? Did Versallo think that a pat on the back was sufficient? Did he think that Mendoza was indeed that nineteen-year-old asshole and that a word of approval from the big boss was going to keep him happy and off the streets along with maybe a five dollar bonus at the end of the week? The hell with him. The hell with the whole thing.

The rage built within him as he went to the guardhouse. He did not know that so profound a layer of resentment was within him; it was no layer but rather a multiple series of humiliations and resentment, peeling away like an onion—the deeper he got the more rancid, then, the core. He had been putting up with this in one form or another for ten years now, wiping Versallo's ass, functioning not only as his detail man and hard guy but as the one who held the big man's hand and wiped his behind when circumstances got the better of him as they so often did. Frankly, he was fed up. He had left the room heading toward the guardhouse with the vague idea that he was going to snatch that valise from them, take it back to Versallo's office, heave it on the floor in front of him and tell him exactly what he could do with his fucking son of a bitching way of dealing with a man who had given him ten years, *ten years* of the best he had to give.

But by the time he had reached the guardhouse, his mind had worked its way down to a more casual, methodical point of view and he was no longer fulminating but simply *thinking*. This was the way it had always been with Mendoza. He alternated between outbursts whose ferocity shocked even him and a methodical, reserved state of mind in which it seemed he was able to see through everything, control everyone. If he had always been the one way he probably would have been killed twenty years ago in a sucker play; if he had been the other all the way he might have been in Versallo's chair a long time ago. Instead he was neither the one nor the other, neither a leader nor a corpse. Maybe it was best this way. Maybe it really was better. You lived in the middle and you let the two ends split.

He walked into the guardhouse. An evil-smelling place. Coombs, the old man on duty, the shotgun lying across his lap. Coombs thought he was on security detail for a trucking firm that was liable to hijack anytime so he had to keep the shotgun ready and control the traffic in and out. Little did he know. But it would have done Coombs no good to know exactly what he was guarding against or what Versallo was; he would not have done his job any better but considerably worse. And Versallo all along the line preferred people who did not know any more than they needed to do their jobs. Another one of his techniques. Versallo was the man.

"How you doing?" Coombs said and looked at Mendoza in a friendly way. Poor old bastard had little enough to do here during the days. Almost anybody who passed by was a potential security risk. He appreciated company.

"I'm doing all right," Mendoza said. He pointed to the valise, shoved off in a corner. "I'll just take that now," he said, "save you the trouble."

Coombs's sunken eyes became strangely calculating. "What trouble?" he said.

"Trouble of having to look at it anymore. I'm going to bring it up to the man now."

"No you're not," Coombs said. "At least I think you're not. Got a call from him just a couple minutes ago. He said hold it here; he's going to send a couple of guys to bring it up."

"Must be some mistake," Mendoza said, working a smile onto his features, looking at Coombs in an open way. He had never had any trouble talking with the poor senile old bastard. "I'm those guys."

Coombs shook his head. He looked confused but determined. "Can't do," he said. "The man specifically said that you weren't to take it. He was sending two from dispatch. I don't know what he had in mind."

Mendoza looked at Coombs. He was the same ignorant, agreeable old bastard he had been nodding to, bullshitting with for three years now. Picked him up out of an alcoholic stupor a couple of times and rolled him home. He could not believe it. "Come on now," he said, "don't be ridiculous. Give me the valise."

He walked toward it, a hand extended. Coombs came to life suddenly and extended the shotgun toward him, more alertness in the old man's expression than Mendoza would have ever suspected. "Cannot do," Coombs said, "I have my orders."

"Now wait a minute," Mendoza said, pointing to himself. "Just forget all of this for a moment and look. This is me, right. Jim Mendoza. You don't know who the hell you're talking—"

"Sorry," Coombs said. The shotgun seemed to have erected like a penis, it was much longer and more menacing than it had seemed to Mendoza when he walked in here. It was just not possible but it seemed as if Coombs might shoot him. Might shoot. Might shoot Jim Mendoza. "Cannot do," Coombs said, "please get out of the way. I don't want to be responsible."

Was this what Versallo did to men? Apparently. Apparently this was exactly what Versallo did. Gentle old Coombs. Who would have believed it? For just a moment Mendoza reconsidered. Maybe not. Maybe it was too risky after all. But no. Coombs would not shoot him. It was impossible for this to happen. "Just stay cool, old man," Mendoza said and reached for the valise, "and let me handle this."

"I warned you," Coombs said, "I warned you—" and levelled the shotgun. In that sickening, compressed instant Mendoza realized that Coombs indeed *was* going to fire and right on the heels of this knowledge the burst came. It unloaded into his guts like a fist and then he felt coins. Of all things, jingling coins were spreading in his belly, moving up and down and he felt a warmth.

"Godamnit," he heard Coombs say, "I told you not to do it. I told you I had my orders. What the hell are you doing this for? Look what you made me do!" The old man lifted the shotgun above his head and threw it violently against the wall. Mendoza heard it snap and then fall in several pieces. The old man covered his eyes. "I didn't want to do it," he said. "I had to do it. What the hell am I going to do now?"

"I'll tell you what you're going to do now," Mendoza said. He was weak, probably shot mortally—his professional sense told him exactly what he had taken—but his strength was not ebbing that rapidly, and if he died it would be from hemorrhage or internal complications, not from the actual impact. Missed the heart, then. He reached inside his jacket and took out his pistol. He pointed it.

"This is what you're going to do," he said and shot Coombs right in the teeth.

Coombs's face pulped, exploded. In an intricate stop-action Mendoza could see the various parts of the old man's features—teeth, lips, cheeks, hair—implode like a tennis ball squeezed roughly and then cascade outward. They showered throughout the cabin. Little pellets of hair or blood hit him.

"Holy shit," Coombs said with what was left of his larynx and palate and fell to the floor in front of Mendoza. He screamed once, quite loudly as he felt the floor and then, as Mendoza stood looking at him, he died.

Mendoza moved slowly toward the valise. Coombs was dead. Get the valise. He felt himself still moving in that sensation of stop-time, his motions infinitely careful and extended. It seemed to take seconds to will the impulse from brain to nerve synapses to fingers. Extend. Extend the arm. Get the valise. He moved toward the valise and stumbled over something. Something was lying on the floor. A man. It was a man lying on the floor.

Mendoza fell over the thing on the floor, his palm against the valise. It was funny what was happening to him. He had been shot a couple of times before and thought that he knew how to come to terms with the wound—shit if it didn't kill you you were all right—but this was something different. Something. Different. Everything before his eyes was in colors, various shades of red, green, pink, yellow, nothing grey anymore although the interior of the cabin had always been dim.

So this was death. This was death, then. Death, like coats, arrived in many colors. He had always thought of dying as a rather dull, flavorless kind of thing but this was exciting. Very interesting. He was dying in the midst of a rainbow.

Mendoza fluttered like a pennant on the floor, his limbs feeling as if they were extending to enormous lengths, becoming transparent in his convolutions. Gelatinous on the floor he rolled and where he stopped rolling he fell to death and the rainbow collapsed over him like a blanket and pulled tight. Strangled in colors he felt the rainbow tightening around his neck. It was a hell of a thing, he thought. It was a hell of a thing to do a job for ten years and the first time you wanted to grab a little edge for yourself ... it was all taken away.

And taken away by a little old man with a shotgun.

Versallo always sent messengers. He would probably die by proxy.

# Chapter 11

"All right," Versallo said. He smiled. "What now, Wulff?"

"I don't know. I was leaving that decision up to you. You seem to have this in pretty good hands and actually I'm more or less free at the moment."

"You're trying to be funny, Wulff," Versallo said. He sighed comfortably and dug for something again below eye level in his desk, emerged with a folder. "The backgrounder on you didn't say anything about you being funny so that's a bit of a surprise. They have you marked as a pretty serious guy."

Wulff said, "May I sit down? I've had kind of a tough trip."

"I guess you have," Versallo said, looking through the folder idly.

THE LONE WOLF #6: CHICAGO SLAUGHTER

"You've been all over the place. But what with your background on the police force, all aspects of police work including tactical police and narcotics, and with that wonderful combat background you had in Vietnam, you should be able to stand up under a little interrogation, eh, Wulff? Later on we can get you a suite in the Congressional Hotel so that you can catch up on your rest."

Wulff looked at the man. The corruption was still there, leaking out in little waves and droplets, but underneath it he sensed something else, a new quality. It was not exactly fear, call it contemplation then or reconsideration, but Versallo was not quite as assured as he had been when Wulff first came in, and Wulff had the clear intimation that he was holding onto the folder in this way to conceal a shaking in his fingers. Maybe. This did not ease the situation; it made the use of the gun in fact only more likely, but it was interesting. It was always interesting to see the advantages shift, to see the way that the balance between people could change. Call it an aspect of police work. "Screw you," he said.

The man laughed, a simple, empty chuckle that filled the room. "My name is Versallo," he said, "you can call me by my name if you want. William Versallo but most of the people I know simply settle for Bill." He paused, shook his head, continued to dig into the folder. "The least you should know is my name," he said, "so just call me old Bill Versallo when you tell me to fuck myself."

"I'm not interested," Wulff said. "I'm not interested in dialogues. What the hell do you want?"

Versallo looked up at him then away, with a restless gesture tossed the folder into the desk drawer and slammed it. "I've got what I want," he said softly, "I've got you. I've been looking for you Wulff. I've been looking for a long time. You've been screwing up, you've been making life unpleasant for a lot of people and I thought that it was high time that we brought this bullshit to an end. I was really glad to get the news that you were coming to Chicago. That made my day, knowing you were coming here. It was too good to be true." He stood abruptly, the gun held in his hand, levelled it at Wulff's chest. "You've just made me very happy," he said. "I've been getting happier and happier all day and having you here in front of me just cinches it. Welcome, you son of a bitch."

Wulff doubted it. He doubted the happiness. He looked at the gun calmly and then into Versallo's eyes and what he saw was not the aspect of a man who would shoot. No. He did not think that Versallo would do it; this was the kind of man who sent messengers to do the job. If he was going to be shot it would be Mendoza who would do it. This and other things enabled him to meet Versallo's eyes. "The trucking line is a good dodge," he said, "it's an honest cover. Most of the guys I've been dealing with so far have been into corporate accounting or stock-brokerage or they don't really seem to do much of anything at all. But you've got a good industry here, you work hard. Why not dump the drugs and get into it all the way? You'd probably do better."

"Probably not," Versallo said calmly. "Have you looked over the books recently?"

"Probably not," Wulff agreed, "because you wouldn't know what to do with yourself if you weren't in shit. You love it; you love breaking people's heads and screwing around. That's what's going to finish you off in the long run."

"I don't have to listen to your shit," Versallo said hoarsely. His face had changed colors; the red flush had yielded to a blue undertone and his breathing was suddenly not regular, the smooth flow of his speech pattern broken. "You're some kind of crazy self-appointed judge and jury who's going to clean up the fucking world, aren't you? Well you're not doing so good, Wulff. Let me tell you something; the world's as mucked up and filthy as it was before you began."

"Of course it is," Wulff said. "You're still in it."

Versallo's face clotted further and he seemed about to scream, then checked himself. That strange smile began again, plucking tentatively at the corners of the mouth, then centering. "Really?" he said. "You really think that that's so, Wulff? Let me tell you something, I'm answering a human need, that's all. And that's all everybody in this business is doing; we're just servicing people. We didn't create that need, we had nothing to do with it and if it were to go away or if the government was to handle it promptly we'd go right out of business. But the way it is, friend, if it wasn't us it would just be someone else and that's about the size of it. Ex-narco, huh? Then you know all that."

"London solution," Wulff said bitterly, "the British policy. Open up a clinic on every corner. Throw smack into every drugstore, let any twelve-year-old walk in there and buy it to order, give it to all of his friends. That would suit you, wouldn't it, Versallo?"

"No," Versallo said, "it wouldn't suit me at all. It would put me out of fucking business, that's all that it would do. I wouldn't get anywhere so I like it just the way it is and so do you, you ex-narco, filthy son of a bitch. Crusader, where would your crusades be if they just gave the stuff away?"

"You tell me," Wulff said, "I'm not here to solve your life for you."

"Aren't you?" Versallo said. He put the gun on the desk neatly, leaned himself across the desk his hands straddling the gun, nowhere in a position where he could not reach it before Wulff's lunge but wanting the position for emphasis. "Let me tell you something you vigilante Christ-loving son of a bitch. I used to be on the shit myself, do you know that?"

"Good," Wulff said.

"I was on shit for twenty fucking years," Versallo said. "*Twenty* years, and I kicked it myself without any help or any drugs or any assistance at all. Probably the only guy in history who ever kicked it cold and all the time went on living his daily life, just like he had before with no one knowing what was going on. And do you know something? That was six years ago, when I kicked it. Nineteen hundred and sixty-eight on June fourth was the last day I ever took any horse and there hasn't been a day since then, there hasn't been one fucking minute when I haven't been dying for it. All right?"

"All right," Wulff said. "I'm very moved."

"Dying," Versallo said again. His cheeks had sunken in; momentarily he looked both younger and older, wrapped in some cloak of recollection which made his face translucent. "*Dying* for a fucking shot of horse. So don't tell me that I don't know what the fuck I'm doing. I know what I'm doing, I know what I'm dealing with."

"You're dealing with death."

"Maybe," Versallo said softly, "maybe you could call it that. But death is only part of it." The translucence faded; his features were again opaque as he took the gun and caressed it. "The thing with you fucking narcos, you Christ-loving clean-up-the-world men," he said, "is that you ought to take a little shot or snort yourself before you go around taking it away."

"I know someone who took a little shot or snort."

"Oh," Versallo said in an abstracted way. "Oh year, that." He tapped the desk drawer as if referring to the brochure. "You're referring to that cunt, Marie Calvante, the one you were supposed to be engaged to, who was found OD'd out in shit city and was supposed to be so very pitiful that it got you started on your crusade. Seeing ain't doing, friend, and if you had shot it up with the little cunt instead of denying what you probably could have seen, she might be alive today and you might be in some gallery somewhere."

Wulff did not contrive what he did then. There was no way that forethought could have allowed it; it was an insane act but talking to him about Marie Calvante had been insane too: mad of Versallo to do it, he surely should have known that no one talked about Marie Calvante to Wulff. *No one*, not even David Williams who had been in the patrol car that night, had seen the girl lying on the floor, had been with Wulff to see what had happened, no one talked about it and yet here was

Versallo, an armed man standing in a locked office with Wulff, having him totally at bay, calling the girl a *cunt*. This could not be. If it was so, if Versallo could be permitted to get away with this then Wulff was a fool, everything that he had done so far had been a fool's act because it had been based on a lie. It was intolerable. The man, no man could be permitted to get away with this.

Wulff sprang at Versallo.

He sprang at him without forethought, without measuring the situation at all, and this is probably what gave him a chance at the start because Versallo was alert and he would have seen the calculation in Wulff's face an instant before the spring. That would have been all that he would have needed to have used the gun. But Wulff had not calculated; his spring was almost as much of a surprise to him as it was to Versallo and so he was able to take the man off guard, at least a little, rammed a knee over the desk and, with a hand extended, was at Versallo's throat before the man could prepare himself.

But Versallo did have the gun. He had the gun and for a man of fifty-three he had extraordinary reflexes and even as Wulff was in midair, his body arched, one hand extended to seize Versallo by the throat and wrench the life out of him, Versallo had snatched the gun off the desk and had fired. The bullet went high, passing just above Wulff's wrist and then the second shot came with booming impact, aimed toward Wulff's belly. Somehow, though, Wulff had been able to turn his body away from the line of fire so that he was falling upon Versallo from a sidewise angle and this shot, too, missed, roaring into the wall opposite. Dull splinters rained out of the ceiling and then Wulff had fallen upon the man, the force of the dive carrying them both to the floor. He had his palm outstretched flat to Versallo's forehead. As the man hit the floor hard on the back of his head he could feel his palm going into the forehead and could feel something literally *splattering* within there. Softness lurched against Wulff's palm, he could feel a moistness—which he took for a moment to be brains but it was not, it was only blood— exploding upward from some open part in the rear of Versallo's skull and quickly he felt his hand palpating with warm, red glue.

At the least Versallo had a concussion; he might have a skull fracture. Nevertheless the man was strong, desperately so; almost reflexively he reared up against Wulff, bringing a knee toward the groin, missing, settling for a dull impact in the belly and Wulff heard a sound like a sack hitting wet sand, realized that it was the sound of Versallo's knee into his belly and almost simultaneously the pain opened within him as the secondary impact of Versallo's fist came up from the floor, striking him on the cheek. The man was fighting desperately, singlemindedly, no thought of going for the gun undercutting his counterattack. Versallo, concussion or not, was functioning coolly and splendidly under the circumstances. He was a murderous alley fighter. Now his other knee was battering up, still seeking Wulffs groin, settling for another part of stomach, and Wulff raised his hand, chopped the flat of it hard into the adam's apple, heard Versallo gag, squawk like a bird and then vomit into his hand as he used his full weight to pin the man like an insect underneath him.

Versallo fluttered and squawked, his feet kicking away at the floor, and then he made one final effort, bringing up both legs simultaneously, getting Wulff in the solar plexus and thus breaking the interlock. Wulff fell away from him, momentarily blinded with pain, went into a full-roll and came halfway to his feet to see Versallo staggering into the corner, all arms and legs and angles, looking desperately for the gun. He was still squawking and cackling but these were the sounds of his breath, Versallo was not the kind of man who would waste his time with cries of pain. Pain would have to be wrung out of him.

He had the gun almost in his hand when Wulff got over there, shambling, crawling and took it away from him by breaking Versallo's left wrist in two places. He could hear it go, double-break, *one, two,* and now the squawks were no longer breaths but real cries of despair. The man was fighting and bucking against him, the heaves of his body then going suddenly gelatinous and Versallo folded underneath him like a sheet, all of the angles of his body disappearing into that gelatinous huddle, still he was going desperately for the gun, grinning in a rictus of pain and revulsion when Wulff levelled the gun and shot him. He levelled death into the man's temple and heart, two shots, both of them mortal, compounding death to ease the man's passage and when that was done Versallo was still, like a dismembered frog, thrashing around on the floor as if on wire.

Wulff threw the gun into the corner with all the force that he could muster, and then, wandering behind the desk in little circles like a pained animal, vomited there, heaves of pain and hatred forcing a mixture of fluid and blood out of him. Weeping he vomited into the carpet, a spreading stain of vomit running through the room and puddling around the corpse's head and finally he was done. He took out a handkerchief and wiped off his mouth and lips slowly, trying through the deliberate slow inhalation of breath to bring himself back to normal. But the effort was still beyond him; he found himself vomiting again, although this time not so much in wrenching heaves as in gentle sobs and outputs which steadied him, slowly.

After a little while he was able to think once again.

He went over to the place near the wall where the gun had fallen and slowly picked it up. It was warm, still stinking of its discharge and he shook it out carefully, then split the chamber and took out the remaining rounds. A point forty-five, a police revolver, a killer, the best professional weapon, and all oiled up for death. Versallo had planned to kill him; there was no doubt about that. He would have said what he intended, gotten out of Wulff what he could and then he would have disposed of him as casually and definitively as he would have ordered a group of trucks dispatched or put in a requisition for a hundred kilos.

Versallo had been a methodical man. Even dying, the blood still storming from him, he was methodical; going about the business of dying as wholeheartedly and with as much energy as he had with the question of drug distribution. Wulff looked at him, looked away then, revolted. No kill had ever shaken him as much as this; no kill had been dirtier and yet somehow as purifying. *He had called Marie a cunt.* Was that some trigger within Wulff of which he was himself unconscious? He had no memory of leaping. He had made no decision whatsoever to attack the man. It had simply happened and now Versallo, against all of his planning and intention was dead. It must be a great surprise to him. Versallo, in one form or the next, would never get over it.

The question was, what the hell was he going to do now?

He had to get out of here, the sooner the better, but Versallo, no fool he, had been operating on his own terrain and surely every conceivable exit, every aspect of flight had been covered. He had no more chance of walking out of this place alive than Versallo now did. Sooner or later, probably sooner, they would come checking around here, see why the boss had not reported in and that would be the end of Wulff. He had one gun and there were probably a few clips in the desk that he could locate but how was he going to hold off ten, twenty, fifty men? All of them would be in on it once they gauged the situation.

He had no chance.

And yet, he thought, this was not so. He had every chance because he held one advantage; they did not know that Versallo was dead. That was his trump card, that Versallo to them would be alive right up until the moment they saw him, and if he were able to manage this quite right they would not see him, not until Wulff was out of the building and on his way.

He wanted to get out of the building. He wanted to get out of here. He certainly had struggled hard enough to get this far; it would be better to keep on going.

He checked the body out once more, the features of Versallo's dead face almost completely shrouded by blood and then he went over to a side door, opened it, found himself in the private bathroom which had probably been Versallo's one concession in this building, to the way he thought a man of his station should live. The bathroom was surprisingly elegant, walls and mirrors gleaming, a medicine cabinet, half-ajar showing an array of sprays, deodorants, shaving concoctions and male perfumes with which Versallo had doubtless covered himself for certain important interviews. But Wulff ignored all that, concentrated on using the basin and a discovered towel to clean himself off as much as possible. His appearance must be unremarkable; he would be able to get out of this building, if he did, only by cultivating an appearance so unremarkable that he would look like any of the men who had been working on the level below. He doubted if he could do this but at the least he could try.

The water revived him marginally and he was able, by stroking a towel rapidly across his face a few times to bring himself back to a condition of some alertness. Coming out of the bathroom, the taps still running—let there be as much noise in here as possible now—he looked at Versallo; seeing the corpse again sent lurching waves of sickness through him all over again. Of all the kills this had indeed been the worst: the ugliest and the most painful. The manner of that way in which a man gave up life was some comment on how he had held on to it during his time, and Versallo had wanted very much to live. Now, lying still in the posture of death the mouth had fallen open, rigidified into a pained bark of dismay and horror as if Versallo had caught some glimpse of the actual form of death during his passage and had screamed out against it, was maintaining that scream even now. A mystery, Wulff thought, a mystery—life, death, the intertwining of the two, none of it to be ever understood; and yet men attempted to control death in the way that they did, inflicting it, holding it off because only that gave them a feeling of immortality. The heaves started deep in his gut again and he turned away, went to the door. His hands fumbled on the bolt and then he lifted it, pushed it aside and spun the knob until it opened. He eased the door back and very carefully looked down the hall. Empty, murmurous sounds filling the corridor; no note taken of what had happened here. Soundproofed, of course. It would stand to reason that Versallo would have soundproofed his office thoroughly.

Wulff held the gun tightly, made his way slowly down the hall. Nothing interfered with him. He reached the staircase. To the first level then.

He was on the way out. And this time, too, he even thought he knew where he might be going.

# Chapter 12

Randall was about to fuck the girl when the distress signal came in from the guardhouse. It was an ordinary trip signal of the type which set off a blinker and a buzz in the setting on the opposite wall, and he saw it as he was literally poised over the girl, seeking entrance. Her pants were down around one ankle, sweater pulled up to the neck and she was regarding him with an intense look which seemed to work between fascination and terror, which was fine with him. He liked to scare them a little. He didn't actually like to hurt them, that kind of thing wasn't his bag at all, leave it to Versallo, but he *did* like to give them the feeling that they *might* be slapped around; he liked to see the fear rising within them. What the hell. It wasn't like he couldn't get a good hard-on anyway, it wasn't that he couldn't come any way he wanted, he was no pervert for God's sake ... but he liked a little rough stuff or at least the threat of it. It did something for him.

But the light was going crazy, the buzzer was whining. Something had happened down there, that was for sure. "Oh shit," he said, locked against the girl in the posture of entrance. She looked at him dumbly, another secretary, another one of the series of cheap little cunts who Versallo liked to bring in on a fast turnover to keep the troops entertained. All of them fucked. If they didn't fuck they were gone, it was a condition of employment. This one had promised to be one of the best he had fooled around with in months, tense and tight below, the needful suction of her little cunt contrasting with the fear in her eyes in a way that really excited Randall ....

But there was the fucking alarm. Something was going on down there for sure. Coombs was a reasonably competent old guy and he wouldn't have set it off unless things were really going crazy or unless the dead-man backup had been used and someone, not knowing about that alarm, had triggered it simply by standing in the wrong place in the wrong posture. "Oh shit," he said again, closing his eyes, hoping that it would all go away, but of course it did not. These things never did.

Let Versallo deal with it. Except that Versallo would not; the alarm went off in his office and in Versallo's but by clear right of seniority Versallo was the man who would sit back, make preparations while Randall had to go in there and see exactly what the hell was coming off. It wasn't fair, of course. Nothing was fair. Still, that was the employer-employee relationship for you.

All the time he was involuntarily pumping. He was really sealed within her now, he couldn't get out easily. But without his mind on it he couldn't come either.

"What's wrong?" the girl said. Her voice was curiously level for someone who was actually being fucked. Probably she wasn't feeling anything at all; if she was so alert to Randall's reaction it meant that she had been faking participation, faking even the fear maybe. This infuriated him. He felt the rage throughout him and it coalesced, all of it, in his erect penis, making the juncture of the bodies even tighter and more frantic with the need to get out of her, frantic with the need to investigate the emergency. But at the same time, locked into the desperate need to climax, he flailed on top of her, his body contracting like a fist, thrust his teeth against her cheek and then biting, gnawing away at the smooth flesh, battering himself against those surfaces that seemingly he could not enter, Randall climaxed, groaning and emerging in great spurts, each contraction recoiling in a sense of gloom, desperation and waste. He pumped himself dry, the girl lying underneath him, and then slowly he withdrew, his organ already limp, his mind already far away from her, speeding into some alley of circumstance. He had to see what was going on down there.

"All right," he said to the girl, getting off her, going for his clothing, "that's all."

She lay there unmoving, making no attempt to pull her clothing into place. "That's all?" she said. "Just like that?"

"I've got troubles," Randall said, pointing to the wall where the light was blinking, the buzzer continuing its sonorous mumble. "No time for anything now."

"You've got a hell of a lot of nerve," the girl said, still lying there. "You jump on top of me and go in and out, out and in a few times and then tell me to get the hell out. What am I, furniture?"

"I don't know what you are."

"You know," she said, "I'm as willing as the next one to cooperate. I don't really have anything against fucking at all but this is not the way you treat a woman."

"Come on," Randall said. He was already dressed. "Get out of here." Her semi-nakedness offended him now; somehow seeing a woman nude in the aftermath of fucking always bothered him. It was as if their bodies had only one function and they should be covered except when they were performing it. He went to a file cabinet under the window, fumbled around with the catch and opened the second drawer, took out a thirty-two. The girl looked at him with amazement.

"Well," she said, "I've seen a lot of ways to end something like this but that's certainly a new one." She lifted a hand protectively to her face, sat clumsily. "You don't have to shoot me," she said. "I was just leaving." Fucking Versallo and his personnel practices. Bring in women for entertainment but you'd think that he would use at least a little ingenuity in screening them; this one was a fucking lunatic. She had to be crazy, talking that way. Just knowing that she was crazy made Randall feel a little better then. She may have seen his vulnerability but her mind was in such bad shape that she had nothing to hold against him. "Come on," he said, putting the pistol away, turning toward the door, "I've got to get out of here. I want to lock this place up."

"Sure," she said, "sure." She tugged up her pants, brought the sweater down in one motion, somehow the two met in the vicinity of her navel and she tucked one against the other, looked under the couch for her shoes. "This is a crazy place," she said. "I don't think I've ever worked in a place like this. Are you all the same way?" She found her shoes, put them on standing, crossing a leg over and then went to the door, tried it, found it locked.

"All right," she said standing there, not looking at Randall. "I give up. What's the magic word?"

Suddenly he was filled with rage, everything coming to that one pinpoint. This little cunt with her sharp mouth, the fucking alarm going off just when he was beginning to enjoy himself, fucking Versallo himself with his security system and surveillance and his demands that Randall, as his chief of security, function as nothing more than a hired gun, ready to jump into action whenever the alert was sounded. Who the fuck did Versallo think he was? What kind of place was this anyway? How had he gotten himself into something like this?

And all the time the fear beating underneath because he had a feeling that the business in the guardhouse was really bad. You developed instincts after a long time if nothing else, and his instincts told them that this was real trouble, not Coombs getting nervous or someone trying to run the gate. No. It was much worse than that. He went past the girl, yanking at the bolt, tearing away at the knob until the door reluctantly opened, put a hand in the small of her back and pushed her out into the hall.

"Go," he said, not caring if anyone was there to see this, "get the hell out of here." Her weight was slight against his thrust, she felt frail, weak and, as she stumbled into the hallway, tripping, losing her balance to fall with a little squeal, he realized that he had lost his temper, had pushed too hard. The hell with it. He pushed by her, pulling his jacket around him. She wasn't going to be here come tomorrow anyway. He might have to take shit from Versallo and jump when the man sneezed, but he had a few little prerogatives of his own, godamnit and one of them was that he could decide who he was going to fuck. She was getting out. He ran down the hall in the direction away from Versallo's office. His instructions on this were very clear. He was to respond to an alarm by going directly to the point of origin, not pausing to check with Versallo. The hall was filled with activity. It had not been caused by the alarm which was linked into only two offices, Versallo's and Randall's. Nevertheless it was jammed; secretaries had come out of the offices fluttering like birds, supervisors, clerical personnel, all of them, thirty or forty people were in this hallway now, milling around, talking. Randall could catch only a few phrases as he went out there but the clamor stopped, they looked at him, then away, then slowly the clumps began to break up as people went toward the stairwells.

*What the hell is going on? Where the hell is Versallo?* he wanted to bellow at them, scream, demand response but of course this could not be done. Versallo had always insisted that distance be cultivated. Fucking the secretaries was all right, a necessary condition of the job, as he put it; but otherwise he was to have nothing to do with the people who worked on the floor (he did not even know what the hell most of them did; they were tied in with the clerical aspect of the trucking firm which was Versallo's cover, and Randall was not there for the cover-operation of course).

Now it was beginning to tell. They all looked at him as if Randall was merely another aspect of disturbance. What the hell was going on? he did not know; he charged the stairs, two at a time, using his arms like wings to beat employees aside and came onto the first floor, the huge, musty area where the trucks and loaders congregated to find that it too was empty. He went through the dead air of that enclosure, through an open door and then at last Randall was able to see what had happened.

Down range, both dull and bright against the tent of sky, the guardhouse was burning.

It was flaming, sheets of flame reaching up like fingers toward the sky, and the first floor was empty of men because they were already down there, ringing the guardhouse, trying with factory equipment to get the blaze under control. And even as he watched this, the hooter at the top of the gate began to scream—emergency-cut-in from incineration no doubt, summoning the fire department. For Chicago's finest or second finest it would be a routine enough job; for the forces at work, however, it appeared to Randall to be too much. Splinters, pellets, really, of force were being hurled from the heart of the flame, filling the air like shrapnel and the fire was lunging across the gates as well. Randall did not care. He was stricken suddenly by an idea.

It was that idea, not fear of the flames which wheeled him around, sent him storming back into the huge, flat building. The fire meant nothing except that somehow the guardhouse had been overcome, Versallo's point of control had been destroyed but it was merely property and as far as the old man who tenanted that guardhouse during the day, fuck him, Randall was not paid to worry about the lives of lower-echelon employees. His condition as chief of security had been clearly mapped out for him by Versallo a long time ago: *you take care of me, you protect me, you don't give a fuck about what's going on in this building; it's got nothing to do with you at all.* Of course. Randall suddenly understood what had happened. As he ran through the huge, reeking enclosure once again, he did so with dread. *Someone had gotten through to Versallo.*

They had been laying for him for a long time; now they had broken the ring of protection, had gotten to him. There were a lot of people who wanted Versallo. Randall was no fool, he knew exactly what his boss was into. What did Versallo think he was, some kind of idiot? All of it was a cover, the factory, the secretaries, the dispatchers, the clerks—merely a means of providing a cover for the real business in which Versallo was engaged, and Randall knew this perfectly well. Why wouldn't he? He was charged with the man's safety. Versallo was into drugs. He was at the virtual top of the midwestern drug trade.

Randall felt the animal of fear bursting within his throat. It was going to be bad. Oh my God, it was going to be very bad.

He sprinted the stairs, groaning. He knew that they had somehow gotten to Versallo. It all tied together. His groin ached as he ran, little flares of pain like bursting buds along the heel of his thigh, opening sores. Too old for fucking, he thought. Forty years old; he couldn't screw around like this anymore and still expect to do the job he was counted on to do. They had probably broken through while he was fucking. Right when he had been in the saddle they had destroyed security and moved upon Versallo. It was going to be hell. There was going to be hell now.

Back on the second floor. He ran past all the open doors, through the whirring and chattering sounds of electrical equipment which had been abandoned in mid-operation, and toward the end of the hallway. The end of the world would probably be this way. The machinery would continue to hum, only the bodies would be missing. The world was created for machinery now; the bodies incidental. That was where they lived. Even Versallo probably carried on his work by computer.

He came up against the closed door of his employer. For just an instant old instinct prevailed; he felt a hesitancy at jamming himself through and possibly finding Versallo whole, untouched, swearing at him over the desktop. "What are you doing you crazy son of a bitch?" and so on: "you fucking Anglo-Saxon prick ...." He could hear it all, the obscenity spurting like semen from the man's open mouth and then the explanations, the apologies, the babblings from Randall. He would have to tell Versallo that he had been fucking a girl and had not heard. Because Versallo knew everything, you could not lie to him; he would have to confess his shame and the resulting scene would be terrible. There was no saying what Versallo might do then but some colder, harder, more ancient part of the brain pushed away a few levers in there and told Randall, that underneath it all he was full of shit. He was not going to find Versallo in there in any condition to berate him. He knew that, didn't he? Of course he knew it.

He tried the door. Locked. He could have expected that, he dug into his pockets for the spare set of keys, didn't find them, felt an instant of panic when he thought that he might have had them stolen when he was screwing the girl—she was an agent or infiltrator of some sort and that was the only reason she had gone down for him, who else would go down for Randall but someone knowing who he was and needing his confidence?

But then he found the keys—see? he told himself, stop looking for the worst explanations for everything—and slammed one into the door, fumbled, sweated, and pushed his way in and there he felt himself seized by the smell, the smell took him by the scruff of the neck and shook him like a puppy. He had never, never under any circumstances, smelled anything like this. It sent him reeling back. He folded up against a wall, shaking his head like a fighter who had been hit hard but still came back. He came off the wall, his only thought being that he had to open a window.

A window, had to open one, get some ventilation in here, get out the *smell*. A smell of such corruption and decay that it overtook his senses and momentarily his very perception was altered, altered to the degree that he did not even know what he had stumbled against. Something was against his *foot*. Very delicately he took his foot away so that the thing underneath should not trip him again, still thinking about getting to a window so that he could ventilate this place. But this time he looked down, anxious to see, or at least interested in seeing what had tripped him, and it was in that posture, holding his foot clownishly, hopping around, looking away from the window which he was going to open in just an instant ...

... That he saw Versallo and the condition to which he had come.

Randall was not a coward and he had seen death many times in his life, but he had never seen anything like this. I've never seen a man so *killed,* was his first foolish thought and then the horror hit. He did not need to open a window after all. A window would do no good. He went instead to the bathroom and the sickness contracted into one electric wave of pain and shock which went through him and for just the next few moments ... until the cops came on the heels of the firetruck to see exactly what the hell was going on in these offices ... for just those next few moments Randall gave in to a sensation of grief and terror unlike any he had ever before known. Versallo, the un-killable was dead, and only he, Randall was left. And somehow it was all his fault because he had been fucking instead of vigilant.

He *knew* that it was not his fault. He knew that vigilance had nothing to do with what had happened to Versallo and that the fucking was the least of all his sins. Nevertheless he felt that way. He battered against himself. He had a difficult time.

But when the cops came in he became quite composed all over again—cops were always able to bring him back to earth—and he answered everything that they asked quite levelly, explaining as truthfully as he could, leaving out only the matter of the fucking and what he really thought Versallo did for a living. And inside him a crazed little heart of purpose kept pounding, pounding, pounding away: he was going to get the man who had done this to Versallo and he was going to do the same thing to him.

# Chapter 13

Wulff found himself in a light van driving toward downtown and the federal office building complex. He did not even know about the fire at the guardhouse which had spread into the warehouse itself until he put on the radio to listen to any kind of background noise which would take him out of himself for a moment, firm up his purposes. He listened to the bulletins with amazement, struggling with the traffic flow on the parkways, struggling with the floor-shift and trying to understand what he had heard. There must have been a struggle in the guardhouse, that was quite clear, and that struggle had something to do with the valise. The valise, of course. Versallo had sent it away from him before they talked and it must have been conveyed there by someone who had tried to take it away. Or from someone else who had wanted it. It all came down to the valise, though, that was clear. He wouldn't be surprised if Mendoza, the man who had escorted him in, had not decided that he wanted that valise, had been blocked, and had precipitated this. Not that it mattered. The valise was gone. He had resigned himself to that before he had killed Versallo.

He didn't want it anymore. He didn't care; he seemed to have lived the better part of his life linked to a valise and now no more. He was not a valise. He was not a million dollars' worth of smack and after the confrontation with Versallo he wasn't sure that he was the avenger anymore either. He was sick of killing. The kill on Versallo had been vicious, bitter, almost sick in its intensity; looking at Versallo in that first horrid aftermath, seeing the true impact of death not only upon the man but upon himself, Wulff had realized something: he detested death. He had seen enough of it, precipitated enough, now he wanted to perpetrate no more. Death provoked death and the price was too high. So someone else would have to do it.

Go to Patrick Wilson then. Go to the federal buildings, see the investigating staff, tell them everything that he could. Surely they would want to listen to him. If the federal war on drugs was at all serious then they could not ignore what he had to say. But even if the war was nothing but a public-relations mockup, even if the war enlisted for its troops people of the caliber he had had to do on the Grand Central Parkway ... well, even so. So be it. Let them carry the ball from now on. He was done. He was not going to pay the price anymore. It had brought him from New York to San Francisco, back across the continent to Boston, into Vegas and then to Havana, only to sweep him back to New York and the horrors of Chicago. And the journey was becoming bloodier at every turn, the opposition more vicious, the price exacted increasingly higher. No more. He would tell them his story and let them move on from there. And for the rest of it, someone else would have to continue.

He pushed the van harder. Bulletins were coming in at only minute intervals now as further details of the fire and explosion at the warehouse came off the police ticker and from reporters sent to the scene. Two found dead in the guardhouse, one killed, fourteen injured in the panic which spread through the warehouse. The names of the dead in the guardhouse being withheld by police until the families were notified. Of course. Let them sweat it out. Discovered dead in his office, William Versallo, president of the company and alleged racketeer. Called in by the grand jury some months ago. Narcotics trade. Major international connections. Refused to answer questions to the grand jury. Married. Three children. Identified in federal investigation as businessman, head of the trucking firm. Personal details beyond the sketchy biography not available. Family in seclusion. Of course. Wulff nodded again. The families were always in seclusion. Ancient ploy.

Someone cut in front of him on the expressway, a middle-aged Cadillac, children peering through the back window, several adults in the front. The driver had pulled in from a service ramp without checking. Now, as Wulff came down on them, horn squalling, the driver seemed to take cognizance for the first time of what had developed behind. The Cadillac bucked, lurched and then went off the road in a spectacular flourish, bumping and lurching to a point on the shoulder, making a half-spin and finally coming to rest in a burst of steam; Wulff turned to see what had happened in the aftermath but he was already well down the road, the Cadillac invisible. Stupidity. The self-destructive urge was so great in so many people that they would literally stop at nothing in the effort to kill themselves. This had something to do with the drug business also. Wulff shook his head in disgust, clawed at the wheel, righted the van and kept on going. He had not been in Chicago for many years, the expressways were new but the direction was old; he thought that he knew the way to the offices.

Get there. Let Patrick Wilson and his merry men take it from there. Was he being unreasonable? Probably, but Wulff had exhausted any sense of alternative. Here he was on the expressway fleeing yet more destruction; on the expressway were thousands of cars at the same time, any one of which might contain a potential assassin. *They were all out to get him; there was no safety anymore.*

He was so engrossed in the effort of driving, battling off like insects the thoughts of how Versallo had looked dead, that he did not even notice the Cadillac until it had speeded up alongside him in the center lane, the driver rolling down the power window on the right side, holding a level pedal which kept him even with Wulff. "You crazy son of a bitch!" he shouted. Between the driver and Wulff was a female passenger, probably his wife who held a hand against her mouth, held herself low in the seat as if to show by the gesture that she had no part in this whatsoever; it had nothing to do with her. Men's business.

"You want to get me killed?" the driver said. "You some kind of lunatic?" He was a small man in shirtsleeves, his hands bulging on the wheel as he fought for control of the car, his face compressed and reddening. Children in the rear seat bounced and screamed. "I got your license number, I'm going to report you!" the driver shouted.

Just go ahead and do that, Wulff thought, let them trace the van back to Versallo's truckyard and see where it would get them. The driver of the Cadillac could arrest the world as far as Wulff was concerned. But he could not shake the car, the van had poor acceleration and the Cadillac was able to anticipate his movements, stay side by side as if they were welded together. "You son of a bitch," the driver said, pounding the wheel. "You crazy son of a bitch."

Go prove to the man that *he* had cut in, Wulff thought. Well, you could not prove this to him, there was simply no way that you could get people, most of them, to take the responsibility for their own actions. He made a dismissive gesture with his hand, held the wheel of the van steady, waited for the driver of the Cadillac to get tired and pull on ahead, drop back—it made no difference.

But the driver, as if he had finally after years of struggle managed to locate the real enemy in Wulff, the one true cause of all his difficulties which had given him a damaged car, a tight-lipped ugly wife, a backseatful of abusive and uncontrollable children ... the driver was not so easily satisfied.

He lifted a fist, shook it at Wulff. "You ought to drop dead!" he shouted. He had worked himself, successfully, into a tantrum. "Crazy!" he screamed. "Crazy!" and Wulff tried to pull the van out ahead again but the shift would not get into second, the van hung sickeningly in neutral for an instant, rpm's hammering at the sheet metal and the Cadillac, over anticipating the spurt came out ahead of him, opened up a couple of car lengths and then began to slide over into his lane. The driver had an idea. He would cut Wulff off, put him off the road.

Wulff went for the brakes, holding the wheel steady, looking for control. If it had not been for the kids in the back seat he would have plowed right into the Cadillac, let the driver fend for himself. He had more weight than the car ahead of him and although there was no hood between him and the point of impact he did not think that the car would risk collision. Rather, by a little leftward maneuver he could probably sideswipe the Cadillac off the road. Nothing to it; it was an old police maneuver, the kind of thing that he could do in his sleep and had done, in hot pursuit, many times back on the force. In San Francisco, he had put two hoods off the road that way in an old Continental, which had less capacity as a battering ram than this van.

But he couldn't. He couldn't do it. The decision was quickly calculated, instantly made; he wanted to hurt this idiot and hurt him badly because in a way the driver of the Cadillac embodied all of the pointless stupidity of human exchange. But the woman next to him had nothing to do with the driver's insanity and neither did the children, four or five of them scuttling around in the back, visible through the distorted glass of the rear panel. It took him less than a second really to calculate and reject the alternative of striking back at the driver and then he was braking, braking the van down desperately, fighting with the wheel as the light truck responded to the diminished torque by contracting into itself. Wulff had a feeling of reduced dimensions, the truck impacting and then he was coming close to the Cadillac. Too damned close, the brakes were no good on the van and the compression braking was worse, something was definitely wrong with the van's motor. Ring job. *I'm heading for the*

*ditch and making mechanic's judgments!* Wulff thought bitterly but by
then the van was already swerving right, at the point of lost control,
heading—still at thirty or forty miles an hour—toward the guardrail.

He still could have bailed out. That was what he would remember
about this the longest. He had the van still marginally under control;
by downshifting to first and hoping the clutch would catch he might
have regained enough torque to yank the steering wheel left, force
response out of the vehicle. He could have come left in the van then,
shutting off approaching traffic and bailed out by passing the Cadillac
but even as he stared he could see that it would be too close, he would
probably sideswipe the old machine, and that would put the Cadillac
in the ditch.

In an instant's calculation he saw all of this and his foot was reaching
for the clutch, reaching for the maneuver which could keep him on the
road but then, staring intently through the windshield, he saw as in
close-up one of the children at the rear deck. It was a boy, five or six years
old, looking at him with solemn eyes, transfixed by the proximity of the
van, the sight of Wulff bearing down upon them. And what he saw in
the eyes was, at least in that dazzle of light, that imploded moment, the
thing that he had seen in Marie Calvante's as she lay on the floor:
another hurt, vulnerable, tormented creature and he could not do it.

He could not do it. He could do it to the idiot driver and his dumb wife
in a moment but not to the child. Not to children. In the two seconds that
elapsed from the moment all of this began Wulff came to the realization
that there were limits to what he could do, either in vengeance or self-
defense and after finding one pole with Versallo, he had found another
in the child's eyes. He held the wheel grimly, tensely, half-saluted in a
bizarre gesture and almost majestically the van, bearing right, away
from the child and toward the Cadillac's safety hit the soft shoulder,
bounced the guard rail, leaped, flamed, and began to roll.

# Chapter 14

It was not easy to conduct a long series of long-distance phone calls
from a hospital bed, fighting all the way through bureaucracy and the
chain of command to find the man he wanted twelve hundred miles
away, but Williams did it. He was determined to do it. There was, after
all, nothing else to occupy his time and he had decided when he began—
at eleven o'clock Chicago time, high noon in New York—that he would
just not be put off with it and he was going to get through no matter
what. They could send the godamned phone bill to the New York police

department, by whose courtesy he had this very excellent hospital room and surgical benefits and the rest of it. He kept in mind the lesson he had learned through being in civil service himself, which was that nothing they did or said to you was ever personal. Nothing personal at all; it was not him they were grinding to a pulp through their policies and procedures and assistants and inquiries, it was anybody who got between them and their safe little system. Chalk up another one then for Wulff.

He got through, finally. There was a new shift at the door; a couple of sullen rookies who seemed to resent the fact that Williams was lying in there all expenses paid and collecting salary in the bargain; they hinted that Williams had probably arranged the knifing himself so that he could get something free out of the NYPD or maybe that was just the inference they were seeking. He figured these new cops didn't give a shit what he did with the phone as long as he kept it quiet, and the nurses and floor detail had long since stopped trying to do anything with him at all. He was a convalescent case and the hell with him. So he went on with it, doggedly dialing Chicago again and again, going from bureau to bureau, finally, he was able to trap a secretary into giving Patrick Wilson's home phone number and from there on it was easy.

He wasn't able to get Wilson at home but by pushing his wife very hard—she sounded like a real piece of ass but dumb, like all prosecuting personnel or those associated with them, seemed to be, basically just dumb—he dug out the phone number of a place where Wilson might be reached if he wasn't in his office or court during working hours. She called it a conference center but to Williams it sounded like a bar. Only two more calls and he was able to get hold of Wilson himself midway between a court appearance, he said, and an urgent interview with a state witness. He sounded impatient and angry but otherwise unremarkable. Williams didn't know; somehow he had expected more. Superman should have a resonant voice filled with confidence and passion, whereas Patrick Wilson, head of an important federal prosecution sounded like—well he sounded something like an informant. Williams pressed on though. Don't let little details like this mess with your mind. For all he knew the guy had a lot of brains, although he certainly sounded like a schmuck.

"Well, I don't know," Wilson said when Williams had put the case to him hurriedly, bringing his voice to a concentrated point of whispering, "I just don't know. I can't make any definite commitments, that's for sure. It sounds to me like the matter is out of my hands."

"It doesn't have to be."

"Other agencies are obviously looking for your man," Wilson said.

There was a sound of hammering in the background, voices singing off-key, detached obscenities, like dismembered limbs floating in water, seemed to be there as well. "They would probably supersede my authority—"

"Don't you know who Wulff is?"

"I'm afraid I can't go into that kind of material with you over the telephone, even if you are who you represent—"

"You mean to say that you don't know who the man *is?*" Williams said. "How can you be into an investigation like this and not know who I'm talking about?"

"I didn't say I didn't know who he *was,*" Wilson said, "I did say that there's information here which I certainly couldn't release unofficially over the telephone to someone whose identity is unsubstantiated."

"I have reason to believe that this man is coming to you, and that a whole lot of stuff is going to fall into your lap and there should be some guarantees—"

"I can't make any guarantees or representations at all," Wilson said. "All of this would have to be handled on an individualized basis. Certainly if this man is as potentially valuable as you say he is we might be able to make certain allowances, we might be able to at least explore the question of a limited immunity—"

"*Limited* immunity," Williams said. "What the hell are you *talking* about?"

"I don't even know who you are, friend. I'm not going to get into bargaining with you on the long-distance telephone."

"You interested in getting something done out there or is this just more federal agency bullshit like the informants? You people seem to be pretty good at blowing up houses and beating up innocent people but are you really out to *touch* the trade? Sounds to me very doubtful."

"I resent your attitude," Wilson said. "And I don't like your representations. If there's anything to discuss it can be handled in a more direct context."

"You know what I think, Wilson?" Williams said.

"Frankly, Mr. Willman or whatever you said your name is—"

"Williams. I'm a New York police officer."

"Williams. Frankly, Williams, I don't give much of a damn *what* you think."

"I figured that out. I really did now. But I'm going to tell you anyway. I think that if Wulff actually comes to you people he's got at least half a chance of being turned right over to the organization."

"You do, do you?"

"Yes sir," Williams said softly. "I really have come to that tentative conclusion," and he held the phone then, waiting for the prosecutor to hang up. He sat there, his breath in his throat, waiting for the signatory click which would tell him that Wilson had definitely hung up on him. But strangely it did not come. It was as if Wilson was as stunned as Williams by what had just been said. After a little while Williams got tired of this and hung up the phone himself. He did so gently, not to injure the delicate ear of the delicate federal prosecutor and he lay back on the sheets then with a sigh, feeling soiled by the contact, but vaguely cleansed as well.

At least, he thought, at the very least, this would put Wilson on notice not to try funny stuff as he might have otherwise done.

What he wished, what he really wished was that there was some way in which he could reach Wulff and call him off. Keep him from going to Patrick Wilson. Keep him after all, from any involvement with the system.

He had been wrong. He had been dead wrong.

Wilson and the people against whom he was allegedly fighting were interchangeable.

The system was the enemy.

He wished that he could tell Wulff that now.

# Chapter 15

Wulff came out of the wrecked van feeling like little bits and pieces, testing various parts of himself, deciding that he had survived the accident in good repair. A man picked up a certain resiliency sooner or later. Superficial bruises, a pain in the left thigh, nothing that he could not work out. The van had overturned, he had made it out through the side door. Not a moment too soon. Lying on its roof, the surfaces had already started to impact and crumple. The Cadillac way down the road, of course. Doubtful if the driver had even looked back. Why should he? It was out of his hands.

A police car pulled to the side of the road. Cruising, they had seen what had happened, were coming to investigate. Wulff thought for a moment of trying to make some escape through the bushes that were over to his right, leading into another warehouse district but decided not to. He couldn't move that quickly. Also the Chicago police would never let him get away. In addition, he decided, it was just as well to be picked up by the cops now as later, wasn't it? He was headed right into the arms of authority anyway.

The police got out of the car, walked down the little depression toward the van. Big, clumsy men dangling clubs and guns, pointing at the van. Wulff stood there, his arms apart, his hands open. It was doubtful if the police would shoot him simply because he had been in a one-car accident but on the other hand the Chicago police had something of a reputation. They did indeed.

"What happened?" one of them said, leaving the other standing at a distance of some ten to twenty yards back, arms crossed, looking in the distance. Standard technique. Two men to a car but one would do the work, the other stand by. Halve the effort. Next call they might switch. Two to a car, Wulff thought, was the biggest waste of manpower possible but all of the large cities worked that way. Patrolmen's unions; "Two men to a car were necessary for protection," they stated but it meant for all practical intents and purposes that all of the time, half the team was not working. "Lose control?"

"I got cut off," Wulff said.

The cop looked at him with interest. Wulff for the first time in some hours became aware of his appearance; the marks of the struggle with Versallo had really not been sponged off by the quick washing he had done. Spatters of blood were on his clothing; his face was probably ringed by it. The cop's eyes flickered. *Bad news,* Wulff thought.

"Who cut you off?" the cop said.

"A man in a Cadillac. I didn't get his license number, didn't get anything; I was having too much trouble trying to control this thing."

The cop looked over at the van, resting on its roof, already beginning to settle upon it. One of the wheels like a finger stroked at the air. "Let's see some identification," he said.

"Identification?"

"License," the cop said, "registration. Credentials. Proof that you had a right to drive that thing." In what was obviously an unconscious gesture his hand reached down, caressed the police revolver, then went up to his chin as if in a gesture of denial. His partner now was watching the scene intently.

"Don't have it with me," Wulff said.

"You don't look like you have any injuries to me."

"I don't. I was lucky."

"I'm afraid we're going to have to take you in, friend," the cop said. "Who are you anyway?"

"I'm from out of state."

"I gather you are. I gather you're from *way* out of state. You still haven't answered me though."

"I don't think I want to," Wulff said quietly.

The cop was completely involved now. Any indifference that had been in him as he had walked over had been burnt out by curiosity, and what Wulff saw was just a trace of fear. He motioned to his partner who came over slowly, trying to show Wulff how little concerned he was, but Wulff noticed that this one curled a hand around his club.

"No identification, no license, no registration, won't identify himself, won't go into any of the circumstances of the accident," the cop said.

"I told you about the accident. I got cut off."

"Stands mute. Looks to me like he's been in one hell of a fight too. Whose blood is that, friend?"

"Mine," said Wulff, "I got cut when it rolled over."

"I don't think so," the cop said and then turned to his partner. "Think we got to take him in?"

"I think we'd better do just that."

"All right," Wulff said, "let's go then." It was a strange feeling being on the other side of a process that he had gone through hundreds of times, feeling the control of the situation shift completely away from him, feeling now as if he were merely an object which these cops were manipulating, manipulating quite protectively of course. It was always interesting to see things from the other side.

The odd thing was that he still felt like a cop and he wanted to tell them that their procedure was all wrong. In light of this situation; the wreck, his appearance, the complete absence of credentials, they should not be standing here idly discussing his disposition, telling him of their planned move. He could be any kind of a felon. They should have had their guns out and already in the process of handcuffing. But the Chicago police were hesitant. Probably their public-relations department was still working to bring back a sense of confidence in them. They had had a rough time, no one believed in them anymore.

"Let's take him in then," the partner said. He still had his hand on his club, reconsidered this, went at last for the gun and took it out slowly as if he were plucking a grape, showed it to Wulff. "There doesn't have to be any trouble," he said, "all you have to do is cooperate."

"I'll cooperate," Wulff said, "don't worry about that. I want to cooperate to the fullest extent of the law."

"This man is funny," the partner said. "This man has an original and delightful sense of humor. Should we show him what we think of his sense of humor?"

The cop who had made the original approach looked discomfited. He looked for the first time, in fact, as if he had no idea of how to proceed. "I don't want any difficulties," he said to Wulff, "there don't have to be any problems—"

"There aren't any problems," Wulff said. "I want to see Patrick Wilson.

That's the federal attorney's offices."

"I don't know nothing about federal attorneys," the cop said, "I don't know anything about Patrick Wilson." He extended a hand. "I can cuff you," he said, "but if you'll cooperate it won't be necessary."

"I told you I'll cooperate."

"Let's cuff him," the partner said. He looked at Wulff in an unpleasant, sidewise way, his eyes suddenly squinting. "Come on, we've got a man who won't identify himself, has no credentials, looks as if he's been in a violent episode of some sort."

"All right," Wulff said. He extended his arms. The partner stopped in mid-speech, looked at him dubiously. People who assumed the position of being handcuffed were obviously a rarity to him. Either that or he did not particularly like the idea of bringing in Wulff in cuffs and had used this merely as a threat. He seemed to be calculating one thing against the other in his mind: what would they think of this in headquarters? The only thing demonstrable so far was that the perpetrator had been involved in a one-car accident.

While he was thinking about this, Wulff pushed past the two of them, walked toward the police car. He kept his hands up all through this to make clear that there was no attempt to flee. His stride was measured and regular. Comforting. In a way it was comforting to be back in police hands again. He had never realized until this moment how it must look on the other side of the fence, why many wanted apprehension, why there were some cases that literally ran toward you begging to be taken in. It was easy; it sure as hell shifted the responsibility. And that was what he wanted right now. For the moment, he did not want to think.

He moved steadily toward the police car. Traffic on the expressway had not halted although cars tended to slow down as they neared the police car with its rotating blinker, drivers peering out to see if they could catch a glimpse of a corpse or two without holding up commuting schedule. They could hardly be blamed for that, Wulff thought, it broke up the routine. A spectacular highway accident was fun for everyone except the victims: it gave the cops something to do, the insurance companies things to investigate, motorists the chance to feel how lucky they were. He opened the door of the police car, wedged himself in in the center and, folding his arms, waited for the police to come.

They showed up in just a minute, the heavier one slightly out of breath from the climb up the incline. One got into the back with Wulff, the panting one became the driver. Doors slammed and the car came out of the pit at forty miles an hour, accelerating. Within the insulated surfaces, spilling out behind them Wulff could hear the sound of the siren.

"I just want to tell you that we don't like any of this," the cop next to him said, "the whole thing stinks. Why don't you give some identification?"

"I'll give it when I'm ready," Wulff said. "I want to see Patrick Wilson."

"Nobody knows who Patrick Wilson is here."

"You tell them at the booking. Patrick Wilson, do you hear me?"

The cop leaned forward, said something to the driver which under the sound of the siren was inaudible. Probably, Wulff thought, he was trying to find out who the hell Wulff was talking about. Then again, maybe he thought that Wulff was crazy and wanted to split this confidence in the way that cops did every so often.

Either way, it didn't really matter, did it? It was a good feeling to be back in custody, to let the sense of all of this shift from him. He had had enough of coping, let them cope for the moment. Let the agencies worry about the problem; they were well-paid enough. With a sigh, with a felon's sense of gratitude Wulff sank back into the slick material of the rear seat (shiny, cheap and uncomfortable but you could bet that it would resist any attempts to scar it with a knife) and let them take him where they would. The bastards.

# Chapter 16

Calabrese lived in a mansion at the end of Michigan Avenue. Most of the people with his money, at his social level had long since fled to Evanston or Urbana but Calabrese was a city boy, and anyway he liked to keep an eye close on his operations, all of which were in the city. So it was still Chicago. But he was sealed in.

He was sealed in by a twenty-four hour security force that numbered at least ten men (the exact number was a secret of course), by gates, by an alarm system and by one of the nastiest patrol dogs Randall had ever seen, a dog so vicious that it appeared to have its own keeper who was paid to do nothing but stay with the dog full-time and minister to it. It was the keeper with whom Randall started his negotiations; forty-five minutes later it landed him in Calabrese's study where the man himself rolled a cigarette between his thumb and forefinger and studied Randall with a curiously calm, kindly expression. He might have been a whimsical old businessman devoted to philanthropy, who took a fatherly and detached interest in everyone who came to his door, a man who regarded humanity from the sidelines with mingled wonder and scholarly concern, and this was in a sense true although it was not quite all of it.

Calabrese was about seventy years old and was such a remote, patriarchal figure that to the best of Randall's knowledge even *Versallo* had dealt with the old man only over the phone and then, perhaps three or four times a year to get approval for this thing, clearance on something else. Nevertheless, Randall had been able to run the gauntlet and get into the man's presence within forty-five minutes. This was a tribute either to Randall's charm and determination or to Calabrese's whimsical old philanthropist's willingness to humor a would-be visitor but Randall did not think that it all ended there.

He sat on the couch under the old man's gaze and tried to keep himself as calm as possible, forced himself to meet Calabrese's eyes. He had heard it told that Calabrese preferred people who were not in awe of him and not easily intimidated, and he would do the very best that he could to oblige although it was very hard to sit there calmly under the gaze of the most important distributor and chieftain in the midwest, a man who had been to Versallo what Versallo was to Randall. Randall had had a rough day. The shock of seeing his boss dead, the trip to the guardhouse, the interview with the police had left him drained. Still, he had all of *this* yet before him. If he did not succeed with Calabrese everything that had gone before was meaningless, and it would be as if everything had been nothing. Versallo would die unavenged, Randall's future would disappear, everything would fall apart.

He suspected that if he failed with Calabrese he did not, at least, have a long, bitter, lonely future to await him. Calabrese would take care of the future for him.

"I don't understand," Calabrese said now in that gentle, low voice of his. Randall might have thought that Calabrese got it out of the movies except that everyone who had any sense knew that the Calabreses were the reality from which the glittering sentimental fantasies came. "What do you want of me? And how did you get hold of a valise with that amount of uncut heroin?"

"That's part of what I can't tell you," Randall said.

Calabrese's eyes narrowed and he did not, suddenly, look quite so benevolent and whimsical. "If the source of that valise is what I think it is," he said, "it doesn't matter whether you tell me or not. That shipment has caused many people a great deal of difficulty."

"Of course," Randall said, "you can have it."

Calabrese's eyes broke out of their narrowness and widened considerably. "Have it?" he said. "You must doubtless be out of your mind. The unfortunate murder of your employer must have unsettled you completely."

"Of course you want it," Randall said. Already he felt off-guard and helpless. Class was class; he admitted it. He was running out of class with a man like Calabrese. He could not, in any terms deal successfully with a man like this; he would always come out feeling like a fool. The only thing was to go stolidly ahead. This man was not born on Michigan Avenue surrounded by pewter. Once he had been a struggling, sweating little man like all of them. Concentrate on that, he thought. Remember he's the same as you, they all are. This did not help.

"But I don't want it," Calabrese said, leaning forward slightly. "I will talk to you very frankly although I do not want you to think even for a moment that I am conceding to you that I am who you seem to represent me as being. I am just a simple, common businessman who has many interests and I am seeing you as a favor to my staff who you have given quite a difficult time. And besides that," Calabrese said with a little glint that made Randall nauseous, "if you ever cause me any difficulty I will have your heart ripped out from your chest cavity, barehanded. There are people I know who can do this kind of a job and even enjoy it."

"But—"

"But nothing," Calabrese said and raised a hand. "But *nothing*. Assuming that I am what you think I am, why would I want this amount of uncut heroin coming into my distribution sources, eh?"

"I only offered it to you for help you might give me," Randall said stubbornly. Concentrate on the one main objective. "If you don't want—"

"You're stupid," Calabrese said in a slightly louder voice. "All of you men are stupid. It's a miracle that you get anything done. Shut up and think for a moment. Do you know what this supply would do to the market?"

"Make you richer."

"No," Calabrese said, "it would not make me richer." He put the cigarette he had been holding into his mouth and looked at an exquisite gold lighter on the desk before him, then as if rejecting the very concept of smoking, shook his head, broke the cigarette and threw it into an ornate wastebasket to his right. "It would make me poorer. It would be as if a massive convoy of enemy airplanes were to fly over downtown Chicago, dropping millions of dollars of perfect counterfeit currency into the south side. How long do you think the economy would last?"

"I don't know."

"What if they simultaneously appeared in Los Angeles, New York, San Francisco, Dallas? What if a hundred million perfect counterfeit dollars were to fall into the hands of the population of Watts or Harlem? Have you thought of that?"

"I guess," Randall said after a moment's pause and he really did think this through because he saw for the first time what Calabrese was getting at and with it was an enormous and valuable insight, "it would destroy our economy."

"Of course it would," said Calabrese. He fumbled inside his jacket, took out a pack of cigarettes and extracted another, looked at it sadly for a moment and then broke this one too across and threw it into the wastebasket. "It's the only way I can control the habit," he confided. "I go through seven packs an afternoon, just breaking them up and throwing them away like this but it's better than dying, isn't it? I don't believe in drugs, you see. It," he said again in that other, more pedantic tone, "would destroy the economy, because it would utterly wreck the objective medium of exchange which is the clear, visible outcome of the most delicate, profound, wonderful system mankind has ever known, which we refer to crudely as supply and demand. There is less currency than desire at any given moment, you see. *Currency*. However, the transferred desire and energies that would otherwise lead us straight to anarchy are transferred over to the pursuit of the abstract, currency.

"But if you meddle with that," Calabrese said, "you risk destroying everything. That was actually considered and rejected, by the way, as an actual means of sabotage during the Second World War. They were going to flood the Berlin of 1942 with marks. The presses were ready to roll and the best, the most expert counterfeiters the government was able to buy or to take out from the prisons for the war effort had prepared plates which were absolutely indistinguishable from the reality. It went up to the highest levels of the security service and only at the last moment was the plan rejected. Do you know why?"

"I think I'm beginning to."

"I think you are as well," Calabrese said. "Because there are certain means of warfare which are absolutely intolerable, even worse than poison gases, and this would be one of them. It was decided, finally, that it would be better to risk losing the war and still inhabit the world which we do inhabit then to win it in a way which would have changed everyone's reality. Of course," Calabrese said after a pause, "there was also the possibility that if we did it to them they would have the capacity to do it to us, and no one was willing to take even the smallest chance that such would be the case. Decency prevailed, you see. It usually does."

"And that's why you don't want the contents of that valise," Randall said.

"Exactly," Calabrese said, "that is why I do not want the contents of that valise. You have, by presenting it to me, already put me into a nearly impossible position. I must arrange for its disposition, and yet how trustworthy would be even the best of those who I would elect to dispose of it? You are going to send an old man to the lake himself on a very sad journey, Randall, and I am not pleased with that. Also, I hate physical exercise of almost any sort."

Calmly, Calabrese took out another cigarette and broke it with an air of sadness.

Randall sat there, thinking about what the old man had said. When you looked at it the way Calabrese had put it, it was logical, completely pure; why couldn't everyone see it? The market was dependent upon the limitation of supply. It was from that limitation of supply that all other possibility flowed. Open up the supply, change the rules of the game as they applied to a man in Calabrese's position, and his position was threatened, possibly destroyed. Wasn't it? What benefit could Calabrese possibly derive from a million dollars or more worth of junk dumped into his comfortable, carefully-controlled operation? It might, to a much younger or more adventurous man be riskily interesting. But Calabrese was not interested in risk or excitement; as he had already pointed out to Randall, as he doubtless had made clear to Versallo and others many times, he had a business to run.

"All right," Randall said, standing, wondering if he would be allowed to leave this house. "You make your point very well. I understand. I'll take it—"

"Sit down," Calabrese said.

"What?"

"I said, sit down," Calabrese said again in the tone of a man who in mind's eye had already placed Randall back in the seat. Randall did so. There was certainly no way that he was going to break out.

"All of that having been said," Calabrese said calmly, fishing out another cigarette, "I am very interested in the man from whom you took this valise. That is a different issue altogether, that man."

"I didn't take it from him," Randall said. "I came by it indirectly."

"Did you?"

"I'm interested in him too," Randall said. "That's why I'm here. The valise was just an offering."

"Oh?" said Calabrese and broke a cigarette. "Was it now?"

"I wanted your help."

"Ah," said Calabrese. "Everybody wants my help. Everybody wants money, some people like Versallo want money and drugs and some people want money and my *help*. Everybody however wants something; that seems to be a basic fact of that supply and demand we've discussed. Help in what?"

"I want you to help me kill him," Randall said.

Calabrese put the pack of cigarettes on the desk and leaned forward, looking more patriarchal, whimsical and soothing than ever. "Now," he said softly, "at last we are talking on common ground. I think we can do business. Tell me what you had in mind."

Randall's eyes swept the office, then came back to Calabrese's.

"Don't worry about a thing," the old man said, "for a few million dollars, anyone can have absolute security. Just tell me."

Randall told him.

# Chapter 17

Wulff wanted to see Patrick Wilson. He started in at the door of the precinct saying this, repeated it at thirty-second intervals thereafter and stepped up the ratio when the interrogation began. You set it in their minds what you wanted and you kept on pounding at it. Cops were single-minded but you could meet their single-mindedness with an obsessive cast of your own. At least Wulff was willing to play it that way. Their booking procedures were incredibly archaic and clumsy. He had thought that the NYPD was a rotten deal but Chicago operated as if there were no dividers whatsoever between police and ultimate authority. These people not only wanted to enforce the law, they wanted to administer what they thought of as justice.

Under the Miranda Decision, he did not have to say a word of course. But these boys did not seem to know shit about Miranda. "Name, address, identification," the booking sergeant said holding a pencil and repeating it when Wulff stood mute. "Name, address, identification please." He looked sleepy but at the same time capable of going on this way until the end of his shift if necessary. "Name, address, identification," he said again and one of the cops who had brought him in gave Wulff a little encouraging shove between the shoulder blades. "Come on," this cop said, "cooperate. It's just going to get harder if you don't, not any easier. We haven't begun to put the pressure on yet."

Wulff had thought that that stuff had gone out with the 1930's or at least with Miranda, but it had not. In the NYC stationhouse they were at least interested in getting onto some personal level before they beat the shit out of you; that is, they tried to decide whether you were *worth* beating the shit out of, if only for kicks, before it started. Then they kept one eye on the door at all times. But Chicago was a different apple altogether. They were both terribly serious and not serious at all. Wulff expected that in just a few moments one of the cops would begin to laugh uncontrollably and the rest of them would snicker along and send him out the door. No chance. No such chance.

"I want to see Patrick Wilson," Wulff said to the sergeant, "he's a federal prosecutor—"

"I don't know shit about federal prosecutions," the sergeant said. "I'd like some information on you, though." For a fat, dishevelled man he spoke with a curious precision; indeed his voice had delicacy. Perhaps it was that flat midwestern accent; it threw the hell out of easterners.

"The way to get some information out of me is to get me to Wilson," Wulff said. "I'll talk to him."

"I'm afraid you're in no position to pick your spots," the sergeant said comfortably. Someone slammed Wulff with a club in the small of the back. Clumsy, Wulff thought; it had missed the kidney. Usually you went for the kidneys; that was the right spot.

"Nevertheless," Wulff said, enjoying, even through the pain, the *nevertheless*, "I want to see Wilson."

"We want some information on you," the sergeant said. He picked up a piece of paper in front of him. "Arrested in a one-car accident on US 90, dishevelled condition, bloodstained, would produce no credentials of ownership, no driver's license, no identification—"

At least he was unarmed, Wulff thought. As usual he had dumped the pistol leaving the warehouse; he figured that he could always pick up that stuff in transit and in the meantime the less he was risking the better off he would be. The sergeant put down the sheet of paper. "I don't like it," he said, "I don't like your attitude for shit, buddy."

"Let me take him downstairs," the cop behind him said in a bored tone. "We'll improve his attitude."

"Eventually," the sergeant said. He leaned toward Wulff, assumed a confidential air. "It would be much easier if you cooperated," he said. "Really, it would be."

"I'll cooperate when I reach the proper authorities."

"You're making life very difficult," the sergeant said. "Essentially we're not looking for trouble, you know. We like things to be quiet and reasonable here. This department has been bum-rapped."

Wulff stood there, looked at the sergeant levelly and said, "I have nothing more to say, I want to see Wilson," and something hit him in the small of the back again this time painfully and much closer to the kidney. He turned and the cop hit him again this time on the side of the face on the cheekline and Wulff abandoned the careful control with which he had come into the station, let it slide away from him like a cloak and hit the cop in the forehead, a glancing blow that made him stagger. The other one moved in then, a club suddenly extended from his hands but the cop who had been hit, backing away toward the wall raised a hand and said, "No. Don't do it." He was smiling although there was a large, greenish bruise already coming out on the forehead. "This is mine. He's all mine. Let me take him downstairs." His eyes glowed with a quality which might have been warmth if Wulff had not known better. "Come on," he said to Wulff and carefully took out his service revolver, levelled it, "let's take a walk. I'd hate to have to report that you were shot and killed in the process of attempted escape."

Wulff looked back toward the sergeant who sat there quietly, hands folded, then he looked at the two cops, finally he moved slowly toward them. He had handled it wrong, he supposed; coming into custody had been a mistake. He had sealed himself in now. It all started with wrecking the van and letting himself get picked up but, of course, it had happened a long time before that. He had been set on this road from the time he had walked into a building on West 93rd Street. Someone was going to get killed downstairs, he decided, because he was not going to submit. The phone on the sergeant's desk rang. He stood there; the cop put a hand on his shoulder, the sergeant was talking quietly. The cop started to pull him out of the room.

"Hold it," the sergeant said suddenly in a voice of enormous disgust and surprise. "Just hold it." He took his hand off the mouthpiece, continued talking, listened. "All right," he said, "all right, then." He seemed to listen some more, shook his head, replaced the phone with a crash. He stood and Wulff noted that the shoulders and chest gave a deceptive impression of mass, actually the sergeant was a rather thin, spindly man below the waist, the legs seeming barely adequate to hold his weight, his pose showing unsteadiness. Probably retired to a desk position for incapacity.

"Would you believe this?" the sergeant said with disgust. "That was federal offices calling. They want to pick this guy up."

"Who?" the cop said, not releasing Wulff. "Who is this guy anyway?"

The sergeant's mind was still back, apparently, on the injury of the call itself. "I can't believe it," he said, "I can't believe it."

"Just downstairs for a few minutes," the cop said furiously. "Just let me at him for a few minutes."

"Can't do it," the sergeant said. "I cannot fucking do it." His dismay was total. He turned toward Wulff. "Wulff," he said, "we won't forget this. Now sit the hell down."

So Wulff went to the bench against the wall and sat. And did not know, after all, how he approached the issue of salvation. It was good to know that he was headed out of their hands and that he was, after all, getting where he wanted to go from the first.

But how the hell had they found him here?

# Chapter 18

Randall, uncomfortable in the uniform of a federal marshal but otherwise almost at peace, proceeded in the car Calabrese had given him to the city jail, being careful to observe all rules and regulations. Calabrese had made it quite clear to him that once he left the mansion on Michigan Avenue he was completely on his own. "I can set this up and give you what you need," Calabrese had said, "but that's where it ends. If anything happens to you it happens to *you,* and if I'm ever tied up with it you're finished. You understand that? And I don't mean any quick easy death. Do you understand that?"

Randall understood that. Now that he had dealt with Calabrese he had a total comprehension of the man. He arranged things at a distance and then he stepped away. And if you did not realize that, if you tried to carry him one step further than he had gone, you were finished.

The way Calabrese had set the whole thing up was amazing. It confirmed the feeling that working for Versallo had given him over the years: that in all the world there were only five or six men who carried absolute power within their individual specialties, and at these top levels everything was arranged very simply and quickly. It was only when you slipped below the very top that life looked confusing and complex; at the summit everything could be worked out with a couple of phone calls.

Calabrese had sent him out of the room; Randall had sat for twenty minutes in a large, bare area down the hall smoking cigarettes and looking at the traffic in and out of the servant's quarters. Calabrese apparently had a large staff. A woman who might have been Calabrese's wife came over at one point and asked if there was anything he needed and Randall said no, he was fine, he didn't want to trouble anyone. He suspected that Calabrese would not have liked the idea that his wife was involved at all with anyone who saw him professionally and that it would be better to keep his distance. At the end of the twenty minutes Calabrese himself had peered out the doorway at the end of the hall and motioned Randall back in, had told him bluntly, "Your man is at a precinct station on the South Side. I've told them to hold him for your pickup."

"That's good," Randall said.

"It's not so good," said Calabrese, "it's not so good at all, it's a little complicated. He's been trying to see a federal prosecutor named Wilson, your man has. Do you know that?"

"Why?"

"That doesn't matter," Calabrese said, "it's all been arranged. He's waiting there to be picked up and they think that a federal marshal is going to be the one to get him. You'll be the federal marshal."

It was all going a little too rapidly for Randall. "Where does the federal prosecutor come into this?" he said to gain time. "What does this Wulff want with him?"

"That doesn't matter at all. That is all taken care of. You will pick him up at the precinct station in an hour," Calabrese said, looking at his watch, "and you will dispose of him."

"He'll think that I'm a federal marshal?"

"Exactly," Calabrese said, and permitted his eyes to take on one, small glint of satisfaction, as if he allowed himself one of these at rare occasions out of some defined quota. "That is all arranged."

"Will I have any help?"

Calabrese looked at him impassively, the glint gone. Everything back to normal now in that face which was both impassive and at some deep level completely observant. "You do not need any help," he said. "Help was never spelled out to be any kind of requirement."

"All right," Randall said, feeling an uneasy excitement, "I'll do it alone. I want to get the son of a bitch."

"I know you do."

"I'm supposed to be dressed as a federal marshal?"

"You will find clothing in the trunk of the car you're being loaned. Go to a gas station and change there. Afterwards disposition of the car is entirely up to you, Randall. I would prefer however," Calabrese said, "that this car not be found. A word to the wise."

"All right," Randall said again. "Tell me where he is, that's all."

"You will be advised of your destination by the guard as you leave the grounds," Calabrese said, "which I suggest that you do immediately."

Randall shook his head in honest wonderment. "You don't leave anything to chance, do you?" he said.

"I try not to. In my business chance would merely be a complicating factor. Our business is done, Randall, we have finished our discussion and I would prefer that you leave by the door nearest to you at the hallway." Calabrese went for the pack of cigarettes again, broke one and then, as if allowing himself a special treat, in the first display of emotion which Randall had yet seen from the man, he plucked out another and broke that as well, giving out a little *ah!* of pleasure.

"What about the valise?" Randall said at the door. "Do I take that with me?"

"The valise? What valise?"

"The valise that I brought in; the valise that I offered—"

Calabrese stood in one casual gesture, looked at Randall. Randall had not realized it; he was quite a tall man, over six feet, slightly stooped in the way that tall men are when they edge above their sixties, holding in his stomach in that tight, self-conscious way which meant that he probably had a paunch. He looked cadaverous in this posture but the way in which he held himself told the tale. *Don't smile,* Randall thought and this was really an unnecessary warning because looking at the eyes of the man any impulse to look for humor vanished. He had never seen eyes like this. Calabrese had kept them shrouded throughout their dialogue so far, it was as if he had held himself down, had *contrived* a look for himself. But now a different Calabrese peeked cautiously out of his face and decided that he did not like what was seen. "I know nothing about the valise," Calabrese said.

"All right," said Randall, "that's okay; I had only offered—"

"I remember absolutely nothing about any valise. Did you come here with a valise? You came here with no valise. You came here empty handed with a request, and out of the goodness of my heart I listened to you. Now you are about to leave and you mention a valise. You must have a false memory, and this would be a very dangerous thing, Randall, for you to go around giving people the impression that you came here with goods and that Calabrese sent you away without them. That would be a slur upon my reputation, which as you know is excellent. Do you remember any valise, Mario?" Calabrese said, and a short, deadly-looking man holding a gun suddenly appeared behind Randall in the doorway, looking at Randall with great interest. "This man seem to be claiming that he came here with baggage."

"I don't remember nothing," the man said.

"Mario's memory is excellent," Calabrese said. "He is paid to notice and to observe many things and I am absolutely dependent upon him for what might be called detail work. You remember no valise, however, do you Mario?"

"None," the man said.

"You see?" Calabrese said. "Your false impression has been corrected. Surely you admit your mistake now, do you not?"

"Of course," Randall said. Once again that feeling of being entirely out of his class assaulted him. It was true; it was true. He could not deal with this man; he was not even at a point where Calabrese truly had to acknowledged him. He was, in Calabrese's mind, merely a construction, like Mario, upon which certain requests like confetti were tossed. Versallo had been tough but not at this level. Randall had never dealt with anything like this.

"I think that Mario will help you to the car in which you came," Calabrese said. "You appear to be a little confused and in need of an escort."

"I came with no—"

"This man thinks that he did not drive up in a car, Mario," Calabrese said, "he seems to have lost his senses completely; claiming not to have a car, claiming to have a valise. What help do you think this man needs in finding his memory?"

"I'm sure we can think of something," Mario said and gave Randall an enormous smile, one of such sweetness that Randall imagined that he would see flies buzz out of the man's mouth in an instant, the same flies that would fester around a cake in a decayed room. "Why don't you come along and we'll work things out?"

Randall stood his ground, not believing that this was happening to him, not willing to accept the fact that he had come to Calabrese as an equal, to appeal for help and was going to end up being mugged and shot by one of Calabrese's men but then, the old man smiled himself, an odd, uneven, wintry little smile that seemed to break down the component parts of his body: slouch, paunch, concave chest, high forehead seen as individual parts floating around the nexus that was Calabrese, rather than assembled into a whole, and Randall saw he had been set up for this like a child and that Calabrese was amused. This was the old man's sense of humor; he was playing. He found it amusing that Randall would think that now he was going to be shot. Calabrese raised a hand and pointed. "Mario will take you to your car," he said, "and I'm sure that your memory and powers of recall will sharpen on the drive. Go now. Go."

So Randall went. Mario led him through the hallway and into the rear of the grounds where he found himself in an enormous garaging area; acres of land which never could have been seen or sensed from the front, cars and trucks scattered through this acreage in all states of repair and preparedness. Calabrese had almost as much area back here as Versallo had had in the warehouse. Of course that was a common tactic, Randall understood; the chieftains would buy up acreage adjoining their own houses for whatever exorbitant price was necessary and would often demolish what structures had been on this acreage ... simply for privacy. So he should not have been as surprised as he was by the sheer dimensions of Calabrese's holdings but then again he *was,* that was all, it reminded him—if he needed reminding at that point—that Calabrese meant business. He had taken the valise and put him in a car, given him instructions on where and how to get Wulff ... and now, he was supposed to do the job. The Calabreses of this world or any other did not extend themselves to efforts of this sort unless they intended completion. If he failed ...

Well, he would not fail, Randall thought, yanking the wheel of the small Falcon viciously, almost past his exit, pouring the car down the ramp at the last possible moment, all six cylinders whining and screaming beneath him. The Falcon had even been overlaid with a federal seal on the right passenger entrance; a deep khaki color it looked like every expressionless vehicle which he had seen on Army posts or outside the federal buildings. Calabrese was a careful man; no detail was beyond him.

In the uniform, in fact, Randall felt somewhat official himself; if the uniform indeed was the man, shaping and framing the personality as theory had it, then he did not feel like anything so much as a federal marshal at this moment. He was going in his capacity as a federal marshal to pick up Wulff and convey him to the office buildings where the grand jury was in session. He even *thought* like a federal marshal, and it occurred to him that if he could go on thinking in this way it would be very easy, could continue being quite easy right up until the moment when he killed Wulff.

Which he would. He would do this because he wanted to avenge Versallo, that was the original impulse and not to be discounted, but beyond that he would do it for another reason: he did not want to think of what might happen to him from Calabrese if he did not. Calabrese was serious. How he had located Wulff, how precisely he had made the arrangements for the pickup he did not know but he knew this: any man who was willing to extend this kind of effort was not to be trifled with.

It was either Wulff or him now. It was that simple.

Randall brought the car to a stop in front of the precinct, wedging it within a row of illegally-parked private vehicles with police stickers, and went up the steps and into the grim, green reception area and found that his man, flanked by two cops, was already waiting for him. He had never seen Wulff before but he would have recognized him anywhere. There was no trouble in knowing the man, not only from the photographs which had been passed around through channels with the bounty offer some weeks ago. No, there was in the eyes of this tall man, flanked by cops, and waiting for him, an intensity not unlike that which he had seen in Calabrese's. Yes, Wulff was of the same stripe as Calabrese; here was another one who believed in himself, believed in his ability to control situations and who, no doubt, was able to convey that intensity so well that there were almost no situations which he was *not* able to control. State of mind, state of will. One of the cops stepped forward and said, "You took long enough."

"Did the best I could," Randall said, feeling uncomfortable. Were the cops in it or not? Did they know that this was a setup or did they take him for federal staff? It was best to play it completely straight, of course. "We have to work on schedule too," Randall said, trying to think like a federal marshal would. "We've got a caseload."

"I don't give a shit about your fucking caseload," the cop said, pushing Wulff forward as if he were a bag of fruit. Wulff took a calm pace forward, looked at Randall levelly. "Just get him the fuck out of here right now." So the cop was pissed off, to be sure, that Calabrese had taken away his play for an afternoon, that was clear. "I said now," the cop said and Wulff kept that level stare on Randall.

"All right," Randall said, "I'll do the best I can." He took a pair of handcuffs that had been dangling from his waist and maneuvered them off his belt buckle with some difficulty, held them out. Wulff, still giving that amused, level stare extended his hands, held them that way and Randall put the cuffs around them.

He had never realized until this moment how *difficult* it was to cuff a man; it always looked easy when cops did it and the movies made nothing of it at all but it was a strange, sweaty job. The cuffs seemed too small for the wrists, they would not come all the way around and then he was unable to lever them in properly, he tried to compensate by adding more pressure but pressure simply buckled them. They slipped away from his grasp and fell to the floor with a little clang. The cop with a detached grin stood there saying nothing. Feeling inept, Randall bent over, picked up the cuffs and tried again. "No," Wulff said as Randall tried to loop one wrist. "That's not the way. You've got to work against the pressure point," and then, one-handed showed Randall what he was talking about. Randall, feeling that he was beginning to blush let Wulff help him and at a certain point the cop came over and finished the job. Wulff's hands, cuffed, fell to stomach level.

"It's generally better to do them behind the back," the cop said, "that way they can't come up over their head high," he pantomimed this, "and then come down on your head," and he made a sweeping gesture which just missed Randall by an inch or so. Randall felt a moment of fury and resisted an insane impulse to seize the gun from his jacket and begin to shoot. He could certainly get Wulff and the cop before anyone here knew what was happening. He decided that he did not want to do this however. He restrained the impulse quickly, noting that five or six cops who had been lounging around the desk were fastening profound stares on him. "That's all right," Randall said, "he won't do anything."

"You mean, you really know how to take them into custody," the cop said, "all of that fine training under federal auspices, right?"

Wulff said, "The man's only trying to do a job, officer. Give him a break," and the cop gave Wulff a look of hatred, his hands coiling unconsciously into fists. There had undoubtedly been difficulties before he had even walked into this one, Randall thought. Calabrese had done the job but maybe it had not been necessary after all; these cops might have killed Wulff themselves and saved him all of this trouble. He decided not to dwell on the irony of this, it did not appeal to him. He pointed the gun at Wulff. "Come on," he said, "let's go."

Wulff shrugged and began moving. Randall let him pass, then moved in behind him. The cop gave Randall a swat on the buttocks as they moved toward the door.

"You show him the real stuff," the cop said and all the others around the desk laughed. They really did not like federal personnel here, that was clear. Fuck them. Fuck all of the sons of bitches. Randall fell into line, took Wulff down the steps. Now he was on his own, a strange, vacant barren feeling hitting him along with the wind. At the door Wulff paused, waiting. Randall opened the rear door and Wulff slid in.

"I'm going to let you sit that way without restraint," Randall said.

"I'll cooperate."

"I'll assume you'll cooperate," Randall said. "I'll be driving one-handed with the gun out and I can see everything in the rear-view mirror. I want you to sit at the extreme right of the rear seat."

"I'll do that," Wulff said, "I'm not going to make any trouble at all." He sounded almost meek. This was not the man that Randall had been reading about; it surely did not sound like the kind of man who could kill Versallo as Versallo had been killed. "I want to get where we're going as badly as you do," he said.

"Then cooperate," Randall said. "Just be reasonable and there'll be no trouble at all," and slammed the door on Wulff, walked around the other side and got behind the wheel, holding the gun in a good, light grip all the time.

How well did Wulff know Chicago? If he knew it well there would be hell to pay when he realized that they were heading in the wrong direction. But even so he had a few moments clearance until he hit the expressway, heading toward the marshes. After that, as Calabrese had said, he was on his own. All right, he was on his own.

Randall started the car. He felt the killing lust once again firm within him. He put the car into gear. He drove.

# Chapter 19

Wulff knew early on that he had put himself into a box. Who did this clown in front think that he was fooling? He was no federal marshal and this was no federal car. Nor were they going in the proper direction. It was one of the crudest fake-up jobs of a vehicle he had ever seen; on the other hand, maybe it was a pretty good job, it was just that he had seen so many of these doctored vehicles in the NYPD that it seemed laughably obvious to him. Maybe not to the men that had done it though. Give them credit.

He knew that he had been sucked in, phonied in somehow, but he found the situation so interesting that for the time being all he did was sit back, his wrists beginning to ache slightly within the clamp of the handcuffs, and take in the situation. The audacity of the ploy was amazing to him; also if he was not being taken to Patrick Wilson, exactly where *was* he going? And how deeply was Wilson involved in some kind of illegality if a trade-off like this could be maneuvered? It was fascinating; it also, he knew, probably involved his life but he would get to that soon or sooner. In the meantime, he and the driver were working in accord, and that was to their benefit. Both he and the driver shared one overwhelming purpose; they were getting him away from the Chicago cops. That was a good thing. That was really the most that Wulff could have asked, to have gotten out of that precinct house at the time that he did. The situation, menacing at best, had shown signs of deteriorating into an irretrievable ugliness and he was not sure, ultimately, that he would have been able to have gotten free of this one. Maybe. Maybe he would have finally gotten himself booked and thrown into a cell but he suspected that there was a good deal that would happen to him before then. Booked into a hospital bed, most likely.

He leaned back in the seat, his wrists aching progressively from the handcuffs and looked at the back of the driver's neck. This was not the neck of a federal marshal either; there was a certain aura which came off people like this which, dealing with them as he had, no one could miss. It would be just possible, he thought, to lean forward and strike the man before he would have a chance to react. This could be done. But what then? The car would lurch out of control and the driver would certainly have the presence of mind to make the accident a devastating one. That determination would be communicated to Wulff, as a deterrent of course.

"How soon will we be there?" Wulff said.

The driver said nothing. He yanked the wheel left and right and they were on a flat open avenue, East St. Louis, Wulff guessed, heading north at forty or fifty miles an hour. "Is this the right direction?" Wulff said. The driver still refused to talk. Wulff leaned forward, jamming a knee into the seat in front of him and said, "I have a right to know, I think."

"No conversation," the driver said. "I told you that."

"I'm not making conversation. I asked you one question."

"Keep your fucking questions to yourself," the driver said. He reached across the seat, hefted the gun, showed it to Wulff by raising it against the windshield. "I mean that."

"That's not too bright," Wulff said, "showing a gun in a crowded area. We might get pulled over. The cops here are very alert."

"Shut the fuck up," the driver said and moved the car faster. He seemed to be afflicted with a kind of sullenness, a dangerous, deteriorating gloom spreading out from him. Wulff caught it. That gloom probably had something to do with the fact that the driver was considering the true implications of what lay ahead of him. Up until this moment he had never really confronted the necessity to murder Wulff *mano a mano*. He had been possessed with the excitement of getting him out of the precinct and into the car. My sympathies, Wulff thought, and just to keep the man preoccupied said, "I've got a lot of information to give, you know."

"I don't know anything."

"That's why I wanted to get to Patrick Wilson, you understand. There are a lot of important details I can give him, specifics for the investigation." Would he really talk this way if he did not know what was truly going on here? Probably not. He warned himself to cool it.

"I told you and I tell you the last time," the driver said, "I don't want no fucking conversation."

He hunched over the wheel, holding the gun like he might a cigar and concentrated on speed. The car burst free of traffic lights and, as was so common in even the densest of the metropolitan areas, found itself on what had become a flat highway, low buildings and barren land around them, flowing out of the city. There was no city that man could construct so complex that it did not, ten to fifteen miles in most directions away from its central point, fall away.

Wulff looked out the rear window where he could see the buildings of Chicago wrapped in smog and filth. If the junkies had their shit, then the cities had pollution. Same thing. Shroud events, corrupt realities. The car swerved to the side. They had come suddenly into a deserted, abandoned area; the car curving on a side-road now almost hidden from the main, a few dismal buildings poking up from the flats around which the car circled. It looked like an abandoned dispatch station of some sort; years ago before the cars and suburbs destroyed public transportation, buses or trolleys must have been sent out of this area; there were still the remains of tracks, gutted and porous, lying half-exposed in the mud and ancient ruts left from tires. Twenty years ago this must have been a very busy place, Wulff thought, hundreds of men must have worked here moving out the network. But now, as they came close on the crumbling buildings, looking through open spaces in the ruined concrete to the patches of darkness inside he decided that it was no such place anymore. Places like this served only one function and that was murder. Thirty or forty years ago the gangs had had to load their victims into cars and take them to Evanston or Joliet to dump them ... now they could do it in the inner city. There was an irony in there somewhere, Wulff supposed, if he wanted to bother looking for it.

The car stopped, shuddering a little. The man in the front tilted down the sun-visor, took the pistol, turned on Wulff. The handcuffs were really biting in now. The cop may have laughed in the precinct but the man had done a good job. He knew his work. Clumsily applied the handcuffs had almost stopped circulation not only in the hands but moving up to the shoulders as well. Wulff felt that he was close to losing control of his arms. "All right," the man said, holding the gun on him, "everybody out."

"This is no marshal's office."

"You noticed that."

"This is no federal building," Wulff said, "and you're no marshal."

"Is that so?" the man said. With the gun in his hand, turning to face Wulff fully without the distraction of having to handle the car he seemed to have come to some full sense of himself, indeed seemed to be enjoying things. "You noticed that."

"You must think I'm some kind of fool," Wulff said.

"Oh no. I don't think you're any kind of fool at all. You're Martin Wulff and the last thing I'd call you is a fool. Get out of the fucking car," the man said.

"And if I don't?"

"Then I'll shoot you right in the back seat and let the bloodstains puddle out. But I'd rather have the car to get back where I'm going and I figure that it's worth a minute more of life to you to cooperate with me." The man brushed hair out of his eyes, sweating lightly. "Get out of the car," he said again.

He was right, of course. You could talk about death as an abstraction, calculate your willingness to accept death in the face of many things or even as a gesture. But people, almost all people, when they were forced right down to it would do almost anything at all for an instant more of life. They would suck cock, dig their own graves, slobber and beg, dance in circles or lie in a terminal bed in a hospital ward somewhere, juice dripping into their veins like heroin while they wheezed and gasped against the life supports for just one more breath. Just one more breath, steer clear of death; we know life, Wulff thought, but we know nothing of what is contained outside of it. Life is only a fraction of experience, this is true, but it is that fraction we know and that is why, righteous or evil, pious or profane, even the most fanatical preacher would deny God under gunpoint just so that he could have enough breath to deliver that denial. Sadness, sadness: he had learned more about death than he ever wanted to know and this man had not misjudged him. Oddly, however, he did not have a sense of crisis. This man was a professional but Wulff was pretty sure that he could not kill him. It was just a question of feeling.

"I can't move," he said, "I've lost circulation in my arms. Besides, how am I supposed to open the door?"

The man had not thought about it. He was so involved with the gun and murder that the simple logistics of the thing had escaped him. His face contracted with thought, "All right," he said, "that's a point. I'll get out and go over and open that door near you and then you'll come out." He turned, opened the driver's door and ducked to move his head below roof-level. "Don't try any shit," he said.

Wulff, poised behind the seat, brought all of his weight down on his buttocks and lashed out with a heel. He had been concentrating on this for several moments, gently working his legs up against the seat, getting his kneecaps almost to the top and then away so that he would have an angle of impact. Now, his foot, pointed sidewise, connected with the man's neck just below the medulla. It was a sidewise impact, the man seeing it, already ducking away, trying to get his gun on Wulff. But the blow was stunning and he was unable to make coordination between hand and gun, his hand shaking on the trigger, finger palpitating against the trigger; then finally he got off a shot, ill-aimed, smashing into the rear window above Wulff's head and the recoil of the shot atop the momentum of the kick sent him spinning all the way out into the dirt, head-first. Wulff yanked desperately at the lever on the left side trying to get at the man but his arms had almost been deadened by the handcuffs; from wrists to neck he felt little more than a numbing ache where his arms had been. The man hit the ground and rolled, came up.

He came up slowly with an expression of terror but when he saw what had happened, that Wulff was still battering helplessly at the door, struggling with the lever to get out, the terror went away, running out of him like blood and in place of it came a slow, eager smile which was like the one on the face of a child about to be offered an illicit gift. His eyes were stunned but slowly they came into focus looking at Wulff and then, as if he had all the time in the world the man paused, shook himself and began very casually to knock the dirt from his clothing, brushing from thigh to knee, knee to raised instep, instep to ground and only then, when his appearance had met some internal standard, did he look downward, spot the gun, pick it up and then walk slowly toward Wulff. There was a jauntiness to his step, a brightness to his carriage. He might have been walking forward to receive communion.

Wulff stopped trying to work on the lever two-handed. Instead he remembered an old trick from judo training at Fort Bragg many years ago: find the pressure-point. The least force is the greatest if applied at the proper juncture. He put his index finger into the space between the lever and the door and rather than trying to force it up through arm movement used just the tip of the finger, keeping the finger rigid, using his arm as pivot to ease it up.

It opened and the door unhinged just as the man with the gun was walking toward him, the gun already in the process of being levelled. Wulff inhaled, drew back both legs and in that moment before the door could click closed again, kicked out ferociously, slamming the door so hard that it almost broke free of its hinges to go spinning into the marshes beyond.

Instead, the opening door hit the man.

It hit him squarely across the stomach and he gasped, gave an *uh!* of surprise and pain and then went stumbling back, his eyes wheeling, his mouth opened like a dog's, struck in the solar plexus. Barely able to breathe he dropped the gun in order to gather breath, the gun twinkling away from him and Wulff leapt upon him then, closing the ground in a heavy, chopping run which tore his own breath from him and then huddled against the man in brief but horrid embrace, looking once again for that pressure-point.

He had no arms, really, and the man, as hard-hit as he was, had two but there was the recollection of judo training once again to remind Wulff that what mattered was not strength but leverage, not condition but distance ... and if he could close upon the man tightly, face to face with him, hold him within that limited range, then he had cancelled out the only real advantage the man had. Distance for the enemy was strength; it would enable him to bring his arms into play, get at the gun again. But if there was no distance there would only be equality and Wulff closed that gap to less than an inch, breathing against the man, feeling the storming, gasping breath of the man hit in the plexus coming back at him. It was an intimacy of a sort, almost the kind of intimacy one might have with a woman, the bodies shoved against one another, engaging in an exchange which was horrid rather than graceful but equally total.

Wulff brought his arms, completely numb now, above his head and used them as a wedge to bring them down upon the man in a battering smash, the man cried out and tried to drop back a pace but Wulff straightened him with a knee to the jaw and now, looking at him in sudden anguish the man's face exploded blood like a pulped fruit, running. He screamed, a scream of mingled hopelessness and pain as he realized that he would not be able to get to the gun before Wulff destroyed him. He struck out feebly and Wulff dodged the blow, brought a knee up again to the damaged plexus and the man fell to his side in the mud, gasping. He opened his mouth and tried to vomit but absolutely nothing would come out. Wulff was reminded of Versallo. "Son of a bitch," the man said, grasping for the syllables like twigs, breaking them off, painfully, one by one. "You dirty son of a bitch."

"The key," Wulff said. He kept the man pinned, knee-to-thigh. "Get the key."

The man shook his head back and forth in agony. Tears were in his eyes. "No," he said and then struggled for breath once again, reaching deep into himself. Little sand puffs came up around them. "No. No."

"Get the key and get these off," Wulff said, "or I'll hit you in the stomach again."

The man's eyes registered horror but still he shook his head. He was a tough one, all right; in full possession of himself he had been the toughest that Wulff had yet faced in this miserable, tormented city. Not at all like Versallo who was completely surface; shake him and he turned inside-out. "I won't do it," he said, "you'll kill me."

"I'll kill you anyway," Wulff said. "Don't you think I will? Can't you believe that." And the man shook his head but his eyes said *yes, I believe that, I believe you would kill me,* and Wulff saw himself rimmed in those tiny, credulous eyes, unspeakably ferocious, leaning over the man. He saw how he must have looked and the effect was terrible. The man's hands were fluttering all over his body, ducking and diving into various little crevices, his eyes now contracting against the sand. "Can't find it," he said hoarsely.

"Find it," Wulff said and slapped him across the face. The man's jowls quivered, the blow knocked ten years off him and suddenly he was fifty, haggard, squirming and struggling in his pockets like a little old man looking for a subway token. Then, in a palm like a pearl, there was a key.

Wulff extended his braced arms. "Unlock them now," he said.

The man resisted feebly, shaking his head again. "No," he said, but it was only the squalling, balking resistance of the imbecile. Wulff brought him back to attention by slapping him on the face again. Now the man looked ashen, senile; the key dipped in his grasp and then he aimed it toward the handcuffs. Wulff held his arms there, waiting. They had moved beyond deadness to a strange, clinging warmth as if there were moisture or oozing fluid within. That was the next to last stage, he knew, before circulation failed completely and he would be left with gangrene regardless of what happened next. The man had braced him in this way deliberately, counting on getting Wulff eventually even should he fail. It had been a foolproof plan indeed but he simply had not counted on poor luck and lack of foresight. Somehow he got the key in. Wulff inverted his wrists and let the key turn.

The cuffs fell away; they bounced off the man's forehead and then onto the ground. Wulff stood, walked away from the man then and walked twenty yards or so to where the pistol lay, picked it up, and put it in his pocket. Then he walked further from the man, behind a little hedge, the only touch of vegetation in this blasted area and there he stood awaiting for the pain of returning circulation to hit him.

It took a minute or two for the blood to begin its motion, and for the next three or four minutes—as he had thought—he stood there absolutely helpless. The pain was exquisite and tormenting, so much so that if Wulff had been alone he would have screamed from the sensation much in the way that he screamed during sex. But screaming was the wrong thing to do. The man lying on the ground was in pain but he was not in the least stupid; if he deduced that Wulff was helpless he might, despite his own agony, chance making a rush at him, and Wulff, not able to move his arms without agony, doubted that he would be able to reach the gun. The man might have a chance of overcoming him. Smart of him to pick the gun off the ground anyway. He could have kicked the man into unconsciousness first but he did not want to do this. Wulff needed information.

At length, in little sobs and squirts of anguish the pain began to subside. He was able to focus his eyes once again, was able to move his arms, was able to see and care that the man uprange had dragged himself to his knees and was now regarding Wulff from that crouched, penitential position with a look of hate as profound as he had ever seen. Wulff walked in that direction, took the gun out of his pocket and pointed it at the man.

"All right," he said, "now we're going to talk."

The man could breathe a little better; his voice was under control although very soft. "No we're not," he said.

"Yes we are."

"Make me."

"What's your name?"

"I won't tell you. I won't tell you anything."

"Why did you want to kill me?"

The man, amazingly, smiled. "Doesn't everyone?" he said.

"I don't know. I don't keep statistics. You did. Why?"

"I'm not talking. I told you that." The man weaved in the ground, got a foot underneath him. He half-rose.

Wulff stepped forward and hit him in the mouth. The man weaved and collapsed to the ground. Wulff kicked him in the shins.

"Come on," he said, "talk. Tell me."

On the ground, the man shook his head. His agony had transported him; his face, incredibly, held confidence. "No," he said, "we won't talk."

"We're going to sooner or later. Why not now? Who sent you? Did Wilson send you himself? Is this a setup?"

The man held himself in frieze. "I won't tell you," he said.

Wulff reached out, feeling the restored circulation in his arm, seized the man by the collar and dragged him neatly upwards to face level. "You're going to talk," he said. "Otherwise I'm going to kill you. You know that, don't you? You know I'm serious."

Sweat was all over the man's face and pain had long since given the skin an impacted density but his voice was low and controlled. "You killed Versallo," he said, "because of that I was going to kill you. I still would if I had the chance. You know that."

"You worked for Versallo?"

"No more," the man said. "I've told you all I'm ever going to."

"Who gave you the car? The uniform? Who set this up? Who paid off Wilson? Is Wilson in on it?"

The man kept that expression on him. His lips were set. "I've never had a wife," he said. "I have no family, no children, I've never been able to enjoy a normal scx act with a normal woman, everything I've had was lent to me by other men for whom I was working. But I have one thing and that's honor. You can't take that away, Wulff and you know it. You'd have to kill me. You *will* kill me, but I won't talk."

Looking at him, Wulff saw it. He knew that the man was telling the truth. He could kill the man but he could not break him. If nothing else this man had that, and looking at him, seeing the stubbornness, something close to the divine in it—if only for the most profane of purposes—Wulff could feel admiration. The man had strength. If nothing else he had that will, that interior which had to be respected.

No wonder, he thought, that Versallo had used him. Versallo knew what manner of avenger he would have.

Wulff looked at the man and he looked away and he realized that he could not kill him. Killing was all right, although the one of Versallo had turned him inside out for a while in its sheer brutality and horror. Still, killing was all right, it was a necessary means to an end and dealing at this level of the culture it was often the only effective tactic. But you killed only for gain. You could not kill in a vacuum, simply for the pleasure of killing because that made you no better, in fact it made you worse than them, because for them as well killing was only an administrative act, part of the operating equipment of a business. No, he could not do it. Wulff turned in disgust, broke open the gun, removed the cartridges left and threw it in the hedge. Behind him, the man drew in a deep, groaning breath and then expelled it as laughter. Wulff did not want to look at his face. He was not ready for that, not just yet.

A car slewed into the yard in one shrieking slide, a Buick Electra 225, and three men in suits and hats came out of it quickly, lightly. All of them held guns and all of them looked confident. Wulff, caught short, without a weapon, could do nothing. He stood there and then in utter disgust, spread his palms.

Damaged as he was, his assailant was now laughing. The tallest of the three men turned that way and the laughter stopped. "Randall, you stupid son of a bitch, you can't do anything right," the man said and Randall looked at the ground. "You really fucked this one up," the man said, shook his head, looked at Wulff, looked away. "What a fuckup, Randall," he said, and then he nodded to the two others and they closed quickly. Wulff felt swift and sure hands upon him and then, quickly, he was bound.

"Personally," the man who had been speaking said, "I'd like to kill both of the bastards right here but orders are orders. So let's take them in."

Wulff felt himself being prodded toward the Electra. Randall, being handled more roughly, was clouted behind the ear by the man guarding him, fell into the back in a screaming dive.

The rest of them got into the Electra, roomy and cavernous inside, air-conditioning clamoring away. And the three men brought them in.

# Chapter 20

Calabrese knew that Randall was going to fuck up. Of course he was going to fuck up; the man always had, anyone who worked for Versallo was a loser from the start. Versallo ran a lousy operation even though, for some reason, he had a lot of employees and got loyalty from them. The sympathy felt for the man who is really soft inside, Calabrese decided. Still, he had to give Randall enough rope. If this was going to work out in the optimum way, then he at least had to give Randall the *opportunity* to do the job. But Calabrese took no chances. You did not get where he was, become what he had become, by working on any margin at all.

He sent men to trail Randall.

Now it had worked out just as he had feared it would. Here they came up the drive, past the guardhouse, the Electra filled with bodies, the guard already reporting over the intercom phone that not only Randall but Wulff had been brought back in the car. That meant only one thing, that Randall had fucked it up. Because if he had not, Wulff would have already been dead, the following *soldat* would have noted that with pleasure, would have disposed of Randall as per their instructions and would then have cleaned out of the area. But their instructions otherwise were explicit, and the *soldat* did not get or keep their positions by being creative. If Randall had not done the job, disposed of Wulff within an hour ... pick them both up and bring them here.

The trouble was, Calabrese thought, that old sayings were true ones: the only way to be sure of getting a job done the way you wanted it was to do it yourself. He should not have dispatched Randall on this errand. It was too dangerous and the man's record which Calabrese had studied carefully indicated that he was beyond his depth. Still, it had seemed too easy; he could not have really passed up what fell into his lap. Here was a chance to get rid of Wulff, who was a source of much despair to Calabrese, with minimum risk. He would not even have to use one of his own men. His own men would be tied only to disposition of Randall, which was routine work. But *now* look at it. Gloomily he watched the men spill from the Electra, Wulff bound up, yet somehow still strangely possessed of himself just as Calabrese would have known him to be, Randall showing all the signs of a bad beating, staggering from the car, being supported by two of the gunmen as he almost fell. That had been some beautiful job Randall had done, all right. Instead of being killed by Calabrese's men, he had been saved by them. Son of a bitch.

Calabrese went back to his desk and waited. The instructions were explicit, bring up Wulff, dispose of Randall at once. It would have to be done on the grounds here but in a clean, efficient fashion. He wanted nothing more to do with Randall; he had had only one potential purpose and had failed. Now the thing was to make sure that he was dead. Wulff on the other hand he wanted to see. He had hoped that he would never have this confrontation but as he waited for the men to bring the man up he succumbed to a weird anticipation. Yes, it was true. He had actually been waiting to see this man for a long time. It may have worked out for the best after all, because he badly wanted to see the man.

He wanted to see the man who had killed Cicchini, killed Marasco, smashed up a townhouse, sunk a freighter, bombed out the Paradise in Vegas, cut up half of Havana too. This was a remarkable man; he should not, after all, have the opportunity of meeting him taken away. *Everything for the best,* Calabrese thought, without irony. Randall had done him a favor after all.

He would see the son of a bitch.

The two *soldat* who had been accompanying Randall came in with Wulff, having switched. One would be sufficient to dispose of Randall in his condition, the *soldat* had decided, and Calabrese would want two men in the room with him at all times while he dealt with this one. That was good thinking. That showed the kind of independent thought and ability to make individual decisions which Calabrese tried to drill into his troops, to take a little initiative, share some responsibility. More than anything else, he thought, it was the secret of his power. You had to know how to run a shop and when to run it, but you also had to know how the hell to delegate authority. Failure to understand that simple fact had destroyed most of the organization throughout the country ... might finish off his, he thought grimly, after he could no longer oversee it. "Sit down," he said to Wulff.

The man, still bound, shook his head. "No," he said in an expressionless tone, "I'll stand."

"Much easier if you sit," Calabrese said. He nodded to the *soldat* covering him. "Unbind the man," he said.

"That's a good idea," Wulff said without emotion, "I'm going to get fucking gangrene if you don't."

Calabrese looked at the man with something near amusement as the *soldat* unbound him. It was really a shame, he thought. A man like this could have been so useful; he could have done so many things for his interests. (Calabrese did not think in terms of anything so rigid as *organization;* there were only interest-groups functioning along defined lines of power). He could have been such a credit to what Calabrese represented. And yet this man was lost to him. Wulff believed himself to be implacably opposed to everything which Calabrese represented, he would probably fight to death any implication that he and Calabrese shared characteristics in common. Yet they did, they always had: the outcome of a man was not so much his convictions, Calabrese had always felt, as his circumstances. Wulff might have, in another world, been him, he might have been Wulff. But it was too late to try to impress that on the man now. Still, what a *soldat* he would have been! Doubtless the man lacked that capacity for organizational grasp and abstraction which was the key to getting to the very summit, but oh my could he have carried out a command! It was a shame, that was all, a damned shame.

"I brought you in here to talk to you," Calabrese said. "I've heard a lot about you, I wanted to see if you were real."

Wulff did not react. He looked down at the floor. The *soldat* murmured and came to his sides, ready to help Wulff show the proper attitude of respect. This was impossible; they would stay in the room throughout the entire interview and try to impose their will upon Wulff. That was not what he wanted, Calabrese thought. No, not at all: he wanted to impress his will upon this man himself. He looked up with sudden decision. "Get out," he said to the *soldat*. "Leave me a weapon."

They knew better than to discuss the issue with him. The near one gave him a forty-five automatic which Calabrese sniffed, opened, checked with satisfaction. At ready. He put it on the desk near him. "Please sit down," he said to Wulff as the *soldat* left the room without looking back. Trained personnel. Of course if Wulff were to overcome him they would be out on the streets within the hour to sell their services but that was all right. A man was no good at all unless he was an opportunist. These men would work with him as long as he was alive; that was all Calabrese could ask. Besides, Wulff was not going to overcome him. It would not be that simple, he thought. The struggle was on other levels.

"I don't want to sit," Wulff said. "Do you see any reason why I should?"

Calabrese motioned toward the easy chair over in the corner of the study. "Come on," he said with a gesture, "be reasonable. Cooperate. I have no intention of killing you, I want to tell you that right now. I did not bring you into this room to kill you, if that was my plan don't you think it would have been done already? I want to talk. I think that we can have some understanding between us." He looked at the gun on the desk, near him. "That doesn't matter," he said, "I know how to use it and I will of course use it on you if you make it necessary. But I don't think it is." He gestured again. "Come on," he said. "Sit."

Wulff went over to the chair, sat uncomfortably, faced Calabrese with that mixture of appraisal and calculation which Calabrese had sensed from the first. The man would kill him if an opportunity presented itself. But that was purely reflex; actually Wulff had larger things on his mind. Calabrese could see this. He could respect it. It could have been me over there, he thought. Except that it isn't but it could have been and he knows it too. Wulff sat.

"I know of your adventures," Calabrese said.

Again Wulff said nothing. It was not precisely resignation; that was not his attitude at all. It was a profound patience operating here. The man would wait him out.

"Your adventures are remarkable," Calabrese said. "I find them hard to believe except that all of them are verified. You are a one-man army. It is a pity that you have misunderstood the situation from the beginning and that you are battling in a futile cause, because your energies are remarkable."

"I've been looking for you for a long time, Calabrese," Wulff said in a monotone. "I didn't know your name but it's been you all along, hasn't it? I've been looking for someone big enough to kill. Don't give me a chance. I'll kill you."

"I'm sure you would," Calabrese said.

"Randall wasn't good enough to kill me but you are. I advise you to do so. It would be far better if you got rid of me because if I ever have the chance—"

"That's all nonsense," Calabrese said flatly. He made a dismissive gesture. "Killing, not killing, all of these threats and aggressions: you understand only the most superficial matters. Obviously you are beyond killing, Wulff, or you would have been taken care of a long time ago. But you still see things in those terms. Do you think that you can have any effect on what I'm doing, who I am?"

"Let me have that gun and I'll show you."

"Nonsense," Calabrese said, "the gun has nothing to do with it. What I represent, what I do can't be eliminated by a gun; there would only be someone else with less compassion. I don't think of the gun at all, Wulff."

"But you're using it on me, aren't you?"

Calabrese spread his hands, showed the palms. "I'm demonstrating the gun to you," he said quietly, "because that's the only thing you understand. You know, Wulff, when Randall was unable to kill you—and I really knew all along that the man wasn't capable of doing it—I decided that I wanted to talk to you because you interested me a great deal and it was time to see exactly what you had on your mind, what would drive you to your remarkable undertakings. But I'm beginning to feel differently about this now. You're disappointing me, Wulff. Do you really have such a simple view of reality?"

"Come on," Wulff said, "kill me. Get to it. I'm going to jump you soon just to get it over with, I swear this."

"I believe you," Calabrese said, fondling the forty-five, "and I believe everything that I've heard about you too; you *are* crazy, the rumors were not wrong. Patrick Wilson means nothing to me, do you understand that?"

"I don't know what you're talking about."

"Of course you do Wulff, you know exactly what I'm talking about. Patrick Wilson is meaningless, I can handle him with a telephone call. But you are a little tougher than that. You're a challenge, Wulff."

"It's all tied together, isn't it?" Wulff said. He showed interest for the first time since he had been brought into the room. "The whole godamned thing is fucking tied together. Patrick Wilson works for *you*, doesn't he?"

"More or less," Calabrese said, "but I really don't want to brag. A man like me tries to live carefully and give the impression of being a responsible businessman—which of course, Wulff, is exactly what I am. The rest is all rumor. Patrick Wilson, he respects me. He listens to my advice. His superiors have given him latitude and he knows who is worth listening to and who is not. We have a relationship. But you aren't listening to me Wulff. You have learned nothing."

"I've learned everything."

"You *think* you've learned everything but in truth, Wulff," Calabrese said, "you understand almost nothing. You are an angry man who has settled upon indiscriminate destruction as the answer. But actually it is not. It is far more sophisticated than you think."

"No it isn't," Wulff said, "it's very simple. There's no mystery to it at all. It all stinks, it's all rotten and it all ties together. You're a fucking murderer, Calabrese. You're killing children. You can hide behind walls and buy off federal grand juries but you're a child killer. So it's very simple." He held his hands together, clasped them until Calabrese could hear the knuckles curdle and then crack. "Fuck you, Calabrese," Wulff said. "If I had a chance I'd kill you right here and then let them kill me. I don't give a damn. I'm already a dead man. I was killed a long time ago."

"Ah," Calabrese said. "I've heard that line too. About how your fiancée was supposed to have been found by you in Manhattan, dead of an overdose and it was this which set you off on your private war—"

He stopped. Wulff's face had become very cold and pale, had even seemed in some trick of light to contract. The man was hunched over, perfectly still, only the hands moving. It was perfectly clear that this man was going to leap upon Calabrese in an instant and damn all of the consequences. The fact that he would be shot dead meant nothing to him. Calabrese had touched the trigger.

He came off it quickly. He did not want to kill Wulff if he could help it. Already he had decided that it was fortunate that Randall had fucked up (and he knew that the man would; subconsciously he had known it all along, hadn't he? and that was why he had allowed Randall to go to begin with) and that Wulff was not to be killed if at all possible. He might be useful. He might even be brought around, in time, to the right point of view. "All right," he said, "I can see that this is sensitive and highly-charged material. So I'll drop it."

Wulff said nothing. He was still at that deadly pitch of preparation. "I said I'd drop it," Calabrese said, "now stop carrying on that way; you're completely wrong you see. You've tied Marie Calvante's death into us in some way but I want you to know that this has been checked through very carefully, in fact frantically, by some of our best people and there is absolutely no connection. None of our people had anything to do with this at all. If the girl was overdosed she was murdered by some street criminal, completely outside of the upper levels. And it's possible that she was on drugs and miscalculated, Wulff. This kind of thing happens, you know. You'd be surprised how often it happens."

"Shut up," Wulff said quietly. Coming out of it a bit Calabrese thought. "Don't talk about her."

"I *have* to talk about her," Calabrese said reasonably. "I have to talk about everything, Wulff, because, you see, your so-called war on the international drug trade is not only futile and pointless because there *is* no international drug trade, merely a group of businessman who are trying to service an extant need which is very strong among all of us, but because your so-called war is also misguided. It comes from a fundamental error. Your motivation is all fucked up, Wulff," Calabrese said flatly, leaning across the desk. "We had nothing to do with Marie Calvante at all."

"Drugs did," Wulff said quietly.

"Yes," Calabrese said reasonably, "that may be true but if she had died of natural causes would you go on a campaign against heart disease? or cancer? If she had jumped out of a window in a fit of depression would you have declared war on the international suicidal and depressive tendency cartel?" He leaned back. "It's perfectly ridiculous," he said and went to his inside coat pocket. For the first time during this absorbing interview, one he had walked through in his mind many times before it finally happened, he needed to break some cigarettes. He found the pack, took out four cigarettes in a lavish gesture and, *one, two, three, four!* cracked them and spilled them across the desk. "And the thing is that you're a remarkable man," Calabrese said. "You could have been of some real use to us."

Wulff said nothing. He sat there, his eyes locked to some screen within his head, probably flashing pictures, Calabrese thought. He was making pictures of the girl behind the brain. Good. Get him back there. Make him think, make him come to terms with what he had become.

"But instead you're just making a lot of difficulty," Calabrese said. "On the other hand I can't deny the fact that you've done us some good." Wulff looked up with interest at this. "Or at least *me* some good," Calabrese added. "The organization was getting very complacent, things were becoming sloppy, a lot of incompetent people had succeeded to positions which were utterly beyond their means but no one sought to depose them. You've washed out some of the weaker elements and you've tightened and firmed up the remainder. You've made us lean and battlehard and the survivors won't be so complacent for a long time."

"If I really believed that," Wulff said, "I'd kill myself right here."

"Well, don't do *that,*" Calabrese said, "I'd hardly feel right having something like that on my head. You know what I'm going to do with you, Wulff? I'm going to send you out of the country. I'm not going to kill you at all; that would be entirely wasteful. Instead of think we're just going to send you away for a while, under supervision of course, so you can get a look at how the other side of the globe lives. And meanwhile we'll carry on here, somehow, without you."

"You'd better kill me," Wulff said, "because if you don't someday I'm going to kill you. You realize that, don't you?"

"Of course I realize that," Calabrese said, "I know you want to murder me and even think that you have a chance. But I'm not going to kill you Wulff, I'm through trying to kill you for the time being because you're just too useful and interesting. We're going to send you out of here and put you where you can't bother any of us for a long time. And maybe after a while when you've had a chance to think things over, you may even see that you'd do better working with us. We could use you. And you really have nowhere else to go. Do you think that you have any life above ground left in this country? Every law-enforcement agency in the world has a bounty for you."

"I'd rather die than work for you."

"You'd rather die than a lot of things, Wulff," Calabrese said and took out another cigarette, "but I think that I'd like to keep you alive."

"Why?"

"Why?" Calabrese said. "Do you really want to know why? Well, then, I'll tell you Wulff: because things get very boring and stultifying here for an old man who has probably seen all of the real action that he's going to see in his entire life. Who wants to sit on a mountaintop and wait for the deathbirds to come and pick me to pieces? No, there has to be more to life than just waiting for the end, reliving what has already been done. And you're my option, Wulff. I want to know that you're still alive and out there and that you want to kill me." He broke the cigarette and flung it in Wulff's face. "It's interesting," he said in a shaking voice, "it gives an old man something to think about."

The cigarette glanced off Wulff's cheekbone, fell to the floor. Neither of them looked at it. Calabrese stood and found that he was shaking: from head to toe his body was betraying him and he was moving uncontrollably. His bowels felt loose and he had a sensation of shame: was he going to deaden and cheapen himself forever by having an accident in front of this man? Abruptly he felt tears come to his eyes. He had not meant to say what he did. It had just come out. It had not even been there five seconds before he had said it and then, when it came out, it did so with the solidity of absolute truth and Calabrese knew that it had been this way all along and that this was the reason why he had cooperated with Randall, made the call to Wilson, had Randall tracked and finally brought Wulff in here. He had never intended to kill him at all. He had just been looking, every step of the way, for a means of bringing him in here and saying what he had to him ... without revealing to himself until this moment what he had really had in mind.

"Get out of here," Calabrese said, his voice still shaking. He picked up the phone on the desk. "Get him out of here!" he said. "What?" a voice said and Calabrese screamed, *"Get him out!"* seeing the smile that came to Wulff's face, seeing the mirror of his own discovered weakness in Wulff's face, his own shame beating like a heart within him and *soldat* came in, seized Wulff by the arms, started to carry him out of there, roughly. Wulff kept those flat, dead eyes on him all through this. The *soldat* struggled with one another and one of Wulff's arms was twisted but the man let go no sound. "Don't hurt him," Calabrese said, "take him downstairs and put him into confinement. I will have instructions shortly." To Wulff he said, "You will be escorted out of the country. You will be informed of your destination later."

"I'll kill you when I can, Calabrese," Wulff said and the *soldat* twisted at him again. Wulff made leverage, turned with the twist, his face impassive. "I said leave him alone!" Calabrese screamed in a rage and the *soldat,* ashen-faced, put Wulff into a standard escort pin and led him from the room, not looking back at Calabrese. The door closed quietly.

Calabrese stood there, not moving. The cigarettes lay open on his desk. In a brutal gesture he took one from the pack and rammed it into his mouth like he would have rammed his prick, when it worked ten years ago, into a woman, held it there and then dug in his desk for matches, removed them, struck a flame with three and lighted the cigarette. He inhaled immediately, sulphuric fumes coming in with the tobacco and gasped, then held all of it in his chest for a long time, the sickening mass beating like a fist, clawing like a dog on the inside, near his heart. He felt that bird of shame battering away within him and it was like fire, like darkness, crying out all the sounds of the night. Surely everyone could hear it ... except that he knew, no one could. All of it was contained inside. Always, always: a man lived within the depths of himself.

Wulff had measured him.

# Chapter 21

That was the day Williams got out of the hospital. No one saw any point in holding him further and the NYPD was pulling off surveillance which seemed to be the signal to the hospital to quit. He could rest at home on full leave for three or four weeks depending on the doctors and then they would see. They would indeed see. His wife held his arm as he walked unsteadily down the stairs and put him in the passenger seat of the car, then went around to the driver's side, opened it and found Williams already sitting there with a shy, tentative, embarrassed grin. "I'm sorry," he said, "I just can't sit. I'd rather drive." She gave him the keys and got back on the passenger side.

Driving, Williams saw all of it again but it was like seeing it for the first time. Metropolitan Hospital adjoined East Harlem and rather than ducking right for the East River Drive, heading toward the Triborough Bridge and home, he stayed on First Avenue up to 125th, seeing all of it. At about 110th the junkies became visible in clumps rather than as isolated, staggering forms. They stretched out on pavements, huddled in doorways, a few of them were weaving across First Avenue in the midst of traffic. Williams rolled up all the windows.

"Why are you going this way?" his wife said and Williams gave her one sidelong glance and in his eyes she saw the answer and said nothing else. He kept the car at an even fifteen for the progressive lighting, looking at what was going on. He had seen it a thousand times but he had never seen it before. At 125th, finally, he cut east to the bridge approach. Traffic was sparse. He took the Impala up to forty. Twenty-two payments left on the thing, as he recalled. Five hundred down and one hundred a month for the rest of your life. The car was a piece of shit. That was the way the system worked. His side ached.

"Wulff's right," he said.

"I know," his wife said, "you've said that already."

So he had. He had said it to her several times, passionately from the hospital bed when he had started to put all the pieces together. He was embarrassed. He should have known better than to have thought that she had forgotten. "I'm sorry," he said, "it just occurred to me again."

"All right."

"He was always right. It's all shit."

"Does it make any difference to us?"

"I don't know," Williams said, holding the wheel steady as they headed into the filth toward Queens. He threw a quarter into the exact change slot, barely halting. "I just don't know if anything makes any difference."

"You have to go on," his wife said. Unconsciously she looked down at herself. She was six months pregnant now. She looked up again. "You do have to go on."

"For what?" David Williams said. "To what?" and the car sailed on into Queens, little foul clouds from Flushing Bay drifting toward them, the stupendous and brutal skyline of that evil city to the east and Williams, hunching his head into his shoulders didn't know: he didn't know. He didn't know.

His wife leaned against him.

THE END

*Afterword:*
# The Truths
# of the Matter

By Barry N. Malzberg

> A pretty dismal life. Wulff could imagine the three of them jammed into the old car, moving silently on their sullen pursuit. Now and then they would pause for gasoline, less frequently they would pull into some bleak hotel for the night, the leader making sure to get receipts at every stage of the journey so that he could put in for governmental reimbursement. They would stay at the cheapest places, of course, and watch the budget. But then again, considering the backgrounds of these men and what appeared to be the general level of their intelligence, it was possible that they were doing quite well. Federal agents usually exceeded their possibilities which had always been low.
>
> —*Chicago Slaughter*

By *Chicago Slaughter*, the seventh of a series I had almost considered doomed after the forced hiatus after the third novel. I felt I had begun to begin to find my way in the series; the protagonist was mad but not incongruous, the situation was impossible yet credible and the brutality was absolute... the country, the Lone Wulff, his targets, the methodology had reached a point of fusion and every incredulity, any damage seemed to feed into that larger circumstance which I felt I had grasped from the outset. The country was bad. Wulff was mad. The drug racket and its chattels exacerbated the madness. There were not three persons occupied in this pursuit but three hundred, three million.

Stylistically, *Chicago Slaughter* was at a level of brutality touched but not fully exploited in the first five novels; there was a certain hesitance, how far could I go with this, how far could Wulff? Were there limitations on the madness? But the green light from Berkley (which never further interfered in any way) was a certain assurance which became a psychic cloaked around the flailing characters and that assurance led to what even might have been a kind of bravura. Wulff was getting away with this, Berkley obviously felt that I was getting away with it too. Oh, what a brave new world with such people in it!

There was another factor which now crawled behind these novels and informed my own rage and that of its protagonist: in the exhaustion and tension surrounding the pledge to deliver ten novels in ten months (with an unwanted *tacet* of nearly a month after the first three) I began to formulate a theory of the Vietnam War, the Vietnam action, the struggle against the creeping dominion destroying the West if the South fell to the invasion of the North. The theory was stark and frightening in its banality: this was a drug war. It was all about commerce, it was all about supply lines.

The war was triggered by North Vietnamese determination to close off the routes of transmission from North to South and then to all the nations... there had been a clear route, a lively trade from North to South and then, with the cooperation of Madame Nhu and her puppets, all the way through the world. This had become intolerable to the West in its false entrapped patron, the government of South Vietnam. The West wanted the drug flow to continue unmolested; Ho Cho Minh took it as a point of honor that he would now obstruct this humiliation of his nation in every way he could, by having his troops go forward into the South and shut down the nation as anything other than an adjunct. The international drug cartels and their employees, the leaders of South Vietnam were not going to abide this audacity.

And thus the War against the North Vietnam blockade to keep those damned drug lanes open. That was the real reason for all of it: the escalation, the bombs, the slaughter, the ravaging of ever-heightening draft calls in the United States. All that simple and terrible.

Well, it all could be seen as the early morning bar ravings of an exhausted and inevitably paranoiac novelist under great pressure but it made as much sense as I blazed through *Chicago Slaughter* as any rivalled explanation and of course over a decade later the Contra scandal would lend more than a hint of credibility to the speculation... the apparent proof that the Central Intelligence Agency was crucial in facilitating the flow of drugs unmolested, unchecked, so that they would reach California and other nations and that the funds paid over by the cartels in tribute would be used to finance the Nicaraguan contras who were having a great deal of trouble trying to oust a revolutionary government which looked unkindly upon drugs. Cadre and officers were being strafed and murdered on the fields of fire, 18 year olds were dying in the mud, the polity and possibilities of the United States were being subjected to this so that the drugs' movement would not be molested. It was all one of those absurdist, frightening, faintly credible Hubbard, Phil Dick or Van Vogt novels in which the Grand Master of the Invasion turns out to really be the leader of the Resistance.

It was enough, that exhaustion-laden parsing of the Domino Effect as the first lie, the basic lie of the war itself, an Occam's Razor cutting mercilessly to and beyond the truth... it was enough to keep me attentive and enraged as I alternately blazed and crept through *Chicago Slaughter* and the eight novels which followed. It was one thing to know from the beginning that all of it was a lie, was manipulation, was public relations... but stumbling upon a True Cause as banal and childishly grasp and greed, that was a remarkable occurrence. It might even have been to Don Pendleton or the various editors and publishers on the profitable Vigilante Express. I put none of this speculation on the page, I was not that kind of dummy... but it was impetus. It was stern and flagrant impetus as *Chicago Slaughter* burned on, as Nixon flailed at the release of the tapes, as Goldwater and several grim accompanying Republican Senators trudged upstairs to deliver Tchaikovsky the news. "Sayonara" was the news and on my 35th birthday the tapes were released and the news was finally delivered. "Well," the bartender at Rosoff's, a big Nixon guy with whom I had intermittently argued in occasional visits over the past year, "Well, okay. Okay. But you got to admit that he really fought." Just trudging the Ho Cho Minh trail, boss.

January 2022: New Jersey

# Barry N. Malzberg Bibliography

## FICTION (as either Barry or Barry N. Malzberg)

Oracle of the Thousand Hands (1968)
Screen (1968)
Confessions of Westchester County (1970)
The Spread (1971)
In My Parents' Bedroom (1971)
The Falling Astronauts (1971)
The Masochist (1972, reprinted as Everything Happened to Susan, 1975; as Cinema, 2020)
Horizontal Woman (1972; reprinted as The Social Worker, 1973)
Beyond Apollo (1972)
Overlay (1972)
Revelations (1972)
Herovit's World (1973)
In the Enclosure (1973)
The Men Inside (1973)
Phase IV (1973; novelization based on a story & screenplay by Mayo Simon)
The Day of the Burning (1974)
The Tactics of Conquest (1974)
Underlay (1974)
The Destruction of the Temple (1974)
Guernica Night (1974)
On a Planet Alien (1974)
Out from Ganymede (1974; stories)
The Sodom and Gomorrah Business (1974)
The Best of Barry N. Malzberg (1975; stories)
The Many Worlds of Barry Malzberg (1975; stories)
Galaxies (1975)
The Gamesman (1975)

Down Here in the Dream Quarter (1976; stories)
Scop (1976)
The Last Transaction (1977)
Chorale (1978)
Malzberg at Large (1979; stories)
The Man Who Loved the Midnight Lady (1980; stories)
The Cross of Fire (1982)
The Remaking of Sigmund Freud (1985)
In the Stone House (2000; stories)
Shiva and Other Stories (2001; stories)
The Passage of the Light: The Recursive Science Fiction of Barry N. Malzberg (2004; ed. by Tony Lewis & Mike Resnick; stories)
The Very Best of Barry N. Malzberg (2013; stories)

## With Bill Pronzini

The Running of the Beasts (1976)
Acts of Mercy (1977)
Night Screams (1979)
Prose Bowl (1980)
Problems Solved (2003; stories)
On Account of Darkness and Other SF Stories (2004; stories)

## As Mike Barry

Lone Wolf series:
Night Raider (1973)
Bay Prowler (1973)
Boston Avenger (1973)
Desert Stalker (1974)
Havana Hit (1974)
Chicago Slaughter (1974)
Peruvian Nightmare (1974)

Los Angeles Holocaust (1974)
Miami Marauder (1974)
Harlem Showdown (1975)
Detroit Massacre (1975)
Phoenix Inferno (1975)
The Killing Run (1975)
Philadelphia Blow-Up (1975)

**As Francine di Natale**

The Circle (1969)

**As Claudine Dumas**

The Confessions of a Parisian
Chambermaid (1969)

**As Mel Johnson/M. L. Johnson**

Love Doll (1967; with The Sex Pros
by Orrie Hitt)
I, Lesbian (1968; as M. L. Johnson)
Just Ask (1968; with Playgirl by Lou
Craig)
Instant Sex (1968)
Chained (1968; with Master of
Women by March Hastings & Love
Captive by Dallas Mayo)
Kiss and Run (1968; with Sex on the
Sand by Sheldon Lord & Odd Girl
by March Hastings)
Nympho Nurse (1969; with Young
and Eager by Jim Conroy &
Quickie by Gene Evans)
The Sadist (1969)
The Box (1969)
Do It To Me (1969; with Hot Blonde
by Jim Conroy)
Born to Give (1969; with Swap Club
by Greg Hamilton & Wild in Bed
by Dirk Malloy)
Campus Doll (1969; with High
School Stud by Robert Hadley)
A Way With All Maidens (1969)

**As Howard Lee**

Kung Fu #1: The Way of the Tiger,
the Sign of the Dragon (1973)

**As Lee W. Mason**

Lady of a Thousand Sorrows (1977)

**As K. M. O'Donnell**

Empty People (1969)
The Final War and Other Fantasies
(1969; stories)
Dwellers of the Deep (1970)
Gather at the Hall of the Planets
(1971)
In the Pocket and Other S-F Stories
(1971; stories)
Universe Day (1971; stories)

**As Eliot B. Reston**

The Womanizer (1972)

**As Gerrold Watkins**

Southern Comfort (1969)
A Bed of Money (1970)
A Satyr's Romance (1970)
Giving It Away (1970)
Art of the Fugue (1970)

**NON-FICTION/ESSAYS**

The Engines of the Night: Science
Fiction in the Eighties (1982;
essays)
Breakfast in the Ruins (2007;
essays: expansion of Engines of the
Night)
The Business of Science Fiction: Two
Insiders Discuss Writing and
Publishing (2010; with Mike
Resnick)

The Bend at the End of the Road
(2018; essays)

**EDITED ANTHOLOGIES**

Final Stage (1974; with Edward L.
Ferman)
Arena (1976; with Edward L.
Ferman)
Graven Images (1977; with Edward
L. Ferman)
Dark Sins, Dark Dreams (1978; with
Bill Pronzini)
The End of Summer: SF in the
Fifties (1979; with Bill Pronzini)
Shared Tomorrows: Science Fiction
in Collaboration (1979; with Bill
Pronzini)

Neglected Visions (1979; with
Martin H. Greenberg & Joseph D.
Olander)
Bug-Eyed Monsters (1980; with Bill
Pronzini)
The Science Fiction of Mark Clifton
(1980; with Martin H. Greenberg)
The Arbor House Treasury of Horror
& the Supernatural (1981; with
Bill Pronzini & Martin H.
Greenberg)
The Science Fiction of Kris Neville
(1984; with Martin H. Greenberg)
Mystery in the Mainstream (1986;
with Bill Pronzini & Martin H.
Greenberg)

Made in the USA
Middletown, DE
27 December 2022

20540555R00129